DEBBIE MACOMBER

The Inn at Rose Harbor

A Novel

Copyright © 2012 by Debbie Macomber

All rights reserved.
Published in the United States of America by
Random House Large Print in association with
Ballantine Books, New York.
Distributed by Random House, Inc., New York.

Grateful acknowledgment is made to Universal Yarn for permission to reprint the Jo Marie's Crochet Shawl pattern and instructions designed by Ellen Gormley for Universal Yarn, the Jo Marie's Knitted Shawl pattern and instructions designed by Michael del Vecchio for Universal Yarn, and the accompanying photos by Shane Baskin/Black Box Studies. Patterns and photos are reprinted by permission of Universal Yarn.

Cover Design: Belina Huey and Shasti O'Leary Soudant
Cover images: Kathy Michael (inn and harbor), Shutterstock (roses), Iskra (rose ornament)

The Library of Congress has established a Cataloging-in-Publication record for this title.

ISBN: 978-0-7393-7828-1

www.randomhouse.com/largeprint

FIRST LARGE PRINT EDITION

Printed in the United States of America

10 9 8 7 6 5 4 3 2 1

This Large Print edition published in accord with the standards of the N.A.V.H.

To
my special friends from
Knitter's Magazine
and the
Stitches Conferences,
Benjamin Levisay
and
Rick Mondragon

THE INN AT
ROSE HARBOR

Chapter 1

Last night I dreamed of Paul.

He's never far from my thoughts—not a day passes when he isn't with me—but he hasn't been in my dreams until now. It's ironic, I suppose, that he should leave me, because before I close my eyes I fantasize about what it would feel like to have his arms wrapped around me. As I drift off to sleep I pretend that my head is resting on his shoulder. Unfortunately, I will never have the chance to be with my husband again, at least not in this lifetime.

Until last night, if I did happen to dream of Paul, those dreams were long forgotten by the time I woke.

This dream, however, stayed with me, lingering in my mind, filling me with equal parts sadness and joy.

When I first learned that Paul had been killed, the grief had been all-consuming, and I didn't think I would be able to go on. Yet life continues to move forward, and so have I, dragging from one day into the next until I found I could breathe normally.

I'm in my new home now, the bed-and-breakfast I bought less than a month ago on the Kitsap Peninsula in a cozy town on the water called Cedar Cove. I decided to name it Rose Harbor Inn. "Rose" for Paul Rose, my husband of less than a year; the man I will always love and for whom I will grieve for whatever remains of my own life. "Harbor" for the place I have set my anchor as the storms of loss batter me.

How melodramatic that sounds, and yet there's no other way to say it. Although I am alive, functioning normally, at times I feel half dead. How Paul would hate hearing me say that, but it's true. I died with Paul last April on some mountainside in a country half a world away as he fought for our nation's security.

Life as I knew it was over in the space of a single heartbeat. My future as I dreamed it would be was stolen from me.

All the advice given to those who grieve said I should wait a year before making any major decisions. My friends told me I would regret quitting my job, leaving my Seattle home, and moving to a strange town.

What they didn't understand was that I found no comfort in familiarity, no joy in routine. Because I valued their opinion, I gave it six months. In that time nothing helped, nothing changed. More and more I felt the urge to get away, to start life anew, certain that then and only then would I find peace, and this horrendous ache inside me ease.

I started my search for a new life on the Internet, looking in a number of areas, all across the United States. The surprise was finding exactly what I wanted in my own backyard.

The town of Cedar Cove sits on the other side of Puget Sound from Seattle. It's a navy town, situated directly across from the Bremerton shipyard. The minute I found a property listing for this charming bed-and-breakfast that was up for sale, my heart started to beat at an accelerated rate. Me own a bed-and-breakfast? I hadn't thought to take over a business, but instinctively I realized I would need something to fill my time. As a bonus, a confirmation, I'd always enjoyed having guests.

With its wraparound porch and incredible view of the cove, the house was breathtaking. In another life I could imagine Paul and me sitting on the porch after dinner, sipping hot coffee and discussing our day, our dreams. Surely the photograph posted on the Internet had been taken by a professional who'd cleverly masked its flaws. Nothing, it seemed, could be this perfect.

Not so. The moment I pulled into the driveway with the real estate agent, I was embraced by the inn's appeal. Oh yes, with its bright natural light and large windows that overlooked the cove, this B&B felt like home already. It was the perfect place for starting my new life.

Although I dutifully let Jody McNeal, the agent, show me around, not a single question remained in my mind. I was meant to own this bed-and-breakfast; it was as if it'd sat on the market all these months waiting for me. It had eight guest rooms spread across the two upper floors, and on the bottom floor a large, modern kitchen was situated next to a spacious dining room. Originally built in the early 1900s, the house looked out on a stunning panorama of the water and marina. Cedar Cove was laid out below along Harbor Street, which wound through the town with small shops on both sides of the street. I felt the town's appeal even before I had the opportunity to explore its neighborhoods.

What attracted me most about the inn was the sense of peace I experienced the moment I walked inside. The heartache that had been my constant companion seemed to lift. The grief that I'd carried with me all these months eased. In its place came serenity, a peace that's difficult to describe.

Unfortunately, this contentment didn't last long, my eyes suddenly flooding with tears and embarrassing me as we finished the tour. Paul would have loved this inn, too. But I would be managing the inn alone. Thankfully the real estate agent pretended not to notice the emotions I was struggling to disguise.

"Well, what do you think?" Jody asked expectantly as we walked out the front door.

I hadn't said a word during the entire tour, nor had I asked a single question. "I'll take it."

Jody leaned closer as if she hadn't heard me correctly. "I beg your pardon?"

"I'd like to make an offer." I didn't hesitate—by that time I had no doubts. The asking price was more than fair and I was ready to move forward.

Jody almost dropped a folder full of detailed information regarding the property. "You might want to think about it," she suggested. "This is a major decision, Jo Marie. Don't get me wrong, I'm eager to make the sale; it's just that I've never had anyone make such an important decision so . . . quickly."

"I'll think about it overnight, if you want, but there's no need. I knew right away that this is it."

The instant my family heard that I intended to quit my job at Columbia Bank and buy the B&B, they all tried to talk me out of it, especially my brother, Todd, the engineer. I'd worked my way up to assistant manager of the Denny Way branch, and he feared I was throwing away a promising career. Todd knew that I would eventually be named manager. I had given almost fifteen years to the bank, had been a good employee, and my future in banking was bright

What the people around me failed to understand was that my life as I'd known it, as I'd wanted it, as I'd dreamed it, was over. The only way I could achieve fulfillment was to find myself a new one.

I signed the offer for the inn the next day and not for an instant did my resolve waver. The Frelingers, who owned the B&B, gratefully accepted my offer, and within a matter of weeks—just before the holidays—we gathered together at the title company and signed all the tedious, necessary paperwork. I handed them the cashier's check, and accepted the keys to the inn. The Frelingers had taken no reservations for the last couple of weeks in December as they intended to spend time with their children.

Leaving the title company, I took a short detour to the courthouse and applied for a name change for the inn, christening it with its new name, The Rose Harbor Inn.

I returned to Seattle and the next day I gave Columbia Bank my notice. I spent the Christmas holiday packing up my Seattle condo and preparing for the move across Puget Sound. While I was only moving a few miles away, I might as well have been going halfway across the country. Cedar Cove was a whole other world—a quaint town on the Kitsap Peninsula away from the hectic world of the big city.

I knew my parents were disappointed that I didn't spend much of the holidays with them in Hawaii, a family tradition. But I had so much to do to get ready for the move, including sorting through my things and Paul's, packing, and selling my furniture. I needed to keep occupied—busywork helped keep my mind off this first Christmas without Paul.

I officially moved into the house on the Monday following New Year's Day. Thankfully the Frelingers had sold the inn as a turnkey business. So all I needed to bring with me were a couple of chairs, a lamp that had belonged to my grandmother, and my personal items. Unpacking took only a few hours. I chose as my room the main floor bedroom suite the Frelingers had set aside as their own area; it had a fireplace and a small alcove that included a window seat overlooking the cove. The room was large enough for a bedroom set, as well as a small sofa that sat close to the fireplace. I particularly enjoyed the wallpaper, which was covered in white and lavender hydrangeas.

By the time night descended on the inn, I was exhausted. At eight, as rain pelted against the windows and the wind whistled through the tall evergreens that covered one side of the property, I made my way into the master bedroom on the main floor. The wild weather made it feel even cozier with a fire flickering in the fireplace. I experienced none of the strangeness of settling into a new place. I'd felt welcomed by this home from the moment I'd set foot in the front door.

The sheets were crisp and clean as I climbed into bed. I don't remember falling asleep, but what so readily comes to mind is that dream of Paul, so vivid and real.

In grief counseling, I'd learned that dreams are important to the healing process. The counselor described two distinct types of dreams. The first and probably the most common are dreams about our loved ones—memories that come alive again.

The second type are called visitation dreams, when the loved one actually crosses the chasm between life and death to visit those he or she has left behind. We were told these are generally dreams of reassurance: the one who has passed reassures the living that he or she is happy and at peace.

It'd been eight months since I'd received word that Paul had been killed in a helicopter crash in the Hindu Kush, the mountain range that stretches between the center of Afghanistan and northern Pakistan. The army helicopter had been brought down by al-Qaeda or one of their Taliban allies; Paul and five of his fellow Airborne Rangers had been killed instantly. Because of the location of the crash it was impossible to recover their bodies. The news of his death was difficult enough, but to be deprived of burying his remains was even more cruel.

For days after I got the news, hope crowded my heart that Paul might have actually survived. I was convinced that somehow my husband would find a way back to me. That was not to be. Aerial photographs of the crash site soon confirmed that no one could have possibly survived. In the end, all that really mattered was that the man I loved and married was gone. He would never return to me, and as the weeks and months progressed I came to accept the news.

It'd taken me a long time to fall in love. Most of my friends had married in their twenties, and by the time they were in their mid-thirties, the majority had already started their families. I was a godmother six times over.

On the other hand, I had remained single well into my thirties. I had a busy, happy life and was involved in both my career and family. I'd never felt the need to rush into marriage or listen to my mother, who insisted I find a good man and quit being so picky. I dated plenty but there was never anyone I felt I could love for the rest of my life until I met Paul Rose.

Seeing that it'd taken me thirty-seven years to meet my match, I didn't expect love to come to me twice. Frankly, I wasn't even sure I wanted to fall in love again. Paul Rose was everything I'd ever hoped to find in a husband . . . and so much more.

We'd met at a Seahawks football game. The bank had given me tickets and I had brought along one of our more prominent clients and his wife. As we took our seats, I'd noticed two men with military haircuts sitting next to me. As the game progressed, Paul introduced himself and his army buddy and struck up a conversation. Paul told me he was stationed at Fort Lewis. Like me, he enjoyed football. My parents were keen Seahawks fans, and I'd grown up in Spokane watching the games on television after church on Sundays with them and my younger brother, Todd.

Paul asked me to have a beer with him as we left the game that afternoon, and we saw each other nearly every day after. We learned we shared much more than a love of football: we shared the same political inclinations, read many of the same authors, and loved Italian food. We even had a Sudoku addiction in common. We could talk for hours and often did. Two months after we met, he shipped out to Germany, but being separated did little to slow our budding relationship. Not a day passed that we weren't in contact in one way or another—we emailed, texted, Skyped, tweeted, and used every other available means we could to stay in touch. Yes, we even wrote actual letters with pen and paper. I'd heard about people claiming to have experienced "love at first sight" and I had scoffed. I can't say it was like that for Paul and me, but it was darn close. I knew a week after we met that he was the man I would marry. Paul said he felt the same way about me, although he claimed all it took was one date.

I will admit this: love changed me. I was happier than I could ever remember being. And everyone noticed.

At Christmastime a year ago, Paul flew back to Seattle on leave and asked me to be his wife. He even talked to my parents first. We were crazy in love. I'd waited a long time and when I gave him my heart, it was for forever.

Right after our wedding in January, Paul got orders for Afghanistan. The helicopter went down on April 27, and my world imploded.

I'd never experienced this kind of grief and I fear I handled it poorly. My parents and brother worried for me. It was my mother who suggested grief counseling. Because I was desperate to find a means to ease my pain, I agreed. In the end I was glad I attended the sessions. Doing so helped me understand my dreams, especially the one I had that first night at the inn.

Contrary to what I'd been told about visitation dreams, Paul did nothing to reassure me he was at peace. Instead, he stood before me in full military gear. He was surrounded by a light that was so bright it was hard to look at him. Even so, I found it impossible to turn away.

I wanted to run to him but was afraid that if I moved, he would disappear. I couldn't bear to lose him again even if this was only an apparition.

At first he didn't speak. I didn't either, unsure of what I could or should say. I remember that emotion filled my eyes with tears and I covered my mouth for fear I would cry out.

He joined me then and took me in his arms, holding me close and running his hand down the back of my head, comforting me. I clung to him, unwilling to let him go. Over and over he whispered gentle words of love.

When the lump in my throat eased I looked up at him and our eyes met. It felt as though he was alive and we needed to catch up after a long absence. There was so much I wanted to tell him, so much I wanted him to explain. The fact that he'd had such a large life insurance policy had come as a shock. At first I'd felt guilty about accepting such a large amount of cash. Shouldn't that money go to his family? But his mother was dead, and his father had remarried and lived in Australia. They had never been especially close. The lawyer told me Paul had been clear in his instructions.

In my dream I wanted to tell Paul that I'd used the money to buy this bed-and-breakfast and that I'd named it after him. One of the first improvements I wanted to make was to plant a rose garden with a bench and an arbor. But in the dream, I said none of that because it seemed like he already knew.

He brushed the hair from my forehead and kissed me there ever so gently.

"You've chosen well," he whispered, his eyes warm with love. "In time you'll know joy again."

Joy? I wanted to argue with him. It didn't seem likely or even possible. One doesn't heal from this kind of pain. I remembered how my family and friends had struggled to find the right words to comfort me. But there are no words . . . there simply are no words.

And yet I didn't argue with him. I wanted the dream to last and I feared that if I questioned him he would leave, and I wanted him to stay with me. A peaceful feeling had come to me, and my heart, which had carried this heavy burden, felt just a little lighter.

"I don't know that I can live without you," I told him, and it was true.

"You can and you will. In fact, you'll have a long, full life," Paul insisted. He sounded like the officer he'd been, giving out orders that were not to be questioned.

"You will feel joy again," he repeated, "and much of it will come from owning Rose Harbor Inn."

I frowned. I knew I was dreaming, but the dream was so vivid I wanted to believe it was real.

"But . . . " My mind filled with questions.

"This inn is my gift to you," Paul continued. "Don't doubt, my love. God will show you." In the next instant he was gone.

I cried out, begging him to come back, and my own sharp cry woke me. My tears were real, and I could feel moisture on my cheeks and pillowcase.

For a long time afterward I sat upright in the dark wanting to hold on to the feeling of my husband's presence. Eventually it faded and almost against my will I fell back asleep.

The next morning, I climbed out of bed and traipsed barefoot down the polished hardwood floor of the hallway to the small office off the kitchen. Turning on the desk lamp, I flipped through the pages of the reservation book the Frelingers had given me. I reviewed the names of the two guests due to arrive that week.

Joshua Weaver had made his reservation just the week before I took ownership. The former owners had mentioned it at the time we signed the final papers.

The second name on the list belonged to Abby Kincaid.

Two guests.

Paul had said this inn was his gift to me. I would do my best to make both guests comfortable; perhaps, in giving of myself, I would find the joy Paul had promised. And maybe, given time, it would be possible for me to find my way back to life.

Chapter 2

Josh Weaver never thought he'd return to Cedar Cove. In the twelve years since his high school graduation he'd been back only once, and that was to attend the funeral of his stepbrother, Dylan. Even then he hadn't spent the night in town. He'd caught a morning flight, rented a car, showed up at the funeral, and left directly afterward, arriving back in California at the job site the same day. He'd barely spoken to his stepfather.

For that matter, Richard hadn't bothered to acknowledge him. It was exactly what Josh had expected. Although Dylan and Josh had been close, his stepfather hadn't seen fit to ask Josh to be one of his son's pallbearers. The slight had cut deep. He'd come anyway to pay his respects to his stepbrother.

Now Josh was back again and not out of any desire to spend time in Cedar Cove. This town meant nothing to him other than the fact that it contained his mother's grave site and Dylan's.

Born just a year apart, Josh and Dylan had been tight. Dylan had always been a daredevil. Josh had marveled at Dylan's complete lack of fear ever since they met. Still, it had come as a brutal shock when word reached him that Dylan had been killed in a motorcycle accident. That was five years ago now. Seven years after Richard Lambert had kicked him out of the house and forced Josh to find his own way in the world.

Now it seemed it was the old man's turn to meet his Maker. The sole reason Josh was back in town was because the Nelsons, who lived next door to Richard, had contacted him. Michelle Nelson and Dylan had been in the same grade in school, with Josh a year ahead of them. Following graduation, gentle-natured Michelle had gone on to become a social worker. Josh remembered that she'd had a big crush on Dylan, but she was overweight and Dylan hadn't returned the sentiment. In his mind, Josh linked her thoughtfulness in looking after Richard to her affection for Dylan.

"Richard is in a bad way," Michelle had told him

during their brief telephone conversation. "If you want to see him alive you'd better come—and make it soon."

Josh had no desire to see the old man. None. They shared nothing other than a mutual dislike. Josh agreed to make the trip for two reasons. First, he was between job assignments as a construction manager. He had just finished one project and was waiting to hear about the next. Second, while he didn't consider it important, or really hope it was possible, it'd be nice to make peace with the old man. Then, too, there were certain things he hoped to collect from his stepfather's house. While he was in Cedar Cove, he wanted to retrieve a few personal possessions that his mother had brought into the marriage. Nothing less than what should rightfully be his and certainly nothing more.

"I'll be there as soon as I can get away," Josh had replied.

"Hurry," Michelle urged. "Richard needs you."

Josh wagered his stepfather would keel over dead before he'd admit to needing anyone, particularly Josh. Apparently the neighbors had forgotten that Richard had taken delight in kicking Josh out of the house only a few months after his mother's death. Josh had been just weeks away from his high school graduation. When he left he hadn't been allowed to take anything more than some clothes and his schoolbooks.

Richard had claimed Josh was a thief. Two hundred dollars had been missing from his wallet and he was convinced Josh had stolen it. The fact was, Josh knew nothing about the missing money, which left only Dylan. Richard would never believe his own flesh and blood was guilty, though, so Josh had accepted the blame. What he hadn't expected was for Richard to demand he leave so close to graduation.

In retrospect, Josh accepted that the missing money was just an excuse. Richard had wanted him out of the house and out of his life, and until now Josh had been more than willing to comply.

He was back in Cedar Cove, but he felt no sense of homecoming as he eased his truck into the driveway of the address scribbled down on a piece of paper. The B&B had surfaced in a hasty online search he'd conducted, looking for a location convenient to his stepfather's house.

One thing was certain: he couldn't stay with Richard. As far as Josh knew, Richard didn't even know he was coming, which suited him just fine. If everything went well, he'd be in and out of town in a day or two. He didn't want to stay any longer than was absolutely necessary. And when he left Cedar Cove this time, Josh had no intention of ever looking back.

Once he parked in the inn's small lot, he climbed out of the truck, and reached for his overnight bag and laptop. The sky was overcast and it looked like rain, which was par for January in the Pacific Northwest. The charcoal-colored skies were an adequate reflection of his mood. He'd give just about anything to be somewhere other than Cedar Cove—anyplace that didn't force him to confront the stepfather who had detested him.

No need putting off the inevitable, he decided. He lugged his carry-on and his computer case up the porch stairs and rang the doorbell. Hardly a minute passed before a woman answered the door.

"Mrs. Frelinger?" he asked. She was of medium height and much younger than he'd expected when he booked the reservation. Her thick brown hair was shoulder length with a part down the middle. Her eyes were a piercing shade of blue not unlike a summer sky. When he'd booked the reservation the woman on the other end of the line had sounded older, as if she were in her sixties. The woman standing before him was young, mid-thirties at most. She wore a colorful red bib apron over casual pants and a long-sleeve sweater.

"Sorry, no, I'm Jo Marie Rose. I recently took over the inn from the Frelingers. Please, come in." She stepped aside, making way in order for him to enter the large home.

Josh entered the foyer and was instantly warmed. A small fire crackled in the fireplace and the scent of freshly baked bread set his mouth to watering. Josh couldn't remember the last time he'd smelled bread direct from the oven. His mother had baked bread but that was years ago. "Something smells wonderful."

"I've always enjoyed baking," Jo Marie said as if she needed to explain. "I hope you have a good appetite."

"I do," Josh said.

"You're my first guest," Jo Marie told him, welcoming him with a bright smile. "Welcome." She rubbed her palms together as if she wasn't sure what to do next.

"Would you like my credit card information?" Josh asked, as he removed his wallet from his hip pocket.

"Oh yes, that's probably a good idea."

She led the way through the kitchen and into a small office. Josh suspected the area might have been a pantry at one time. He withdrew a credit card.

Jo Marie stared at the card. "I'll need to jot down your number for now—I have an appointment at the bank later." Looking uncertain she raised questioning eyes to him. "If that's all right?"

"Not a problem," he said and she wrote down his credit card information and handed the card back to him.

"Would it be all right if I got the key to my room now?" he asked.

"Oh sure . . . sorry! Like I said, you're my first guest."

Josh wondered just how long she'd owned the business. Jo Marie must have read his mind because she added, "I signed the final papers just before Christmas."

"Where did the Frelingers go?" Josh didn't remember ever meeting them when he'd lived in town, but he wondered why they would sell.

Jo Marie returned to the kitchen and lifted the coffeepot, silently asking if he wanted a cup.

Josh nodded.

"Apparently the Frelingers have decided to travel across the country in their motor home," Jo Marie explained. "It was loaded and ready to go the day I took over the inn. They handed me the house keys and were off to join their two daughters in California for Christmas as their first stop."

"They certainly weren't letting any grass grow under their feet," Josh said as she handed him a steaming mug of coffee.

"Do you take sugar or cream?" she asked.

"No, black is perfect." He'd gotten accustomed to drinking it that way when he lived with Richard.

"You have your choice of rooms," Jo Marie told him.

Josh shrugged. "Any one is fine. This isn't exactly a pleasure trip."

"Oh?" She seemed openly curious now.

"No, I'm here to set my stepfather up with hospice."

"I'm so sorry."

Josh raised his hand to stop her from expressing

sympathy. "We were never close and frankly we didn't have the best of relationships. This is more out of duty than anything else."

"If there's anything I can do?" she offered.

Josh shook his head. At this point there wasn't anything to be done. If he could have, he would gladly have avoided this altogether, but unfortunately there was no one else to take responsibility for Richard.

Jo Marie showed him a room on the second floor. It had a large picture window that overlooked the cove, and the Puget Sound Naval Shipyard was directly across the way. There were several ships and a moth-balled aircraft carrier visible, and the sky reflected the battleship gray of the navy vessels.

Richard had worked at the shipyard for most of his working career, Josh remembered. He'd served in the navy during the Vietnam war, and after being honorably discharged he had found work as a welder in Bremerton. Dylan had worked at the shipyard, too, until the accident that had claimed his life.

Stepping away from the window, Josh didn't bother to unpack his bag. He took out his cell phone and logged on to his email account to collect his messages, hoping for word on the next job. He hadn't even seen Richard yet and already he was planning his escape.

The first one that popped up was an email from Michelle Nelson, Richard's next-door neighbor. She'd sent it only a couple of hours earlier.

Josh read the message.

From: Michelle Nelson (NelsonM@wavecable.net)
Sent: January 12
To: JoshWeaver@sandiegonet.com
Subject: Welcome Home

Dear Josh,

I'm expecting you to arrive in Cedar Cove anytime now and I wanted to make sure we connected first thing. My parents are visiting my brother in Arizona—he's a new father—and I'm staying at their home to feed the dog and keep close tabs on Richard. I'm off work the next couple of days so give me a call once you're settled in at the B&B and I'll go with you to see Richard if you'd like.

Michelle
360-555-8756

Josh settled against the back of the chair and folded his arms over his chest. He remembered how Michelle's obvious infatuation with Dylan had been an embarrassment to his stepbrother. Still, Dylan had never been cruel to Michelle like some of the other boys in school had been, taunting her with names and off-color remarks and jokes.

He appreciated her offer to accompany him when he went to visit Richard for the first time. It would be great to have another person there to act as a buffer. Josh punched out the phone number Michelle had listed, and she picked up almost right away.

"Michelle, it's Josh."

"Oh Josh, my goodness, it's so good to hear your voice. How are you?"

"Good." Michelle's enthusiasm felt like a balm. He hadn't expected anyone to be pleased that he was in town. While Josh had had plenty of friends in high school, he hadn't kept in touch with any of them. Following his high school graduation he'd joined the army and headed almost immediately for basic training. Then he'd linked up with a construction company and worked his way up to project manager. He didn't mind the travel, so he bounced from town to town and from job to job, never staying longer than a few months in any one place. He'd seen a good part of the country and hadn't put down roots anywhere. In time, he'd settle down, he supposed, but he didn't feel the burning need for that to happen anytime soon.

"You sound wonderful," Michelle continued, her voice soft with what seemed to be remembered affection.

"So do you," he murmured. Josh had always liked Michelle, even though he'd felt sorry for her because of the extra weight she carried. "I suppose you're married by now with a passel of kids," he joked, confident that she'd found someone who would appreciate her.

He remembered her as being generous and kind. It didn't come as any surprise that she'd become a social worker, looking after others.

"No, unfortunately." Her voice echoed with regret and a tinge of sadness.

Josh was sorry he'd asked.

"What about you? Did you bring your wife and children with you to see your old stomping grounds?"

"No, I'm not married either."

"Oh." She sounded surprised. "I asked Richard about your family and he didn't know."

No reason he would—they hadn't spoken in years. "How's the old man faring these days?" he asked in order to change the subject.

"Not so good. He's both stubborn and foolish. He insists he doesn't need any help from anyone, although he's willing to let me take him meals and check in on him every now and again."

Same old Richard: unreasonable, cantankerous, and constantly in a bad mood. "Does he know I'm coming?" Josh asked.

"I didn't tell him," Michelle said.

"Would your parents have mentioned it before they left for your brother's?"

"I doubt it. None of us were sure whether you'd show or not."

Apparently the Nelsons knew him better than he realized. "I wasn't sure I would either," he admitted.

"Stop by my parent's house first," Michelle offered.

"I'll meet you there and we can go over to Richard's together."

"I appreciate the offer," he said.

Michelle hesitated and when she spoke her voice went soft, almost wistful. "I've thought about you often through the years, Josh. I wish . . . I wish we'd had more of a chance to talk at Dylan's funeral."

Josh couldn't remember seeing Michelle there although she would have surely attended. His own participation had been so brief there hadn't been time to really talk to anyone. It'd stung that Richard had discounted the strong relationship Josh and Dylan had shared. It was just another slight to add to all the rest, but as it stood now, Josh was Richard's only living relative.

"When would you like to stop by?" Michelle asked.

"I'll get settled in and be there in about an hour. Does that suit you?" The sooner he confronted the old man the better. Putting it off wouldn't make seeing him again any easier.

"Perfect. I'll see you at my parents' house then."

"See you," Josh said and disconnected the call. It felt good to have one ally in town, someone he could talk to freely. He'd forgotten how just being in this town, close to Richard, made him feel under siege.

His truck keys jingling in his hand, Josh started down the staircase.

Jo Marie met him at the bottom of the stairwell. "I'm going down to the bank this afternoon, but the key to your room unlocks the front door as well, so if I'm not here feel free to make yourself at home."

"Thanks, I will. I'm heading out now," he said. "I'm not sure when I'll be back." Josh had decided that he would drive around town before heading over to the Nelsons'. It would be interesting to see what changes the years had brought to Cedar Cove. He hadn't noticed that much when he'd exited off the highway. From the view in his room, the waterfront area didn't appear any different than what he remembered. He expected much had remained the same as well.

"I'll see you later, then."

"Later," he concurred. Leaving the B&B, he paused long enough to zip up the jacket he had yet to remove. The cold hit him hard as he walked outside. Rain had started to fall, a steady drizzle that was so common in the winter months around Puget Sound.

He headed for the high school and saw that other than a few more mobile classrooms, everything was as he remembered it. He parked the truck and walked around the back of the school to the track and football field. The track looked like it had been resurfaced recently. He'd run track in high school and done fairly well, but Dylan was the real athlete in the family—he'd even been on the Homecoming Court his senior year. By then Josh had been in the army, and he remembered how proud he was when Dylan had told him he'd been nominated.

Josh hadn't attended his own homecoming or, for that matter, the prom. He couldn't afford it and Richard wasn't likely to pay for anything beyond his most basic needs. After his mother died, Josh knew he couldn't depend on Richard for anything more than a roof over his head, and he'd been right. In the end Richard had been unwilling to provide even that.

From the high school, Josh drove down Harbor Street and was pleasantly surprised. The library was adorned with a freshly painted mural and the Chinese restaurant was in the same place he remembered. But several businesses were gone, including the dog-washing shop where he'd worked one summer between his junior and senior years in high school.

Finally he decided it was ridiculous to put his reunion with Richard off any longer and headed for his old neighborhood. Needless to say, he wasn't anxious to see his stepfather, but he was determined not to let the old man intimidate him any longer.

Josh parked on the street outside the Nelson house and reached for a pen and paper, quickly compiling a list of things he wanted to collect from the house. His mother's Bible was the first item he noted, along with her cameo. He'd give that to his daughter, if he were to have one. He also wanted to retrieve his letterman jacket and his high school yearbook from his senior year, both of which he'd paid for himself. He'd been unable to take them when Richard had kicked him out of the house. His stepfather wouldn't allow it.

An hour after his phone call with Michelle, Josh rang the doorbell to the Nelsons' house.

"Josh?" she asked, greeting him with a welcoming smile.

Surely there was some mistake. The person standing on the other side of the glass door couldn't be Michelle. The woman who stood before him was tall and slim and . . . strikingly attractive.

"Michelle?" he asked, unable to disguise his shock.

"Yes," she laughed softly, "it's me. I guess you haven't seen me since I lost the weight, have you?"

It was all Josh could do to close his mouth and not stare.

Chapter 3

Josh followed Michelle into her parents' home, still trying to assimilate the fact that the beautiful woman in front of him was Michelle Nelson. It was difficult to believe that the overweight teenager he remembered and this svelte woman were one and the same.

"Coffee?" she asked as she headed into the kitchen.

"Ah, sure." Josh's head continued to buzz. He wanted to ask her what had happened, but realized it might be rude.

Michelle filled a mug and handed it to him.

Josh had a difficult time keeping his eyes off her. He suddenly realized why he hadn't seen her at Dylan's funeral—he simply hadn't recognized her. She could have been standing directly in front of him, and for all he knew they might even have spoken. He remembered briefly talking to several people, a couple of whom he hadn't been able to place.

Josh continued to stare at her from above the rim of the coffee mug.

"Are you so shocked?" she asked, grinning widely. She stood on one side of the kitchen counter and he remained on the other.

He nodded, hardly knowing what else to say.

"I'm not the same girl I was in high school," she assured him. "And frankly, I'm glad."

"Clearly, you've changed." He pulled out the stool and sat down.

"We all do, don't you think? You're not the same as when you left Cedar Cove, are you?"

Josh conceded the point. "No, and like you, I'm grateful." As a teenager he'd been hotheaded and angry. He'd just lost his mother and his stepfather had rejected him. He didn't want to think about those days, and was glad he didn't need to repeat them.

"What can you tell me about Richard?" he asked.

She took a moment to consider the question. "Not much has changed about Mr. Lambert, personality-wise," Michelle said.

"You mean he's still cantankerous, stubborn, unreasonable, proud, and difficult?" Although Josh made it sound like a joke, he was serious. That was the Richard he remembered. If anything, Josh assumed Dylan's death and old age had probably intensified his stepfather's negative traits, although he hoped otherwise.

"Basically, yes," Michelle laughed, holding on to her coffee mug with both hands, halfway to her mouth. "He should be in a nursing home or some other care facility, but he won't hear of it."

"Same old Richard." Josh knew his stepfather must have put up quite a fight to remain in his own home. He couldn't fault Richard for that—he would have done the same.

"Same old Richard," Michelle echoed.

"What about hospice?"

Michelle lifted one slender shoulder. "He's refused to discuss it. He told me he doesn't want a bunch of people drooling sympathy, hanging around waiting for him to die."

Josh shook his head. He'd expected that Richard would be difficult even though he was close to death. Why change now?

He took one last sip of his coffee and set the mug on the counter. "No need to keep putting this off, let's go on over." He couldn't help thinking that the shock of seeing him might be enough to cause Richard to keel over. He felt slightly guilty for being so negative and was surprised by his own attitude, especially since it felt a bit like wishful thinking on his part.

Over the years Josh had worked hard not to resent

his stepfather. Yet he hadn't been in town for more than a few hours and he found himself reverting back to the same negative feelings he'd harbored when he'd left as a teenager. It was as if no time had passed whatsoever, and he was eighteen all over again—proud, immature, and angry.

"I'll grab my coat and be right back," Michelle said, setting her mug down as she left the room.

Josh stuffed his fingertips into his jean pockets. "I appreciate you going over with me."

"No problem." Michelle's words echoed from the hallway leading to the bedrooms.

When she returned, she was wearing a bright red jacket and a white knit scarf was draped around her neck. Outside, Josh was again struck by the cold winter wind cutting through him. Thankfully, the two houses were close together. The Nelsons had lived next door to his family ever since his mother had married Richard.

"Anything special I should know before I see him?" Josh asked, wishing he'd thought to ask sooner.

Michelle's steps matched his as they walked side by side in the drizzling rain. "He looks much older than his actual age. I first noticed the difference about six months after Dylan died. I don't think he's ever been the same since burying his son."

To his surprise Josh experienced a twinge of sympathy. Richard had lost two wives and his only son. His last remaining relative was a stepson he'd never liked. Everyone who had ever been important to him was gone. And after Dylan's death, Richard had no legacy to pass on to the next generation.

They climbed the steps onto the house's small porch. The carefully tended flower beds that his mother had pampered had been completely crowded out by the encroaching lawn. Josh had done his best to keep the beds weeded while his mother had battled breast cancer, and after she'd died, too. He'd been the only one to care. He looked away, refusing to allow something like a neglected flower bed to undo him.

"Mr. Lambert keeps the door locked most of the time." Michelle reached into the mailbox and extracted a house key. She unlocked the door and then replaced the key. It landed with a ping when it hit the bottom of the metal box.

"Yoo-hoo," Michelle called as she opened the front door. "Anyone home?"

"Who is it?" Richard asked in a voice that Josh found only vaguely familiar. His stepfather sounded as if he were in the family room off the kitchen.

"It's Michelle."

"I'm fine. I don't need anything."

"Good," she called back, leading the way. "Because I didn't bring you anything." She laughed and it was clear she was good at letting Richard's grouchiness run off her back.

They entered the room and Josh's gaze immediately went to the old man sitting up in the recliner.

It was the same one Richard had favored when Josh had lived with him.

The old man looked small and frail in the chair, and he had a blanket over his lap. He'd never been a robust man. By the time Josh was sixteen he had stood six feet, two inches taller than his stepfather, and he had grown another inch the following year.

What he lacked in height, Richard made up for in bravado. He'd never gotten overly physical with Josh, but the verbal abuse had been nonstop. It had gotten much worse after his mother's death.

Richard looked up and when he saw Josh, shock registered in his eyes. For just an instant his gaze seemed to soften, but any indication that he was pleased to see his stepson swiftly vanished.

"What are you doing here?" he demanded.

Josh stiffened, surprised that a dying man still had the power to intimidate him. "I came to see how you're doing and to get a few of my things."

"What things? You will take nothing, do you understand? Nothing."

Josh bristled and bit back an angry response, amazed at how quickly Richard could rile him up.

Michelle placed a restraining hand on Josh's arm. "Can I get you anything, Mr. Lambert?"

"No," Richard barked. He tossed aside the blanket and attempted to get out of the chair.

Before he could do anything to injure himself, Michelle rushed forward. "Mr. Lambert, please."

Richard eased back into a sitting position. He'd gone pale and he looked as if he were about to pass out. The sound of his deep, staggering breaths filled the room.

Josh felt terrible. He hadn't meant to bait him. He hadn't realized how fragile his stepfather was.

"I won't take anything without your approval," Josh assured him.

"You're nothing but a vulture," Richard said once he'd regained enough breath to speak. Even then it wobbled and was wispy. He pressed his hand over his chest. "You've come to circle overhead, just waiting for me to die so you can steal from me the same way you did when you were a teenager."

"I don't want anything from you," Josh insisted. Five minutes with his stepfather and his blood was boiling.

"If you're looking for a handout, then—"

"I want nothing from you," Josh insisted, cutting him off.

"You'll get nothing."

"Do you honestly think I would want anything of yours?" Josh asked. "Do I look that desperate?"

"You were desperate enough to steal two hundred dollars from me. You don't get much lower than that."

Josh knotted his fists. If he didn't leave now, he would do or say something he'd regret. Turning on his heel, Josh slammed out of the house and paced on the sidewalk as he struggled to deal with his outrage.

Michelle followed a few minutes later. By then Josh had regained his composure.

"Are you all right?" she asked.

Josh ignored the question. "How is he?"

"Weak, but okay."

Josh exhaled slowly and closed his eyes. "I don't think that could have gone much worse."

"Mr. Lambert isn't himself."

Josh snorted. "You're wrong. He hated me as a teenager and his feelings haven't changed." It must tighten the old man's jaw to realize that Josh was his only living relative.

"What's this about two hundred dollars?" Michelle asked.

"I didn't take the money," he answered vehemently.

"The missing money was the reason he kicked you out of the house, isn't it?"

He stuffed his hands in his pockets, hunched his shoulders, and nodded.

"Who took it?" Not waiting for a response, she answered herself. "Dylan?"

"He must have. I can only assume he intended to return it, but Richard discovered it was missing before he got the chance."

"And Mr. Lambert naturally assumed it was you."

It wasn't a question but a statement of fact. Josh

doubted that he'd ever forget that scene. Dylan had been in the kitchen when his father had stormed into the family room where Josh was studying. Shouting and cursing, Richard had grabbed Josh by the collar. Dylan had stood frozen with terror, shocked speechless while Richard literally kicked Josh out of the house.

Although Josh and his stepfather had never gotten along, Richard had never manhandled him before.

Later, Dylan had come to him. Josh knew that Dylan had taken the money, and Dylan knew that Josh knew. But he told his stepbrother that it was time for him to leave anyway, and that they should let things lie. Even if Dylan had confessed, it wouldn't have mattered. The missing money was just the excuse his stepfather had been waiting for.

What Richard didn't know was that Josh had already enlisted at the army recruiter's office. He was due to leave for basic training within a week of his high school graduation. He'd never planned on returning anyway, so clearing up the issue hadn't seemed important.

Michelle placed her hand on his sleeve. "Are you okay?"

Josh wasn't sure how to respond. Was he? "I'm surprised, is all. Surprised that Richard still has the power to rile me and shocked that he still has this much control over my emotions."

"What can I do to help?" she asked.

Even if he knew, Josh doubted he could answer. Even more shocking than the anger that had consumed him was the sadness that threatened to overwhelm him.

In his own way, Josh had made peace with his past. He didn't ever expect to be bosom buddies with his stepfather. Yet deep down, a part of him had hoped—had anticipated—that perhaps there was a chance they could finally come to terms. He didn't hate Richard; he never really had. The old man was at the end of his life and even now, even with only weeks to live, it seemed unlikely that he would be open to settling their differences.

"Josh?" Michelle asked again.

"Nothing, thanks. I'm grateful you were there."

"I think it might be best if I was with you next time you see Richard, too," she offered.

Josh concurred with a nod. "That's probably a good idea."

"Have you been to the Pancake Palace yet?" she asked, after a pause.

The question seemed to come from out of the blue. "I beg your pardon?" The Pancake Palace, which served a wide variety of food, but specialized in breakfast, had been the gathering place for teens following high school football games, but he hadn't thought about it in years.

"Have you had lunch?" she asked pointedly. "I'm always grumpy and easily upset on an empty tummy."

"Lunch?" he repeated, still caught in the throes of the confrontation with Richard. "I guess I haven't."

"Me either, and I'm famished. Join me?"

She seemed to assume his answer was yes because she wrapped her hand around his elbow and led him toward his truck. "It's after three already and I haven't eaten since early this morning," she said.

Josh doubted that he could down a single bite, but he needed to get away from Richard and the thought of returning to the bed-and-breakfast and sitting in his room held little appeal.

"Pancake Palace, it is," he said, opening the passenger door for Michelle and helping her inside.

He walked around the car and joined her. When he went to insert the key in the ignition, her hand stopped him. "That must have been difficult. I'm so sorry, Josh, so sorry."

He appreciated the gentle touch of her hand on his and the tenderness of her gaze. He found himself mesmerized by the changes in her. Not just the physical—although they were dramatic—but what struck him was her wisdom and maturity, neither of which came without dealing with some deep emotional pain.

Josh had his own issues, his own scars. Richard seemed determined to leave matters as they were between them and to die alone. If that was what his stepfather wanted, then far be it from Josh to stand in his way.

Chapter 4

I got everything situated with the bank so that I could accept credit card payment from my guests. I'd meant to take care of that earlier, but had put it off because so many other things required my attention.

I was back at the inn within a couple of hours after one quick stop at the grocery store. I spent the rest of the afternoon preparing the breakfast I intended to serve the next morning.

My one guest, Joshua Weaver, didn't return that afternoon, but he'd left his things in the guest suite, so I assumed he would show up in due course. Because

I was new to all this I wasn't quite sure how much or how little I would be expected to entertain.

According to the reservation book the Frelingers had left me, a second guest was scheduled to arrive at some point this afternoon or evening. Abby Kincaid. I readied a second room, fluffed up the pillows, and made sure everything was prepared. If I were to stay at a B&B, this was exactly the type of room I would choose for myself. I found the lavender walls inviting and comforting. The room had a queen-size canopy bed with lots of embroidered pillows, and at the foot of the bed was what my grandmother would have called a hope chest. I'd already checked inside and found extra blankets. The window seat was similar to the one in my own room, overlooking the cove with an excellent view of the marina where the watercraft gently bobbed in the slate-green waters.

Satisfied, I walked down the stairs just in time to see a vehicle pull into the parking area reserved for guests. Several minutes passed but no one came to the front door. Glancing out the window, I saw that my visitor was still seated in her car. My guess was that she was uncertain she had the right address. I was half-tempted to venture outside and reassure her she was at the right house.

If it hadn't been raining, I might have done just that. However, I wasn't eager to get wet and the afternoon was quickly growing dark. I turned on the gas fireplace and returned to the kitchen and slipped on my apron. I'd decided to bake a chicken potpie for dinner. While at the grocery store I'd picked up a roasting chicken, which I deboned, setting the meat aside.

After making a white sauce, I added poultry seasoning, chicken broth, plus several fresh veggies before stirring in the meat and leaving it on the stovetop to simmer. I was just getting ready to measure out the flour for the pie crust when the doorbell rang.

After quickly rinsing my hands, I hurried for the front entrance.

A woman who looked to be in her early thirties stood on the other side of the threshold, a suitcase by her side. Her dark hair was sopping wet, as if she'd been standing in the rain, which I couldn't understand because it was a short walk from the parking area to the porch.

"Hello," I greeted warmly. "You must be Abby Kincaid."

She nodded and offered me a weak smile.

"Come in, come in," I urged, ushering her in from the porch and out of the rain.

Abby walked into the foyer and glanced around, her gaze darting from one area to another. "I was here once, years ago," she explained. "That was before the Frelingers bought the house and turned it into a B and B."

"Oh, you must tell me what it was like," I said, eager to learn what I could about the history of the house. I knew that it'd once belonged to a prominent Cedar Cove family headed by a banker, which was somewhat ironic since I had given up my position at a bank to take over the house. The house had fallen into disrepair and the Frelingers had purchased it, refurbishing it from the basement to the attic and then turning it into a B&B. That, however, was the extent of my knowledge.

"A . . . friend of my mother's knew the owner. Everyone in town loved this old house. It's quite a bit different now." Her gaze continued to roam over what she could see of the downstairs.

From what I knew, the Frelingers had made extensive repairs and had changed all the electrical wiring and plumbing, adding updates from room to room. Mr. Frelinger had done much of the work himself. Clearly he was a master craftsman who had managed to save the period details while modernizing the house.

"So you're familiar with the area?" I didn't mean to appear overly inquisitive. Not knowing the town all that well myself, Abby might be able to enlighten me on its history.

"I was born and raised in Cedar Cove, but I . . . I haven't been back in several years. My parents moved away shortly after I graduated from college and, well, there wasn't any reason to return."

"So it's been awhile," I said conversationally.

"More than ten years."

I thought to ask her about friends, class reunions, and such but held back. She seemed edgy, uneasy, and I didn't want to add to her obvious anxiety.

"Would you like to fill out the paperwork before I show you to your room?" I asked, leading the way through the kitchen to my office. "I have you down for three nights, is that correct?"

"Yes," Abby said and hesitated. "I might . . . I hope to leave early, but I don't know what your policy is on that."

"It's no problem." I knew that some hotels charged a penalty for early departures, but as of that moment I didn't plan to. Because I was still getting my feet wet in this business I was willing to be more flexible.

"I'm in town for a wedding," she volunteered. "My older brother . . . I think Mom and Dad had just about given up hope that Roger would settle down and marry. We're all so happy for him and Victoria."

"That's wonderful."

Abby handed me her credit card. I quickly took down the information and set it aside. "Would you like me to show you your room?" I asked.

"Please."

Abby paused on the way toward the stairs and looked out over the lights of the city.

"It's lovely here at night," I told her. "And the view during the day is even better."

"I know . . . I always loved the view of the cove from this street." She reached for her suitcase and followed me up the staircase to the room down the hall from Joshua Weaver.

"There's only one other guest," I told her. "You'll probably meet him at breakfast tomorrow morning."

She nodded, but she didn't look overly interested in meeting anyone. After bringing her to the room and showing her where to get fresh towels and an extra blanket if she needed them, I returned to the kitchen and assembled the chicken potpie.

Once I got the pie in the oven I realized there was enough to feed an army. No need for me to eat alone. I set the oven timer and climbed back up the stairs to Abby's room. The door was closed so I knocked lightly.

"Just . . . just a minute."

I stood in the hallway for several moments before Abby unlocked the door. She held it only partially open. She didn't meet my gaze but I could see unshed tears glistening in her eyes. Rather than embarrass her, I quickly said, "You're welcome to join me for dinner, if you don't already have other plans."

"Oh, thank you, that's thoughtful. My family doesn't know I'm here . . . I came in a day early, but I . . . I'm not the least bit hungry."

A day early and she hadn't told her family. That seemed odd, especially since she was in town for such a joyous occasion.

"If you need anything, don't hesitate to ask."

"Thank you, but everything is fine."

The door was already halfway closed and it was clear she wanted to be alone. I respected that, since I'd felt that way myself many times in the last nine months, and was determined to leave her be until morning.

Still, I remained curious. Abby Kincaid had flown in from Florida, which was about as far away from Cedar Cove as a person could get while remaining in the continental United States. She appeared to be happy for her brother and his bride, but she didn't seem pleased to be in town. She'd mentioned that it'd been over ten years since she was last in Cedar Cove, but surely there were school friends she'd want to see.

The timer dinged and I brought the pie out of the oven. The crust was a perfect golden brown and the sauce bubbled up from the slits I'd made in the top. I left it on the counter to cool while I washed up the few dishes I'd dirtied.

One of my favorite spots in the B&B was a three-sided shelter across the driveway from the house. At one time there'd apparently been an outbuilding there, a much smaller residence I suspected. All that remained of the original building was the three walls, a roof, and a fireplace.

The Frelingers had turned it into a cozy space for sitting with chairs and stacks of wood for a fire. The rain had stopped and the night stars were out. I felt drawn outside. After I ate my dinner, I tucked my arms into my coat and ventured outside to the alcove.

Everything was ready for a fire to be lit in the stone fireplace and so I struck the match and watched as the paper immediately caught. Soon the kindling was crackling. I propped a small log on top and then settled into the chair and placed my feet on a stool. I had a blanket with me, and I spread it across my lap.

How peaceful it was. If I closed my eyes I could almost pretend that Paul was sitting by my side. This was how I'd dreamed we would spend our evenings, sitting together in front of a flickering fire that was warming us. We would discuss our day and find something to laugh about. I don't think I've ever laughed with anyone as much as I did with Paul.

His quick-witted comments were what I enjoyed most about him. He had such a wonderful sense of humor. He wasn't the kind of man who would ever be the life of the party; his humor was dry and subtle, little comments he made on the side, most of the time under his breath. I smiled at the memory.

I rested my head against the back of the chair and closed my eyes. I missed him so. A hundred times a day, even now, all these months later, I continually thought of him. Would it always be like this? I wondered, and guessed that it would. Paul would always be a part of me. It would have been our first anniversary this week and already I was a widow.

Well-meaning friends told me that in time I would love again, but that wasn't my expectation. I could imagine someday reaching a feeling of contentment again. Eventually this ache I carried with me like an extra layer of skin would gradually ease away. But fall in love again? I sincerely doubted it was possible. As for finding true happiness, experiencing joy again, that, too, remained a question that only time would answer.

The fire crackled gently and the warmth wrapped its way around me like a soft hug. Sitting there quietly, I mulled over the last couple of days and my first two guests at the inn.

In my dream that first night at Rose Harbor Inn, Paul had come to me and said I would feel alive again. I could see that he was right. My first two guests had arrived and both seemed to be carrying their own burdens. Perhaps I recognized it because I, too, carried a heavy load.

I thought about Abby sitting upstairs struggling to master her emotions over something, I knew not what. Joshua, too, appeared anxious, which was no surprise given the circumstances of his visit.

With my eyes closed I murmured a silent prayer that Abby Kincaid would find whatever it was she needed during her time in Cedar Cove and that Joshua Weaver would as well. While I was at it, I said a prayer for me—that the joy and contentment that had once been mine would return.

"Jo Marie." Abby said my name, stirring me from my reverie. I think I must have been half asleep.

"Yes?" I said, looking up.

"I hope I didn't wake you."

"Not at all, I was wool gathering," I joked, smiling up at her. "Would you care to join me?"

Abby hesitated and then sat down on the wooden chair next to mine. But she sat close to the edge, without relaxing against its back. She seemed wary, as if it might be necessary to flee at any moment.

"I . . . I saw you here from my window upstairs . . . you looked so peaceful."

Peaceful. In an instant I knew she was right. I did feel at peace. This was something new for me. It seemed impossible that in the depth of my grief I could find peace. The two words seemed like an oxymoron, seemingly contradictory. Not so, I'd discovered.

"I . . . I didn't pack toothpaste," Abby said as if this were a small tragedy. "I don't know how I could have forgotten it."

"I'd be happy to lend you mine for tonight since the stores are all closed, but I don't have any extra. There's a pharmacy on Harbor Street that will be open in the morning."

"Oh." Her shoulders sagged as if that was the last thing she wanted to hear. "Thanks, I'll walk down in the morning then," she said.

"I left a slice of chicken potpie out for you in case you changed your mind."

"No thanks, like I said I . . . I don't have much of an appetite."

"Well I hope you're hungry in the morning." I had big plans for my first official breakfast. I'd assembled the casserole earlier. The recipe said to let it rest overnight in the refrigerator. I planned to serve it with fresh fruit, home-baked muffins, fried bacon, and orange juice. I also had steel-cut oatmeal, if anyone was interested.

"What time is breakfast?"

I told her and then she quietly returned to the house; I mentioned I'd be close behind her.

And yet, lulled by the flames, comfortable and at peace, I wasn't sure how long I remained by the fire before turning in. I savored the warmth, thinking about the new life I was about to settle into.

Chapter 5

Abby Kincaid grabbed the sheet and tugged it over her shoulder. She forced her eyes closed but they quickly flew open. Shadows danced across the walls, taunting her. This was what she'd feared most about returning to Cedar Cove. Already the demons were at play, choking off her breath and any possibility of sleep.

The moon was full and bright, making it even more difficult to relax. Abby sat up and looked out over the cove. Moonlight shimmered across the water's smooth surface. At any other time she would have lost herself in the beauty of the scene before her. Not tonight though. Not tonight.

Abby had to sleep. It'd been days, no, weeks since she'd had a full night of uninterrupted rest. Her eyes burned and still her mind refused to stop spinning. Dreading her return to Cedar Cove, she'd fretted nonstop over her brother's upcoming wedding. She would give anything to have found an excuse to stay away. But how could she? This was her brother. Her entire family was planning to attend the wedding. Aunts and uncles . . . cousins, too, many of whom she hadn't seen in years.

Why, oh why, had Roger fallen in love with a woman from Cedar Cove? Abby had yet to meet her future sister-in-law, although she'd spoken to Victoria a couple of times on the phone. She seemed like a perfectly fine young woman. A gentle, kind person . . . and if she knew about the tragedy that hung like a dark cloud over Abby's life, Victoria had thankfully never mentioned it.

Although they were little more than strangers, her future sister-in-law had asked her to participate in the wedding, which Abby had agreed to do, albeit reluctantly. She would serve the wedding cake.

The only flaw that Abby could find in Roger's bride was the fact that she had chosen to be married in the last place on earth Abby ever wanted to see again.

She hadn't been in town twenty-four hours and already the temptation to pack her bags and return to Florida was stronger than ever. The fact that she'd been forced to arrive an entire day early complicated everything. Somehow, in her reluctance and nervousness, she'd made a mistake when booking her reservation. For her arrival date, she'd meant to put in Friday, arriving in time for the rehearsal and dinner. The wedding was early Saturday evening, and then, of course, the reception would follow. She'd purposely not chosen the motel her family had booked, preferring to remain away from the hubbub of activity. Her return was booked for the earliest flight out Sunday morning. She planned to be in and out of town as quickly as possible.

Here and gone.

No such luck.

By the time she realized that she'd booked her arrival on Thursday rather than Friday it was too late and too expensive to change her flight dates. All the seats were gone for the Friday flight. Although she hated the thought of it, arriving on Thursday made more sense. Abby had gritted her teeth and flown in early. Just what she wanted least—an extra twenty-four hours in Cedar Cove.

She hadn't told her brother or her parents about her mistake. It was probably better this way, in case she did run into anyone she knew from back then . . . before Abby had caused the death of her best friend and watched as the town of Cedar Cove sat in judgment of her.

For more than ten years, Abby had managed to avoid returning to her hometown. Eventually even her parents had found it necessary to move away. Oh, they'd used a convenient excuse, careful not to lay blame at her feet. But Abby knew the truth even if they were too generous to admit to it. No one needed to spell it out for her. Her parents hadn't been able to face their friends, or the Whites . . . especially the Whites.

Her father claimed he'd accepted early retirement from the shipyard, the largest employer in Kitsap County, and shortly afterward her parents had settled in Arizona. Her brother was already living in Seattle by the time of the accident, a corporate executive at Seattle Best Coffee. Of all the women he'd dated over the years, why oh why couldn't he have fallen in love with a woman from Seattle or Alaska . . . or Timbuktu? Anyplace other than Cedar Cove.

Well, there was no help for it. Abby was here now, like it or not. Here and miserable and afraid, so very afraid. A counselor she'd talked to years ago had suggested she confront her fears. Good advice, she supposed, as those fears were currently front and center. She'd run away from them for so long and now the awful memories were nipping at her heels, keeping her awake with the nightmare she'd spent the last fifteen years trying to forget.

It'd all started out so innocent, so fun. Abby and Angela had been best friends all the way through high school; Abby's mom had nicknamed them "The A Team." BFFs for sure. Angela was the best friend

Abby had ever had. They were both on cheer squad, both in soccer, both in drama classes, and were practically inseparable all through high school. It was more than being best friends though. Angela had been the one person in the world Abby felt free to share anything and everything with, knowing she'd never be judged. They could talk for hours, and often did. And oh how they could laugh.

Following graduation, Abby had headed for the University of Washington in Seattle while Angela attended Washington State University in Pullman, the arch-rival school and her mother's alma mater.

Even though they were an entire state apart, they'd communicated daily, and both of them had looked forward to Christmas break. Abby had saved a hundred things to tell her best friend, but mostly she wanted to update Angela on her relationship with Steve, her brother's roommate, whom she'd recently started dating. It'd only been a couple of months, but Abby was sure this was love, she was absolutely convinced of it. Real love. In retrospect, Abby realized she had known nothing about love . . . and even less about loss.

Over the years a few friends from Cedar Cove had attempted to stay in touch, but Abby hadn't responded to their letters or returned their Christmas cards. She hadn't kept in touch with Patty, Marie, Suzie, or her other good friends since she'd moved away.

How would she ever be able to celebrate Christmas again? Abby did her best to ignore the holiday completely. It was the worst time of the year for her and it never seemed to get better.

For a time she had made an effort to keep in touch with Angela's family, but they wanted no reminders of what had happened to their daughter. The truth was, they wanted nothing to do with her ever again. Although she desperately needed to hear from them, her letters were returned unopened.

When Abby could stand it no longer she asked her mother about the Whites, worrying as she did about them, but Linda Kincaid sidestepped her questions. When pressured, her mother confessed that matters had been difficult between the two families. Strained.

Not more than six months later, Abby's father announced that he'd taken early retirement and the family home was on the real estate market. Abby had long suspected that her father's retirement and the sudden desire to move had been prompted by what had happened that fateful December night. Both denied it, but Abby feared her parents were looking to protect her from the truth.

Either way, it no longer mattered. With her parents in Arizona, Abby had heaved a giant sigh of relief. She'd been grateful to put Cedar Cove behind her. Her parents' retirement plans were the perfect excuse to put that part of her life behind her and strive to look forward.

Only Abby had never quite succeeded in forgetting. Really, how could she forget Angela? Or shove her to the back of her mind as if her life had been of no importance? She'd been the one driving. She was the one responsible. The blame was squarely on her shoulders. What it took her years to realize was that she'd lost far more than her best friend that night. Right along with everything else, Abby had lost her soul.

The carefree happy teenager she'd once been had died that night right alongside her best friend. Her entire life had changed afterward—even her personality. Before the accident she'd been gregarious, outgoing, and fun-loving. These days she was much more subdued, intense, and quiet. She dated, but not much. It seemed grossly wrong that she should continue on with a happy life while Angela was dead. And from everything she'd learned about the White family, they'd never recovered from the loss of their only daughter.

Eventually Abby had graduated from college and left Washington State, but she was never the same. She had few friends; she avoided getting close to anyone, for it always felt like a betrayal of Angela. She lived in regret, or so her counselor had once told her. Nothing she did, good or otherwise, would ever be enough to wash away the burden of guilt she carried.

Through the years, the fact that she was responsible for killing her best friend had become part and parcel of who she was, who she was destined to always be.

After obtaining her degree, Abby had accepted a job in management at the QVC fulfillment center in Port St. Lucie, Florida. Florida was just about as far away from Cedar Cove as she could get, both physically and otherwise. Living in a place of ninety-degree winter days, humidity, and alligators made it almost possible to believe that a small wooded town on a cove in the Pacific Northwest was just a dream.

With her parents living elsewhere and her only brother in Seattle, there'd never been a reason to revisit her childhood home. Until now.

The family was excited for Roger. He'd been in and out of relationships for years before he met Victoria. Their mother had been ecstatic with the news when Roger and Victoria announced their engagement. This was Linda and Tom's best shot at being grandparents.

Everyone, Abby included, accepted that she would probably never marry. In many ways she felt like her entire life had been placed on hold following the accident. She'd grown accustomed to living in this emotional bubble.

Rubbing the sleep from her eyes, she glanced at the bedside clock radio for the tenth time. It was after six now and still pitch dark. She'd slept, if she could even call it sleeping, for a grand total of three hours.

Turning on the lamp by the bed, Abby reached for a book she'd brought with her. Immersing herself in a good story would occupy her for a while, keep her

mind busy until it was time to go downstairs and join Jo Marie and the other guest for breakfast.

Later she would venture into town to find the pharmacy Jo Marie had mentioned, and hope she didn't run into anyone she knew in the process. Then, this afternoon, she would hook up with her parents and her brother for Roger and Victoria's wedding rehearsal.

Abby was genuinely happy for her brother and resolved to put on a smile for his sake.

Chapter 6

Josh didn't sleep well. Little wonder—the dreadful scene with Richard played continuously in his mind, like a movie that refused to be shut off. Despite his best efforts the confrontation had gone even worse than he'd imagined it would. If anything, Richard seemed to dislike him even more intensely. It made sense. Richard had every reason to resent Josh. He was alive but the favored son—the son he'd fathered—was dead.

Breakfast was on the table when Josh came down the stairs. Jo Marie greeted him with a bright, "Good morning." Her natural cheerfulness caught him off guard. Just seeing her helped lighten his mood. Although she'd said he was her first guest since taking over the B&B, she was a natural. As far as he could tell she was the perfect hostess, seeing to his care, allowing him to set the parameters of how much attention he wanted.

Josh returned her greeting, then sat down at the table in the formal dining room. The room was bathed in sunlight, as if in reflection of Jo Marie's enthusiasm for the new day, and a welcome change from the gloom of the day before. His mother had been a morning person, Josh remembered. She'd sometimes woken him for school by singing to him. He grinned at the memory. Her chipper mood had irritated him at the time. Grumbling, he'd bury his head beneath his pillow.

Richard had been a different person back then. He'd always been in a rush to get out the door in the mornings and he often ate his breakfast standing up, gulping down one last sip of coffee before heading out the back door. No matter how much of a hurry Richard had been in, he'd always taken the time to kiss Teresa good-bye. Sometimes they kissed with such enthusiasm that Josh had been forced to look away. His stepfather had been a happier man back then.

Hearing footsteps behind him, Josh glanced over his shoulder. Jo Marie had mentioned another guest would be joining them. The woman looked about the same way as he felt. She kept her gaze lowered and smiled faintly when Jo Marie called out her cheery morning greeting.

The other woman didn't seem to notice him until she sat down at the table. Surprise registered on her face when she looked up.

"Morning," he said. While he didn't really feel like making conversation he didn't want to be rude.

"Morning," she replied with what seemed to be a certain reluctance.

"Josh Weaver, meet Abby Kincaid," Jo Marie said as she returned to the dining room, carrying a pitcher of orange juice.

Josh noticed that his coffee mug was already full. The casserole rested in the middle of the table along with a plate of crisp bacon, a stack of buttered toast with an array of jellies and jams, and home-baked muffins.

"Orange juice?" Jo Marie asked him.

"Please."

"None for me, thank you," Abby said.

Josh discovered he was ravenous. He hadn't eaten dinner the night before, although he'd enjoyed a late lunch with Michelle. They'd stayed at the Pancake Palace for nearly three hours, talking about everything under the sun, other than Richard. Pride wouldn't allow him to show how upset his stepfather had made him.

After he'd dropped Michelle off at her parents' house, Josh had driven around for another couple of hours, familiarizing himself with the town and the outlying areas around it once again. Cedar Cove was the only real home he'd ever known, and it felt strange to be back.

Michelle hadn't exaggerated the situation with Richard. Josh didn't doubt that his stepfather was dying and, odd as it seemed, he felt a twinge of loss. The end of an era, even if not a happy one. The end of his chance to make things, if not right, then different than they had been.

Perhaps his sadness was related to the fact that he would be all alone in the world once Richard died. And yet, that didn't make sense, because basically he already was alone. The two hadn't spoken in years.

Still, there it was, this feeling that he was on the verge of losing something important. He barely remembered his biological father, an alcoholic who'd abandoned him and his mother when Josh was five. His mother had died thirteen years later and then his stepbrother.

Josh noticed that he'd been staring sightlessly out the dining room window and ignoring everyone else. He spooned a large serving of the egg dish Jo Marie had brought into the room and ate it with gusto.

The meal was delicious. Josh had two helpings, which was unusual for him. By contrast, Abby barely touched her breakfast. She just shuffled food around on her plate when she assumed someone was watching. Josh doubted she'd swallowed more than a bite or two, if that. He guessed she hadn't experienced such a great night herself.

It seemed like they had each come to Cedar Cove weighed down with burdens. He didn't speak of his and she didn't either, which suited him just fine, although they exchanged polite conversation.

"Will either of you be available for dinner?" Jo Marie asked, sweeping into the dining room with a fresh pot of coffee.

"I don't have dinner plans," Josh confirmed. "But don't count on me."

"I'll be with my family," Abby returned apologetically.

"It's not a problem," Jo Marie assured them both and laid a hand on the top rung of the ladder-back chair behind Josh. "Is everything to your liking?"

After the scrumptious breakfast she had prepared, Josh could again hardly believe she was new to this. "It's wonderful."

Abby didn't respond; she seemed to be caught up in her own thoughts.

"Abby," Jo Marie prodded gently. "Anything more I can get you?"

Abby made an effort to smile, and failed. "Everything was . . . perfect. Thank you so much."

"No problem."

Jo Marie was like a bumblebee flirting from flower to flower, buzzing about the room. "I had the most wonderful night," she said as if she couldn't hold it in a moment longer. "I sat by the fireplace and soaked up the quiet. I can't remember an evening that peaceful in a very long while."

Josh was pleased that someone had found solace. He doubted it was possible for him while he was in Cedar Cove. He would like nothing better than to retrieve the few things he wanted and, if possible, leave that very morning.

He left the B&B shortly after breakfast. Michelle had said she'd meet him at her parents' house to try again with Richard. Josh appreciated her company.

As he drove toward his old neighborhood, he realized that while he and Michelle had spent a good portion of the day together, he still didn't know that much about her. He hadn't realized it at the time, but he'd done the majority of the talking. Michelle had seemed curious about his time away from Cedar Cove. She'd asked about his stint in the army and plied him with questions regarding his schooling and his jobs around the country. Josh couldn't remember a time he'd had a three-hour conversation with anyone that wasn't job related. Afterward he'd felt close to her, closer than he had to any woman in a very long while. He wasn't sure what to make of this, if anything, but it played on his mind.

Josh had never married, but it hadn't been a conscious decision. He'd dated plenty over the years and had been in three serious relationships. Eventually they'd fizzled out.

Josh wasn't sure why, other than the fact that he had never stayed in one place for long. One broken relationship was understandable, two was questionable, but three times? Really, that said it all. Clearly the trouble rested squarely with him. Josh supposed he was a prime candidate for counseling. No doubt he had unresolved issues regarding the father who had deserted him, and the depressing relationship he had with his stepfather.

When he arrived at the Nelsons', Josh noticed that the lights were on inside the house. Not so with his stepfather's place. Instantly alarmed, he started toward the run-down family home and stopped himself in the nick of time. If he rushed into the house and found Richard sitting up in a chair, he'd appear a fool. Best to stick with the plan. Get in. Get out. Get away.

Michelle opened the front door as he strolled up the walkway to her house. She held a mug in both hands. "Morning," she called out.

"Morning." Even now it was difficult to get used to the fact that this lovely woman was Michelle. The girl he remembered had been shy and retiring, seemingly uncomfortable in her own skin. They'd taken the school bus together for years.

She'd had friends. Josh was sure of that, but he simply couldn't remember who they were. What he did remember was the names the other kids called her. Michelle had ignored them, but still that must have hurt. A couple of times he'd put an end to it, but that had backfired on him. The kids had started to tease him, saying he was sweet on her.

"How about a cup of coffee?" Michelle asked.

"Sure." He wasn't so much interested in coffee as he was in delaying the inevitable—another confrontation with his stepfather. He followed Michelle into the kitchen and sat at the kitchen counter while she filled his mug.

"How long ago did you lose the weight?" he asked. That was probably not the best conversation starter, but it was the one question that kept popping up in his head.

Michelle shrugged as though it was no big deal. Josh wasn't fooled, it had been a major turning point in her life; it must have been.

"It's been a few years now."

Knowing how much she'd loved Dylan from afar, he asked, "Did Dylan ever see you . . . like this?" He wasn't sure how to phrase it and he hoped he hadn't insulted her.

"I'd lost quite a bit of weight by the time of his accident, but I doubt he noticed."

Josh found that hard to believe.

"Dylan wasn't living at home at the time," she clarified. "I didn't see him that often; he was involved with Brooke."

"Brooke Davis?" Josh asked. Dylan had been attracted to Brooke in high school. She was a wild child with bright red hair and a temperament to match. As far as Josh was concerned, Brooke was bad news. She'd brought out the worst in Dylan.

"They were living together?" he asked.

Michelle nodded. Josh realized he'd been naive to assume that Dylan had remained at home. It had always been understood that Josh was expected to move on as soon as he was out of school, but for Dylan it'd been a different story, and Josh had never thought otherwise.

Hiding his reaction to the news that Dylan had been living with Brooke, Josh sipped his coffee. Discussing his stepbrother upset him and so he abruptly changed the subject. "We talked a lot about me last night. What about you? You're not married either, right?"

"Not now."

"But you were?" This, too, came as a surprise, although it shouldn't have. Again he'd made a false assumption. Since she was so close to her family and helping out around the house, he'd naturally thought . . . well, he'd been wrong.

"I was briefly married," Michelle continued. "It was a mistake that I regretted almost immediately. I married Jason when I was twenty and we were divorced by the time I turned twenty-one. He's since remarried and moved out of the area."

"I'm sorry," Josh said, not exactly sure what to say. Although she made light of her failed marriage, he supposed it had cut deep emotional wounds in her heart.

"Yes, so am I," she said with a shrug.

Josh noticed that she didn't make excuses, lay blame, or list the reasons for the divorce like some of the women he'd dated tended to do. He considered that a sign of maturity on her part. He took another sip of coffee. "After I dropped you off, I realized I hardly asked anything about you."

"What do you want to know?" she challenged.

"Well, for one, where do you live?"

"I have a condo on the water in Manchester."

Those must be new. Josh didn't remember any condos over there. "Do you enjoy your job? It can't be easy to be in social work when so many people need help."

"Actually, I love my work. I'm fortunate to work on the adoption end, and to be in charge of finding permanent homes for children who need them. It's rewarding on a number of levels."

He hesitated, not wanting to make her feel like he was grilling her with questions. "I'm grateful you're helping me with Richard . . . I want you to know that. I'm hoping today will go better."

"I hope so, too." She offered him a gentle smile.

Josh had a hard time looking away. She really was a beautiful woman. She'd always been beautiful, both inside and out, but he'd been too blind to see it. Everyone had.

She set her mug in the sink and seemed uncomfortable under his gaze.

The atmosphere had gotten a bit thick so Josh filled the silence with words. "And I really appreciate how you and your parents have been keeping tabs on Richard. You were always good neighbors." He recalled how Michelle's mother had brought over meals when his own mother was so desperately sick.

Michelle lowered her gaze. "Richard and my mother had a falling out a few months back. When she took a meal over to him, she found him on the floor and dialed nine-one-one. Richard got upset and ordered her out of the house and told her not to come back."

Foolish man. But that sounded just like Richard.

"Your father's been checking on him then?" Josh asked.

"No. The only one he'll allow in the house is me."

In response Josh shook his head and did his best to hold back a smile. Apparently his stepfather wasn't immune to a pretty face.

"I think it all goes back to my high school crush on Dylan. Seeing me makes it easier for him to deal with his loss somehow. I don't know why, but mostly he's pleased when I stop by."

"Does Brooke ever come around?"

She snickered softly. "Never. She didn't even attend Dylan's funeral. From what I heard she spent the day getting drunk, crying in her beer."

"Is she still around town?"

"Don't know," Michelle murmured. "I don't really care to know."

Josh didn't really care either. "Richard's gotten all the more difficult, hasn't he?"

She didn't bother to hide the truth. "I'm afraid so."

While Richard wouldn't appreciate it, Josh felt he had to ask. "Is there anything I can do for him?"

Michelle mulled this over, briefly nibbling on her lower lip. "I . . . don't think he'd accept help from you."

Josh figured as much. Having her say what he already suspected did little to cut the disappointment. Despite their negative history, he did want to help the older man.

"Have you spoken with his doctor?" he asked.

"Some. I've tried to phone a couple of times. Like I said earlier, Richard shouldn't be living by himself, but he insists that if he's going to die, he wants to be in his own bed."

"Thank you for being such a good friend to him," Josh said, and he meant it.

"I would have done it for Dylan . . ."

"You loved him, didn't you?"

She hesitated. "At one time perhaps, but you didn't let me finish."

"Sorry."

"I did it for Dylan . . . and for you."

Chapter 7

I was busy cleaning up in the kitchen when the doorbell rang. Setting aside the dish towel, I walked toward the front door. On my doorstep, smiling at me, was a striking woman with salt-and-pepper hair. She was dressed in a raincoat and a bandanna and she was holding a tray of what looked like muffins.

"Hello, I'm Peggy Beldon."

Beldon, Beldon. The name rang a vaguely familiar bell.

"I believe the Frelingers might have mentioned that I would be stopping by. Sandy called and asked if I had time to chat with you about the bed-and-breakfast."

"Oh, of course." That was where I'd heard her name. The Frelingers had mentioned that they'd asked their friend and fellow B&B owner to stop by to answer any questions I might have about the business. They'd been eager to start their new life, but didn't want to leave me without support. I appreciated their thoughtfulness.

"Please, come inside," I said, and opened the door for the other woman. It'd started to rain again, which certainly wasn't uncommon for this time of year.

"I brought you some freshly baked blueberry muffins. The berries are from my own bushes. I had to fight the deer for them last summer but I managed to get enough to freeze." She pulled off her bandanna and stuffed it in her pocket, and then removed her coat. "My husband and I own Thyme and Tide on Cranberry Point."

"Welcome," I said.

"I meant to phone before I came, but I was headed this way anyway, so I thought I'd just drop by. My husband is getting his teeth cleaned and the dentist is just around the corner from here. I hope it's not an inconvenient time?"

"Not at all. In fact, it couldn't be more perfect. I was just about to take a break." I brought her into the kitchen and set about assembling a pot of tea. "I'm still bumbling around a bit." Up until now, I'd been acting on instinct, and I welcomed the opportunity to speak to someone with more experience. I was sure there were tricks of the trade I needed to learn.

My mother was a wonderful hostess and I'd inherited her knack of making people feel at home. I figured running a bed-and-breakfast couldn't really be that much different from having overnight guests. Could it?

I poured the tea and brought out a plate for the muffins. I'd served my two guests breakfast, but I hadn't taken time to have anything myself beyond a glass of orange juice. Breakfast was my least favorite meal of the day, and I was usually satisfied with a latte or juice. By ten-thirty, however, my stomach had started to growl.

Peggy blew into the teacup, trying to cool the steaming liquid. Her elbows rested comfortably on the tabletop. "So, how are you settling in?"

"Everything seems to be going well thus far, but it's only been a few days."

"Good. I hope you don't mind if I make a few suggestions."

"Oh, of course. You're the one with the experience." I settled back in my chair with my tea, savoring the ginger-mint scent, and reached for a blueberry muffin.

"Have you gotten your food handler's license yet?" Peggy asked me.

I was ashamed to admit I hadn't. "Not yet, but I plan to soon."

"The sooner, the better," Peggy urged. "It doesn't take as much time as you'd think and you can take the training that's offered online easily enough."

That was welcome news. I'd had it on my to-do list to research the options, but I hadn't gotten there yet. With so much to do, it'd been easy enough to put that off.

I could see that Peggy had a lot to offer in the way of experience, and I didn't want to rely on my memory. "Excuse me for just a moment, I want to take notes."

"Oh, sure."

I scooted out of my chair and went into my office, where I collected a small yellow tablet and a pen.

Peggy waited until I'd settled back down before she spoke again. I noticed that she'd helped herself to a muffin while I was away. I took a bite of my own and it was delicious.

"I understand you're new to the area," she said as she peeled away the paper wrapper from the muffin.

"To Cedar Cove, yes, but not to Puget Sound."

"That will help."

"Oh?" I asked.

"It's important to familiarize yourself with Cedar Cove. Bob and I grew up here, and although we'd been away for several years we thought we knew this town. We did, but not as well as we should have. You need to view it through the eyes of your guests."

I licked crumbs from my fingertips. The muffin

was still warm in the center. "I'm not entirely sure I know what you mean . . .through the eyes of my guests?"

"Take the time to become acquainted with local businesses and the area's attractions. Visit the Chamber of Commerce or, better yet, join yourself. We have a Visitors Center, too. Get to know the local restaurants and make a binder with their menus. That will give your guests options when they need a recommendation. Bob and I had small maps made so our guests will have an idea of where they are in town."

"That's a wonderful idea." Reaching for my pen, I made a note on the pad.

"Find out what you can about local events, too," Peggy advised. "We discovered that our guests thoroughly enjoyed Concerts on the Cove last summer. They take place every Thursday night at six. Various entertainment groups are brought in and are paid for through donations from local businesses. You'd be amazed at the talent and the variety. People bring lawn chairs because the seating fills up so quickly. And a lot of families take picnic baskets as well."

"That does sound like fun."

"It is and it's a good way to meet your neighbors. We all tend to get busy and isolated. Because Bob and I live out on the Point, we don't have close neighbors, and I miss that."

Being in town, then, was a bonus for me. "I haven't had the chance to meet anyone just yet."

"You will," Peggy assured me. "Sandy and John were such a wonderful couple and they were much loved in town. I'm sure they spread the word that you'd be taking over for them. People will want to meet you.

"Why don't you host an Open House?" she suggested all of a sudden. She sat up straighter. "Really, you should. That would give the neighbors an opportunity to meet you and for you to meet them."

"Well, yes, that does sound like a fun idea, but there are a few things I'd like to take care of first."

"Of course. Anything I can help with?"

My head was spinning with ideas and a list of items I wanted to accomplish. "Well, for one, I've changed the name of the Inn."

She nodded as if that was understood. "That will mean a few expenses but it'll make it your own."

I understood a name change would mean having new brochures, business cards, and stationary printed and that sort of thing, but I'd never feel that the B&B was completely mine until I renamed it. "I've decided to call it Rose Harbor Inn."

"Rose Harbor Inn," Peggy repeated and frowned slightly.

"You don't like it?"

Peggy set her teacup on the saucer. "It's not that—I think it's a perfectly lovely name, but Sandy doesn't have any rosebushes."

"I noticed. Rose is my surname. I've started a to-do

list and I plan on planting a big rose garden, one with an arbor and a bench where my guests can sit. Some of my favorite roses are the antique ones . . . I have access to several plants and their scent is incredible." I knew I was chatting on, giving her far more information than necessary, but I couldn't seem to stop myself.

"You'll need a new sign and those can be pricey; you should know that up front."

I'd already looked into having a sign made and been shocked at the cost.

"Have you thought about hiring a handyman?" Peggy asked.

"Not yet . . . " I'd known that eventually I'd need one, but hadn't started looking just yet.

"Let me give you the name of a reliable man. Bob does a good portion of the work around Thyme and Tide, so we've only needed Mark on rare occasions. Mark does woodwork as well. I'm sure he could give you a competitive bid for a new sign."

I reached for my pen once more.

"His name is Mark Taylor. You'll like him . . . but," she hesitated.

"But?" I prodded.

"He can be a little prickly at times. Rest assured his bark is worse than his bite. He moved into town a few years back, but no one seems to know that much about him. While he might not be Mr. Personality, he does good work at a fair price."

Well, I mused, all I needed in a handyman is a skill with tools. I didn't care if he was a conversationalist or not.

"I have his phone number in my cell phone contacts." Peggy reached for her purse and rummaged through it until she retrieved her mobile phone. Pushing a few buttons, she gave me his number. I'd give "Mr. Personality" a call later and perhaps arrange a meeting so he wouldn't be an unknown quantity when an emergency arose.

Peggy reached for her tea again and I did, too. It had finally cooled and I sipped the comforting brew.

"Anything else I should know?" I asked.

Peggy thumped her fingers against the tabletop as she considered my question. "Do you have a marketing plan?"

I did, and we briefly discussed my ideas. She seemed to approve and I smiled at the way she had assumed a big sister role already, even with a touch of well-meaning bossiness.

"You'll soon discover that word of mouth is important. You'd be surprised by how much damage one dissatisfied guest can do. I have the name of a great website designer if you need one. Don't overspend on this when you don't need to, okay?"

"Okay."

Peggy relaxed against the chair. "Sorry, I get a bit opinionated at times. Just ask my husband."

I didn't take offense. I'd already seen to that and

had in fact been working closely with a web designer almost from the day I'd signed the final papers. At least that was one thing I'd accomplished. I was determined to make this venture successful, and yet I wasn't going to let her make me feel overly anxious.

"There are national, state, and local B and B associations. Join them."

"Do you belong?" I asked.

"We do. My husband and I have been active on the local and state level. I'll let you know when the next meeting takes place; I'll bring you myself."

"Thank you, I'd appreciate that."

"My pleasure," Peggy said. "One last thing."

"Yes?"

"How comfortable are you around computers?"

"Very."

"Good. Get familiar with your software programs. You're going to need them for accounting and for record-keeping purposes. There's a wonderful program Bob found for taking reservations. I'll get the name of it for you."

"Perfect. That would be great." I thought about the Frelingers' reservation book and agreed that I could probably afford to be brought into the twenty-first century.

"There's also some excellent software available for property management."

I took a deep breath and renewed my vow not to panic at the to-do list. One step at a time.

Peggy finished the last of her tea and then checked her watch. "Bob should be finished by now, so I'd best get back to the dentist's office. It was a real pleasure to meet you, Jo Marie."

"You, too." I resisted the urge to hug her. Although the visit had been quick, I felt as if Peggy and I had been friends for a long while. Her take-charge manner was comforting, and it made me smile. "Thank you for the muffins, too."

"I'll pass along the recipe if you'd like." She reached for her coat and then started for the front door.

"I would love the recipe," I said, trailing along after her. I was convinced my guests would enjoy these wonderfully flavorful muffins. Then again Peggy might not take kindly to me sharing her special recipe with my own guests.

As if she read my mind, Peggy grinned. "Not to worry, I've handed this recipe out all over town. The secret, at least in my opinion, is the home-grown blueberries. That's one of the reasons I'm willing to fight off the deer every summer. Deer might be lovely creatures, but they can be real nuisances."

I hadn't seen a live deer in more years than I could remember—not since I'd been a teenager. I'd thought they were magical creatures when they appeared at dawn or dusk. It surprised me that people who lived outside the city thought of them as pests.

"By the way, you might want to do something to

protect your roses, once your garden is planted. Roses happen to be one of deer's favorite eats."

"Deer venture into town?"

"They do. They're more prevalent outside the city, but it certainly isn't unusual for them to make their way from one backyard to another, munching on everything in sight."

I'd find a way to protect the roses. This garden was too important for me to willingly hand it over to the area wildlife.

Peggy slipped her arms into her coat. "Be sure and give Mark a call. He's always busy, so it would be a good idea to give him a heads-up about the sign. I know he'll do a good job. Just don't be offended if he barks at you."

"Okay, I won't." I held open the front door for her.

I watched as Peggy quickly walked to where she'd parked her vehicle. Our visit had lasted less than thirty minutes, but I felt as if I'd gotten a year's worth of information and advice. I planned to put everything into action as quickly as possible.

Energized by Peggy's visit, I headed back into the house and, reaching for the phone, punched in the number for Mark Taylor, the handyman she'd recommended.

He answered on the fourth ring, just before the phone switched over to voice mail. "Yeah, what is it?"

he demanded breathlessly, as if he'd rushed to get to the receiver in time.

"Oh hi," I said, "my name is Jo Marie Rose."

"Who?"

"Jo Marie Rose. I'm new in town," I babbled nervously. "Peggy Beldon gave me your name."

"What do you need?" he asked with more than a hint of impatience.

"Well, as it happens, I need help with a number of projects."

"How old are you?"

"Excuse me?" The man certainly didn't lack for nerve.

"Your age," he repeated. "Frankly, you sound like you're still in high school."

"Well, I'm not and what should that matter anyway?" I got the distinct feeling that I wasn't going to like this man. He was far too brusque to suit me, but then again Peggy had warned me.

"Your age will tell me how far down to put you on the list."

I grew more agitated by the moment. "I don't think my age is any of your business."

"Okay, fine, don't tell me."

"I have no intention of doing so."

I heard him mutter under his breath, "Would you like me to guess?"

"No, what I'd like is an estimate for a new sign for the B and B I recently purchased from the Frelingers."

"When do you need it?"

"The estimate or the sign?"

"Both."

"As soon as possible." I wasn't sure I was going to be able to work with this man. "Have you done work for the Frelingers before?"

"Plenty."

"When can I expect to see you?"

"I'll put you on the list. I heard the Frelingers had found a buyer," he said.

I noticed that he didn't offer his welcome. What an unpleasant man.

"You're not from these parts, I heard," he said.

"From what I heard, neither are you," I returned. I could give as good as I got.

He ignored that. "I can probably stop by sometime later today."

"Okay, but call first. I have errands to run and I might not be here." Nor did I have any intention of waiting around for him all afternoon.

He chuckled as if I'd said something amusing. "Call first? Do I sound like the kind of man who enjoys making phone calls?"

I had to admit he didn't. "Take your chances then."

"I will."

I was tempted to make a sarcastic comment like "nice talking to you" but resisted. I did have to admit, though, that I was curious about Mark Taylor.

Chapter 8

Josh stared at Michelle and wondered what she'd meant. She'd been a friend to Richard because of how she felt about Josh? That made no sense. They had no relationship. Oh sure, he'd been sympathetic when they were teenagers. He'd helped her dad paint the garage one summer and she'd brought him a glass of iced tea and they'd chatted a bit, but Josh had never thought of her as anything more than a friend—in part because he had always assumed she'd set her sights on Dylan. He looked at her with fresh eyes, somewhat astonished that he'd been so blind.

For now, Josh decided to ignore the comment. It

was better that way. Less complicated. Less troubling. He couldn't focus on anything other than dealing with Richard; anything else would be distracting.

Interrupting his thoughts, Michelle asked, "You ready to slay the dragon?" She seemed anxious to let the comment slide as well.

Josh had never thought of himself as a dragon slayer, but he liked the analogy. "Ready as I'll ever be."

Grabbing his jacket he walked with Michelle across the yard toward Richard's home. Josh noticed that the house was showing a lot of disrepair. The gutters needed to be cleared and it looked like it was well past time to have the roof checked for leaks. The siding could use a paint job as well.

Richard had always been a stickler about keeping the house and yard neat—he'd taken great pride in it.

It seemed his stepfather had given up on just about everything after Dylan's death. The neglect also said that Richard had been unwell for a long while.

Michelle didn't bother to do more than politely knock before she opened the door and let herself into the house.

"Richard, it's me," she called out as she led the way inside.

"**He's** not with you, is he?" Richard called.

By **he,** Richard must mean Josh.

"I'm here," Josh shouted back, trying to keep it light.

They found Richard in the family room, sitting in his recliner, his feet up and his legs covered by a knitted afghan. It was the dark blue one his mother had knit the year before she died. Josh remembered how she'd struggled with getting the cables all to face the same direction. Funny how little things like that stuck in his mind like a protruding nail in a floorboard, catching on things. For an instant Josh experienced a sense of overwhelming loss. He was a man of well over thirty, but he missed his mother. He shook it off before either Richard or Michelle could see his sadness.

"What do you want now?" Richard demanded. His voice was gruff and weak, as if he'd wanted to shout but didn't have the strength or the breath to manage it.

"Just a couple of things that belonged to my mother," Josh said, keeping his voice level and calm.

"Like what?"

"Her cameo." His mother had worn it nearly every day. She'd loved the small broach that had been passed down to her from her mother.

Richard frowned and shook his head as if to say he didn't remember any cameo. "I don't know what you're talking about."

Josh was convinced his stepfather had gotten rid of it just to spite him. "This cameo," he clarified and grabbed a photo of Richard and his mother off the bookcase and handed it to Richard. "See, there on her blouse. It belonged to her before she married you and I'd like to have it to remember her by."

Richard stared at the framed photograph for a long time before he answered. "I buried your mother with the pin . . . I didn't think."

Josh frowned. He tried to remember seeing his mother inside the casket and couldn't recall what she'd been wearing or the jewelry she'd had on at the time.

"The funeral director would have given it back to you," he insisted. "Right along with her wedding ring."

Richard stared back at him and slowly shook his head. "I . . . I don't know where it is, and even if I did . . ."

Josh didn't stay to hear anything more. Not even five minutes inside the door and his temper was ready to explode. The two of them couldn't be in close proximity without an angry outburst.

"Where are you going now?" Richard called after him.

Josh ignored the question and headed up the stairs to what had been his bedroom at one time. He heard footsteps behind him and he knew Michelle was trailing after him. Being in Cedar Cove again was proving to be so much more difficult than he'd ever anticipated.

"Josh?" Michelle reached him just before he entered his old room.

He heaved in a deep breath in order to center himself. His emotions had gone from grief to anger so quickly that even he was shocked. This entire trip had him on an emotional roller coaster. Josh wasn't accustomed to dealing with these sharp ups and equally rapid downs. His heart pounded hard against his ribs while he struggled within himself.

"I apologize, Michelle," he said, turning to face her and planting his hands on her shoulders. "I don't know what it is about Richard that makes me so angry. I didn't mean to blow up like that."

"It's a volatile situation," she said. "I understand."

Josh stuffed his hands in his pockets. She was right; it was that all right, and more.

"If you want I'll ask Richard if I can look through his bedroom for your mother's cameo."

Josh shook his head. "It would probably be better to just wait."

"You mean . . ."

She didn't say the words out loud. She didn't need to complete the thought for Josh to know what she was asking.

"Yeah," he confirmed. Josh wanted to wait until Richard was dead to find the cameo, if it was to be found. No sense unsettling the old man any more than he already had.

"So which room was yours?" Michelle asked as they stood in the middle of the narrow upstairs hallway. Dylan's bedroom was on the right and Josh's on the left. The bathroom they'd shared was at the end of the hallway. The master bedroom was downstairs. Josh wondered if Richard had taken that into account when he purchased the house years ago, anticipating that he wouldn't have the strength to climb the stairs in his old age. He couldn't now; otherwise he would have followed Josh up the staircase.

Instead of answering Michelle's question, Josh opened his bedroom door. The room looked exactly as it had when he'd been in high school. The bedspread was the same one that had been there when he'd left—correction—when he'd been kicked out.

The dresser and mirror were also exactly as he remembered them. He walked over and opened the dresser drawer and frowned. Instead of his T-shirts being in the top drawer where he always kept them no matter where he lived, he discovered his socks and underwear. They were stuffed haphazardly inside, which was just the way he'd left them—in a different drawer. The second one down held the T-shirts.

"Do you want to pack up any of these clothes?" Michelle asked. "They look almost brand-new."

Josh shook his head. "I'd prefer to give them all to charity . . . except," he paused and smiled at Michelle. "I want my letterman's jacket." He'd earned that letter his senior year in track. Dylan had been the athlete who all the girls had pined for, but Josh had made his mark on the track field. He wasn't a great runner, but he'd been good enough to make the team.

"Where'd you keep it?" Michelle asked, sounding excited herself.

She'd made a point of attending all the school's sporting events, including the track meets. Josh remembered how she used to cheer the team on from the sidelines, and was grateful. A couple of times he'd gotten a ride home with her. His mother had been too sick to attend the meets and Richard, well, he couldn't be bothered. Even driving to pick Josh up after an event had seemed to be a huge burden for him, and he'd always complained. So much for parental support.

Josh slid open the closet door. A couple of shirts remained and a good pair of slacks, the very ones he'd worn to his mother's funeral. Then he saw his letterman's jacket.

"Oh, Josh." Michelle's hand flew to her mouth.

Someone had taken a razor blade to the sleeves, ripping them open, slashing away at the leather.

Someone?

Josh was able to narrow that **someone** down to a single individual in less than a second.

Richard.

It could only have been Richard. For an instant he saw red. Josh wasn't about to stand by and ignore this. He didn't care that Richard was sick, this was destructive and immature for a grown man. Josh started out of the room when Michelle placed a restraining hand on his arm.

"Why?" Josh demanded. "What did I ever do to Richard that would give him reason to destroy the one thing I was most proud of accomplishing in high school?"

"Oh Josh, I hardly know what to say . . ."

"Why?" he demanded again. "What could I have possibly done for him to hate me this much?"

Josh sank onto the end of the bed. Michelle sat with him and reached for his hand, gripping it with both of her own.

"I think he did it the day he learned Dylan was dead," she said.

"How would you know?"

"I don't for sure. It's an educated guess. He was in such pain that he lashed out."

"At me? But why? Explain it to me if you can, because frankly it looks pretty sick."

"Because you were alive and his son was dead," she explained. "You were only here on the day of the funeral, but I was around afterward and it was bad for Richard. So bad that my parents called me and asked me to talk to him. Richard was inconsolable, in such terrible grief that no one seemed to be able to reach him. My family thought I might be able to help. You have to understand that he didn't come out of the house for days. He didn't eat, didn't bathe."

"I was alive and his son was dead."

"I realize that makes no sense." Michelle squeezed his arm in consolation.

Josh wanted to lash out at his stepfather, make him sorry for what he'd done; instead he forced himself to calm down.

"In other words, punishing me for being alive made sense to Richard," Josh said.

She leaned against him. "Letting your anger get the best of you now wouldn't do either of you any good."

Josh knew she was right. As difficult as it was, he'd need to simply let it all go. "Actually, in some way it doesn't come as that much of a shock. Richard never liked me. I was little more than an encumbrance that he had to tolerate while my mother was alive."

"Your mother loved him, though, despite his flaws," Michelle said.

"She did." Josh sighed and realized Michelle was right. His mother had been happily married to Richard. Josh's father had abandoned the family when he was barely five and Teresa had struggled as a single mother, doing the best she could. She viewed Richard as an honorable man. And to her, he had been all that and more.

Unfortunately, Josh's stepfather had never taken a liking to him. Josh tended to think that Richard had never tried. He'd married Teresa and found in her a wife and a mother for the son he loved. As it happened, Teresa had come with a bit of baggage in the form of a son, whom Richard did his best to ignore.

It hadn't taken very long for Josh to figure out the lay of the land. Dylan was the apple of his father's eye.

It was always Dylan, and nothing Josh accomplished would ever measure up in Richard's eyes. Josh had been a fatherless boy, longing for a male figure in his life, which only made it worse. While Dylan didn't excel academically, he was a star in both football and basketball. Josh helped him get a passing grade in geometry, earning his stepbrother's respect. The two got along just fine.

Not so with Richard and Josh. They locked heads often, and although Josh was almost always on the losing end, it didn't stop him from challenging his stepfather.

"He was good to my mother," he said, deep in thought.

"I see this same scenario in my work again and again. Richard loved your mother, but wasn't at all loving with you."

In response Josh snickered. "You could say that."

"Did he . . . did he ever abuse you?" she asked. Being a social worker, this was probably a subject she dealt with far too often. It'd been bad, but never as bad as that.

"Never with his fists."

"Verbally?"

Rather than meet her stare, Josh looked away. "Every chance he got."

"Didn't your mother—"

"He was careful around her and she never heard the things he said." Nor had Josh told her. His mother had been happy and Josh wasn't about to destroy the little bit of contentment she'd found in her marriage to Richard Lambert.

Josh stood and opened the drawer in his nightstand. He'd placed his senior year high school yearbook there. He breathed a sigh of relief—it was still there. He set the book on his lap and ran his hand over the slim hardcover as if looking for damage.

"Did he destroy that, too?" Michelle asked.

Just from the feel of the annual, Josh knew something was wrong. Opening it, he quickly discovered that several pages had been ripped out. His graduation picture for one, and several others as well. Josh guessed that Richard hadn't sat down and methodically flipped through the book until he found what he wanted, but had blindly ripped pages from the yearbook in a rush of anger and grief. It was all a little nuts—the violence of the act—even all these years later. Josh found it disturbing to be so loathed by his stepfather, although it shouldn't come as a shock.

"What are you going to do?" Michelle asked again with trepidation, as if she were afraid of his answer.

"Nothing."

"That's wise," she assured him. "You're a much more sophisticated, emotionally secure man than he is."

Richard would like nothing better than to get an angry reaction from him. Michelle was right; he had to let this go. If he had responded reflexively with rage, it would have only compounded the problem. As difficult as it was, Josh refused to give his stepfather that much power over him.

Michelle leaped to her feet.

"Don't worry," he assured her. "I don't intend to say a word to him."

"Good."

"You know that's what Richard wants, don't you?"

She nodded. "He'll be looking for your reaction."

"I'm not going to give him one."

"He's sorry, you know."

"Richard? I doubt it."

"Actually, I believe he is. He didn't want you to go upstairs and this is why. He's embarrassed by what he did, but he couldn't make it up the stairs to hide the jacket or the yearbook."

Josh wanted to believe his stepfather regretted the rampage that had destroyed his things, but he wasn't sure that he could.

"He's sorry," Michelle repeated. "If you can find it in your heart to let it go, then do."

She made it sound easy. He paced the room as though his anger was too hot to hold inside of him. "This is wrong on so many levels. How could Richard do something like this? What kind of grown man does this?"

He didn't give Michelle the opportunity to respond. He felt himself getting fired up again. It was hard to rein in his anger and stay coolheaded.

"How can you say he regrets any of this?" he challenged.

She continued to sit on the edge of the mattress and stared up at him, perfectly calm while he vented his outrage. "Did you notice how the yearbook was neatly tucked back inside the drawer?"

"So what?" he snapped.

"He cleaned up the torn-out pages."

"Big deal." But still Josh felt the anger leave him. He appreciated Michelle all the more for talking him down. He resisted the urge to take her into his arms and simply hold her.

"At some point Richard returned to the room and cleaned up the mess."

She was right. No one else would have been up here. Richard lived alone. Gradually his pulse returned to normal. Losing Dylan had been hellish for Richard. He could only guess what other damage his stepfather had done when he learned that he'd lost his only child. Whatever it was had been righted to the best of Richard's ability. No doubt Josh's dresser drawers had been emptied, too, and then everything had been returned to some semblance of order. That would explain why his socks were in the top drawer and not the second one where he'd always kept them.

Josh's letterman's jacket was hung up, too, which told him that at some point Richard had returned to the room and replaced it on the hanger.

"Richard probably didn't expect me to find any of

this until . . ." He didn't complete the sentence. The older man assumed he'd be dead and buried before Josh discovered this damage.

Michelle couldn't seem to stand still. "Let's go someplace and talk this out," she suggested.

"Where do you want to go?" His time in town was limited and he wanted to settle matters so he could leave. This was no vacation.

"I need to get away from here . . . just a few hours. I still think you can retrieve the things you want of your mother's and say your good-byes, but we need to take it slow."

"All right," Josh agreed.

They came down the stairs and found Richard standing in the hallway, leaning his weight against the wall as if he were braced for a confrontation with Josh.

"We'll be back later," Josh said, avoiding his step-father's glare.

Richard frowned, almost as if he were disappointed, and then slowly nodded and shuffled back to his recliner.

Once outside, Michelle looked at him, her frown as deep and dark as Richard's had been moments earlier. "You're a better person than me," she said.

Josh sincerely doubted that. "Come here," he whispered. When she stepped closer he brought her into his arms and hugged her close. It would have been a simple matter to kiss her, but he didn't. All he wanted was to absorb her softness. He closed his eyes and rested his head against the top of her head. He wasn't sure what he was doing, but the fatherless son in him didn't care. He craved comfort.

"It'll be okay," she said when he released her.

"I know," he admitted. "Thank you, Michelle. I mean that. Thank you for everything."

Chapter 9

Abby waited in her room at Rose Harbor Inn until almost eleven before she gathered the courage to venture outside to buy the toothpaste and hairspray she needed. Staying inside the inn until it was time to meet her family was just plain silly. Eventually she'd need to leave the protection of her room, and it might as well be now. Besides, Jo Marie needed to get into the room to make up her bed and bring in a fresh set of towels.

As Abby descended the stairs, she smelled cookies baking. Chocolate chip? The scent was heavenly. She paused just inside the kitchen doorway to find

Jo Marie lifting freshly baked cookies off the cookie sheet and placing them on a wire rack to cool. She glanced up and offered Abby a reassuring smile.

"You're going out?"

"I thought I'd walk down to the pharmacy you mentioned."

"Good idea. It's only a few blocks away. I have an umbrella by the door that you're welcome to use," she offered. It'd been sunny earlier, but now it looked like rain. The weather in Cedar Cove changed on a whim, especially during the winter months, Abby remembered.

"Thanks, but the rain doesn't bother me. It's more mist than real rain anyway." Abby had thought she was an expert when it came to rainfall when she moved to Florida—after all, the Pacific Northwest was known for its rainy weather. That assumption had been wrong. In her entire life she'd never seen rain come down the way it did in Florida. Many times Abby had been forced to pull over to the side of the road because her car wipers were unable to keep up with the downpour.

Jo Marie busied herself by scooping dough onto the empty cookie sheet. "Have a good walk."

Abby headed for the door, closing it softly, tentatively, behind her. She stepped onto the front porch and froze. Her heart raced like a NASCAR engine. Really, this was ridiculous. So what if someone recognized her? The accident happened years ago. Just because she hadn't moved past it didn't mean that the rest of the world was in the same holding pattern.

This fear, this terror, was absurd. Abby couldn't even name why she was so afraid. True, meeting up with old friends who'd known both her and Angela might be awkward. And she could run into Angela's parents. Whatever the case, it would be better to deal with it now rather than during her brother's wedding.

The first step down the porch steps was the most difficult. Drawing a deep breath into her lungs to stave off a panic attack, she made it all the way down to the sidewalk. So far so good.

With her hands safely tucked inside her coat pockets, she started walking. This wasn't so bad. In fact, she breathed a bit easier. The wind, coming from the north, chilled her and she hunched her shoulders. Living in Florida she wasn't accustomed to temperatures that dipped into the low forties. Then again, she would have been chilled by anything below sixty-five degrees. She hadn't acclimated yet, but it wouldn't take long. She grinned. By the time she was accustomed to the cold, it would be time to fly back to West Palm. She'd already gotten through almost a whole day in Cedar Cove, which meant she only had two more to go.

Thankfully the walk down to the Harbor Street Pharmacy was all downhill. It was a bit steep, but she had on her boots and her footing was secure. The

Wok and Roll was still in business, which pleased her. Angela and Abby had thoroughly enjoyed the steamed dumplings there. The service had always been a bit slow, but every bite was worth the wait.

Angela had been able to eat the dumplings with chopsticks, but not Abby. The last time they'd shared an order, Angela had teased Abby about her lack of coordination, flexing her wooden chopsticks with an agility Abby could only envy. Frustrated, Abby had been ready to snap her own chopsticks in two. She finally just speared one dumpling and stuck it in her mouth while her best friend accused her of cheating. Abby smiled at the memory. Even now, all these years later, those moments with her best friend remained vivid in her mind.

The flower shop on Harbor Street was the same, too. Her mother had been good friends with the proprietor. Yvonne? Yvette? Abby couldn't remember her name.

The candy shop was new. The dress she'd purchased for the wedding was a bit snug, otherwise Abby would have been tempted to venture inside. Unable to resist, she stared into the window and saw something that made her smile.

Seagull plops. White chocolate with green swirls. And only available in Cedar Cove. Again Abby was hit with memories of her and Angela.

Every spring, Cedar Cove held its annual seagull calling contest, and one year Angela had participated.

The winner was determined by how many seagulls he or she could attract with their unique call. Angela had lost out to a fourteen-year-old boy, but she'd accepted defeat with good humor. She'd always been a good sport about everything. The whole day had been such fun; the two of them had laughed until their sides hurt.

Moving on down the street, Abby spotted the pharmacy. It was small and cozy—definitely the kind only found in small towns. It was a one-stop shop with both a small post office and liquor store included. If it had been there while she was in high school, she didn't recall. Once inside it didn't take her long to find the things she needed. She collected both and took them to the counter.

The woman behind the counter stared at Abby, who recognized her instantly—this was Patty, a friend from high school. One of the very friends Abby had cut off contact with following the accident.

"Abby?" Patty whispered almost as if she couldn't believe it was actually her. "Abby Kincaid?"

Abby hesitated before briefly nodding. "Hi, Patty." She felt the compelling urge to turn and run away.

Patty must have sensed it because she stretched out her arm and said, "Don't go."

While Abby stood frozen in place, Patty came around the counter to face her. Her eyes were bright and her smile was wide and eager. "I don't believe it," she cried out excitedly. "It's really you."

"In the flesh." The comment came off with a sarcastic edge Abby didn't intend.

"My goodness, where have you been all these years?"

She shrugged as though it shouldn't be that big of a mystery. "Around."

"You live in the area?"

"No," Abby admitted with a certain reluctance; she realized she'd braced herself for blame and accusation.

"Where?"

Abby hesitated.

"It doesn't matter," Patty said. "Oh my goodness, it's just so good to see you." Impulsively she reached for Abby and hugged her. Abby stood with her arms stiffly at her sides, hardly knowing what to make of this reception.

Patty had been a good friend. They'd met in fifth grade and gone through seven years of school together. For a couple of years their families had lived on the same block and they'd walked to school every morning together. Later Patty had moved, but their friendship continued all through high school.

"Are you married?" Patty asked.

"No," she said, and then—drawn in by the warmth of Patty's smile—she asked. "You?"

She nodded. "It's Patty Jefferies now."

"You work in the pharmacy?"

"I'm the pharmacist. My husband, too. Things are

a bit slow at the moment, so I help out front when I can. It's difficult for a small pharmacy to compete with the big box stores, but we manage."

"You and your husband own the pharmacy?"

Patty grinned. "We do, and thanks to the local support, we're surviving."

"Good for you," she said, and meant it.

"Abby, it's just so good to see you. Tell me everything."

Unnerved, she lifted her hands. "Like what?"

"I can't imagine why you're still single."

Abby shook her head. "Too picky, I guess, at least that's what my mom says." Right away Steve Hooks, her brother's college roommate, came to mind. Following the accident she'd shunned him, too.

"How long are you in town? Did you know that there's been all kinds of speculation at our class reunions about where you were living? No one has seen or talked to you for so long. Someone said they'd heard you'd joined a commune."

"A what?"

"A commune," Patty repeated. "I thought it sounded silly, but you never know. We weren't able to find you for our fifth or tenth year reunion. And we looked. It was like a Where's Waldo hunt," she teased.

Actually, Abby had heard her perfectly fine the first time. Her join a commune? The suggestion was so outrageous it'd been an instinctive question. Why in the love of heaven would anyone assume she'd done anything so out of character? Well, she had no one else to blame; she'd left her whereabouts open to speculation.

They hadn't found her because Abby hadn't been interested in being found. Her brother knew better than to answer questions about her, and her class-mates probably didn't know where her parents had moved to.

Her parents.

From what Abby understood, her mother and father had severed contact with a number of their friends from Cedar Cove. Whenever Abby asked about a certain longtime family friend, she got the same response: "Well, you know, honey, people change. It's hard to maintain long-distance rela-tionships. We have a new set of friends in Arizona now."

New friends, because it was too difficult to face the old ones, Abby realized with a pang. Her parents had worked hard to shield her, but she knew that the car accident had cost them.

"It's just so good to see you," Patty said. "Everyone wondered where you'd gone. Why didn't you come to any of the reunions?"

Abby just stared at her. The answer should be ob-vious.

"It just wasn't the same without you." Patty

sounded amazed and a little hurt. "Obviously it was hard after the accident, but you just disappeared! You were always so upbeat and fun and cute . . . and to learn that you're not married. I assumed you'd be settled down by now with two or three kids."

Abby wasn't about to get into the reasons she was single.

Patty beamed with pleasure. "What brings you to town?"

"My brother's getting married. Do you know the Templeton family?"

Patty's forehead compressed with a frown as she reviewed the name. "Templeton . . . Templeton? I can't say that I do. Was she in our graduating class?"

"No . . . she's a couple of years younger than us."

"That would have made her a sophomore when we were seniors, right?"

"Right," Abby agreed. Victoria was five years younger than Roger and a career woman in her own right. They both lived and worked in Seattle now.

"It was good to see you, Patty," she said, ready to be on her way, back to the safety and security of the bed-and-breakfast.

"How about a cup of coffee?" Patty suggested. "Like I said, business is a bit slow right now and Pete wouldn't mind if I took a short break." Standing on her tiptoes, she looked toward the pharmacy in the back of the building.

Abby hesitated. "Ah . . . "

"Please say you will. It would be so good to catch up."

Abby wasn't allowed to refuse. Patty wrapped her arm around her elbow and led her toward the back of the pharmacy. The area contained a small round oak table and two matching chairs. A coffeepot sat next to the sink. Before Abby could decline, Patty filled two mugs.

"It's fresh," she said as she placed the cup on the table. "I made it myself . . . yesterday."

Abby had been ready to take a sip but she stopped, the cup halfway to her mouth.

"I'm just kidding."

Patty had always been something of a smart aleck, and she loved to party. Abby would never have guessed that Patty would end up as a pharmacist.

All at once Patty thrust her arms into the air. "I have an absolutely fabulously great idea."

Abby clung to the coffee mug with both hands. She was almost afraid to ask what scheme was circling around her former schoolmate's head.

"We should all do lunch; Marie is still in town and a couple of our other old friends live here, too. You can, can't you? You must. It will be such fun . . . "

"I can't." Abby response was immediate.

"Why not?" Patty wasn't taking no for an answer, at least not easily.

It simply wouldn't work. "I'm only in town for a couple of days, Patty. I wish . . ."

"When do you leave?" she asked.

"Early Sunday." She had to get to the airport and check in two hours before the flight, which meant she'd need to leave the B&B by 5:30 a.m.

"That leaves Saturday." Patty wouldn't be easily deterred. "And . . ."

"Saturday is the day of the wedding," Abby finished for her.

"What time is the wedding?"

"Six."

Patty's smile lit up the room. "That's perfect."

"Perfect?"

"I'll get the word out that you're in town. Leave everything to me. I'll make all the arrangements. All you need to do is show up for lunch."

"Patty. . ."

"I'm not taking no for an answer."

"But the wedding," Abby insisted.

"You'll have plenty of time to get ready. Are you in the wedding party?"

"No."

"That's even better. We'll all meet up at noon at the Pancake Palace. Everyone loves the Pancake Palace."

"Ah . . ."

"Your mother will be in town, won't she?"

"Well . . . yes."

"Perfect. Bring her along, too, and I'll bring my mom, if she's available. She's been volunteering like crazy ever since we lost my dad. Our mothers were in PTA together, remember?"

Abby didn't remember, but she didn't have a chance to say so because it was difficult to get a word in edgewise.

"We like to do this, you know?" Patty continued undaunted.

"Do what?"

"High school friends. We meet for lunch on occasion. All we need is an excuse and you're the best possible excuse. Oh Abby, everyone is going to be so happy to see you."

Abby wondered if that could possibly be true. Angela had been their friend, too, and Abby had taken her from them all. She couldn't believe they didn't harbor resentment or bitterness toward her. The one reassurance she had was that Patty had included Abby's mother. No one would ask Abby uncomfortable questions about Angela or the accident if her mother was there to run interference. She was a bit old to cower behind her mother, but her mother had been her fierce protector following the accident and it was nice to know she'd be there.

"We invited our mothers to join us about six

months ago . . . which, come to think of it, was the last time we got together. We all had such a good time and our mothers have as much in common as we do."

Abby bit into her lower lip. Her mother would enjoy this. The accident had cost her, too. Abby didn't know if it was possible to put the tragedy behind her, but maybe . . . just maybe it was.

Chapter 10

The anger that had consumed Josh only a short while earlier now seemed pointless. He sat at a table by the window of the Pot Belly Deli, and watched the traffic flow down Harbor Street in a steady stream. Michelle sat across the table from him; he was glad she was there.

"Do you want to talk about it some more?" she asked.

He glanced up and saw that Michelle was waiting for him to respond. "There's nothing to be done at this point. It is what it is." He'd leave town and return after Richard died to settle the estate.

"You're angry and you have every right to be upset, but I think there's something to salvage here."

"This isn't life and death, Michelle," he said, downplaying his outrage. "I'm over it; now if you don't mind I'd rather not talk about it."

"Okay," she said slowly, reluctantly. "I just think there's a chance for you and Richard to connect on some level. It's hard when someone dies and you haven't said good-bye and made your peace. Even with someone you've had a very difficult relationship with."

"I don't think that's going to happen," he said, loud enough that several people turned and looked in their direction. Immediately he regretted his outburst. She was right. But he just wasn't ready to talk about anything having to do with his stepfather. Too much was happening and too quickly for him to fully comprehend its meaning. The best thing for him to do now was simply leave.

"You want me to forgive Richard."

"In time, or at least let go of your anger and his power over you."

Josh didn't realize he'd spoken out loud, but he must have for her to respond. **Forgive** was a powerful word. He would like to think he was man enough to overlook what his stepfather had done, but Josh wasn't sure he'd reached that point. Perhaps one day he'd be able to release the resentment he'd stored up against Richard, but not today.

She stared at him for a long time, as though there was more she wanted to say. Michelle appeared to be weighing her options, considering if this was the right place and time.

"What is it?" he asked.

She arched her brows in question.

"You want to tell me something, but can't decide if you should or not. Just say it."

"I don't know that now is the best time." She set the menu aside and leaned ever so slightly toward him, pressing her stomach against the edge of the table.

"Sure it is."

"I'm concerned about you," she said finally.

"Really? And why is that?" Her comment amused him.

Once more she hesitated. "I believe I know what you're thinking. You want to leave Cedar Cove and come back after Richard has died."

That was exactly what he was thinking. Josh could see that it wouldn't do much good for him to hang around town. The two men would never see eye to eye, and as Michelle had witnessed, they didn't respect each other. Josh had just finished managing the construction of a strip mall and had encountered one complication after another. He was both physically and emotionally ready for a break, and he wasn't keen on spending his free time butting heads with his stepfather. Richard would prefer to have him out of

his life, and Josh was more than willing to accommo-
date the dying man.

"I'm right, aren't I?" she prodded.

He responded with a sharp nod of his head. "I've
given it some consideration."

"Don't," she advised.

"Can you give me one good reason why I should
stay?"

"I can give you more than one."

He snickered and pretended to read the menu.
"Did you happen to read the specials on the board
when we came in?" he asked in an abrupt change of
subject.

"No. Do you want to hear my thoughts or would
you rather bury your head in the sand?"

His appetite gone, he set aside the menu. "Do I
have a choice?"

"Of course you do."

Josh would prefer to put his stepfather out of his
mind, but he could see that was impossible, especially
since Michelle was so keen to see this through.

He folded his arms and leaned back, prepared to
listen. She didn't disappoint him.

"As much as neither one of you wants to admit it,
you need each other," she said point-blank.

Josh nearly laughed out loud. He didn't need Richard and his stepfather sure as hell didn't need him.
"You've got to be kidding me."

"You're all Richard has left in this world . . ."

"Like he cares," Josh rebutted. It didn't matter that Josh was Richard's last remaining relative.

"And Richard is your last relative, too, and whether you want to admit it or not, the two of you are linked together. Richard is dying, and he's afraid and alone. He would never ask you to stay but he needs you. And you need him, too. Josh, he's the only father figure you've had in your life, and even if the relationship was a terribly disappointing one, you need to find closure. If you leave now, I'm afraid you'd always regret it."

Unsure, he mulled over her words.

"By the way," she added.

He looked up. "Yes?"

"The specials are cream of broccoli for the soup du jour and a shrimp basket for the entrée." She read off the list that was posted on the countertop and smiled her dazzling smile.

A sudden childhood memory flashed before Josh. He must have been around ten years old at the time; this was before his mother had met Richard. It'd been just the two of them back then and his mother had taken him down to the Saturday farmers' market on the waterfront. A boat had docked at the marina, selling fresh Hood Canal shrimp.

His mother had bought two pounds and they'd brought the shrimp home and boiled it in a mixture of spices. In all his life, Josh had never tasted more succulent shrimp. The two of them had feasted on the shrimp with homemade hush puppies and fresh coleslaw. Teresa had found some Cajun music and they'd done a silly jig around the living room. It was one of the happiest memories of his childhood . . . a childhood with far too few such memories.

"Josh?"

He looked up from the menu to find Michelle staring at him. "Sorry, my mind wandered away for a moment." He realized he was too much in the habit of keeping everything to himself and so he described the memory to her. Once again he was reminded of how much his mother had loved Richard.

"What do you remember about your father?" Michelle asked.

Josh guessed she was offering him the opportunity to compare his birth father to his stepfather.

Josh shrugged. "I have only vague recollections of him from when I was small. The only thing I really remember is Dad throwing something at my mother and her screaming, grabbing me, and then running into the bathroom and locking the door."

Michelle simply shook her head and didn't comment.

"I never saw him again after that. Well, not that I remember, anyway."

Michelle placed her hands in her lap. "You've never looked him up?"

Josh leaned back in his chair and crossed his arms over his chest. "I did when I was discharged from the army. Apparently he died when I was seventeen. It wasn't that long after I lost my mother . . . six months I think. He was living somewhere in Texas at the time and had remarried."

Not once had Teresa said a negative word about Josh's father. Not a single word. No need really. What little Josh remembered of his father said it all.

The waitress came to their table. Josh ordered the shrimp basket and Michelle asked for the soup.

"You're not eating much," he mentioned when the waitress left their table.

Michelle hesitated. "I'm so upset with Richard that I could scarf down half the menu in one sitting. But I know better than to let emotional eating get the better of me."

Josh admired her ability to gauge the difference between real hunger and emotional hunger. It occurred to him that she was much more self-aware than he was.

"You said that Richard had a hard time after Dylan passed," he said.

Michelle set her fork and spoon next to each other in perfect alignment. "He's never been the same."

Josh had suspected as much.

"He retired from the shipyard and hibernated," Michelle continued. "He sat in front of that television day in and day out. My mother and father tried to draw him out but Richard wasn't interested, and eventually he started resenting their help. When he stopped mowing the lawn my dad knew something wasn't right."

"It made him think of my mother," Josh whispered, hardly aware he spoke out loud.

"He used to make you work in the yard, too, remember?"

Josh chuckled. "I'm not likely to forget. You know what's funny?" Michelle would probably laugh, but he didn't care. "I have a rental house in San Diego and my yard is the best-looking one on the block." He didn't realize he'd picked up his enjoyment of yard work from his stepfather as well as his mother. If Richard ever found out, he'd get a good laugh out of it for sure.

Their food arrived and for the moment they were distracted from conversation.

"My mother's death was hard on him, but losing Dylan, well, that must have been more than Richard could take," Josh said as he reached for a deep-fried shrimp. He dipped it in cocktail sauce before plopping it in his mouth.

Michelle's spoon hovered over her soup. "Dylan wasn't as wonderful as everyone thought."

"Oh?" Josh asked, looking up. He reached for another shrimp, waiting for her to elaborate.

She didn't.

Josh decided not to push her. If Michelle had something to say, then she'd do it when the time was right; when she was ready.

"You were kind to me at a time when I needed kindness, and I want you to know I've never forgotten what you did," Michelle said.

"You mean on the bus that time." The teasing incident remained vivid in his mind.

"No, what happened in the hallway at school."

Josh's mind was a complete blank. He didn't remember anything happening with her at school that involved him.

"Don't tell me you've forgotten?"

"Refresh my memory."

Smiling, she leaned back in her seat. "Does the name Vance Willey ring a bell?"

It did. Vance had been a bully. A loser who preyed upon anyone smaller and weaker than him.

"I remember Vance," Josh admitted.

"He thought I was too ugly to live and he decided to humiliate and embarrass me in front of half the school."

That sounded like something Vance would have done. "What happened?"

She squared her shoulders. "You stood up to him and told him to cut it out."

"I did?" Josh still had no recollection of the incident.

"You said if anyone was ugly it was him, and that was sad because outwardly he was okay, but the ugly part was on the inside. You nailed him," she said, smiling with the memory. "You told him that the only way he felt powerful was by putting other people down."

"I said that?"

"Every word. You could have heard a pin drop in that hallway, too. And then you said you felt sorry for him. Everyone held their breath wondering what Vance would do."

"He walked away, didn't he?" Josh whispered as a vague memory wormed its way into his consciousness.

"He did, and I don't think anyone was more shocked than Vance. I saw him later and you know what?"

Josh couldn't venture a guess.

"Vance apologized to me."

Josh found that almost impossible to believe. "Now that's cool."

"I thought what you said was the wisest thing I've ever heard," Michelle confessed. "You didn't leap to my defense; you didn't fight him. Instead you hit him with the truth and he backed down."

It took Josh a moment to connect all the dots. Michelle had a specific reason for recalling the story. "You're more or less doing the same thing with me, aren't you?"

She set the spoon aside. "Josh, don't make the mistake of deserting Richard. If you do, you'll find yourself dealing with unresolved issues. Richard's being cruel because he doesn't want to need you and admitting that he does is far too difficult. Look beneath the surface of his behavior and be as patient with him as you can."

Josh knew she was right, although she was asking him to stay when every instinct told him it was best to turn his back on the old man and walk away. "I actually feel sorry for him," Josh admitted.

"You'll stay?" she asked.

After a moment he nodded. He didn't like it, but he knew she was right.

Michelle reached across the table and grabbed hold of his hand, squeezing his fingers tightly. "Thank you."

She was the one who deserved his appreciation.

When they'd finished their meal, Josh paid and together they returned to Richard's house. Stepping inside, he called out, "We're back."

No response.

"Richard?"

Josh found his stepfather in the chair, struggling to breathe. "Richard?" he said again.

His stepfather gasped for breath; he looked like he was having some sort of attack.

"Call nine-one-one," Josh shouted.

A moment later, Michelle assured him that an ambulance had been dispatched. They should arrive soon.

Josh just hoped they would get there before it was too late. He rushed into the master bathroom and thrust open the medicine cabinet. The shelves were lined with row upon row of medications. It took him a heart-stopping minute to find what he wanted.

Aspirin.

Shaking four mini-dose tablets into the palm of his hand, he hurried back into the family room and placed the tablets in Richard's mouth.

"Chew them, Richard," he demanded. "Chew and swallow. Get them down as quickly as possible."

The ambulance arrived and transported Richard to the Bremerton Hospital. Josh and Michelle followed behind in his truck. After Josh filled out the necessary paperwork, Michelle sat with him in the ER. He reached for her hand, needing an anchor. They waited for nearly an hour before a physician approached them. His badge identified him as Dr. Abraham Wilhelm.

Josh stood to meet the physician eye to eye. "How is he?" he asked.

The doctor's concerned look said far more than any words the man might have uttered. "Stable for now. The bottom line is that he doesn't have much longer in his weakened condition. I'd like to admit him, but he refuses."

"When you say he doesn't have much longer, what exactly does that mean?" Michelle asked.

"I wish I could be more precise, but I can't. His heart is in bad shape."

"Did he have a heart attack?"

"Actually he's had several."

"What about surgery?" Josh asked.

Dr. Wilhelm shook his head. "His heart is far too weak to sustain surgery. I think it's time for hospice."

"Hospice," Josh echoed. "Richard agreed to that?"

The physician cracked what resembled a smile, although Josh couldn't be sure. "When I mentioned hospice to Mr. Lambert, he said he wanted out of the hospital. His words were, and I quote, 'Get me out of here. I don't care what you have to do but I want out. People die here.'"

Josh chuckled. "I see what you mean."

"Mr. Lambert prefers to die at home and so I urge you to take him there. I'll arrange for hospice to make a visit as soon as possible."

Josh nodded. "Thank you."

Dr. Wilhelm slapped him across the back. "He has a strong will."

"He's stubborn all right," Josh agreed.

"You're family?"

"His stepson, but I'm all the family he's got."

Dr. Wilhelm nodded. "In that case, I'd say he's fortunate to have you."

Chapter 11

I'd just finished changing the towels in Abby Kincaid's room when the doorbell chimed. I bebopped down the stairs, thinking it might be someone looking for a room, which would be nice.

When I opened the door I discovered a rather tall, thin man standing on the other side of the threshold. He wore coveralls over a thick flannel shirt in an orange and brown plaid and was easily six-three or six-four, which was a good seven or so inches taller than me. His eyes were dark brown, and the instant he saw me, he frowned.

"Can I help you?" I asked, unwilling to let him

into the house until I knew exactly who he was and why he was at my front door. I drew myself up to my full height—not that it did any good—and stared at him, unwilling to flinch under his glare.

"You called me."

I relaxed. "You're Mark Taylor?"

He nodded, and I stepped aside. He came into the foyer and stopped to sniff appreciatively. "You've been baking."

"Chocolate chip cookies. You interested?"

"Does a bear . . ." He stopped talking abruptly and cast me an apologetic look. "I can't remember the last time I had home-baked cookies. You have coffee to go with that?"

"Does a bear . . ." I teased. I hadn't been sure what to expect of the handyman Peggy Beldon had recommended. He'd seemed a bit of a grouch . . . or at least an odd duck. Seeing him now, he was outwardly exactly what one would expect a handyman to look like.

To my surprise I actually liked him. We hadn't started off on the right foot—I'd found my phone conversation with him more than a bit disconcerting. But despite my hesitation I was pleased I'd decided to give him a chance. His eyes were dark but honest, and while he wasn't exactly Mr. Personality, he seemed, in a word, interesting.

His hair was a dark blond and a tad long. I could tell it bothered him because his bangs fell into his eyes and he impatiently brushed them aside a couple of times.

"You take your coffee black?" I asked when he followed me into the kitchen.

"Please."

I carried two mugs to the kitchen table and piled cookies onto a plate and brought those over, too.

Mark sat down and reached for a cookie while I retrieved from my office the sketches of the sign I'd envisioned.

Mark stood when I returned. The gesture surprised me. I wasn't accustomed to such old-fashioned but thoughtful behavior in men. Then again, perhaps he was just looking to make a good impression to get my business. It was an odd contradiction with his gruffness.

After I sat down, he relaxed in the chair, leaning against the back of it. "So, what do you have in mind?"

"I need a new sign made for the front of the inn."

"Not a problem. I enjoy woodwork. Show me what you want."

I'd drawn up a couple of ideas. I wanted it freestanding in front of the short driveway so that guests who were driving to the inn would know that they'd reached their destination as soon as they came down the street. I wanted it painted white to match the house, with red lettering, and red roses painted on each side of ROSE HARBOR INN.

Mark looked over the drawings and asked a few questions. "You want this to stand, what, five feet high?"

"Yes, I think that would be perfect . . . with lettering that's legible from the street."

He nodded.

"What would that cost me?"

He named a figure that I found more than reasonable. Mark's quote was half that of the estimate I'd gotten before I took possession of the inn.

"How soon could you have it done?"

Mark finished his cookie, brushed the crumbs from his hands, and reached inside the pocket of his coveralls for a small black book. He licked his finger before he turned several pages.

I looked away in an effort to hide my amusement. Before smart phones, most little black books were used for women's phone numbers instead of jobs. It begged the question of whether there was a love interest in Mark's life.

"I could have that for you by the end of the month," Mark told me, after flipping several pages. Apparently he already had plenty of jobs lined up over the next few weeks.

"That long?" I hated the thought of waiting three weeks to identify the inn. Although I feared the more expensive estimate might require even more time.

"I'll see what I can do to make it happen sooner," he suggested.

"I'd appreciate that. One question. Did my age move me up or down the list?" I teased.

He grinned. "Do you want me to go ahead, then, with the sign?"

"Please," I said, the decision made. Peggy thought highly of Mark and his work. He was local and I liked doing business with the neighboring merchants. It was good practice. I wanted to establish myself in this community, especially since I planned to live here a good long while.

Mark removed a stubby pencil from his shirt pocket and listed my name in his little black book. "I'll do a good job. I guarantee all my work."

The new business sign wasn't the only job I had in mind. "Do you know anyone who's willing to do yard work?" I asked. While he leaned back I leaned forward, resting my elbows on the tabletop.

"I can."

He didn't seem overly keen on the idea, though.

"You sure?" His body language said otherwise.

"If it's something I'd rather not do, I'll tell you, okay?"

"Fair enough," I said. "Perhaps you'd like to recommend someone else."

"First tell me what you want done." Another cookie disappeared and he reached for a third.

"A rose garden," I explained. "I want to plant a big, beautiful, and rather elaborate rose garden." I handed him the sketchbook I'd used and flipped it open to the appropriate page. I'm no artist, but I felt I'd done an adequate job of illustrating what I wanted done. My idea would require a large portion of the lawn to be removed. I wanted an arched entry into the garden and a stone pathway between the flowering bushes. In addition, I hoped to have benches along the pathway, and perhaps, if it wasn't too elaborate, a gazebo. Not right away, but once I was more established. A gazebo would be perfect for special occasions, even weddings.

Mark studied my drawings for several moments. "This is quite the rose garden."

"I know. It'll be a large project."

He nodded. "It makes sense you wanting a rose garden planted seeing that you renamed the inn Rose Harbor Inn."

I agreed, but didn't mention Paul. "Do you think this is a project that would interest you?"

He frowned. "I don't know that much about roses."

Fact was I didn't either, but I certainly intended to learn what I could. "I'll purchase the roses and plant them myself. I want to get as many antique rosebushes as I can find."

"Antique roses? I've never heard of such a thing."

"They're older, obviously, stock from before growers started cross-breeding them. The flowers tend to be smaller but they're especially fragrant. I'd also like to plant a few hybrid bushes. I thought it would be a nice touch once the garden is complete to place a bouquet of roses in the rooms of my new guests."

"That would be nice; a little something extra; a welcome to Cedar Cove and your inn."

"So, what do you think . . . about the garden I mean?" I'd need to get an estimate from him regarding that as well. This would be a large project requiring lots of time and it'd be expensive.

"I'd say I'm your man."

"Great." I relaxed. "Put together an estimate and I'll look it over."

"I might see about finding someone else to come in and remove the lawn and prepare the soil. And if you plant the bushes yourself it'll cut down on the expense."

"I'd like an arched trellis leading into the garden, too," I said and pointed to my drawing. "Maybe more than one . . . but I'll need to get a price first." It would be easy to go overboard on this, and I'd hoped to keep the costs down as much as possible.

"No problem; I can build you as many as you want."

"What about benches? Could you build those, too, or would it be more economical for me to just buy them ready-made?"

He mulled over the answer. "If you're looking to save money, buy the benches, but I need to tell you that if you decide to have me build them, then I guarantee it will be as solid as they come and will last longer than anything you could purchase."

Again, it depended on price. "Add it to the estimate and I'll make that decision later."

He nodded and reached for another cookie. The plate, however, was empty. He'd stuffed down six cookies, one after the other, with barely a pause in between. These weren't small cookies, either. I wasn't about to let him gobble up the entire batch so I didn't offer to refill the plate. He was probably one of those fortunate people with a high metabolism who could eat anything they wanted and still remain as thin as a pogo stick.

He sipped his coffee and studied me as he raised the mug to his lips. "You're younger than I expected."

"Funny, I was just thinking the same about you."

He shrugged. "Most people assume I'm older, retired, making a little extra income on the side. Fact is I'm busy all the time. I've got more projects going than I can handle."

"Where did you work before?" I speculated that he'd been an employee at one of those big box hardware stores. From what Peggy Beldon told me, Mark knew enough about electricity, plumbing, and carpentry to build his own home, which he'd apparently done.

"I didn't."

"You've never had a job?" I found that hard to believe.

"I was military."

That caught me by surprise. "That's a job." I've always had huge respect for the men and women of our military and the service they provided for our country, even before meeting Paul.

"In a manner of speaking, being in the military is a job, but it's much more than that. I had a few issues when I was discharged so I decided I preferred to be self-employed."

"Thank you for your service to our country," I said simply. Whatever his issues had been, he clearly didn't want to elaborate. That was fine by me. Everyone had issues. I certainly had my own and it seemed my two guests did, too.

He looked away as if my appreciation made him uncomfortable.

"What's your story?" he asked.

I shrugged. "Nothing special. I came into an inheritance and decided to make a career change. The idea of opening a bed-and-breakfast appealed to me and so I went for it."

"With no experience in this particular area?"

"None." I had to admit it did sound rather foolish. "I'm a quick learner and I've been reading everything I can get my hands on about owning and operating a bed-and-breakfast."

"So you've met Grace?"

"Grace? No, sorry, I can't say that I have. Who's Grace?"

"Grace Harding, the head librarian. You should introduce yourself. I did some work for her after her husband disappeared. I get a lot of my work from widows and single women."

"Her husband disappeared?"

"That was years ago now. She's since remarried. Harding is the name of her second husband. Good people, you'll like Grace and Cliff."

"Thanks." I'd intended to get down to the library before long.

"At some point you'll probably meet Grace's best friend, too. That would be Olivia Griffin. Her husband's the newspaper editor."

I doubted I'd be able to remember all these names. "Where does Olivia work?"

"Courthouse. She's a family court judge. Have you eaten at the Pancake Palace yet?"

"No." I'd been cooking, trying out new recipes I hoped to serve at the inn, so I hadn't been to any of the restaurants in town.

"Try their coconut cream pie when you do."

"I will."

"Best in town."

"Good to know." I was rather fond of coconut cream myself.

The handyman took another sip of his coffee. "I'll have the estimate to you before the end of next week."

"Perfect."

"If you decide you want to go ahead with it, I'll

need to know when you'd like it completed so I can get it listed in my book."

That little black book of his. I hadn't researched when the best time was to plant rosebushes, but spring sounded like a good time. "March," I told him. "Maybe April, after the last frost."

Mark stood, reached for his mug, and carried it over to the sink. "I'll get those figures to you first chance I get."

I walked him to the foyer.

"Have to tell you, I've tasted a lot of chocolate chip cookies in my day, and yours are some of the finest."

I blushed with his praise. "Thank you."

He left then, following the walkway. The parking area was empty, which meant he'd come on foot. Then I remembered that Peggy had told me he lived just a few blocks over. He was an unusual man, that was for sure. If I were to guess his age, I'd say mid-forties. And I couldn't help but think that there was much more to him than met the eye.

Time would tell.

Chapter 12

Abby checked her watch and saw that she was right on time. Her brother had asked her to meet him and his fiancée at a coffee shop—a place that had opened after she moved away. So much had changed over the years. The coffee place was in a strip mall that had been a vacant lot the last time she was in Cedar Cove.

Abby parked in front and she immediately spotted her brother just inside the shop. He looked wonderful; happy and a bit anxious as he paced the area, waiting for her and Victoria to arrive.

When he saw Abby, Roger swung the door open

and held his arms out to her. "Abby." He embraced her, squeezing hard. "You look . . . fabulous. I'm so pleased you're here."

"I am, too." And she meant it. The time she'd spent with Patty Morris—oops, Jefferies—had gone surprisingly well, and meeting up with her classmate had encouraged Abby. Maybe, just maybe, she could put the accident behind her for at least this one weekend. The wedding was supposed to be a joyous occasion. She couldn't—wouldn't—allow her fears to rule every waking minute. So what if someone mentioned Angela or the accident? If they did, Abby would deal with it like an adult instead of running away or hiding under a rock.

"Victoria will be here any minute," Roger said. "She said I should order a latte for her."

"I'm so looking forward to finally meeting this paragon who has managed to steal my brother's heart."

"She's anxious to meet you, too." The siblings walked inside and out of the cold. The latte line was long. It always surprised Abby to read how popular these places were in the Pacific Northwest. She couldn't think of a single latte stand in Florida, other than Starbucks, and in Cedar Cove there was one on practically every street corner. Coffee was hot stuff here.

"When did you get in?" Roger asked, joining the line.

"A while ago," she said vaguely. Roger would

feel bad if he knew she'd been in town for nearly twenty-four hours without contacting him.

Her brother reached for his wallet as they approached the counter. "What would you like?" he asked.

Because she so rarely had anything other than plain old black coffee, Abby wasn't sure what to order. The menu on the wall listed a number of drinks and she found it all a bit confusing. "Just a latte, I guess." As it was, she'd already had three cups of coffee this morning.

"What about mixing it up a little?" he suggested.

Abby kept her gaze focused on the menu. There were dozens of different flavors to choose from. Dozens. "Just get me what you're ordering for Victoria," she said, fearing her hesitation was holding up the line.

"Good idea."

The barista was ready for their order. "Three hot vanilla chai lattes with a shot of espresso plus a mocha twist with caramel, no whipped topping."

The woman grabbed three cups and quickly wrote out the order in shorthand on them, and then her fingers flew across the cash register's keyboard. The total could have bought them lunch.

Roger paid and then they scooted down to where the drinks were being assembled and delivered. The sound of gurgling milk filled the compact room. After they collected their drinks, Roger found them a table by the window.

Abby tasted her vanilla chai tea with espresso and had to admit it was good. The drink probably had as many calories as a full sandwich, which was fine. She hadn't planned on eating lunch anyway.

"So how does it taste?" Roger asked, watching her expression.

"Not bad," she admitted.

Her brother had only just sat down when he abruptly stood again. "Victoria's here." His eyes brightened as he focused his gaze at the parking lot.

Abby glanced over her shoulder to where her future sister-in-law was climbing out of her car. She'd parked next to Abby's rental car. Victoria was just as lovely as her picture, perhaps even more so. Her hair was as dark as Roger's, shoulder-length and tucked behind her ears. She was petite and slim and she wore a soft pink sweater and white slacks under a long gray wool coat that she'd left unbuttoned. Abby took another sip of her drink and then stood to meet the woman who'd snagged her brother.

Roger greeted his fiancée with a gentle kiss on the lips and then, with his arm around her waist, he led her toward the table where Abby waited.

"Victoria, this is my sister, Abby. Abby, my soon-to-be-wife, Victoria." His eyes were warm with love and pride.

"I'm pleased to meet you," Victoria said. "Roger has told me so much about you."

Abby frowned, instantly afraid that Roger had told

her about the accident. Naturally he would have. Victoria was to be his wife; she would need to know, if she didn't already. It seemed to Abby as though her entire life had been rent in two by that fateful night.

Before the accident.

After the accident.

And between that chasm, was a huge pile of "what ifs." Abby stuffed down the regrets, the guilt, and the pain, refusing to allow the feelings to surface.

It took an awkward moment for her to realize that Roger and Victoria were awaiting her response. "I'm so very pleased to meet you, too," she finally managed to blurt out.

Roger pulled out a chair for Victoria. "Did you get everything settled with the caterer?"

Victoria expelled a deep sigh and nodded as she settled into the chair and shucked off her coat. "Thank goodness my mother kept the receipt."

"What happened?" Abby asked.

"Nothing important, just finalizing everything for tomorrow." Victoria reached for Roger's hand. "My mother has been working on this wedding for weeks . . ."

"Months," Roger interrupted.

"She's the organized one in the family and it's a good thing."

"What about the rehearsal dinner tonight?" Abby asked. With her parents living out of state, it would have been difficult for her own mother to arrange such a large dinner. Nor could Abby remember her mother mentioning it.

"Not to worry, I took care of that." Roger looked downright proud of himself.

"You?" Abby asked, laughing.

"Hey, it was a breeze. I booked the banquet room at the Lighthouse restaurant and—"

"Just a minute," Abby said, raising her hand to stop him. "I thought Mom told me that the Lighthouse burned to the ground."

"It did," Victoria answered on Roger's behalf. "But it was rebuilt."

"And under new ownership, too," Roger added. "They have a large banquet room that will fit the wedding party plus an assorted group of relatives."

"I helped choose the menu," Victoria whispered, "otherwise Roger would have ordered pizza and beer."

"They have great pizza," Abby's brother countered.

"Pizza? You wouldn't have?" Abby teased. "You're not serious."

"I am serious," Victoria said, smiling.

Abby enjoyed the banter between Roger and his fiancée. The two were so obviously in love, so obviously right for each other.

"Have you been down Harbor Street yet?" Victoria asked after sipping her drink.

"Well, yes . . . a ways, why?"

"Did you see the Victorian Tea Room?"

"Ah." Abby didn't think so. "I don't know. Is it new?"

"Very. It opened last year. The couple who owned the Lighthouse sold it and built the tearoom instead. It's become one of the most popular places in town for breakfast and lunch. Be sure and give it a try before you leave . . . or at least drive by."

"I will," Abby promised.

"Where are you staying?" Victoria asked next, her hand gripping her latte.

"Rose Harbor Inn."

Victoria frowned. "I don't think I know it."

"It was originally the Frelingers' place."

"Sandy and John's? They sold?" Victoria sounded surprised. "Well, good for them. I remember Mom saying something about the place being up for sale, but that was months ago. Is it still as lovely as I remember?"

"It's amazing, and the new owner is very nice." Thoughtful and considerate, too, but Abby didn't want to sound like she was gushing, or let on that she'd been there long enough to become acquainted with Jo Marie.

"I can't tell you how pleased we are that you're here," Victoria said, holding Roger's hand. "It means the world to us."

"I wouldn't miss my big brother's wedding." Abby would never admit how difficult it'd been to make this simple decision. Her parents had more or less guilted her into attending. Guilt was one emotion she responded to well, although it was sad to admit.

"When do Mom and Dad arrive?" Abby asked next. She already knew but she wanted to change the subject. It would be uncomfortable if Victoria started asking questions she didn't want to answer. Questions about why it had taken so long for her to commit to serving the wedding cake. Questions about why she hadn't booked her flight until it was almost too late.

Roger checked his watch. "Their plane landed ten minutes ago."

"Was it on time?"

Her brother pulled out his cell phone and typed in a few words. After a couple of minutes he glanced up and announced, "Right on the nose."

"When do you expect them to arrive?"

"By the time they get the rental car and check into the hotel, it'll be a good two hours. Mom said she'd phone if they were going to be any later than five," Roger explained.

"Mom suggested we meet up at the church just before the rehearsal," Abby added.

"They told me that, too."

Victoria sighed as though she was exhausted. "I better get back. My mother is working herself into a heart attack. I'm meeting her at the florists in"—she glanced at her wrist—"ten minutes."

"I know everything must be hectic so close to the wedding," Abby said. "Thank you for taking time out to come meet me."

"I've been looking forward to it for weeks. It's going to be so nice to have another sister." She stood and reached for her drink to take it with her.

Roger stood, too, and so did Abby.

The two women briefly hugged, and then Roger walked Victoria to her car. They chatted for a couple of minutes outside before he returned to the coffee shop.

"Oh, Roger, she's wonderful."

"I know." His gaze followed Victoria as she backed the car out of the parking space and turned onto the street.

He relaxed and turned his attention back to Abby. "You okay?" he asked.

"Of course, why wouldn't I be?" Silently she prayed he wouldn't bring up the accident. For once, just once, she wanted to pretend it had never happened.

"It's been a lot of years since you've been back."

Abby sat up at bit straighter. "You'll never guess who I ran into," she said, forcing enthusiasm into her voice. She didn't give Roger time to guess—"Patty Morris," she said.

Roger frowned and shook his head. "Who?"

"Patty Morris. We went to school together. We were good friends."

He went still, as if he was afraid of what she'd say next.

"Patty married Pete Jefferies. You might have known him."

Roger shook his head.

"She and her husband are both pharmacists. They own the pharmacy down on Harbor Street. I forgot to pack toothpaste and so I walked down there and ran into Patty." She didn't mention how disconcerting it had been to see her old friend, but Roger seemed to know just by looking at her.

"That's good, right?" It was just like her big brother to worry. He knew she'd avoided people for years.

"Everything was wonderful."

"Good."

"Patty and Pete have twins. A boy and a girl. They're six and in first grade."

Roger seemed distracted but he nodded.

"She invited me to lunch tomorrow afternoon."

He reverted his attention back to her and frowned slightly. "You okay with that?"

"I'm fine," she said, making light of it. "Apparently several of my old friends still live in the area. Patty insisted they would skin her alive if she didn't let them know I was in town. We're all meeting at the Pancake Palace."

Roger's gaze remained dark and steady. "You and your high school friends?"

Abby nodded. "Mom's invited, too."

Roger shifted as if suddenly uncomfortable. "Are you sure that's such a good idea? I mean, I think it's great you meeting up with your friends and all, but it's cutting it close to the wedding, don't you think?"

His concern, Abby realized, was that something might be brought up at lunch that would upset her. "It'll be fine. Patty seemed so pleased and excited to see me. Apparently I was missed at the reunions . . . people have asked about me." Which in retrospect was probably pretty natural considering the circumstances.

Roger nodded and sipped his latte. "I'm glad, Abby. It's time to settle the past once and for all."

Her past. That meant the accident. Angela's death. The guilt she carried.

"I'm glad the wedding brought you back to Cedar Cove and I'm thinking maybe this lunch with Patty and the others will go a long way toward giving you the peace of mind you need."

Abby lowered her head and swallowed against the thick knot in her throat. Heart-to-heart talks with her brother were rare and his encouragement meant a great deal to her. "Thanks," she whispered.

"Having Mom with you is a good idea, too."

"I thought so, too . . . it was Patty's idea. To tell you the truth I'm a little concerned."

"Everything will be perfectly fine," Roger assured her. "Have fun with your friends. Enjoy yourself,

Abby. You deserve that. You have lots of friends. You always have."

Tears blurred her vision as she looked up at her brother and smiled. At one time she did have plenty of friends. Maybe she would again.

Chapter 13

"Let me die in peace," Richard insisted, as soon as Josh and Michelle returned with him from the hospital.

Josh ignored the comment as he came around to the passenger side of the car and helped his stepfather into the house. Michelle climbed out from the backseat and hurried ahead to open the front door.

As much as he hated it, Richard was forced to lean against Josh in order to walk. His feet shuffled, and by the time they reached the third step onto the porch, his breathing was labored. Josh walked with him, keeping his arm tucked around the older man's waist. Michelle held open the door and ushered them inside.

It went without saying how difficult Richard was finding it to accept help from Josh. He needed a walker, but he refused to use one. Any display of energy seemed reserved for verbally lambasting anyone within reach of his voice.

Josh helped Richard back into his favorite recliner. The old man collapsed into the chair and expelled a deep breath as though it had cost him every ounce of energy he possessed to make it this far. Ignoring Josh, he automatically reached for the television remote, turning on a twenty-four-hour news station.

"Can I get you anything?" Josh asked, stepping back.

Richard simply shook his head.

By the time he entered the kitchen, Michelle had the teakettle on the stove. "Can you doubt that Richard needs you now?" she muttered under her breath.

Josh didn't respond to the obvious. It was doubtful that Michelle could have managed to get Richard up the porch steps on her own. Not that looking after his stepfather was her responsibility. He wanted to remind her that it wasn't his either—that he didn't owe Richard anything. It would serve the older man right if Josh turned his back and walked away. The thought was tempting, but he couldn't do it. Not because Richard deserved his help, that was for sure. Josh knew that staying was what his mother would have wanted him to do, and it was for her sake that he said, "Don't worry, I'll stay in Cedar Cove for as long as I can."

"Thank you," she whispered and gently squeezed his upper arm.

He rested his hands on her shoulders, grateful for her wisdom and encouragement.

"I don't think I ever realized how bad things must have been for you here," she said.

True, the years Josh had spent with Richard certainly hadn't been any picnic, Josh was more than willing to admit it. The tension in the house, especially after his mother's death, had been volatile at times. Thankfully he'd had Dylan as a buffer; otherwise the situation would have been impossible. Now both his mother and Dylan were gone and only Michelle was here to keep matters from becoming explosive.

At the same time, Josh was forced to admit he wasn't completely innocent when it came to his stepfather. As a teen he'd enjoyed egging the older man on. Richard had made his dislike all too obvious, so rather than working toward building a positive relationship with his stepfather, Josh had gone out of his way to goad him.

If it was garbage day, and it was his job to get the can to the curb, Josh would purposely plant it in the middle of the driveway so Richard would need to get out of his vehicle and move it before he could leave for work.

If he was assigned to wash the dinner dishes, he'd do exactly that and nothing more. Milk was left on the table and the countertops were left cluttered. If there were leftovers that he knew Richard intended to take for lunch the following day, he would make sure they got dumped. Since Richard had made it clear that Josh could do no right by him, Josh hadn't seen any reason to be helpful.

"I was at fault, too," he whispered.

The teakettle whistled and Michelle reluctantly moved away to lift it off the burner. She had the ceramic teapot ready and poured the boiling water into it. Josh recognized it as the one his mother had brought with her into the marriage. Where it had come from, he didn't know. It might have been a wedding gift or a family heirloom. Josh wouldn't ask about it now for fear that Richard would purposely destroy it. That sort of attitude was what he'd come to expect, and it saddened him to admit it.

Michelle left the tea to steep while she brought down three mugs.

Since a volunteer from hospice would be stopping by later that afternoon, Josh went back into the living room and started picking up the newspapers that littered the carpet. He fluffed up the pillows and set them at the corners of the couch.

"What are you looking for?" Richard demanded. He reached for the TV remote and lowered the volume.

"I'm not looking for anything. I thought I'd straighten up the room before the hospice volunteer arrives."

"You want something."

Josh glared at his stepfather. "I was straightening the room. I don't have an ulterior motive."

"I don't believe it. You're looking to steal from me. The least you can do is wait until I'm dead."

Josh squeezed his fists at his sides as he responded. "Think what you like, but I don't want or need anything from you." The anger that seared through him was enough to make him clench his teeth. Just seconds earlier he'd been willing to admit his own part in the animosity that existed between them. Yet one brief comment from Richard and his anger shot to the surface so fast it felt like a brain freeze. Before he said something he would later regret, he walked out of the room.

Richard's toxic personality made him feel like he was a teenager all over again, determined to stand up to the old man, to find some way to lash back at him for the hurt he'd so effortlessly inflicted.

Lost in thought, he was surprised to find Michelle in the foyer; her hand on his arm. "You okay?"

Rather than explain, he simply nodded. "I'm fine."

He glanced over his shoulder and saw that his stepfather was holding a cup of tea, his focus on the television.

"Does he need anything to eat?" he asked Michelle.

"I offered but he claimed he wasn't hungry."

Despite himself, Josh smiled. It would be just like Richard to go on a hunger strike to spite him.

"You need something in your stomach," Josh said as he returned to the living room, purposely disrupting the news program. "I'll heat you some soup," he offered, testing out his theory.

"I don't want any soup. Like I said, I'd prefer to die in peace, so why don't you do us both a favor and go back wherever it is you came from." This was quite a speech for a man who was supposedly failing fast.

"I will—all in good time, all in good time."

Richard completely ignored him then.

This was another tool in his stepfather's arsenal, Josh remembered. When Richard had realized that nothing he said or did affected Josh more than the silent treatment, it had become the older man's favorite form of torture. He'd simply pretend Josh wasn't in the room or the house. It had driven Josh nuts. Within an hour he'd do whatever was necessary to get a reaction out of his stepfather, even if it meant destroying something he knew Richard enjoyed, like his favorite magazine or the television guide for the week. Anything that would bring him recognition.

"That won't work on me now. I'm an adult," he told Richard. "You can ignore me from now until kingdom come. Actually, I'd be grateful."

Richard didn't so much as blink, his attention riveted to the newscaster.

Ignoring the older man, Josh found a can of soup in the cupboard and opened it. Funny that he could remember his way around this kitchen as if it was just yesterday that he'd walked out the door.

He searched through the cupboard until he located a pan and set it on the still warm burner that Michelle had used to heat the water for tea. Unfortunately, the cupboard where his mother had kept the soda crackers was empty. That was fine. Richard would simply have to do without.

He poured the soup into the pan and added a can of hot water, then left it to heat. Seeing what he was doing, Michelle walked into the other room. Josh saw that she was busily clearing off the cluttered TV tray that sat next to Richard's recliner.

"What are you doing?" Richard demanded, snatching the television remote.

"Clearing a space so I can bring you a bowl of soup."

"I already told you I don't want anything to eat."

"You need something," she insisted.

Richard's gaze narrowed. "You're siding with him, aren't you?"

Michelle reached for his hand, taking it between her own. "It isn't a matter of taking sides."

"Either you're my friend or you're his," he told her. "You can't be a friend to both of us at the same time. You choose." Even from his vantage point Josh could see this was an emotional moment for Richard. His eyes seemed to cloud with tears. "I . . . I know how you always felt about Dylan. He liked you, too. I believe that if he'd lived he would have come to see how beautiful you are."

"Mr. Lambert . . ."

"You choose, understand. It has to be one or the other."

Michelle straightened. "Like I said . . ."

Josh eased forward one step, unwilling for her to take any heat on his behalf. Richard needed her, even though he'd be hard-pressed to admit it. Michelle was the one link that remained between him and Dylan—she was the one person who still remembered Dylan and remained a part of Richard's life. Josh couldn't allow her to put that at risk. He raised his hand, wanting to stop her from choosing. In a day or two Josh would be out of both of their lives; it wasn't worth the trouble, the loss.

Michelle seemed to read Josh's mind. "Let me think on it, okay?" she said to Richard.

The older man frowned and it went without saying that her answer had upset him. He leaned his head back and closed his eyes, blocking her out.

Once the soup was warm, Josh poured it from the pan into a bowl and brought it into the other room.

He half expected Richard to sweep it off the tray and hurl it across the room.

"I need to run an errand," Josh announced as he reached for his jacket. He felt an urgent need to escape the house. The atmosphere was oppressive.

He was halfway to the door when Michelle joined him, her own coat and purse in hand. "I'll go with you."

Josh hesitated, uncertain of whether they should leave Richard alone. "You sure you should?"

"I want to," she insisted, her gaze holding his steady.

He acquiesced and headed out the front door. Although the thermostat in the house was set unnaturally high, Josh felt chilled to the bone. Being around Richard was like standing over a toxic dumpsite. He couldn't be close to the other man without it affecting him negatively.

"Where are you headed?" Michelle asked, managing to keep pace with his much longer stride. He regretted agreeing to her tagging along. He needed to be alone. She climbed into the passenger side of the truck and closed the door behind her as if to say that nothing was going to change her mind about this.

"Richard needs a walker." That was a convenient excuse to get out of the house. A valid one but also convenient. No matter what happened, Josh would be leaving in a few days, and although she'd been wonderful to Richard, Michelle couldn't check on him every day. Seeing how weak he was, although Richard took pains to disguise it, Josh wanted to buy his stepfather a walker.

They rode in silence as Josh headed for the pharmacy where he hoped he'd be able to locate what he needed.

"What Richard said about me and Dylan . . ." she hesitated. "At one point I thought the world of him; I was crazy about him all through high school until our senior year."

"All the girls in school were half in love with Dylan, and with good reason. He was a star athlete, personable, and an all-around nice guy."

"No, he wasn't," Michelle countered softly.

Her voice was low, but she'd captured his attention just as surely as if she'd shouted. He took his eyes off the road for long enough to glance at her in the passenger seat next to him. "I beg your pardon?"

"He wasn't everything you said."

"Oh?" That was the way Josh remembered Dylan.

"I've kept this secret for over ten years, Josh, but I'm going to tell you."

He eased to a stop at the red light. "Tell me what?"

"The year we were seniors, Dylan had trouble in English class. We each had to write a term paper."

"I remember. I did mine on Jim Ryun, the first high schooler to run a four-minute mile." The paper had required a lot of research. Because it was a subject that interested Josh, he'd actually enjoyed it.

He'd received a high grade, but he'd never told his stepfather.

"If Dylan didn't get a passing grade on his term paper then he wouldn't have been allowed to play basketball that season."

While Dylan was popular for all the reasons he'd noted earlier, his one shortcoming was his dismal grades. Dylan hated studying. Josh remembered that his stepbrother still hadn't managed to memorize his times tables in high school. His spelling was atrocious and he'd often flat out ignore homework. He'd barely skidded from one grade to the next.

Teresa had spent copious hours helping Dylan with his assignments, but it had done little good. After she became sick those nightly sessions quickly fell by the wayside.

"I wrote the term paper for him," she murmured.

"You did?"

"We struck a deal. I knew no boy would ask me to the prom . . ."

"Michelle, that's not true—"

She interrupted him with a sharp laugh. "Don't kid yourself. I was the fattest girl in the class . . ."

"Did Dylan promise to take you to the prom?"

"No," she said and shook her head for emphasis. "I realized no one would believe that Dylan would ever ask someone like me to the junior-senior prom, but I wanted to go in the worst way. A bunch of us girls decided we would band together and drop by all on our own. All I wanted from Dylan, all I asked in return for writing his paper, was that he ask me to dance with him. Just one dance. He agreed, and I wrote it for him, making enough grammar and spelling errors to make sure Mrs. Chenard would believe it was his.

"Dylan turned it in and then he completely ignored me at the dance. Really, how would it have hurt him to dance with me just that once?" she asked.

"He didn't?" For sure Dylan was no saint, but Josh had trouble believing that he would renege on his promise to Michelle.

"I confronted him later and he said he forgot."

The excuse sounded lame to Josh. Still, he felt obligated to defend his stepbrother. "I'm sure there was some misunderstanding."

"There wasn't. Later I heard through the grapevine that Dylan bragged to his friends about how he'd manipulated me into writing his term paper with the promise of a single dance. He told them that he just couldn't bring himself to do it. He said he wasn't sure he could get his arms around Dumbo."

From the way Michelle's voice dipped, Josh knew that this was still a painful memory for her. It seemed like his stepbrother had taken delight in embarrassing her. "I'm so sorry," Josh whispered.

"You have nothing to regret, Josh. You didn't do

that to me." She managed what looked like a forced smile. "My one consolation was that he got a B instead of an A because of all the intentional typos."

Josh smiled, too, and, reaching for her hand, gave it a gentle squeeze.

"I'm telling you this so you'll realize that Dylan wasn't the saint you and his father have painted him to be. In many ways he was wonderful, but he could also be heartless and cruel."

Josh knew that to be true. Dylan was his father's son.

Chapter 14

While my guests were away for the afternoon, I decided to run a couple of errands. I wanted to stop off at the local bakery and check out their sweet rolls. My original intention had been to bake my own, but I know myself well enough to realize that that might not always be possible. I enjoyed baking, but there were bound to be days when I simply couldn't.

The drizzle continued to fall, but having lived in Seattle all these years I was undeterred. I grabbed my raincoat, scarf, and gloves, locked the front door, and headed down the hill. The sky was darkening even though it was barely two in the afternoon. The cove was thick with fog, making Bremerton and the navy shipyard directly across the cove completely invisible.

The sidewalk was steep but I figured that by walking I could offset the additional calories I'd be consuming when I sampled sweets at the bakery. A warning to watch my weight was another gem Peggy had shared. As B&B proprietors, it was far too easy to get into the habit of sampling our own cooking, she'd said. The first year she and Bob had owned Thyme and Tide, Peggy confessed that she'd gained ten pounds.

My resolve weakened the minute I opened the door to the bakery. They apparently had just taken bread out of the oven because the smell filled the room. A scent like this was more hypnotic than French perfume. Paul claimed that he decided to marry me the first time I baked him a loaf of homemade bread. I'm no dummy. I knew the way to a man's heart, and he'd already captured mine so I used all my baking skills to woo him.

"May I help you?" a young woman asked as I stepped up to the counter.

I'd barely had a chance to look. The glass-enclosed shelf contained row upon row of delectable delights. The macaroons looked amazing, as big as my fist and golden brown, just the way I like them. Peanut butter cookies were another favorite of mine, and Paul's, too.

"I'll take a dozen cookies," I said before I could change my mind. "Mix and match, okay?"

"Sure thing." The girl behind the counter instantly brightened. "We have eight varieties today."

"Make that two dozen then to even everything out," I said, completely disregarding Peggy's warning.

I scooted down the case and glanced at the cakes on display. They were huge. The coconut cake looked like it contained five or six layers, and it stood nearly as tall as a wedding cake. The same could be said of the carrot cake, which was decorated with chopped nuts and tiny orange carrots made of frosting that circled the top in an artful display. The chocolate cake was elaborately decorated with a large white bow, as if it were a gift to be shared and enjoyed. Before my mouth started to water, I looked over the selection of pies.

"Is there anything else?" the girl asked, following my gaze.

"Ah . . ." I hesitated, and then reluctantly shook my head. I'd take the cookies back to Rose Harbor and set out a plate for my guests, in case they returned later that afternoon. Sandy Frelinger had recommended that I offer a mid-afternoon refreshment. My cookies resembled golf balls compared to these baseball-size wonders.

The bell above the door chimed softly as someone else entered the bakery.

"We're also offering a special today," the young clerk announced to me and the second patron. "Buy one cake or pie and get the second for half off."

"Oh dear, you do make this hard to resist." Then I remembered my original intent. "Where are your sweet rolls?" I asked.

"Sorry, we sold out of those before ten this morning. We almost always do. If you want breakfast sweets you'll need to get here early, or order them the day before."

"Okay. Then maybe I should place an order for sweet rolls for tomorrow."

"A dozen?" the clerk asked, grinning.

"Just six for now. I only have two guests at the moment, so that should be more than enough. What time do you open?"

"Seven. We make great lattes, too."

I'd noticed the espresso machine when I entered the shop.

"Excuse me," the other patron said from behind me. "Are you Jo Marie Rose?"

"Yes." I was surprised that anyone in town knew my name.

"You bought the Frelingers' B and B, right?"

Again I was pleasantly surprised. "I did."

She held out her hand. "I'm Corrie McAfee; Peggy Beldon is a good friend of mine. She mentioned that she was hoping to chat with you soon. Welcome to Cedar Cove."

"Peggy stopped by this morning." I was warmed by how friendly everyone was.

"My husband and I moved from Seattle several

years ago. Peggy mentioned that you're from there, too."

I nodded, liking Corrie right away.

"Do you have time for a cup of coffee?"

I glanced at my watch. There wasn't any reason to rush back to the house. I knew Abby Kincaid had a rehearsal dinner to attend for her brother's wedding. Josh hadn't mentioned his plans but he'd said that he'd be out until late afternoon.

"I'd love a cup of coffee," I said. The bakery had a small sitting area with round tables.

"Great, and it's my treat."

"And I'll provide the cookies to go with it," I suggested.

Corrie nodded enthusiastically. "That's an offer too good to refuse."

After I finished my order for the sweet rolls and paid for everything, I selected a table close to the window. Corrie got our coffees and joined me.

I held open the pink box of cookies and let her make her selection. Like me, she opted for a macaroon.

"I have a weakness for these."

"I do, too," I confessed.

We each simultaneously took our first bites. The macaroon was just as delectable as it looked. We both took a moment simply to savor it.

Corrie spoke first. "Roy and I have come to think of Cedar Cove as our home now, despite the years we spent in Seattle. Our son and his wife are here with our granddaughter. Our daughter lives in North Dakota with her family."

I envied Corrie her husband and extended family. "I'm a widow and unfortunately I don't have children." And it looked like I probably wouldn't have children. Accepting that was one of the most difficult parts of losing Paul.

"When I get a chance, I'll introduce you to my husband," Corrie said, picking up the conversation. "Roy's a retired police detective who works as a private investigator now and again."

"I'll look forward to meeting him."

"If you ever have a problem—and I doubt that you will—please don't hesitate to contact Roy or me."

"Thank you," I said, struck again by the way this small town had already gathered me into its arms.

We spoke for a while longer and finished our coffee and macaroons. I told Corrie how Peggy had urged me to get to know the town well. I could see now this was valuable advice, and I asked lots of questions about the businesses around town.

Corrie and I left at the same time. My new friend headed for the library and—as Mark had done earlier—she suggested that I stop in and meet Grace Harding. I made a mental note to get over to the library sooner rather than later.

I huffed and puffed my way up the steep hill to Rose Harbor Inn. By the time I was at the top, I was panting and the back of my calves ached. I'd worked off that macaroon for sure. I paused as I caught my breath. I'd need to work an exercise regimen into my daily routine.

I was halfway up my driveway before I noticed that a car was parked in the special area reserved for guests. Because I hadn't expected anyone, I'd spent far more time away from the inn than I'd originally planned.

Picking up my pace I approached the car to find a man sitting there, apparently awaiting my return. I tapped lightly against the window, and he turned to look my way, automatically breaking into a huge smile.

He seemed vaguely familiar, but I couldn't place him. He opened the car door to climb out as I stepped back.

"Jo Marie, how good to see you."

My mind was busy trying to piece together how I knew this man. Unfortunately I came up blank.

"I hope I didn't keep you waiting long?" I said. He knew my name so clearly he wasn't a guest whose reservation had somehow gotten overlooked.

"I've only been here for a few minutes," he assured me. He followed me up toward the house, chatting as we walked. "I can't wait for the rain to stop. Nothing depresses me more than one rainy day after another," he said affably, although the cheerful tempo of his voice belied his words.

"I was at the bakery," I explained as I led the way

into the house. I set down the cookies and paused for long enough to hang up my coat and scarf. He removed his own coat and hung it next to mine.

My mind remained a blank, but the longer he spoke, the more convinced I was that I knew him. Then it hit me. This was Spenser Wood—he'd been in the same unit as Paul, and they'd been stationed at Fort Lewis together.

"You're back," I said, feeling much more comfortable now that I recognized Spenser. If I remembered correctly, he had been in Afghanistan with Paul.

"Yes. A friend from our unit told me you'd moved here. I wanted to stop by and tell you how sorry I am about Paul. He was a good man."

"Thank you." The words caught, but he didn't appear to notice and I was glad. "I have coffee on if you'd like a cup."

"Please, that would be wonderful."

He followed me into the kitchen, locking his arms behind his back as he looked around, giving the room an intense appraisal. "This place is really something."

"I fell in love with it the minute I saw it," I confessed.

"Paul would have loved it, too."

I agreed with a short nod. I hadn't spoken to anyone who knew Paul for several days now. I found it rather awkward for Spenser to mention his name, though I hadn't felt that way with others who wanted to talk about him.

"You were in Afghanistan with Paul, right?" I asked, leading him into the living room by the fireplace. It was lit by gas so when I flipped the switch the fire instantly roared over the logs.

Spenser sat on the sofa and I took the chair. He set his mug down on the wood coffee table before I could get him a coaster.

"You know how close Paul and I were," Spenser said, his face falling in his own grief over the loss.

To the best of my memory I'd only met Spenser once. I didn't remember Paul mentioning him in his emails or any of his other correspondence. While he was deployed, Paul and I had had the opportunity to talk now and again on our cell phones. I searched my memory and couldn't bring up any mention of Spenser.

"I'm grateful for all of Paul's friends," I said, sidestepping the question.

Spenser gripped the coffee mug with both hands. "He was like a brother to me . . . a brother I never had. We were tight, especially after we landed in Afghanistan."

I looked down, avoiding eye contact. For reasons I couldn't explain this conversation was making me uncomfortable. I felt myself tensing up. I wasn't sure where Spenser was headed.

"He talked about you a great deal," Spenser went on to say. "He was crazy about you."

"I deeply loved my husband."

"And he loved you more than anything."

A lump filled my throat as I fiddled with my coffee mug. An awkward silence followed and I glanced up. Spenser had scooted closer to the edge of the cushion and was leaning forward.

"I imagine you're wondering why I'm here. It pains me to come to you like this . . . it's rather embarrassing, to be frank. Unfortunately I've gotten myself into something of a financial mess and . . ."

My gaze shot up. Could it be that Spenser had come to me looking for a loan?

He gestured weakly with his hands. "I know that as Paul's wife you're the recipient of his life insurance policy. The army takes care of their own and . . ."

"And this concerns you how?" I asked.

"Seeing how close Paul and I were, I was hoping you could help me out."

I was too stunned to speak.

"I apologize for hitting you with this, but the truth is that I could use a little financial help. It would only be a loan for a short while. I wouldn't even think to approach you if Paul and I weren't like brothers . . . like family."

Dumbfounded, I tried to think about how Paul would have wanted me to handle this situation.

Before I could speak, Spenser added, "If Paul were alive I know he'd lend me the money without question. Like I said, we were really close."

"Spenser," I said as gently as I could. "I'm not a bank."

He nodded and seemed to accept my decision. "I understand, but I felt I had to ask. Paul and I often helped each other out of financial jams. More than once I've lent him money . . . and he did the same for me. I wouldn't want you to think I came to you out of the blue. I'd do this for Paul in a heartbeat . . . and now that he's gone, I'd be more than willing to help you, if our situations were reversed."

I didn't know how to answer. I hadn't been aware that Paul had ever borrowed money from friends, and that surprised me. I teetered, wondering what I should do.

"I know what it means to get caught in financial difficulties," I said, sympathizing with him.

"Then you've been in the same spot?"

I nodded, remembering what it was like when I was on my own for the first time. "I've been there myself." After getting my first credit card, despite warnings from my family, I'd charged more than I could afford to spend. When the bill arrived I'd been shocked by exactly how much I'd managed to run up in a single month.

It got much worse before I came to my senses and destroyed the card. For a while I could ill afford to pay the interest on the debt, let alone make headway toward the principal. Then my hours were cut and all I earned went toward rent, groceries, and utilities. I didn't sleep. I fretted and worried. It was the most awful feeling not to be able to pay those bills. I never wanted to endure that again.

"Then you might reconsider . . . if you've been where I'm at, you must understand how humiliating this is."

"I—"

I wasn't allowed to finish my thought.

All at once the front door burst open and Mark Taylor walked in unannounced. He paused in the foyer and took one look at Spenser and me. His eyes darkened as he headed directly for Spenser.

Spenser stood.

The two men stood nose to nose. "I believe we need to talk," Mark said gruffly and then added. "Outside. Now."

Spenser looked at me for an explanation, but I had none to give him. "Ah . . . Mark," I started.

He ignored me. "Now," he repeated in a tone that didn't leave room for argument.

Spenser shrugged his shoulders and walked toward the door.

Mark followed, grabbing Spenser's coat off the peg on the way out.

I stood and looked out the window. I couldn't see either man, but I could distinguish raised voices. Hard as I tried, I couldn't make out what was being said.

After only a few minutes, I heard footsteps, followed a minute later by the sound of a car engine.

Spenser was leaving. Without a single word of farewell.

The next thing I heard was the sound of gravel crunching as he backed out of the driveway and drove away.

I hurried toward the front door to confront Mark and find out why he'd rushed into the inn like an angry mother bear protecting her cub.

Only he had left, too, his retreating figure moving quickly.

Chapter 15

Abby had been worried about meeting Roger's fiancée, but Victoria had been sincere and gracious and so clearly in love with Roger that Abby couldn't help but like her. How fortunate her brother was to have found someone he was willing to commit to for the rest of his life.

The afternoon was speeding by and Abby wanted to change clothes before the rehearsal and the dinner that was scheduled to immediately follow it. Before leaving her brother, she'd learned that their cousin, Lonny, was serving as Roger's best man and his parents were staying at the same hotel as Abby's parents.

With every detail she realized how much distance she'd put between her and her family. In retrospect, she couldn't believe she'd been so caught up in her own worries about the wedding that she hadn't even asked whom he'd chosen as his best man.

As she pulled into the driveway of the Rose Harbor Inn, Abby was struck again by what a lovely place this had turned out to be. The structure itself was amazing, overlooking the cove. However, it was far more than the beauty of the place that drew her to it. Abby felt like she was coming home each time she returned. Just being in the house seemed to affect her in a positive way. It was as if she was shucking off the burdens of the past right along with her wool coat when she walked in the door.

As Abby entered the foyer, Jo Marie stepped out of the kitchen to greet her. "Oh hi, I wondered when you'd be back," she said. "Did you have a good afternoon? When's the rehearsal?"

"I did." It was true. Abby had enjoyed herself. Running into Patty had been unexpected. Her one-time friend's reaction had gone a long way toward boosting Abby's spirits and her confidence. She was beginning to tentatively feel that coming home had been the right thing to do. As much as Abby had dreaded this wedding, she now found herself flirting with a sense of hope, of anticipation that putting the accident behind her just might be a possibility.

When Abby looked up, she realized Jo Marie was

looking at her. "I'm sorry, did you say something? I zoned out for a moment."

"Please, don't worry. I'm a little zoned out myself," Jo Marie said and then shook her head. "You'll have to forgive me. The oddest thing just happened. A . . . former acquaintance stopped by and then someone else, someone I barely know, popped in. Then they both stepped outside and before I knew it they were gone. As far as I know they'd never met each other before and . . . I . . . I hardly know what to think."

Abby was grateful to have the subject shift away from her. "That is rather strange, isn't it?" she said, sympathetically.

"Really weird," Jo Marie said, shaking her head as though she was utterly perplexed by the entire event. Still seeming distracted, Jo Marie returned to the kitchen.

Glad to avoid any further delay, Abby headed up the stairs. In an effort to bolster her self-confidence, she'd splurged on two new outfits—one for the rehearsal and dinner and another for the actual wedding. She'd chosen a pink and white pant suit for the rehearsal. It had cost more money than she felt comfortable spending, but the salesclerk had raved about how good it looked on her, so Abby had succumbed.

If ever there was a time to feel positive about herself, it was now, facing her family and friends. The mental preparation was as important, if not more so, than the physical one.

Abby quickly changed clothes, refreshed her hair and makeup, and then sat on the edge of the bed, hands folded in her lap as she struggled to calm her pounding heart. It was all about to begin now. Within the next hour she'd be with her parents, visiting with relatives she hadn't seen in years.

After several minutes, Abby felt she was as ready as she was ever going to be. For good measure she squirted on her favorite perfume and headed out the door, amused by the thought that a squirt of expensive perfume would give her an edge.

"Have a wonderful time," Jo Marie called after Abby as she left the inn.

"Thank you." Abby's response was automatic, yet she wondered if enjoying these festivities would be possible. Her nerves were already on high alert, and she could feel the muscles along the back of her shoulders tightening with tension.

Abby arrived at the address Roger had given her, although she already knew where the Catholic church was located. It was the same church they'd attended when they lived in the area. The sanctuary, however, was new. A large cross dominated the front of the sprawling structure, centered on the roof above the double-wide doors leading into the building.

The church lot was almost deserted. Abby parked

close to the entrance and heard laughter and good-natured banter floating down the hall from the sanctuary. Abby recognized Victoria's voice and realized that part of the wedding party had gathered in a room off the vestibule. Abby knew that Tamara, Victoria's younger sister, was the maid of honor, and that Victoria had chosen several close friends as her bridesmaids.

As soon as Abby entered the room, Victoria broke away from the wedding party and came to greet her. With her arm around Abby's waist, she brought her close and introduced her. "Everyone, this is Abby Kincaid, Roger's sister."

She was greeted with a chorus of welcomes and was instantly subjected to a number of questions.

"What was Roger like as a kid?" Tamara asked. "I mean, Victoria and I fought something terrible. Did you and Roger get along?"

Abby grinned, remembering how grateful she'd been to have a way to meet boys, all thanks to her brother. "We did in our own way . . . he was the source of most of my early dates." Immediately Steve came to mind, her brother's college roommate. Like Patty and other friends, he'd made a number of efforts to connect after Angela's death but she'd ignored him, the same as she had everyone else.

"Roger and I argued a lot as kids, but it wasn't so bad when we got older."

"No, because he needed you in order to meet girls,"

her future sister-in-law joked. "That street goes two ways."

Abby tilted her head to one side and smiled again. How right Victoria was. "Exactly."

Abby found a chair in the corner and sat. She felt more comfortable sitting back and observing than she did being the center of attention. Watching Victoria with her friends was an endless source of entertainment. While Abby didn't know these women, she liked the way they fussed over Victoria, teasing and laughing together. Abby laughed, too, drawn in by their happiness.

Her parents were due to arrive any minute. By now they must have had time to drive to their hotel, check in, and change their clothes.

Briefly Abby wondered if her father still had the same double-breasted suit he'd worn to every formal occasion she could remember. One suit, he claimed, was all he would ever need. Abby's mother had talked up a storm in order to convince him to invest in another, but Tom Kincaid had insisted that wasn't necessary.

After a few minutes, Abby made an excuse and left Victoria and the other women in the wedding party. Without conscious thought she wandered into the church, drawn in by the sanctuary.

Standing in the middle of the center aisle, she looked around, taking in the modern features. Gone was the statue of the Virgin Mother holding the baby

Jesus, her eyes gentle with a look of complete serenity. Jesus hanging on the cross, blood dripping from his pierced hands, was nowhere in sight either, although a large crucifix dominated the area behind the altar. The Stations of the Cross had a more modern look than she remembered. A lot had changed in the years she'd been away.

The altar was completely different, too. The elaborate marble top had been replaced with a wooden structure.

Abby tried to remember the last time she'd been to mass, and couldn't. After the accident she'd drifted away from the church, and from God.

She slipped into a pew in the back of the church and sat, soaking in the calming silence. Abby closed her eyes. The exhaustion she'd experienced that morning was gone and in its place had come a sense of anticipation.

Anticipation, not dread.

The realization struck her and once more she experienced a feeling of hope, a thin seedling of optimism, of . . . healing. The tension she'd felt across her shoulder blades gradually eased.

She thought about praying the memorized prayers of her youth, but wasn't sure she would remember all the words. Praying, talking to God, felt foreign, awkward. She wasn't sure what to say or how to say it. Wasn't sure she even could.

When she'd first heard that Angela hadn't survived the car crash, Abby had cursed God. If anyone had to die, it should have been her. She'd been the one behind the wheel . . . the one responsible. Anger had gripped her. A holy anger. A righteous anger. God had failed her. He'd failed Angela, too. It wasn't fair that her friend should have been killed and that two families had been torn apart.

Funny how time scrubs away such agony, weathering it through the years, like water rushing over rocks gradually smooths away the sharp, painful edges. What they said about time being the great healer was true, Abby realized. She had a long way to go, she knew, but she had made progress. This one small step, returning to Cedar Cove, had taken courage even if she'd been forced into it by this wedding. It felt as if God was telling her it was time to use the momentum of this visit to continue to pick up the pieces of her life.

The door to the sanctuary opened and Abby turned to see her mother peeking her head inside the door.

"Mom," she whispered. As a child she'd been taught never to speak out loud inside a church.

"Abby." Her mother walked inside and met Abby with open arms.

The two women hugged, their embrace tight as if they'd been lost and then found.

"I didn't know what to think when I couldn't find

you," her mother whispered. "Victoria didn't know where you'd gone . . . the sanctuary was the last place I thought to look."

"I've only been here a few minutes," Abby said, amused by her mother's reaction. A quick look at her watch told her she'd been in the sanctuary far longer than she realized. Almost half an hour.

"Oh look at you," Linda Kincaid whispered, leaning back to get a better view of her. "Oh, honey, you look just wonderful."

"Thank you." That salesclerk had been right. The pink and white outfit complemented her dark hair and eyes.

"It's just so good to see you," her mother continued, her eyes shining with unshed tears.

"It hasn't been that long."

"Two years," her mother contradicted. "Two very long years."

Had it really? Abby found it incredible that the months had come and gone so quickly. It seemed like only a few weeks ago that her parents had flown to Florida for a visit.

"Christmas two years ago."

"I'm here now," Abby countered.

Again her mother hugged her. "It means so much to Roger and me that you agreed to attend the wedding. I . . . I know how hard this is for you."

"It's better, Mom, much better," she said. "I ran into Patty."

"Patty Morris?"

"She's Patty Jefferies now and she's a pharmacist."

"Oh that's just wonderful. I'm surprised. I can remember you and Patty pouring over your biology books and her claiming she just didn't get it. And now she's a pharmacist?"

Abby nodded. "She and her husband, Pete, own the pharmacy."

"That's amazing." Her mother's smile was wide and approving. "Who would have believed it?"

"She seemed genuinely pleased to see me."

"Of course she was. You two were close all the way through school."

"Oh, Mom," Abby said, struggling to hide her amusement. Her mother was her constant support, her anchor. How could she have kept her at arm's length for so long?

"How is Patty?" her mother asked.

"She's fabulous and she has twins."

"Twins. I'm telling you, Abby, if you or Roger don't make me a grandmother soon, I don't know what I'll do. I need grandchildren to spoil." Her laughter died away and she grew serious. "Are you dating anyone?" Within a matter of seconds, Linda pinned Abby with her laser look.

"Mother! No, I'm not dating, and if I was, I wouldn't tell you."

Linda shook her head as though thoroughly disgusted. "I don't know what it is with you kids," she lamented. "By the time your father and I were your age we had two children and a mortgage. When are you going to meet a nice man and settle down?"

Good question, and if Abby knew the answer she would have enjoyed sharing it with the rest of the world.

"Mom, listen. I told you about meeting up with Patty for a reason."

"Oh?"

"Patty's organizing a lunch with some of my old friends who still live in the area and she asked that you come, too."

"Me?"

"Yes, you. She's hoping to have her mother join us." Abby rattled off the names Patty had mentioned.

"I was on the school board with Kathy Wilson," her mother said. "She's Kelly Wilson's mother."

"I know Kelly," Abby said, amused now and struggling to disguise it.

Once again her mother hugged her. "I knew this wedding would bring our family back together again. I just knew it."

Abby wasn't ready to go quite that far, but she felt it was a start.

Chapter 16

"It's thoughtful of you to do this for Richard," Michelle said as they loaded the walker Josh had purchased at the local pharmacy into the trunk of his rented vehicle.

"Knowing how stubborn he is, Richard will probably refuse to use it." It would be just like his stepfather. "Still, it's worth a try. I don't like the idea of him trying to walk on his own. It would be far too easy for him to take a tumble."

"I've been saying the same thing for weeks."

When they arrived back at the house, Josh found Richard sound asleep in his recliner. He didn't wake up, which told Josh that the trip to the hospital had exhausted the older man. To Josh's surprise it looked as if Richard had managed to eat a little of the soup. At least he'd made the effort. That boded well for the walker. Maybe, just maybe, Richard would be willing to accept this small gift from him. The purchase hadn't been made out of love, but out of respect for his mother.

Josh carried the boxed walker into the kitchen. Michelle came with him. He would need to assemble it, although it didn't look like there was much to it.

"I'll find you a screwdriver," Michelle offered.

Josh doubted that he'd need one, but he didn't stop her from leaving. While she was out of the room, he opened the box and removed the pieces. He hadn't had time to process what she'd told him about Dylan. In all the years he'd known his stepbrother, Josh couldn't remember Dylan ever being intentionally cruel. He enjoyed practical jokes, Josh remembered. Slapstick humor seemed to amuse him the most, so he had to admit it didn't seem impossible.

It hurt Josh to know that Dylan had wounded Michelle's tender heart. He was sorry it'd happened. Her pain had vibrated off of her as she'd recounted the details of the dance. What took him completely by surprise was that he'd felt the heady urge to take her in his arms and comfort her, to lean over and kiss her and tell her how bad he felt that something like this had happened. If he could have, he would've turned back the clock and escorted her to the prom himself.

Having Michelle leave the room for a few minutes gave him some badly needed breathing room. The physical awareness between them had heightened after her story. He sensed it and was fairly certain that Michelle did, too, but there was no point in dwelling on it. A relationship between them would be impossible. His work took him all over the country. Although he had the house in San Diego, he was rarely there. By contrast, Michelle's life was here in Cedar Cove. When he left town this time, it would be for good. He had no intention of returning.

Josh had the walker fully assembled by the time Michelle returned with a screwdriver.

"You did it?"

Josh grinned. "It was easy."

"Maybe for you," she joked.

"I see you found a screwdriver."

"I got it from my dad's garage." She held it up for him to examine. "I was stunned by how many there were. I chose this one because it looked like Dad used it the most."

"Then you'd better take it back before he discovers it's gone."

"Yeah, good idea." She left once more and returned a few minutes later.

Josh stood, thinking that with Richard asleep, it

would be a good time to seek out the other things he wanted to collect.

"Where are you going?" Michelle asked.

Josh hesitated, not sure if he should tell her. "Richard's bedroom."

She frowned as though she wasn't sure she approved. "Why?"

"I want to look for something . . ."

Still she hesitated. "I want to come with you."

"Are you afraid I'll ruin something precious in retribution for what he did to my things?"

"I don't think you're capable of that."

Her high opinion of his intentions humbled him. "Don't be so sure." Then, because he knew he might have a hard time controlling his temper if he found anything else of his that Richard had destroyed, he held out his hand, inviting Michelle to join him.

The master bedroom was in the hallway off the kitchen. The door was slightly ajar. It creaked when Josh swung it open. He hesitated and glanced over his shoulder, fearing the noise might have woken his stepfather. From where he stood he couldn't see Richard. Josh had to believe that if the old man was awake, he would do something to try and stop him.

The room was exactly as he remembered it. The bed was in the same position, but unmade. His mother had been a stickler about Dylan and him making up their beds every morning. To find the very one in which she'd slept such a mess of sheets and blankets somehow seemed wrong. Odd that he should feel compelled to straighten it.

He walked around to his mother's side of the bed and opened the drawer of her nightstand. It was empty. Disappointment hit him and his shoulders sank.

"Did you find what you wanted?" Michelle asked.

He shook his head. "It isn't here."

"What are you looking for?" she whispered. "Maybe I can help."

"No need to whisper," Josh assured her. "If Richard could hear us he would have called out by now."

"What is it you're looking for?" she asked again, unwilling to let him sidestep the question.

He hesitated and then told her. "My mother's Bible. In the last days of her life, she kept it at her side twenty-four/seven. I don't have anything that was hers and I'd like to have that Bible."

"A Bible," she repeated. Michelle glanced around the room. "Where do you think Richard would have put it?"

If Josh had any idea, he'd be looking there now. "I don't have a clue."

"Check the top shelf in the closet," Michelle suggested.

Josh slid open the door only to discover the closet was jammed full of clothes, extra blankets, and a multitude of . . . stuff. If Richard had tucked the Bible in there, it would take all day to uncover it.

Discouraged, he shook his head.

"You could just ask Richard for it," Michelle offered.

Josh turned to face her. Apparently she hadn't learned anything from his shredded jacket and year-book. "Do you honestly think he'd tell me?"

"Why wouldn't he? It was your mother's Bible. You have every right to it."

"Don't you understand?" he said, nearly losing his patience. "If Richard learns I want that Bible, he'll do everything within his power to make sure I never get it. He'd see that it was destroyed before he'd give it to me."

Michelle opened her mouth as though to argue and then abruptly snapped it closed, conceding the point.

"You're right," she whispered. She turned to him and slipped her arms around his waist and hugged him, the side of her face pressed against his chest. She twisted her head to look up at him and their eyes met and held. For an extended moment they simply stared at each other. Josh didn't breathe and he was fairly certain Michelle didn't either. The air between them seemed charged with awareness and need. Need to comfort. Need to console.

Plain, raw need.

After what seemed like years, Josh closed his eyes and lowered his mouth to hers, no longer able to resist. The kiss started off gentle; gradually it became something else, something more. Something deeper.

Josh wound his fingers into Michelle's hair, bringing her tighter against him as he ground his mouth over hers, wanting to claim as much of her as he could, giving, taking.

When he broke off the kiss, they were both breathless and panting, their shoulders heaving.

Josh wanted to say something, but words refused to formulate in his mind. What crowded his thoughts was how he'd never meant for this to happen, and at the same time, how right it'd felt to have her in his arms. The contradictory feelings canceled each other out, leaving him speechless and bewildered.

She stuffed her fingers in the back hip pockets of her jeans. "Oh boy," she whispered, and walked away. She took a moment, apparently to compose herself and then turned back to face him.

"I still think I should approach Richard about the Bible," she said, picking up the conversation as if there had been no interlude. No kiss. No urgency between them.

"Michelle . . ."

She raised her hand, stopping him. "I won't come out and ask him directly."

Okay, fine. If she wanted to pretend nothing had happened then that was fine by him; easier all the way around. And if she had a plan on how to get his mother's Bible then Josh was eager to hear it. "Okay, what's your idea?"

"I'll be subtle about it. I'll . . . I'll ask him if he'd

like me to bring him a Bible. He knows he's dying and he might want one."

"And if he doesn't?"

"I . . . I don't know. I haven't thought that far ahead. One step at a time, Josh. I've dealt with situations like this before. We'll get you your mother's Bible one way or another."

While Josh appreciated her efforts, he wasn't willing to suspend his search. "Maybe he's already felt the need to read the Bible," he said and walked around to the other side of the bed, to Richard's nightstand. Opening the drawer he discovered a bunch of loose coins and a couple of paperback novels.

No Bible.

He headed for the chest of drawers next, convinced Richard had purposely hidden the Bible in an effort to thwart him. The top drawer was filled with what looked to be dirty laundry. The second one down proved equally unfruitful.

Michelle stopped him by setting her hand on his shoulder. "Josh, give me a chance," she whispered.

As much as he wanted to believe her, he had legitimate doubts. Richard had made it plain earlier that Michelle had a choice to make. It was either side with him against Josh, or never enter this house again.

She must have read the hesitation in him because she raised her hand to his face, cupping the side of his jaw. "Josh."

The way she whispered his name—the soft pleading quality of her voice—gave him pause. His eyes searched hers.

Then, as though to prove her intent, she raised up on the tips of her toes and kissed him again. Josh had yet to recover from the first kiss. He'd wanted to think this through before anything else happened.

Well, it had, and here he was caught in the flow of an emotional stream with a current so swift he feared he would be knocked off his feet. With every ounce of resolve he possessed, Josh broke off the kiss.

"I don't think this is a good idea."

"What?" she asked, her eyes burning into his. "Us kissing?"

He nodded.

"Okay." She started to turn away, but not before Josh saw the disappointment and hurt reflected in her eyes.

"Wait . . ." He caught her by the shoulder and brought her back into his arms. If the first exchange of kisses had been hot, this second round was strong enough to scorch his senses. He felt a powerful surge of desire and need so strong, he feared he was about to crush Michelle with his bare arms.

Thankfully, before it got out of hand they were interrupted by the doorbell.

They broke apart like guilty teenagers caught making out. Josh stared accusingly at the partially closed bedroom door.

"Who could that be?" Michelle asked.

Josh already knew. "Hospice."

"Right, hospice," she repeated. "I forgot they were coming."

Josh pulled himself together first and walked out of the bedroom. Michelle wasn't far behind him.

When he opened the door a professional-looking woman smiled back at them. "Hello, my name is Ginger Cochran. I'm with hospice."

"Come in, please," Josh said, holding open the door for her.

As soon as she was inside the house, he closed the door to keep the cold air at bay. Richard was awake now, Josh noted, the old man's eyes fluttering as he struggled to focus.

"Who are you?" Richard asked.

"My name is Ginger. I was just telling your—"

"Stepson," Josh inserted. They hadn't had a chance to introduce themselves yet. "And this is Michelle Nelson, Richard's next-door neighbor. She and her family have been looking in on him for the last several months."

"I know why you're here, but I'm telling you right now you made an unnecessary trip," Richard told Ginger, ignoring Josh and Michelle. "You can leave."

"Mr. Lambert," Michelle protested.

"I said you can go now," he repeated with surprising strength. "I don't want you here." He pointed a shaky finger at Josh. "Take him with you. He intends to rob me . . . he isn't even waiting 'til I'm dead. He's already started rifling through my things."

"Mr. Lambert," Michelle stated calmly. "That isn't true."

"You think I didn't notice that you two just came out of my bedroom?"

Josh laughed and slowly shook his head.

"I'm not here to upset you," Ginger Cochran said as she reached for her purse. "I came to make you as comfortable as possible. If you want me to leave, I will."

"Good. Leave."

"Mr. Lambert," Michelle protested again.

"I told you earlier, I want to die in peace. My house has become like Grand Central Terminal with people coming and going. Get out of here. All of you. Just leave me alone. What does a man have to do around here to die in peace?"

"I'm sorry," Michelle whispered to Ginger as she turned to leave.

Josh stood back as Michelle escorted the other woman to the front door.

Richard's gaze narrowed as he pointed at the walker. "Where did that come from?" he demanded. Josh had brought it into the room and set it by the chair.

"I don't have a clue," Josh said.

"It wasn't here when I got back from the hospital."

"I don't recall if it was or wasn't. Perhaps Santa brought it . . . a delayed Christmas gift. You know how slow the mail can get at this time of year."

What might have been a smile briefly flitted across Richard's face, but it disappeared so fast that Josh doubted what he'd seen. His stepfather closed his eyes again, blocking them all out.

Stubborn old fool, Josh mused. They were both far too stubborn for their own good.

Chapter 17

This had been by far one of the most perplexing days of my life. Spenser, a man I barely remembered, had shown up unexpectedly at my front door. I hadn't thought to ask him how he'd found me, which left yet another question unanswered.

And that was just the beginning. Mark, a man I had only recently met, had stormed into my house like a raging bull and escorted Spenser outside, and they'd both left without another word. It'd all been so strange, so odd. So shocking.

I was determined to find out what had happened and the only person I could ask was Mark. I dug out the business card he'd given me and walked over to the phone. I held the receiver for several moments while I figured out what I wanted to say, then dialed his number.

To my disappointment, it rang four times and then went to voice mail. I listened to the recorded message and waited for the beep, which seemed to take forever.

"Mark, this is Jo Marie Rose, could you please call me back?" I hesitated before replacing the receiver, hoping that Mark would somehow pick up. My curiosity over his behavior was like the itch of a pesky mosquito bite. I simply couldn't ignore what had happened.

Thankfully, I didn't have long to wait. No more than ten minutes later the phone rang.

"Rose Harbor Inn," I said.

"It's Mark. Sorry I missed your call; I had the buzz saw running."

All at once I decided I didn't want to have this conversation over the phone. He'd made it plain earlier that he hated talking on the phone. And I wanted to see Mark's face when we talked. Over the phone it might be too easy to put me off and I had the distinct feeling that he didn't want to explain himself. Otherwise he wouldn't have run off the way he had without offering any explanation.

"Would it be all right if I stopped by this afternoon?" I asked.

"Here?"

"At your shop, yes."

"My shop is part of my home and I'm not much for company." He sounded hesitant.

"Would you rather stop by the inn . . . again?" I couldn't help adding that last part.

"No; I'm busy."

"Then I'll come to you."

Mark exhaled audibly and when he spoke there was a hint of sarcasm in his voice. "I don't have time for coffee and cookies."

"I won't stay long . . . I'll only take a few minutes of your time."

He hesitated and seemed to realize I wasn't going to drop this easily. "Fine . . . come over."

I'd certainly had more enthusiastic invitations, but in this instance I would take what I could get. His business card had only listed his mailing address, which was a post office box. "I need your street address."

"Oh, right." He gave it to me. "It's just a couple of blocks from the inn. You can drive but I recommend walking—there isn't always parking close by."

"Oh? Why's that?" Cedar Cove wasn't exactly a bustling metropolis. I'd heard parking spaces on the waterfront were limited, but not in local neighborhoods, at least in my experience so far.

"I live by the courthouse," he explained, sounding impatient to get off the phone.

"This will only take a few minutes," I promised again.

"Whatever."

I bristled but held my tongue. It would be easy to take offense at his brusque manner, but I tried not to let my irritation show.

I docked the phone, grabbed my coat, scarf, and gloves, and within a couple of minutes of our conversation, I was out the door.

Tucking Mark's address in my coat pocket, I headed up the hill in the direction of the courthouse. It was a steep climb and it wasn't long before I was winded. I kept my head down and my shoulders hunched forward. I paused to drag in a deep breath when a vehicle whizzed past me. It looked just like Spenser's car. His speed seemed excessive, as if he was eager to leave town. He drove in the opposite direction of the inn, toward Tremont Street, which led to the freeway. I wasn't sure that it was Paul's friend, but intuitively I thought it might have been. Apparently he'd hung around town for a bit longer, but I could only speculate as to why.

Spenser had claimed that he and Paul were as close as brothers. I didn't know if I should believe that, although to be fair, it wasn't completely implausible. Still, it seemed that if the two of them had been as tight as Spenser had indicated, Paul would have mentioned him more often. My husband had talked about several men under his command, but not Spenser, at least not since he'd been shipped to Afghanistan.

I should know. I'd read my husband's letters and

emails, which I'd printed out, so often I'd practically memorized each word. These notes were my connection with Paul, the one tangible link I still had to him.

I suspected Spenser had exaggerated their relationship as a ploy to get me to loan him money. If Spenser thought he could guilt me into a loan then he was mistaken. And anyway, I'd invested nearly all of the insurance money I'd collected as Paul's beneficiary in purchasing the inn. Thankfully I had my own healthy savings account as a cushion—funds I'd put aside from every paycheck for a number of years.

Standing outside Mark's residence I was impressed by how well maintained his home and yard were. The house itself looked to have been built in the 1950s, and wide concrete steps led to its large front porch. The porch columns appeared to be constructed of river rock.

A buzz saw could be heard in the distance. Perhaps Mark's shop was in the basement. I walked up the steps to the front door, thinking I'd wait to ring the doorbell until there was a pause in the noise. However, when I approached the front door I saw a small sign posted there.

IF YOU'RE HERE SELLING ANYTHING, I'M NOT HOME, it read. Directly below that line was another: IF YOU'RE HERE ON BUSINESS, COME AROUND TO THE SHOP IN THE BACK BY THE ALLEY.

I followed his instructions and took the stone pathway around the side of the house. As I came around the corner I saw a small outbuilding. It looked as if it must have been a garage at one time, although there wasn't a driveway that led to it.

The building's door was open and Mark was inside, at work at a table saw, with his back to me. Thinking it might not be a good idea to distract him, I waited until he turned off the machine. The silence was almost deafening. Mark seemed to know I'd arrived because he removed his protective eye gear before he even turned to face me.

"I see you found me," he muttered, frowning.

"I just followed the noise," I said, feeling completely out of my element. "I realize this isn't the best time and I apologize, but it shouldn't take long."

He didn't agree or disagree. Instead he picked up the piece of plywood he'd cut and carted it over to his workbench.

Undeterred, I followed him into his work area. "How long have you known Spenser?" I'd introduced the two men—or attempted to at any rate—before Mark had interrupted me.

"Never met him before in my life," he mumbled, reaching for a planer. He ran it over the wood a couple of times and then set it aside.

I had trouble not showing my surprise. That didn't make the least bit of sense. Okay, fine, I'd try a different angle.

"Why did you stop by the inn?" I asked.

He shrugged.

"That's no answer. You must have had a purpose." Considering how busy he seemed now, whatever had brought him to the house must have been important.

"No reason."

"No reason," I repeated, all the more perplexed.

"Okay, if you must know, I had just started work when this niggling feeling came to me and wouldn't go away."

"About me?"

"Yeah. And I wasn't happy about it."

I'd already guessed as much. "What kind of feeling?"

He paused then, and turned to confront me. He wore a thick frown. "If I could explain it, I would. But I can't. This feeling . . . this nagging sensation . . . kept telling me that you needed help."

I was as stumped as Mark appeared to be. "That I needed you? But you barely know me."

"That's the point, don't you think?" he snapped, and then seemed to regret his outburst. "I was working and all at once you popped into my brain. That happens sometimes after I've accepted a job. An idea will come to me and I'll stop what I'm doing and jot it down."

"An idea about me?"

"About the job. You wanted me to design a new sign for the inn, didn't you?"

"Yes, and I'm anxious to get it. But this feeling you had didn't have anything to do with the sign, did it?"

I could tell from his stance and his body language that he didn't want to answer the question.

"No . . . I kept thinking you were in some kind of trouble."

"Trouble?"

"Listen, I'm no knight looking to rescue a damsel in distress. I tried to ignore the feeling, but the harder I tried, the stronger the impression came back until it was either get over to the inn or knock my head against the wall."

"I wasn't in any danger," I insisted.

"Maybe not, but whoever that man was, he had less than honorable intentions toward you."

"How do you know that?" While Mark might assume I was defending Spenser, I wasn't. Mark hadn't been privy to our conversation, nor could he have known Spenser's reasons for stopping by the inn. He couldn't have known Paul's friend had sought me out looking for a loan.

"I just know. I suppose you're here because you want me to apologize."

I was about to correct him—I'd come for information and nothing more, but he continued without allowing me the opportunity to speak.

"Okay, fine. I owe you an apology," he admitted gruffly. "I was abrupt and impatient, but frankly I was angry."

"Angry about what?"

He tossed his hands in the air as if he worked in a

pizza factory. "That's just it. I don't know. I took one look at your . . . friend and it was all I could do not to ram my fist down his throat. I haven't felt like that in a long time. I don't initiate fights, but I don't back away from them, either."

His answer confused me all the more. "You're sure the two of you have never met?"

"One hundred percent positive."

I walked around two sawhorses he had in the middle of his work area. "What did you say to him?"

Mark didn't answer right away and when he did a frown creased his forehead. "He asked me what my relationship was to you."

I stiffened. Spenser had no business making such an inquiry. "And you said?"

"I told him it wasn't any of his business."

"Okay."

"Then he said the two of you were having a private conversation and he'd appreciate it if I butted out." Mark picked up the planer again. "Now if you don't mind . . ."

"A couple more questions."

He glared at me and then exhaled. "Go ahead."

"What convinced Spenser to leave when he did?"

"I did. I told him to leave you alone and advised him not to come back . . . ever." He exhaled. "I probably spoke out of turn. If you're looking for an apology, okay fine, you've got one. But if he was a good friend, then I'd say you need better friends."

I bristled. "He isn't my friend." And frankly I felt even more certain that he wasn't Paul's either, despite Spenser's claims.

"Then no harm done." Mark reached for the planer, apparently dismissing me.

"No harm . . . only."

"What now?" Mark said, and set the planer down on the workbench. Clearly my questions frustrated him but I didn't care. I wasn't about to let the matter drop—well, not entirely. "I saw Spenser a few minutes ago."

Mark straightened, and seemed to be on full alert. His gaze narrowed and he started moving toward the door.

"He was in his car. I'm not one hundred percent sure it was him, but it was the same car, same model, same color . . ."

"It was him."

I didn't question how he could be so sure.

Mark set the planer aside and faced me, his frown darkening all the more. "Do you know where he went after he left the inn?"

I shook my head. Frankly, I had no idea, and I certainly didn't appreciate the accusing look Mark sent my way.

"Which direction?" Mark demanded.

"He took off . . ." I couldn't remember the name of the street. Tree-something. "On the main street coming up the hill."

Mark relaxed. "Headed toward the freeway on-ramp?"

I nodded. "**Speeding** toward the on-ramp would be a more accurate description."

"Maybe he'll get a ticket." Mark chuckled, and for the first time since I'd arrived I sensed a smile in his voice.

My curiosity hadn't been resolved. In truth, Mark's answers seemed to raise even more questions. But I'd already outworn my welcome.

"I said I wouldn't stay long and I meant it. Thanks."

He shrugged and returned to his workbench. He reached for another sheet of plywood and carried it to the saw.

I watched him for a couple of moments and when he switched on the saw, spitting sawdust in a perfect plume, I turned to leave. I wasn't more than a few feet from the door when the saw went silent.

"Jo Marie," Mark asked.

"Yeah?" I turned back to face him.

He wore a frown and he scratched the side of his head. "Can I ask you something?"

Seeing how I'd drilled him with questions it didn't seem fair to deny him. "Sure. Go ahead."

"Can you tell me who Paul is?"

Chapter 18

"We need to join the others before the wedding rehearsal starts," Abby's mother said, wrapping her arm around her daughter's waist. "I'm just so happy." She laughed lightly and the joy seemed to fizz up inside her like champagne bubbles. "I can't tell you how long your father and I have waited for this day."

"I've only just met Victoria and I love her already."

"Your father and I feel the same. She's perfect for Roger, just perfect."

They came out of the sanctuary and Abby immediately caught sight of her father. He saw her at the same time and hurried toward her, his arms out-stretched, his face lit up with happiness.

"Abby, sweetheart."

Her mother released her and within seconds Abby was embraced in a huge bear hug. "I'm so glad you're here," her father murmured against her hair.

"I can't remember the last time the whole family was together like this," her mother said.

"All I can say is that it's been far too long," her dad agreed.

Abby knew she was the one to blame. For years she'd avoided her family, made convenient excuses not to see her parents. And yet, when she did see them, she felt enveloped by their love. Protected. Neither of them would bring up the painful subject of Angela's death, but if anyone else did, Abby had the strong feeling that her parents were determined to run interference. Just knowing that made Abby feel like a huge burden had been lifted from her shoulders.

Father Murphy, the elderly priest who would be performing the wedding ceremony, entered the vestibule. Roger, Lonny—the best man—and the three ushers joined him. Abby glanced at the ushers without any real interest. She'd probably met them at one time or another. Deep down she'd hoped that Steve might attend the wedding. She owed her brother's old roommate an apology for the way she'd treated him following the accident. Apparently Roger and Steve were no longer close, though, because Steve was nowhere in sight. Later, Abby decided, she would ask her brother about him. No doubt Steve was married by now . . .

Victoria and the rest of the wedding party joined the group. There was more good-natured teasing back and forth and Abby found herself smiling again. She remained close to her mother's side although she soon realized all the attention was for Roger and Victoria, as it should be.

Gradually Abby felt herself getting caught up in the joy of the moment. It felt so good to be a part of this. It'd been silly and wrong of her to dread her return to Cedar Cove.

Because she didn't have a role in the actual ceremony, Abby slipped into the back pew and waited while Father Murphy gave instructions to the wedding party.

While the priest spoke to Roger and Victoria, Abby's mother slipped into the pew next to her.

"You won't believe what your father did," she leaned close and whispered in Abby's ear.

Linda Kincaid sounded like a teenager, telling tales out of school.

"What did Dad do?" Abby asked.

"He bought a new suit for the wedding."

"Daddy?"

Her mother cupped her mouth. "I told him he

needed to try on his old suit and, well, you know your father. He insisted it was perfectly fine and he wasn't going to spend money unnecessarily."

"That's Dad."

"Well, he put on the suit just to prove how right he was and it was tight across the shoulders."

"Dad's gained weight?" That surprised Abby; her father didn't look as if he'd gained an ounce. He was one of those lucky people whose weight never varied. Unfortunately she hadn't inherited his metabolism.

"His shoulders are a bit larger," her mother admitted. "He's been playing a lot of golf lately and I think he gained muscle mass from swinging the golf club."

"I thought his shoulders looked bigger."

Linda giggled again. "Be sure and tell your father that. He's out on the golf course two or three times a week."

"Daddy?"

"Yes, and he loves it. He swears he's in the best physical shape of his life."

"And he's tan, too."

Her mother wrapped her arm around Abby's elbow. "We're loving retirement."

"It certainly sounds like it."

"I do wish you'd come see us more often," her mother said, sighing.

This was a constant request. "You don't regret leaving Washington?" Abby asked, diverting the conversation away from herself.

"Regret taking early retirement?" Linda repeated as if the question was crazy. "Sweetheart, it's one of the smartest moves we've ever made."

"But all your friends are here."

"We've made new ones. My goodness, your father and I are so socially connected that we hardly have a free night at home. Your father is actually considering joining the country club."

"Dad?" Abby found that hard to believe. Her father had been a blue-collar shipyard worker. Golfing, socializing, clothes shopping . . . that simply wasn't the behavior of the father Abby remembered.

"And you know what else?"

"You mean there's more?" Abby teased.

Linda nodded eagerly. "Your father wants me to take up golf, too."

"Are you going to?"

"Oh, I don't know . . . I'm not much good at that sort of thing."

"You could try, Mom." Abby knew that her mother enjoyed quilting and being part of a book group. She was an excellent cook, too. But she hadn't ever been particularly athletic. With one small exception—when they'd lived in Cedar Cove, Linda had been part of a Jazzercise group.

"Do you honestly think I'd be any good at golfing?"

"You won't know until you try."

Her mother considered Abby's advice and then slowly shook her head. "You're right. I should sign up for classes. Your father even offered to buy me my own set of clubs."

Abby smiled at her mother. Both of her parents seemed genuinely happy. Even if they had moved away from Cedar Cove to escape criticism or speculation, it'd obviously been a positive transition.

"Oh . . . Oh, my goodness I got so caught up telling you about your father golfing that I forgot the best part."

"Do tell," Abby teased.

"I went with your father to help him choose a new suit and . . ." She paused and looked around for fear Tom might be close enough to overhear the conversation. When she spoke again, she lowered her voice to a whisper. "He bought **two** new suits."

"Two?" In all her life Abby had never known her father to walk inside a department store.

Her mother cupped her mouth once again as though she was trying to squelch the giggles. "And a sports coat, too."

Abby felt like laughing herself. "Oh, Mom, that's just great."

"Oops, I'm up." Her mother scooted out of the pew and Abby watched as she approached Father Murphy. "That would be me. I'm the mother of the groom."

While her mother and father were busy with the rehearsal, Abby watched the proceedings. Roger waited at the altar as Victoria walked down the center aisle on her father's arm. Father and daughter laughed and teased each other along the way.

A few years after the accident, when her high school friends had started to marry, Abby had been asked to be a bridesmaid in two weddings. Both times she'd declined because it would have meant traveling back to Cedar Cove. Since she'd lived in Florida, it'd been easy enough to make an excuse. She'd mailed off generous wedding gifts and left it at that. Christmas cards and birth announcements had followed. Abby had ignored those, too, choosing to turn her back on her old life and concentrate on the new one. The life where no one knew about Angela and the accident. A life free of guilt and speculation and pity.

She'd grown comfortable in Florida. Her life was uncomplicated by the weight of the past. Gone was the carefree young woman who'd taken off for an evening of shared fun with her best friend over Christmas break. In an instant, her life had forever changed on a patch of icy roadway. How abruptly she'd transitioned into the reserved young woman who kept her secrets to herself.

Abby was mesmerized by the rehearsal, and she found herself smiling several times. Unrestrained happiness was foreign to her. Joy had become a rare commodity for someone unworthy of contentment. How could she be happy? How could she laugh when her best friend was buried in the ground? Especially when Abby was the one who'd put her there.

"Would it be all right if I sat with you?"

Abby jerked herself away from her thoughts and turned her attention to the man who sat down beside her.

"Oh . . . of course."

"I'm Scott," he said, and held out his hand.

"Abby Kincaid."

He seemed surprised but for what reason she could only guess.

"You're Roger's sister, right?"

"I am."

"The one who lives in Florida?"

She smiled and relaxed. "He only has one sister."

"So I understand."

"Are you related to Victoria?" she asked him.

"Actually no. I'm one of the groomsmen. I met your brother in Seattle after college. We play basketball together."

Abby glanced from Scott to the altar. "Shouldn't you be up there with the rest of the wedding party?"

"Probably. But I've been in a lot of weddings so I'm familiar with what to do. You looked so alone back here that I thought I would join you." He relaxed against the seat and stretched his arms along the back of the pew.

"Scott," Abby said slowly, dragging out his name. "Are you flirting with me?"

He grinned and his eyes flashed with amusement. "I would say that I am."

"I'm flattered but . . ."

The wedding party broke up then and Roger noticed for the first time that one of the groomsmen was missing. Shaking his head, he walked toward Abby and Scott.

"Is Scott pestering you, little sister?"

"Me?" Scott planted his hand over his chest and cast a look of pure innocence toward Roger. "She was making eyes at me."

"I most certainly was not." And then she burst out laughing at the old-fashioned expression he'd used. "Making eyes?"

"You most definitely were," Scott insisted. "I looked back here and you were all alone and I said to myself, 'Self, the most beautiful woman in the room needs you.' "

"My sister is indeed beautiful, but the most beautiful woman in the room at any wedding is always the bride," Roger chastised, "and especially in this case."

"Right," Scott agreed, "but Victoria is obviously not interested in me."

"I would hope not," Roger agreed, chuckling.

"So," Scott explained with perfect logic, "that leaves your sister, and I was simply staking my claim before any of these bozos took the lead."

Roger shook his head. "I don't think Abby's interested, Scott. I actually think someone else has dibs."

"Someone else?" Abby asked.

Roger patted her hand. "Just wait, sis. I have a small surprise for you."

"Which leaves me out in the cold," said Scott mournfully.

"Sorry, Scott," Roger said, without the least bit of contrition.

"Foiled again."

Abby laughed and so did Roger.

Scott was obviously a player. And she was sure that Roger had said someone had dibs on her just to deter Scott from hitting on her.

Her parents joined them and Abby stood. "Do you need a ride to the restaurant, sweetie?" her father inquired.

Before she could tell them she had a rental car, Scott interjected. "She can ride with me."

Abby's father arched his brows.

"Actually, I have a car, but thank you both," she said.

Her parents started out of the church and Abby stood and reached for her purse.

Scott remained stubbornly at the end of the pew. "You could ride with me and I could drive you back to the church after dinner," he suggested, as they walked out of the sanctuary.

"That seems like a lot of unnecessary driving."

"Maybe, but those few minutes alone with you would be worth having to backtrack."

Abby shook her head, both amused and flattered. "You really are a silver-tongued devil, aren't you?"

"You wound me," he said, and pressed his palm over his heart. "Won't you ride with me?"

"I appreciate the offer, I do, but I might want to leave the dinner early."

His eyes brightened. "With me?"

"No. It's been a long day and I'm exhausted."

Scott released a long, exaggerated sigh. "If you must."

"I must," she insisted.

The two walked side by side toward the parking lot. Abby wasn't fooled. Scott was a flirt and way too glib for her to take him seriously. Nevertheless, she couldn't remember an evening she'd enjoyed more. . . and the festivities were just getting started.

Chapter 19

Michelle placed the last of the dirty dishes from their simple supper in the dishwasher while Josh wiped down the kitchen countertops. Richard had managed to swallow down a couple of spoonfuls of soup while Michelle and Josh had sat with him.

Being with Michelle reminded Josh of working in the kitchen with his mother when he was young. She'd made even the most mundane tasks fun. They used to sing silly songs while washing the dinner dishes. She'd never had a dishwasher until she married Richard. Instead, Josh had washed the dishes, and he'd so enjoyed the songs and simply being with his mother that he hadn't minded scrubbing pots and pans.

Kitchen time with his mother had been special. She'd let him mix and stir and on rare occasions they had baked cookies together. Those good times with his mother were memories he'd clung to through the years. He remembered how she'd talked to him while they worked together; how she'd encouraged and praised him. According to his mother, Josh had a brilliant mind and was capable of achieving anything he wanted in life. But she'd never failed to add that he had to create his own opportunities.

Those early years with her had been the happiest of his life.

In the evenings they sat around the table together while he did his homework. She'd look over his work, and because she made him believe he was smart, he always did well in school. To his way of thinking, their lives had been idyllic, until she met Richard.

When his mother and Richard had first started dating, it hadn't been so bad. Josh and Dylan had gotten along well and Josh had thought it was super cool that he might have a brother one day. When Richard proposed, his mother had talked the decision over with Josh. He'd assumed everything would continue as it had been and they would become a regular family.

"You're looking thoughtful," Michelle commented as she closed the dishwasher and pushed the button to start the wash cycle.

"I was remembering my mother." Even now he missed her and he knew Richard did, too. For all his faults, for all he lacked, Josh couldn't fault his step-father for one thing: Richard had loved his mother.

"I remember Teresa." Michelle pulled out a kitchen chair and sat down, as if weighed down by sadness over Josh's mother's death. "She was always such a joyful, happy person. Even after she was diagnosed with cancer, she never failed to be upbeat and positive."

"She was an eternal optimist," Josh recalled fondly. The sky was always blue and the sun was forever bright and shining in his mother's eyes. Life was a gift to be treasured; each day an adventure.

Josh and his mother had struggled financially before she married Richard, but Josh had never thought of himself as underprivileged or poor. He didn't get all the toys he wanted, but the one or two wrapped gifts under the Christmas tree had been more than enough.

"I'll check on Richard," Michelle said.

"I'll do it," Josh offered, "I'm up."

Before he could go Michelle stopped him with a question. "Did you ever tell your mother about the way Richard treated you?"

Josh shook his head. Really, he couldn't see the point. For the first time in his life, Josh had known his mother was content. She loved Richard and worked hard to keep a comfortable home for her new husband and his son. She took pride in a clean house and in preparing healthy, appetizing meals.

"No, I never did."

A frown marred her features. "Why didn't you?"

The temptation had been strong to run to his mother, especially in the early years of her second marriage. The problem was that the verbal put-downs had been hard to pinpoint, especially since Richard's behavior was mostly passive-aggressive. Josh feared that he'd sound like a crybaby if he told his mother Richard had picked up Dylan after school, leaving Josh to walk home alone. If he were to complain, Richard would simply claim he hadn't seen Josh, or make some other phony excuse.

"Josh," Michelle sighed. "I don't understand you."

"What's to understand?" he asked.

After a time, the changes in his mother became even more apparent to Josh. She was genuinely happy. She loved Richard and Dylan, and most important, they loved her. Yes, it meant he had to share his mother with these two other people. While that might have been cause for concern, Josh didn't mind because she deserved happiness.

She hummed when she baked elaborate desserts, and she planted flowers and started knitting again, all the things she'd given up because of tight finances. Richard and Dylan had lived without a woman's influence for several years, and the small female touches of gentleness Teresa brought into their lives made a difference, too. Josh recognized that and so he said nothing.

"My mother was happy," he said after a lengthy pause. "Richard made her happy."

Michelle appeared to look at him with fresh eyes. "You were wise and mature beyond your years, Josh."

If that was the case then Josh had his mother to thank. She was the one who'd raised and nurtured him, who'd instilled a sense of honor in him.

Josh headed down the hallway to his stepfather's bedroom. He made an effort to silence his steps as much as possible as he approached the older man's room. After dinner, they'd given Richard his prescribed pain medication and he'd promptly gone to bed. Within minutes he'd fallen asleep.

The master bedroom door creaked as Josh opened it. He hesitated for fear it would wake Richard.

"I'm not dead yet, if that's why you're here."

Josh slipped into the bedroom and turned on the light. Richard lay half-prone, propped up by two pillows. "I figure you'll live another ten years just to spite me," Josh said.

"I should."

"Don't let me stop you. Do you need anything?"

Richard sat up and glared across the room at Josh. "Nothing you can give me. Why are you here?"

"I came to make sure you're resting comfortably."

Richard snorted and shook his head. "You were looking to rob me blind, weren't you? That was what you did before, so why should I trust you now?"

For an instant the old resentments flared back to life and he retorted sharply. "You know as well as I do that I didn't steal that money."

"You lied to me twelve years ago and you're lying now," Richard spat.

Josh could see that the argument had quickly tired the older man. A pillow toppled from the bed and onto the carpet. Josh came all the way into the room and retrieved it from the floor.

"Do you want it behind your back?" he asked.

Richard hesitated and then nodded.

Josh replaced the pillow and while he was there he straightened the blankets and smoothed the afghan his mother had knitted over the end of the bed.

"Thank you."

At first Josh was sure he'd misunderstood. Richard had actually thanked him. "You're welcome," he said.

Richard exhaled slowly, as though he found it difficult to breathe.

Josh started to leave and was about to ask if Richard wanted the light on or off. Instead he stood near the foot of the bed. "Michelle and I were talking just now and, well, it doesn't really matter what led to this, but I want to tell you something."

"I don't want to hear it," Richard barked. "I'm tired, leave me alone. Now get out of here before I—"

Josh ignored the tirade and spoke over his stepfather. "I wanted to thank you for making my mother happy."

"Oh I'll—" Richard abruptly stopped speaking. "What did you just say?"

Josh was fairly certain the old man had heard him. "My mother was happy when she was married to you . . . perhaps for the first time since she'd had me. You made her happy."

Richard glared back as if unwilling to trust what he'd heard.

Undeterred, Josh continued. "I wanted to thank you for giving her that small piece of joy. God knows she deserved it."

"Your mother was a good woman."

"You were good to her," Josh admitted, "especially toward the end of her life." Richard had taken good care of Teresa and for that Josh would always be grateful. His stepfather had encouraged and supported her, and in the last days of her life, he had simply sat by her bedside and held her hand. Josh had been there, too— on the other side of the bed. He'd wanted to be as close to her as possible, and was afraid of what would happen to him after she was gone.

To his amazement Richard's eyes clouded with tears. "I loved Teresa."

"I know you did."

"She was the best thing that ever happened to Dylan and me."

"And to me, too," Josh added.

Moisture slipped from the corner of the old man's face. "You . . . you looked like your mother," Richard whispered. "I couldn't look at you without being reminded of what I'd lost."

It had never occurred to Josh that seeing him had been, for his stepfather, a constant reminder of all he had lost.

"When she died . . ." Richard was unable to continue. "I thought . . . and then I lost Dylan, too."

"I know," Josh whispered.

"No, you don't," he countered sharply. "You couldn't possibly know what that kind of grief does to a man."

Richard was probably right. Josh had no idea what it was like to lose a child. He didn't think God ever asked more of a parent than to claim one of their children. Richard had lost two wives and his only son; he was bitter and angry, but he was entitled to both emotions.

"I don't want to live any longer," his stepfather whispered.

Josh struggled to make out the words.

"I have nothing to live for."

"I'm sorry," Josh told him.

"No you're not. This couldn't have worked out better for you. Well, I have news for you. You'll get nothing from me. Not one single penny. You stole that money and that was the day I wrote you out of my will. I refuse to leave anything to a thieving step-son."

"That's perfectly fine by me," Josh assured him.

He left then, keeping the bedroom door ajar.

"Get back here. I'm not finished telling you what I think," Richard called, his voice pitifully weak.

Josh pretended not to hear. He started toward the kitchen when Michelle stopped him. "You okay?"

He nodded.

"He doesn't mean the things he says," Michelle assured him.

"I know." And Josh did. "Richard's lost everything that ever mattered to him."

"And he's turned his back on what's left because he's afraid of losing that, too."

Josh would like to believe Richard actually cared about him, but past evidence proved otherwise.

Michelle pressed a comforting hand on his arm, and Josh reached for her and brought her close. She was warm and soft and after confronting his stepfather's grief and bitterness, he needed her gentleness and her beauty to wipe away the old man's hate.

She raised her lips to his, and unable to resist, Josh kissed her again and again, accepting the sweetness and reassurance she offered.

Chapter 20

I took up knitting after I heard the news about Paul. A friend, Judith Knight, told me it would help me with the grieving process. At the time I'd been so desperate I was willing to try anything that would soften the horrendous pain. If learning to knit would do this, then I'd stand on my head in the middle of the street in order to learn. On the way home from work late one afternoon, I stopped at a downtown Seattle yarn store and signed up for a beginner's class.

Hurting as I was, my frustration level was about ten times higher than normal. I wanted to quit, to throw in the towel—if you'll pardon the cliché—any number of times, but with Judith and my instructor's encouragement I stuck with it. I'm grateful I did. Although I'd been knitting for less than a year, I was fearless in choosing my projects, willing to tackle just about any pattern. I'd knit a pair of socks, a hat, taken a Fair Isle class, and I had recently bought yarn for a lace shawl.

What I found amazing was that knitting did help me. I'd been so busy with the move, transitioning from my Seattle home to Cedar Cove, that I hadn't picked up my needles in weeks. That was unlike me; I'd become addicted to knitting. Addicted to the small comfort I felt when I centered myself and concentrated on creating something beautiful.

The repetitive action of weaving the yarn around a needle, one stitch at a time, brought me solace in a way that's difficult to explain. When I sat down to knit I discovered that I could divert my thoughts from the emptiness I experienced after I lost Paul. And yet . . . and yet many a night tears blurred my eyes, and all I could think about was Paul. Nevertheless, I discovered that comfort came with each stitch.

My thoughts were burdened following the events of that Friday afternoon. I recognized that knitting would help my mind make sense of what had transpired and give me a chance to catch my breath. I'd been busy from the moment I set my feet on the carpet that morning.

I was grateful to have met Peggy Beldon and Corrie McAfee. Although I didn't know either woman well, I had the feeling that given time both would become friends.

Sitting in front of the fireplace, I reached for my current knitting project. I almost always had three going at the same time. The socks were easy projects to take with me, which was good because I found I fidgeted if my hands were idle for long.

I have practically no patience. I didn't used to be like this, but since I lost Paul I haven't been able to sit still for long periods. It's the waiting that disturbs me; I can't stand stillness, the silence of inactivity. Knitting helps me deal with this completely unreasonable aspect of my personality. If the dentist is running late or if I'm obliged to sit for several minutes, having a small knitting project with me helps tremendously.

The delicate lace shawl pattern demanded total concentration. I'd chosen a lovely light blue alpaca. At times it felt like I was knitting with a spider's web. To this point it'd turned out beautifully. This evening I would work on the afghan.

I was knitting one in shades of brown and orange and yellow for the foot of one of the guest room beds. This was a much larger, more complicated project. I'd long since memorized the ten row repeat pattern, and I could pick the afghan up at any time and work on it. Ten rows took about an hour, which was perfect. I knew if I sat down I would need at least a sixty-minute time frame.

As I began to knit, my mind returned to the events of that afternoon. Mark Taylor was an enigma. Although I'd seen him three times now, I was still uncertain how I felt about him. He was brash, irreverent, and short-tempered. He couldn't explain why he'd shown up when he did or why he'd taken such a keen and instant dislike to Spenser.

My fingers tugged at the yarn, freeing it from the skein as I continued to work, my thoughts whirling as fast as my needles.

Both my guests were out for the evening and I'd been told not to expect either for dinner. Not having to work in the kitchen had freed me. For my own dinner, I'd toasted a cheese sandwich and called it good. After all the errand running and walking I'd done that afternoon, I should have had more of an appetite, but I didn't.

I thought about my guests and was surprised that I hadn't seen more of them. With Josh it was understandable; he'd briefly mentioned that he was in town because his stepfather was ailing. I hoped everything was going as well as could be expected.

As for Abby, she'd told me she'd come to town for her brother's wedding, but a wedding should be a happy occasion. That didn't explain why she'd been in tears the afternoon she'd arrived.

Both had come back to Cedar Cove, their former home, with burdens. For that matter, I carried more than a few of my own. Each one of us hauled rocks on our backs, some larger than others, I realized. Some people had grown so accustomed to the extra weight that they no longer seemed aware of the baggage. I felt an impulse to help my guests but I wasn't sure if, or how, I could—or if I should even try. Or perhaps they had come to Rose Harbor Inn so they could help me.

The afghan was about half-completed and the weight of it on my lap warmed me. The room was also being heated by the fireplace, and I was so comfortable and drowsy that I found myself shaking sleep off a couple of times. It'd be ridiculous to head to bed this early. The grandfather clock in the foyer said it was barely seven-thirty. Oh dear. For me to be this sleepy, this early, told me the day had been even more taxing than I'd realized.

I finished knitting the row and let my hands rest in my lap as I decided to briefly close my eyes and rest . . . just for a few minutes . . . only a few. Almost immediately I could feel myself drifting into a half-sleep.

Then it happened for the second time since I'd moved to the inn.

I felt Paul's presence and was wrapped in the memories of the first time we met. It had been at a Seattle Seahawk football game. Paul was in the seat next to me, and the first thing I noticed about him was his smile. It didn't come from his mouth as much as his eyes, which were a compelling shade of blue. Big blue eyes. Big smile.

"You attend all the games?" he asked me as I passed him the beer he'd ordered from the attendant.

"I wish," I said, "but unfortunately no. I watch them on TV, though."

"Me, too."

Right away we bonded over football. Throughout the game we talked back and forth, cheered and groaned together. The couple with me, the Andersons, were keeping each other company. Without Paul, I would have felt odd man out.

The Seahawks won the game. As we stood to exit the stands, the Andersons were thanking me profusely for bringing them along. I nodded and was about to exit the row myself, when Paul stopped me with a hand on my shoulder.

"Would you like to have a beer with me?" he suggested.

I was tempted, really tempted, but for a split second I hesitated. After a number of painful disappointments, I'd mostly given up on relationships. To be blunt, I wasn't sure I had the energy for this anymore. I'd already learned that Paul was in the military and only in the area for a brief time. I wasn't sure I wanted to get involved in something that was destined to dead-end in quick order.

In retrospect, even knowing that I would eventually lose him and my heart, I remain grateful that I told him yes that afternoon.

We talked for three hours that first night. Three solid hours. Our connection had been strong from the very beginning. We were close to the same age, and neither of us had been married, each for different reasons. Paul had been married, in essence, to the military.

My reasons were completely different. I'd dated plenty of men but I'd never fallen head over heels in love and I didn't want to settle for comfortable.

My parents claimed I was too picky, and I suppose I was. Not until my second date with Paul did I realize what had held me back from those other relationships.

I'd been waiting to meet Paul.

Deep down I'd known that when the time was right, I'd connect with the man I was meant to love for the rest of my life. I'd almost lost faith.

Half-asleep, I remembered Mark's question from earlier in the day when he'd asked me who Paul was. The question had badly shaken me. I don't remember now what I told him or if I even answered. And now Paul was with me.

I sent Mark, he seemed to be telling me.

Spenser is no friend. He was dishonorably discharged before we left for Afghanistan. I should have told you, but I assumed neither of us would see him again.

Spenser hadn't even been in Afghanistan. It'd all been a lie to dupe me.

And so Paul had sent Mark to protect me? The handyman had said he'd felt compelled to hurry over to the inn. At the time he didn't know why. By his own admission he'd tried to ignore the urge and found he couldn't. He hadn't been happy about traipsing to Rose Harbor Inn . . . and it had showed.

I wanted to ask Paul why he'd sent Mark, of all people. There were any number of others who could have served the same purpose. Corrie McAfee, for instance. Married to a private investigator, she could easily have sent Spenser on his merry way.

Just as I sensed Paul's presence, I sensed his departure. He'd only been with me a few seconds. I wanted to cry and beg him to return, but intuitively I realized it was useless. It was enough that he'd been with me.

I knit for another hour, content because Paul had been by for a visit, however briefly. As my fingers worked the ten-row pattern, I wondered why Paul had chosen to come to me now. Why hadn't he come when the grief was at its worst? Why had he waited until I was in Cedar Cove?

Perhaps he had been with me at other times, but I had been too raw, in too much pain, to feel his presence. On second thought, perhaps it was the inn—this special place, this harbor I'd found—that had brought everything together so we could connect.

It was still relatively early when I set my knitting aside. I ran a hot bath and soaked in the water, savoring the lavender-scented bubble bath and my special soap. When I climbed into bed, the sheets felt cool against my skin.

I reached for the novel I was reading, fluffed up the pillows, and read until after ten. Apparently both my guests were out late.

After receiving the news of Paul's death, I'd been unable to sleep. I'd fall asleep easily enough, then bolt awake, sleeping in fits and starts for the rest of the night. After a month of this I was close to a mental and emotional collapse. I got up each morning with burning eyes, feeling sick to my stomach from lack of sleep. Although I hated the thought of it, I resorted to taking over-the-counter sleep medication.

That night, after my dream of Paul, I didn't take a pill. I finally felt I could wean myself off the medication. To my delight I slept better than any night since I'd lost my husband.

I woke the next morning feeling refreshed and eager to tackle the day. For several minutes I lay in bed, pleasantly surprised by how well I'd slept. I felt so very grateful to have had Paul visit me, if only for those few moments.

Because it was still early, I dressed warmly and walked down to the bakery to pick up my order of fresh sweet rolls. They smelled heavenly, still hot from the oven. I'd make sure they were served warm.

By the time I returned, Abby was up and dressed.

She looked up guiltily when I walked in the front door. "Morning," I greeted her cheerfully.

"I hope you don't mind; I helped myself to a cup of coffee."

"Of course. That's why it's here." After I set the box on the kitchen counter, I removed my coat, hung it up in the foyer on the hook, and then joined Abby in the kitchen.

"I apologize that I wasn't awake when you returned last night. How did everything go?" I hoped I wasn't asking unwelcome questions. It was none of my business, but I couldn't help being curious.

"It went just beautifully," Abby said. "So much better than I'd dared to hope."

"You met everyone in the wedding party?"

"I did. My parents arrived without a problem and several of my aunts and uncles are in town, too. It's the biggest family get-together we've had in more years than I can remember. Roger is so happy and Victoria is a perfect complement to him."

"That's great."

Abby remained in the kitchen, pressing her shoulder against the doorjamb with her ankles crossed, apparently in no hurry to return to her room.

I opened the refrigerator and brought out the French toast I'd prepared the day before and was planning to bake that morning. I sprinkled the top with frozen berries and set it on the stovetop while I waited for the oven to preheat. I intended to scramble eggs, too.

When I opened the oven door, I noticed that Abby was still in the kitchen. She stared sightlessly into space, apparently deep in thought. When the ding told me the oven was fully preheated, I set the dish inside the oven and closed the door.

I debated on whether to ask specific questions of Abby. "Is everything okay?" I asked, keeping my voice low and gentle.

Right away, Abby broke into a smile. "Yes, everything is fine . . . better than I expected." She didn't elaborate, though.

"We run from foolish things, don't we?" The question was out before I had a chance to censor it. I couldn't imagine what had made me ask something like that.

But Abby took it seriously and nodded. "We do; we really do." The thoughtful look was back. "My parents are happy. I didn't expect that. I thought . . ." she paused and smiled. "They're happy and that makes me happy, too."

I didn't know why her parents' happiness should come as a shock. Considering how quickly my mouth got ahead of my brain, I decided it would be best not to ask.

"It's good to see that those we deeply care about are well, isn't it?" I asked instead.

From Abby's expression I could see that she hadn't processed my question, which was fine. I didn't really need an answer.

"I would have given just about anything to avoid this wedding," she commented softly, almost as if she was unaware that she'd spoken aloud.

"You didn't want to attend your brother's wedding?"

"Oh, no. I was eager to do that. What I didn't want was to return to Cedar Cove."

I waited for her to explain.

"I was so certain it would be a disaster . . . It still might be, but I doubt it. My family will back me."

"Good."

"My family," she repeated softly, and again I don't think she realized she'd spoken out loud. Snapping out of it, she looked up and smiled. "I've been so afraid and I shouldn't have been. If I'd faced these demons earlier I would have spared myself a great deal of grief."

"Then you think coming home for the wedding worked out for the best?" I posed the question even though I already knew the answer.

"It did," Abby confirmed. "It really did."

Chapter 21

The scent of cinnamon wafted up the stairwell and stirred Josh awake. He hadn't gotten back to the B&B until after three that morning. Despite his mood, he'd crawled into bed and instantly fallen asleep.

He could hear noises down below and he recognized the voices of Jo Marie and the other guest. Annie? No, that wasn't it. "A" something. Abby. The other guest's name was Abby.

Both women were up and about. Rolling onto his side, Josh glanced at the bedside clock and was shocked to see that it was past eight. He needed to get back to Richard's house. He was concerned about his stepfather.

Before Michelle had left the older man's house the night before, Richard had fallen into a fitful sleep. His breathing had gotten shallow. More than once Josh had been convinced he should call 911. He would have done it, but he knew it would only upset Richard. The old man was determined to die in his own home on his own terms. He was alone in the world and that was the way he wanted to leave it.

Josh didn't know when he'd become so concerned about his stepfather's wishes. He should hate the old man, but oddly he found that he didn't. If anything, he pitied him.

With some difficulty, he'd managed to convince Michelle to go home and sleep. They'd planned to meet again this morning at nine.

He, however, had been determined to stay the night at the house. If Richard knew, he would hate the idea. Part of Josh wanted Richard to hate him; he was accustomed to his stepfather's intense dislike. In fact, he was comfortable with it and as painful and demoralizing as it was to admit, he found a certain satisfaction in seeing Richard weak and nearly help-less.

He'd intended to stay the night in part to help Richard and in part to irritate him.

Josh thought he'd sleep on the sofa. Only he got

worried and ended up pulling a chair into the old man's bedroom and sitting by his bedside. He wanted to be close in case Richard needed him, even though he knew his stepfather would prefer to die than to accept Josh's help. They both knew it.

It'd worked out fine, him being in the bedroom. Josh found himself listening to the old man's breathing, which at times was steady and even, and at times shallow and weak as if his heart had decided to pause for a beat or two.

Josh fell asleep sitting in the chair.

The older man had woken him up sometime later, growling and cantankerous. "What are you doing here?" he'd demanded, eyes narrowed.

"Just checking on you," Josh had assured him.

"Get out. I don't want you here."

"No doubt."

"I mean it."

"Don't worry, I'm leaving. No need to get upset. You want me gone, then I'm out of here."

"Where's Michelle?"

Josh noticed that Richard didn't push himself up on one elbow the way he had earlier. Whether it was because he was too weak or because he was too tired to put much effort into it, Josh didn't know.

"Michelle went home a long time ago."

His frown deepened. "Why didn't you leave at the same time?"

Josh grinned, knowing his answer wouldn't please the older man. "I figured you'd like the company."

"You figured wrong. Now get out of here."

Josh stood and dragged the chair into the other room. He left the door open, thinking he might be able to hear Richard from the living room if he was needed.

After a few minutes he'd settled on the sofa and was almost asleep when he heard his stepfather softly murmur his name. In a flash Josh was on his feet. He scrambled so fast that he nearly tripped in his eagerness to get to Richard's bedroom.

Richard was sitting up and from the glower on his face, he wasn't happy.

"You okay?" Josh asked.

"Damn straight I am."

Josh's own heart raced at double time.

"I told you to get," Richard reminded him.

"I did."

"Get out of the house, understand? I don't want you here."

"Fine, whatever. I'll leave."

"Don't come back, either."

Now that was a request Josh couldn't honor. "Sorry to disappoint you, but I'll be back in the morning."

"You come back and I'll kick you out myself," Richard threatened.

Josh resisted the urge to laugh. His stepfather might

have been able to use physical force against him when he was in high school. Now, however, Richard didn't have a prayer. Not even a sliver of a prayer.

"You heard me."

"You can try," Josh told him.

"Now get."

Josh reached for his coat, slipping his arms into the sleeves. "Go back to sleep; I'm leaving."

"Good."

Josh noticed the water glass at Richard's bedside was empty. He walked over to retrieve it and stepped back when the older man cowered reflexively.

"Richard," he whispered, shocked by his stepfather's reaction. "Did you expect me to hit you?"

His stepfather didn't answer. He turned his head away and closed his eyes.

Picking up the empty water glass, Josh carried it into the kitchen, filled it, added ice, and then returned it to the bedroom. He lingered for an extra moment and then obeyed Richard's wishes and returned to Rose Harbor Inn.

Now it was morning.

Tossing aside the covers, Josh climbed out of bed and headed into the bathroom for a quick shower. While the spray hit his body he mulled over the events of the previous day, specifically the unexpected twist of emotions he was feeling for Michelle.

He'd never intended to kiss her. A little more than twenty-four hours ago he hadn't considered her anything more than the girl who lived next door. Oh, he knew she'd had a huge crush on Dylan, but as Richard had so gleefully pointed out, all the girls had been crazy for Dylan.

Kissing Michelle, wanting her close, finding comfort in her, had come as a shock to him. And yet it'd felt right. And good. She'd fit perfectly in his arms and he wasn't referring just to the physical aspect of holding her.

Stepping out of the shower, Josh quickly dressed, combed his hair, and headed down the stairs, still mulling about Michelle and where these feelings might take them. Nowhere, he decided. Traveling as much as he did, from one job site to another, didn't leave room for relationships. His thoughts and his steps were heavy as he came down the staircase, wishing things could be different, and knowing they never would be.

Abby was sitting at the dining room table and glanced up when he entered the room.

"Good morning," she greeted.

Apparently she was in a much better mood than she'd been the morning before—for that matter so was he.

"Morning," he answered, returning her smile.

"Coffee?" Jo Marie asked as she stepped into the room, a glass coffeepot in one hand and a pitcher of orange juice in the other.

"Yes to both."

She deftly filled his mug with coffee and the glass with orange juice.

"I have French toast and scrambled eggs this morning," she told him.

"And sweet rolls fresh from the bakery," Abby added. "I made a pig of myself and tasted a little of everything."

"Just coffee and juice for now." In the back of his head he could remember his mother insisting that he eat something on his way out the door to school. She'd been a real stickler about that.

"Maybe the eggs, too," he said, surprising himself. His mother would be proud. Although most mornings, Josh escaped to the bus stop with little more than a slice of toast or a piece of fruit, she'd tried to get him to eat protein when she could.

Within a matter of minutes Jo Marie returned with a plate of fluffy scrambled eggs. Josh intended to take a couple of bites and make his excuses. He surprised himself by eating everything on the plate. It must be something in the air.

"I'm off," he said, standing. He started to carry his plate into the kitchen, which was something else his mother had taught him.

Jo Marie stopped him. "I'll take care of that."

He set the plate down and was on his way out of the dining room when he realized that he should wish both women a good day. "I don't know what time I'll be back this evening."

"Then I shouldn't plan on you for dinner, right?" Jo Marie asked.

"Right." If he did finish before then, he'd eat elsewhere. "Have a good day you two."

"I will," Abby returned with a determination that caused him to turn his attention to her.

"Good." He stuffed his arms into his coat, grabbed his scarf, and left the house, bouncing down the steps. Anyone seeing him, he realized, would think he was eager to get to where he was going. Quite the opposite was true.

He was eager, but not to see Richard. The person who lingered in his mind was Michelle. Again the memory of their kisses returned to plague him.

They hadn't talked about what had happened between them. Really, what was there to say? Because of everything that was going on with Richard, Josh was already dealing with a number of different emotions. He couldn't see any reason to further confuse what was already an overly complicated situation.

On the drive over to the house he made a firm decision to say nothing to Michelle regarding those kisses. Hopefully she'd dismiss them as part of the craziness of the day and that would be the end of it.

But was ignoring the growing attraction between them what he wanted? Josh couldn't answer that. He was drawn to her; to her commonsense approach to Richard, her emotional maturity, and her gentle ways.

He parked the rental car in front of the house and saw that Michelle had already arrived. He walked up to the porch, knocked once lightly, and then let himself inside.

Michelle walked out from the kitchen to meet him. She answered his question even before he had the chance to ask.

"He's still sleeping."

"You're sure he's sleeping?" His fear was that Richard would have had the audacity to die during the night, laying a heap of guilt at Josh's feet for having lost his cool and walking out.

"I thought you said you'd be here this morning," she said.

"Richard woke up last night and kicked me out."

"I was afraid that might happen," she said, shaking her head as though she was disgruntled with herself. "I should have stayed with you."

"Richard wouldn't have liked that either. He told me not to come back."

A soft smile brightened her eyes. "I see you don't take orders well."

"Not from him," he agreed. "I haven't given up hope of finding my mother's Bible and her cameo and a few other things I'd like to have that were hers before she married Richard; photos and such."

"Where do you intend to look?" she asked.

Unfortunately the only place Josh could think to check was the master bedroom. "I still think they must be in there." He motioned with his head toward the room.

Michelle groaned. "Richard will have a conniption."

"Tell me about it." Josh dreaded another confrontation with his stepfather.

"I'll ask about your mother's Bible this morning," Michelle promised.

"Thank you." He desperately hoped Richard hadn't purposely destroyed the photos and other memorabilia from his childhood. He reasoned that many of the things he wanted must have been stored after his mother's death. He was convinced Richard had kept them somewhere close by, and the most logical place was the master bedroom.

Richard wouldn't have ruined anything that belonged to her because it would have been precious to him. Even the things that also happened to mean something to Josh would be worth keeping intact. At any rate, that was Josh's hope.

The problem was convincing Richard to tell him where these things were. Josh was fast running out of time to search. A text message had come that morning that his new job was about to start, asking when he would be available.

"What are you thinking?" Michelle asked.

He shook himself from his reverie. "Sorry, I was trying to figure out the best way to handle this. I can't stay much longer."

"What do you mean?"

"My new job is starting. I'll need to head out in a couple of days at the latest."

"That soon?"

He nodded.

"Where?"

"Montana." He explained that the project involved building a strip mall in Billings.

He saw the disappointment in her eyes.

"I could never live here again," he said softly, hoping she understood.

"I wouldn't ask that of you," she countered.

"I'm doing what I can for Richard, but I have my own life, too."

"I understand, Josh, I really do. I guess I just hate the thought of saying good-bye."

He waited a moment, thinking she might be about to add something.

She stayed silent though, and after a moment he realized he hated the thought of leaving her, too. Necessity demanded that he would, but it would be far more difficult than he would ever have thought possible.

Michelle was beautiful, but he'd known other women who were just as attractive. Still, she was different. Being with her made his heart light up. He enjoyed simply hanging out with her, which said a lot given the circumstances of their time together. Another thing he found attractive about her was that she didn't feel the need to fill the silences between them. By the same token, he liked that she spoke her mind. But given his job, he didn't want to toy with her heart when logistically a lasting, meaningful relationship just didn't make sense.

Chapter 22

Abby sat in her car, her hands clenched tightly in her lap. She hadn't left the parking lot of the Rose Harbor Inn yet and already her hands had started to sweat. She'd promised herself she'd do this; promised herself that when and if she ever returned to Cedar Cove, she would visit Angela's grave. Not once since her dearest friend had been buried had Abby found the nerve to actually go to the cemetery.

It was time. Past time.

This would either make or break the entire trip for her. Abby forced her hands onto the steering wheel and sucked in a deep breath. It was now or never.

What made this extra difficult was that Roger's wedding was supposed to be a happy time for their family. Just that morning Abby had told Jo Marie she'd have done anything to avoid returning to Cedar Cove, and that was true.

This was the reason. Years ago she'd promised herself she'd never be back. Because when she returned she would have to go see Angela. Then good ole Roger had chosen to get married in their hometown. It felt as if God was forcing her to confront the past.

In a flash, Abby was eighteen all over again. It was Christmas break and she was dying to see her best friend. It'd been torture not to tell Angela about meeting Steve. She'd been so crazy about him. It embarrassed her now to think of the horrible way she'd treated him following the accident.

Abby remembered that she hadn't been home an hour before Angela phoned. Christmas was just three days away and Angela hadn't done a lick of shopping. Abby agreed to drive her to the mall. Her dad said she could use his car and that the gas tank was full. He'd warned her on her way out the door to watch for black ice.

They'd had a blast that night; shopping, laughing until they were almost sick, trying on clothes. Abby and Angela had been sisters of the heart, born only a few weeks apart. They'd done everything together from the time they were in junior high; it wasn't unusual for them to spend the entire weekend together, barely managing to sleep, staying up all night.

After shopping that night they ate dinner at Red Robin, their favorite haunt, sharing a burger and fries. While they were inside the restaurant, it'd started to snow. Thick, fat flakes that fell from the sky, creating the most beautiful, picturesque scene imaginable. This was Christmas as it was always meant to be. A perfect Northwest Christmas.

Abby called home before they headed out from Silverdale.

"Drive carefully," her father cautioned her a second time.

Abby had been careful. So very careful. Or so she'd thought. But instead of arriving home with gifts to give her family, instead of decorating sugar cookies with her mother and brother, instead of enjoying the holiday, Angela had died that night on a road just outside Cedar Cove.

Abby was never entirely sure how it had happened. She remembered that they'd been singing a Christmas carol along with the radio, and making plans for all the things they wanted to do while on break from school. Angela had teased her about Steve and insisted she wanted to be the maid of honor at their wedding. As if Abby could imagine asking anyone else! They'd made plans for a ski trip between Christmas and New Year's, and Abby had promised that she would ask Steve to join them so that Angela could meet him.

Naturally there would be a get-together with their friends, shopping in Seattle, a movie. Maybe even two. They each had one they were anxious to see.

And while they were chattering like birds on a telephone wire, laughing and singing, Abby had hit a patch of ice.

The car spun out of control, flipping over and over and over. Angela had screamed . . . or maybe that was her, Abby couldn't remember. What did stick in her mind was the sheer terror she'd felt as the vehicle started to roll.

When Abby had awoken, she was in the hospital and her mother was standing over her, eyes red and swollen from crying. Her father and brother were there, too, looking so . . . sad.

"You're going to be all right," her mother had whispered, gripping hold of her hand with both of her own.

Abby's mouth felt dry and the pain nearly blinded her. "Angela?" she'd managed to whisper her friend's name. This stupid accident was going to ruin their school break and all the plans they'd made.

That was when her mother started to sob for real; heart-wrenching sobs that tore at Abby's heart. Was Angela badly hurt? Why wasn't anyone saying anything? Instead of answering her questions, Abby's mother had covered her face with both hands and turned away.

Abby rolled her head and looked up at her father.

He gently took hold of her arm. He, too, she recalled with vivid clarity, had had tears in his eyes. In all her life Abby couldn't remember ever seeing her father cry. He did that night.

"I'm so sorry, sweetheart," he managed in a broken whisper. "Angela was declared dead at the scene of the accident."

Angela dead?

No.

This couldn't be right.

How could Angela be dead when just an hour or two earlier they'd been singing Christmas songs and making plans for the holidays? It made no sense. Abby couldn't imagine a world without Angela in it. Her mind refused to accept what her father had told her.

Angela's funeral was held December 27. That horrible day would forever remain in Abby's memory. Both of her legs had been broken, plus three ribs, but she'd insisted on attending the funeral. Respecting her wishes, her father had gotten permission from her doctor and borrowed a wheelchair. It was the first time Abby would see Angela's parents following the accident. She was terrified to face them, but she knew she had to somehow tell them how sorry she was, how she'd do anything to turn back the clock.

Instead, Angela's mother had gone berserk. As soon as Abby entered the church, Angela's mother had stood up, her red and swollen eyes making her look like a madwoman, and had called her a murderer. She screamed at Abby to leave. Nothing would console Charlene White. Not her husband, not the funeral director, not the priest who was about to say the funeral mass. Abby had been forced to leave—there was no other option.

She'd missed an entire semester of school her freshman year as she slowly recuperated from her injuries. Physically, it'd taken only a matter of months for her to heal, but emotionally . . . emotionally she was never the same again. She'd internalized the hatred in Angela's mother's eyes. Abby felt like a shameful, marked woman who'd committed the ultimate sin; one that could never be redeemed.

Twice more Abby had attempted to talk to Angela's parents. The second time had been the summer following the accident. Angela's father had answered the door and he'd said it would be best if Abby didn't come around again. Their rejection had cut her to the quick—Mr. and Mrs. White had been like a second set of parents to her. Not only had she lost her best friend, but she'd been targeted with every ounce of the Whites' hate and blame.

Every day as she drove through town she passed the spot where the accident had taken place. Someone had erected a small cross. Flowers were laid there on a routine basis. It was a constant reminder to Abby of the accident, salt in the wound.

The roadside memorial was difficult to see, but the

rumors were the worst. Abby's own mother asked her if it was true that the two of them had been drinking that night. Yes, they'd been drinking hot cocoa at the mall, but nothing alcoholic. Word spread that they'd been speeding, too. If anything Abby had been driving below the speed limit. She'd been a careful driver. Snow and ice were to blame, not drugs, alcohol, or negligent driving. The police had cleared her of any wrongdoing, but none of that appeared to matter.

So-called friends stopped by to ply her with questions about what had happened, eager to learn any information that they could spread. It didn't take long for Abby to refuse to see anyone because she didn't know who she could trust. Even Steve. She preferred to remain in her bedroom to study or read.

The summer between her sophomore and junior years of college, Abby had gone on a work/study program to Australia instead of coming home. It was just too painful to be in Cedar Cove, to know that people were staring at her when she walked by. Did they honestly think she couldn't hear what they said? She was the one to blame. Abby had been the driver and now Angela was dead.

Five years following graduation, their high school class held their first reunion. Money had been raised for a small memorial in the city park in honor of Angela.

The memories seemed to wrap their way around

Abby like a lasso, binding her until it became diffi-cult to breathe normally.

Distracted by her memories, Abby had only just started to back out of the driveway when her cell phone chirped. The ring reverberated inside the car until it felt as if she were standing next to a bell in a church tower. She grabbed her phone and checked the Caller ID.

Her mother.

She hesitated and then decided to let the call go to voice mail. If she spoke to her mother now, Abby feared she might break down. Worse, she might confess that she was headed to the cemetery and her mother was sure to try to persuade her to let matters be. This was Roger's wedding day. Abby shouldn't be doing this.

And her mother would be right.

Abby had been in town for two full days. She'd put this off too long already. She should have stopped by on Friday or even Thursday . . . but she hadn't been able to force herself.

Her cell chirped again, indicating that her mother had left a message. Abby would listen later.

She checked her watch. It was nine-thirty.

She had plenty of time.

She had no time.

A lump had started to form in her throat. She wasn't sure what she expected, what she hoped to gain. Absolution? Forgiveness? A blessing? Even now, all these years later, she didn't know why God had allowed her to live and Angela to die.

Considering the crushing weight of guilt she'd carried since the accident, she would so much rather be the one forever sleeping under six feet of soggy ground. She was so tired of feeling terrible about what had happened.

Taking the long route, Abby drove past the high school. She swallowed hard as she looked up at the window of what had been their homeroom their senior year. They'd been so silly and immature; eager to make their mark on the world. As seniors they'd considered themselves hot stuff. Super cool. Over the top. Silly, yes, but innocent, too. Little did Abby guess the rude awakening that awaited her just a few short months after graduation.

When Abby arrived at the cemetery she discovered two tents on different areas of the graveyard, indicating recent burials. Not until she climbed out of the car did Abby realize that she had no clue as to where Angela was buried. It took nearly forty minutes to locate her tombstone. By then her face was nearly numb from the cold.

A tingling sensation moved up her arms when she spotted the marker bearing her best friend's full name, ANGELA MARIE WHITE, engraved in granite. Even now, after all these years, it felt like a bad dream. Beneath the dates of her birth and death were the words **Beloved Daughter.** If only she'd been able to add **Best Friend.**

Not knowing what to do now, Abby continued to stare down at the tombstone. A rogue tear slipped from the end of her nose and splashed against the granite marker. A vase had been added to the grave marker and was filled with plastic flowers. Yellow daisies.

Yellow daisies had been Angela's favorites. Although she didn't know who she'd eventually marry, Angela had said she'd carry a bouquet of daisies down the aisle on her wedding day. And she'd drawn her wedding dress along with her bridesmaids' dresses.

Naturally they'd assumed Abby would serve as Angela's maid of honor and Angela would serve as hers. Abby had helped design her own maid-of-honor dress, laughing over Angela's sketchbook. They had agreed nothing would ever come between them. Not boys, not other friends, not even their parents. They were true BFFs.

Feeling unbearably awkward she sniffled once. "Hello," she whispered.

"It took you long enough."

Abby whipped around—she hadn't noticed anyone close by.

No one was anywhere in the vicinity.

Frowning, Abby turned back to stare at the gravestone.

"Yes, it's me. Did you think the grave would keep

me silent? Come on, Abs, you know me better than that."

"Angela," Abby gasped.

"Don't worry, no one else can hear me. My voice is all in your head."

This was too much. The pressure had gotten to her. Now Abby was hearing things. The voice was simply in her imagination. It had to be. Talking to Angela was . . . impossible. At least that was what Abby told herself, otherwise she'd need to consider contacting a mental health professional.

"Nine-one-one, what's your emergency?" A crisp professional voice would say to her.

"I'm hearing things," Abby would reply.

"What kind of things?"

"Dead people's voices."

"Stay on the line. We're sending help right away."

The entire scenario played out in Abby's head. She could picture the ambulance, siren blazing, rushing into the cemetery and hauling her off to the loony bin. Not only was she hearing voices, she was answering them.

"Oh don't get all excited. It isn't as bad as all that."

"Angela, please stop, you're freakin' me out."

"I wouldn't if you hadn't taken all these years to come see me."

Clearly Abby was simply talking to herself. Her

overactive imagination had stimulated this emotional response. But whether it was real or imagined, she couldn't let this chance to talk with her friend slip away.

"I tried to see your parents after the funeral, but—"

"I know, I know, it's my mother."

"She can't forgive me." That horrible scene played again and again in Abby's mind. She understood their reaction.

"Hey, sweetcakes, you can't even forgive yourself. Don't go blaming my mama."

"I saw Patty Morris; she—"

"I know, Mom told me. Stop changing the subject. Stay on track, okay?"

Abby ignored the comment. "You probably know more than I do then."

"Loads more. My mother still comes to the cemetery every week or so."

"Oh dear."

"Oh, she's much better, actually. It used to be every single day. You wouldn't believe the way she carried on, throwing herself down on the ground, sobbing. It was the most pitiful thing you've ever seen."

Abby covered her mouth and swallowed back a sob. She'd rather not know any of this. "Are you really talking to me, because if it isn't you, then I'd rather this stop, okay?"

"Am I real? Am I real?" Angela repeated, louder the second time. "Hmm . . . I think you'll need to figure that out yourself."

"I can't. I want to believe we can communicate, but I know it's impossible."

"Don't worry about it. It doesn't matter, I'm just pleased you found the courage to come. Finally. I've been waiting a very long time."

"I couldn't before . . ." Abby whispered aloud.

"And why not?"

Abby leaned her head back and stared up at the threatening gray skies. "My brother's getting married this evening."

"There you go again. Quit changing the subject. I want to know why you didn't feel you could come see me."

"Ah . . ." Abby broke down then, swallowing hard against the huge knot in her throat—one so large that for a few seconds she found it impossible to breathe. "I . . . I am so sorry, Angela. So very sorry."

"I know, I know," Angela murmured. "But it's time you got over it."

"Got over it? Are you nuts?" Abby nearly yelled. "I killed my best friend. No one with a conscience . . . with a heart, gets over something like that."

"But you have to," Angela insisted.

Abby didn't know how to respond.

"If you felt so guilty, why didn't you bring me flowers? Yellow daisies would have been perfect."

"Oh my goodness, I should have. I'm sorry."

"Hey, if you want to feel guilty, then go for it. You kept me waiting years and years, and when you finally do show, you don't even bring me flowers."

"I already apologized."

"Don't worry about it. When people do bring flowers they almost always don't have water. You wouldn't believe the stuff folks will put in that silly vase my mother insisted upon. I've had coffee, soda, fruit punch. You name the liquid and I've seen it."

"Oh."

"Okay, you're here and I'm real glad to see you."

"I'm glad I'm here, too."

"You don't look it. Your mascara is running and your nose is all red. You'd better clean up before your brother's wedding or guests are going to wonder who died." She immediately broke into peals of laughter. "Oops . . . bad choice of words there."

Abby looked away.

"Smile, Abby. Smile. I need for you to have a good life. I need to know you've been able to put this accident behind you and that you're enjoying life for the both of us."

"How can I?"

"Because I asked you to. I don't want you carting around this ball and chain of guilt."

Abby didn't want to carry it either.

"You know what your problem is, don't you?"

Abby shifted uncomfortably. "Well yes, I'm responsible for your death."

"No, that's not it. You aren't responsible, and anyway, nothing can change what happened now. No, your problem is that you've grown so comfortable with feeling guilty that you're afraid of what will happen if you don't. Being happy frightens the very life out of you. Oops, there I go again. Listen, everyone dies, so you have to get over it."

"I wish I was the one who'd died."

"But you didn't. You're alive, so enjoy life. Why aren't you married? By now you should have a husband and two or three children and be in tons of carpools."

"I should?"

"Isn't that the life we planned?"

Abby sobbed once. "Nothing turned out the way we planned."

"It seldom does, from what others tell me. Still, that's no reason to wallow in guilt. Now tell me you're ready to get on with life. I want you to live it to the fullest."

"I wish I could."

"Abby!"

"All right, all right," she cried, nearly shouting the words. Thankfully no one was around to hear her.

"Okay, good. But you need to do something first."

"What?"

"You aren't going to like it."

Abby's shoulders sank. "It has to do with your parents, doesn't it?"

"Yup, you need to go to them."

Abby shook her head, immediately dismissing the idea. "I can't, Angela, I can't. They blame me . . . your mother can't even stand to look at me."

"She needs to see you; to talk to you. Do this one thing for me; that's all I ask."

"I can't."

"You have to try again, Abs."

"Next time."

"No. Today. Now."

Abby shook her head. "I have a lunch date with Patty and a few others . . . my mother is coming with me. I don't have time."

"Go after the lunch."

"Can I take my mother with me?"

"No. Go alone. It won't be easy. I can't guarantee that Mom won't say or do something unkind. But this isn't about her, you know. It's for you. Nothing will change if you don't."

"Angela, I can't. I'm sorry, but I can't."

"Then promise me you'll think about it. That's all I ask, okay?"

"Okay, I'll think about it." She reached inside her pocket for a tissue and blew her nose.

"Enough with the tears. You're beginning to sound like my mother."

Abby grinned.

"Hey, that's more like it, now get out of here and have a wonderful day. Tell Roger congrats from me. I always did think he was a cutie."

"I will. Good-bye, Angela."

"Bye," Angela called out after her. **"Remember, you have to have a happy life; you're living it for the both of us."**

Abby turned away from the gravesite. Had that really happened? Had she really just been talking to her dead best friend? Regardless, she felt like a huge weight had been lifted from her shoulders. Still in a daze, she was walking slowly to her car when her cell phone rang again. This time she answered it. "Hi, Mom."

"Sorry to bother you, sweetheart, but I need to know what time you're picking me up for lunch?"

Abby glanced at her watch. "How about eleven-thirty. Patty suggested noon. That will give us plenty of time."

"Perfect."

Her mother hesitated. "You okay, sweetheart?"

"I'm fine, Mom. More than fine."

"I'm glad . . . I've been concerned. Your father, too. See you soon."

"Oh and Mom . . ."

"Yes," her mother said quickly, as if she'd been just about to turn off her cell. "What is it?"

Abby had been about to tell her she'd apparently just had a lengthy conversation with Angela, but she quickly changed her mind. "It's nothing important. We'll have time to catch up before the wedding."

"Okay, and did I tell you I've decided to wear the pink suit instead of the pale green one?"

"You look lovely in pink."

"You think so? That's what your father said. It's such a mother of the groom outfit, but as your father reminded me, I **am** the mother of the groom."

Abby smiled. "You'll be lovely."

"We both will be," her mother insisted.

Chapter 23

I waited until the house was empty before I gathered my coat and purse. I had a few errands to run, but none were really important. My mission was to get to know the town better and meet other business owners.

Peggy Beldon had recommended a dry cleaners and I had a couple of pillow shams I wanted to drop off. They would go nicely on the sofa. I was planning to stop off at the library, too. Two people now had mentioned Grace Harding and I hoped I'd have the opportunity to introduce myself.

I had the shams in a bag and my purse over my

shoulder. Again I chose to walk rather than take the car. One of the nice things about Rose Harbor Inn's location was that I could walk to almost anywhere in the downtown area. But instead of heading down the hill, the way I intended, I found myself walking toward Mark Taylor's place.

I hadn't answered his question about Paul the day before. As soon as he'd asked it, I'd made an excuse and had promptly left. Mark hadn't tried to stop me and I was grateful. In retrospect, though, I felt I owed him an explanation. Besides, I still wasn't satisfied with his answer about why he'd showed up at the inn while Spenser was there.

Just like the day before, I found Mark in his workshop, sanding a lovely cradle. It was a work of art, with intricate carving on each end. He glanced up when I appeared in the doorway, surprise showing in his dark eyes. He wore coveralls over a thick plaid winter jacket. One look reminded me that he wasn't a man who paid a lot of attention to grooming. His sandy blond hair needed to be cut and he didn't appear to have shaved that morning.

"You again," he said, not looking the least bit pleased by my unexpected visit.

"Yup, me again. Do you have a few minutes?"

"Not really."

I ignored that and walked over to where he kept a coffeepot and poured myself a cup and one for him, too.

"Sit with me a while," I suggested.

Mark glowered at me. "What do you want now? You keep interrupting me and I'll never get that sign made."

"It doesn't look to me like you're working on it now anyway."

His frown deepened but he ignored the comment.

"Someone commission you to build a cradle?" I asked.

Reluctantly he shook his head.

"You're building it . . . why?"

"Are you always this nosy?" he growled.

"Sometimes," I admitted. Pretending not to notice his complete lack of welcome, I pulled out a stool, sat down, crossed my legs, and cupped the mug between my hands, letting the hot coffee warm my palms.

Mark appeared to be doing some pretending of his own, acting like I wasn't there. I let him. My gaze automatically went to the cradle. I couldn't take my eyes off the intricate swirls he'd carved at each end. "The cradle is beautiful," I said, admiring his handiwork. Mark was a talented craftsman.

He stepped back and regarded his project with what seemed to be a new perspective. "Thanks."

"Is someone you know pregnant?"

"No." He returned to his project and added begrudgingly, "The idea for it came to me one night."

"And you decided to build it?"

He dropped his hand and glared my way. "Do you have a problem with that?"

"No." I found his gaze intimidating, but I wasn't about to let him know that.

A half smile appeared, but his voice was filled with sarcasm when he spoke. "I'm glad to hear it." He took the chisel to the wood, carefully tapping away at the intricate scroll.

"What do you intend to do with it?" I asked. He didn't have retail space as far as I could see.

He shrugged. "Don't know yet. I'll probably give it away." He sounded less irritated now.

"Give it away?" I repeated. That cradle could be sold for a fortune. Beautifully hand-carved, one of a kind? Nothing about Mark was the least bit usual—I never knew what to expect from him.

I blew on my coffee and then took a tentative sip, fearing it would burn my lips.

"Is there a reason you stopped by?" he demanded. He stepped away and reached for his own coffee.

"Yes."

"Then don't you think you should get on with it? As you might have noticed I'm busy."

Despite his attitude I smiled, and did a poor job of hiding my amusement.

"You find something funny?" he demanded.

"You," I told him.

He scratched the side of his head. "I've been called

a lot of things over the years, but I have to say funny isn't one of them."

"I felt I owed you an explanation regarding Paul . . ."

He raised his hand and stopped me. "It's none of my business. Whoever he is doesn't matter an iota to me, understand?"

I ignored him. "Paul was my husband. He was killed in Afghanistan about nine months ago."

Mark straightened his shoulders and took a step back. "That explains it."

"Explains what?"

He shook his head, apparently unwilling to respond. After a moment he said, "I'm sorry for your loss."

"Yes, I am, too. Paul Rose was a good man. The world is a better place because of him." I bit my lower lip, hoping to keep the sadness out of my voice. I wasn't sure I succeeded.

His look grew thoughtful. "You named the inn after him and you want to plant a rose garden." It was as though everything made sense to him all at once.

"His helicopter went down in the mountains. The crash site isn't accessible so his body was never recovered."

Mark's look held mine. "That's tough."

"For a long time I tried to believe he might still be alive."

"Is he?"

I shook my head. "As much as I want to believe it's a possibility, I don't think it is. The aerial photographs of the crash site show that it would have been impossible for anyone to have survived."

Mark looked away and set his cup aside. Without another word he returned to working on the cradle.

"I apologize if I made a pest of myself," I said, setting aside my own mug.

"You didn't," he said as he continued with the task at hand.

"Thanks for the coffee," I said on my way out of the shop.

"Don't think anything of it," he grumbled.

I left and started down the hill toward town. The cold felt good against my face. I was grateful for my wool coat and the warmth it offered. The wind blew off the water and the scent of salt lingered in the air. I was half-tempted to walk all the way to the marina and look out over the cove. I resisted when my stomach reminded me it was time for lunch.

Although I'd cooked a hearty breakfast for my two guests I hadn't eaten much of anything myself. I'd heard a lot about the Pot Belly Deli and I decided to stop in there for a bowl of soup.

The place was packed. I waited ten minutes for a table and was seated at a small round one by the window, overlooking Harbor Street.

Two women sat at the table across from me. They

were obviously good friends and they chatted back and forth, leaning toward each other and sporadically laughing.

When the waitress came over with a water glass and a menu, I asked for the soup of the day, and was told it was beef vegetable. I ordered that and a cup of tea. It wasn't until the waitress left that I noticed that one of the women at the table across from me had on a name badge. Grace Harding. This was the very person I'd hoped to meet later that day.

She must have caught me looking in her direction because she paused in the middle of her conversation and glanced my way.

Flustered and a little embarrassed, I said, "I apologize if I was staring."

"No, not at all. Are you the young woman who recently purchased the Frelingers' B and B?"

"Yes, I'm Jo Marie Rose."

"Grace Harding, and this is Olivia Griffin."

"Judge Olivia Griffin?" I asked.

"Yes." The judge was an elegant-looking woman with short, stylish dark hair and dark brown eyes. "I'm pleased to meet you both."

"Welcome to Cedar Cove."

I'd felt such a warm reception from the town already. "Practically everyone I've met so far has said I need to introduce myself to you," I told the two of them.

The waitress came by with my soup, a warm crisp

roll, and a pat of butter. The bread smelled as if it'd come straight from the oven and I could feel my resolve weakening. When I looked up I discovered that Judge Griffin was watching me.

"Did you have an unexpected guest yesterday?" she asked.

I started to say that I hadn't and then remembered Spenser. I wasn't sure how to answer. I opened my mouth and then closed it. I couldn't imagine how she would know about him. I didn't think Mark would have said anything, but then again I didn't really know Mark. The more exposure I had to him, the less I knew.

Olivia looked slightly embarrassed. "The reason I ask is that my daughter Justine and I were in town and a man in a car stopped and asked for directions to Rose Harbor Inn. I told him I didn't think there was a B and B in town with that name."

"Yes, I decided to change the name."

"Unfortunately I didn't know you had, and he got rather upset."

"With you?"

"With the world in general." She frowned. "I ran into Sheriff Davis a little later and mentioned the incident. Did the man find you?"

I nodded. "Unfortunately he did."

"Is everything all right?"

"Oh yes." I was half-tempted to mention Mark's unexpected visit but held back.

Olivia stood and reached for her tab. "I apologize if he was a friend of yours."

"He wasn't . . . isn't. I doubt he'll be coming back anytime soon."

"Good." Grace frowned and looked concerned, too. "Both Olivia and I have been single women on our own so we know what it's like. Don't ever hesitate to give a holler."

"Women need to stick together," Olivia added.

I couldn't agree more.

The two left then and I tasted my soup. It wasn't anything exotic or fancy, just good home cooking. The roll remained hot to the touch and when I ripped it open, steam rose from inside. The butter melted and ran onto the plate. It was every bit as good as it looked and smelled.

When I finished my lunch the crowd had thinned out considerably. I paid at the cash register and headed for the dry cleaners, which was a couple of blocks over.

As I walked down the street I noticed several curious glances in my direction. A number of people smiled and nodded as though to acknowledge me.

I found the dry cleaners and left the shams. From there I headed directly to the library, where I intended to sign up for my library card.

Chapter 24

Josh watched as Michelle quietly slipped out of Richard's bedroom, being careful to close the door with the least amount of sound possible. She looked toward him and sighed expressively. "He's much worse than yesterday."

"I thought so."

She lowered her head and was quiet for a moment, as if she was struggling to get out the words. "Despite what Richard says he wants, I think we need to contact hospice. I'm worried that he's in pain, and hospice can help us make his last days more comfortable."

Josh agreed with her. He also knew Richard's thoughts on the matter. "Richard won't like it."

Michelle agreed. "He's in no condition to argue. He's sleeping fitfully, and frankly, I don't think he has much longer. Hospice will have a better perspective than me, though. We need to be sure he shouldn't be taken back to the hospital." Her words trembled with emotion.

Josh walked into the living room and stared out the large picture window. In a matter of only a couple of days he'd witnessed a rapid decline in his stepfather's condition. It was almost as if Richard had waited for Josh's arrival before he was willing to let go.

When Josh had first walked into the house, Richard had had the energy and resolve to shout at him, but this morning, his stepfather barely had the strength left to breathe.

"I'll make us lunch," Michelle said from behind him.

It was that time of day already. Josh wasn't interested in eating. "Don't make anything for me; I'm not hungry."

Michelle acted as if she hadn't heard him. She went into the kitchen and after a few minutes Josh heard the teakettle whistle. She returned moments later with two mugs.

"I called hospice," she said.

Josh took the mug from her hand and they sat across from each other. The recliner where Richard spent the majority of his time remained empty, although he was very much present in their thoughts.

"What did they say?" he asked.

Michelle set the tea down on a coaster and leaned back in the chair. "The woman told me they'd send someone out this afternoon to check on him."

Richard wouldn't like it, but as Michelle had said earlier, the old man was in no condition to protest. He'd asked to die alone, and for just a moment, Josh wondered if they should abide by his wishes. But he suspected Michelle would refuse to leave her neighbor.

Truth be known, Josh would like to climb into his rental car and drive as far away from Cedar Cove as a tank of gas would take him. In the back of his mind he had hoped to spend at least part of his time off at the ocean.

One of the happiest memories of his childhood had been a short trip with his mother to Ocean Shores. Josh must have been around ten years old. After his father had left there'd never been extra money for luxuries like vacations. Finances were always a struggle. Yet somehow his mother had managed to eek out a few extra dollars for gas. They'd packed a cooler, loaded the car with pillows and blankets, towels, plastic buckets and shovels, and driven to Ocean Shores. They couldn't afford a hotel room, so they'd parked on a sandy stretch of beach.

Josh had raced up and down the shoreline, running headlong into the oncoming waves with boy-ish glee. They'd purchased a cheap kite and Josh had loved how the wind had picked it up and carried it so high that it became little more than a speck on the horizon. He'd laughed until he was almost sick with happiness.

Together Josh and his mother had built a huge sand castle and then later that night they made a small fire with driftwood and roasted hot dogs. Even now, all these years later, Josh didn't think he'd ever enjoyed a better meal. That night they'd slept under the stars with the sound of the ocean in the background.

"You've gone quiet," Michelle said.

Josh's gaze shot to her. Caught up in the memories, he had a difficult time bringing himself back into the present. "I was thinking about a trip I took with my mother as a kid."

"Before she met Richard?"

He nodded. "I was ten and we went to Ocean Shores. I'd hoped this matter with Richard would be done by now and I'd get a chance to visit the ocean. I know the town has grown up a lot since I was there, but the memories will never leave me."

"You never returned?"

"We did, once, with Dylan and Richard."

Michelle seemed to be reading his mind. "It wasn't the same, was it?"

Josh had been fifteen and he'd had his driver's per-mit, which enabled him to rent a scooter. Richard had rented a second one and let Dylan drive it along the beach. In the beginning it'd been crazy fun. Josh had loved the freedom of the scooter, racing on the sand with his stepbrother by his side, the wind in their faces. Then Josh had crashed and the bike had been damaged.

Richard had reacted with such fury that for the first time his mother intervened, reminding her husband that it'd been an accident. Still, Richard had insisted Josh pay for the damage and they leave for home immediately, ruining everyone's fun.

The ride home had been intolerable, thick with tension between his mother and Richard. Dylan had been angry with Josh, too, and Josh had felt sick with the knowledge that he was the one responsible.

In retrospect he didn't fully understand Richard's anger. It had clearly been an accident. He'd paid for the damage to the bike from his paper route money and had accepted responsibility for his actions. No one had even seemed to care that he'd been lucky enough to walk away from the wreck. He almost wished he had been hurt. Perhaps then he might have gotten sympathy instead of a tongue lashing.

"You're deep in thought again," Michelle said.

"Sorry."

"No problem."

He hadn't taken a single swallow of his tea. Before crashing his scooter, Josh had seen his mother walking along the beach with Richard. It might actually have been the distraction that caused him to crash—that part he didn't remember.

Teresa had had her arm wrapped around Richard's elbow. She was dressed in a sleeveless summer dress and the wind had whipped the hair about her face. Her skirt was pressed against her legs. Richard was more relaxed than Josh could ever remember seeing him. He'd rolled his pant legs up to his knees and they were both barefooted. The sound of his mother's laughter echoed down the beach, mingling with the cries of seagulls circling above. What had struck him about that moment in time was the fact that Teresa was so genuinely happy and carefree.

All too often Josh could remember his mother sitting at the kitchen table with a mound of bills in front of her. She'd have them stacked in piles as if gauging which ones had to be paid first. More times than he wanted to recall he'd watched her cover her face with both her hands and weep. Just thinking about that made his stomach clench into a hard knot.

Just the day before, Josh had been willing to acknowledge that his mother had loved Richard. And he couldn't help but feel grateful to Richard, despite all his flaws, for bringing joy back into her life.

The doorbell chimed and Michelle went to answer. It was the same woman from hospice that had stopped by the day before.

"I was at another house close by," Ginger explained as she stepped over the threshold.

Michelle took her coat and purse and hung them on the coatrack just inside the door.

"We were just having tea, would you like a cup?"

"Thank you, but I don't really have time. I'll check on Richard and then I need to be off."

"I understand."

"I'll go with you," Josh said, hoping that if Richard got upset, he would take his anger out on Josh instead of the woman who had so graciously volunteered her time.

Michelle cast him a look that said she should probably be the one to escort the other woman in to see Richard. He bowed to her wishes.

The temperature between them had cooled considerably since he'd told her that he would be leaving soon. He was sorry for that, but he didn't want to mislead Michelle. The timing was just all wrong. This was an intensely emotional time and he was confused and unsure if he could trust his feelings. Richard was close to death and the chance to make a clean break from this town and the painful memories was fast approaching.

After a few more minutes of questions and answers, the two women quietly crept into Richard's bedroom.

Josh didn't hear Richard complain, so he speculated that his stepfather was still asleep. Maybe he had even passed away.

Richard dead.

The unexpected shaft of grief that struck him

caused Josh to sink down into a chair. He should be glad all of this was over if indeed that was the case.

Thinking back, Josh tried to remember what it'd been like when his mother had died. They'd known, of course, that the end was near. Richard and Josh had been with her, one on either side of her hospital bed. That was fitting, considering how far apart they were in every aspect except their love for the dying woman.

His mother had been sleeping, and her breathing had gone shallow and whispery. After one last breath, she was gone.

Richard had looked at Josh, tears streaming down his ashen cheeks, his eyes filled with raw grief, and whispered, "She's passed." Then he'd leaned forward, his elbow braced against the bed, and wept loudly.

Josh had been in some sort of emotional shock, he realized now, because he'd felt nothing. Not grief, not pain . . . he'd felt absolutely nothing. He hadn't shed a tear, at least not that he remembered.

Richard's loud wails had brought a nurse into the room. A chaplain had been called, too. By then Richard had gotten ahold of himself enough to function normally. Josh couldn't remember either of them speaking on the way home. After dropping Josh off at the house, Richard left almost immediately for the funeral parlor.

Funny how those memories were surfacing all of a

sudden. What he found even odder was that he had been in an emotional bubble when his mother had died and he was feeling just the opposite now that it was Richard's time to go. He was overwhelmed with sadness and the old man was still alive. Josh could find no plausible explanation.

Michelle and Ginger came out of Richard's bedroom.

"He's awake," Michelle said. "His eyes fluttered open when we entered the room."

"What do you think?" Josh directed the question to the hospice volunteer.

She didn't hesitate. "Less than forty-eight hours would be my educated guess."

"That soon?" Josh wanted to believe Richard was too mean to die. He'd want to beat the odds, prove that he was more powerful than death. "Did you tell him that?" he asked.

The woman from hospice shook her head.

"Was he upset we called hospice again?" Josh asked, looking at Michelle.

"He was, but he doesn't have the strength to yell any longer."

"He wanted you to leave him alone, right?"

She smiled knowingly and nodded. "Oh, there were a few other choice words tossed in as well, but I can't see repeating those."

"That's probably for the best."

"Call me if there's a change," the hospice lady said. "The medication will address the pain. I don't see any reason for him to go to the hospital."

Josh walked her to the front door. As she fastened her coat, she paused. "He could pass soon, perhaps sometime late tonight or early tomorrow morning."

"Okay. Thank you for coming; we appreciate it."

"No problem. I'm glad I was in the vicinity and could stop by."

"We are, too."

The house seemed unnaturally quiet after she left.

Josh hesitated and then went into Richard's bedroom. The door creaked when he opened it.

Sure enough, Richard's eyes opened as Josh walked into the bedroom, stopping at the foot of the bed.

"I thought I told you to stay away," Richard muttered.

Josh moved closer in order to hear him. "I'll leave in due course, so don't worry. I'll be out of here before you know it."

"Go now."

"Okay, if that's what you want."

Richard closed his eyes and inhaled softly, his breath reedy and thin.

"I was remembering when Mom died," Josh said.

Almost instantly Richard's eyes filled with tears. He rubbed his hand across his face and Josh could see he was embarrassed.

"I still miss her," the older man managed to whisper. "Not a day passes that I don't think of Teresa."

"Thank you for the joy you brought into her life. I hope you realize how deeply she loved you and how happy being married to you made her. I'll always be grateful for how you took care of her, especially at the end of her life."

Richard's tears flowed in earnest then, rolling down his deathly pale cheeks, making gleaming tracks as they progressed to his chin and dripped onto the pillowcase.

"Meeting Teresa was the best thing to ever happen to me . . . and to Dylan, too."

He was silent after that, as if he was caught up in the memories. Then, just as Josh was about to leave, Richard spoke again. "I thought I saw her . . ."

"When?" he asked softly.

"Last night. She stood at the foot of the bed, ghost-like. I could see straight through her to the wall."

"Did she say anything?" No doubt it'd been the drugs. The dose of painkillers would have kicked in by then and they were strong ones.

"She didn't speak but . . . it seemed like I could hear her. She told me that she and Dylan were waiting for me."

Josh nodded.

"I'm not afraid of death." The defiant look in

Richard's eyes underscored his words. "I'm ready to go. Anytime."

"Good thing."

"Good thing," Richard repeated and closed his eyes.

For one crazed second Josh thought he'd actually died, but then he saw Richard's chest move as he exhaled, and he was able to breathe again, too.

Just like Josh had thought. Richard Lambert was too ornery to die.

Chapter 25

Abby knocked on her parents' hotel room door and waited. No one responded, so she knocked again, louder. Still no one answered. Fearing she might have gotten the wrong room, she headed down to the front desk. As she neared the counter Abby noticed that the breakfast room was tucked off to the side, and it was crowded with people chatting and sitting around tables. It wasn't breakfast time though.

"Abby." Her mother came through the double-wide doors with her arms outstretched. "We're in here."

"Mom . . ."

"Abby," her aunt Eileen cried, joining her mother. "Oh, sweetie, it's so good to see you." She enfolded Abby in her arms, giving her a hug so strong that Abby feared her aunt would crack her ribs. "It's been far too long," Eileen said.

Her uncle Jake joined his wife. He slipped one arm around Eileen's waist and the other around Abby's. "Come see your cousins."

The last time Abby had seen Sondra and Randall she'd been a teenager and they'd been toddlers. The gangly young man who approached her had a protruding Adam's apple and he stood at least six feet two inches, towering above her.

"Randy?" Abby couldn't believe this was her baby cousin.

"I go by Rand now."

"Rand?" Her eyes widened. "What happened to you?"

He grinned sheepishly. "I grew up."

A lovely young blond woman joined him. "Don't you remember me?" she asked.

"Sondra?"

She smiled, revealing perfect white teeth. "It's me."

"I don't believe it." Abby laughed. "Good grief, I changed Rand's diapers."

"Ah . . . would you mind . . . ?" The youth asked, awkwardly shuffling his feet.

"As I recall we called you Super Pooper."

Rand's boyish face went bright red, and the assembled group laughed.

"Don't worry," Abby promised, "I won't mention it again."

"Thanks," he said, grinning back at her.

"Remember your aunt Betty Ann?" her mother said, steering Abby to the other side of the room.

"Where's Uncle Leon?" Abby remembered that her father's brother always had a camera in hand.

No sooner had she asked the question than a camera flashed.

"Uncle Leon," she said, laughing. Both her aunt and uncle hugged her.

"It's been far too long," her aunt Betty Ann complained.

"You're welcome to visit any time," Abby surprised herself by saying. "Remember, I live in Florida and the winters there are lovely."

"We live in Arizona," Betty Ann said. "We have great winters, too."

"They aren't that far from us," her mother added.

"Oh sweetie, you don't know how good it is to see you."

Her uncle Leon aimed the camera in her direction. "You always were as pretty as a picture." The flash went off three times in quick succession.

"Where are Doug, Craig, and Joy?" Abby asked about her younger cousins.

"They're here. Joy made us grandparents two years ago."

"You're a grandmother, Aunt Betty Ann?" Her mother had probably mentioned it, but she had forgotten.

Abby's mother crossed her arms in a competitive huff. "Don't go there, Betty Ann." She glared at her daughter and then smiled, letting her know she was only joking. "Now that Roger is marrying there's a good likelihood Tom and I will eventually have grandchildren. Unless, of course . . ." she paused and looked squarely in Abby's direction. "Unless Abby finds a young man, settles down fast, and has a baby or two."

"Mom!" Abby protested but not strenuously.

For the next fifteen minutes she was shuffled from table to table to reacquaint herself with a bevy of relatives from both her mother's and father's sides of the family.

She saw Joy and her infant son and met Joy's husband. The family lived in Alaska and had flown down to Seattle for the wedding and to visit other family members. Doug and Craig were both married, too, and Abby met both of their wives. Doug's wife was pregnant and her aunt Betty Ann was thrilled that it was a baby girl, her first granddaughter.

What astonished Abby was how much everyone had changed from the last time she'd been at a family gathering, which had been more years ago than she cared to remember.

At one time Abby had been close to her younger cousins, despite the difference in their ages. Even three or four years had been a big deal back then. Sondra and Rand were the youngest while Doug, Craig, and Joy were only a few years younger than Abby.

By the time Abby followed her mother back to the hotel room to get ready to leave for lunch, her head was spinning with names and faces. "When did everyone grow up?" she asked, shaking her head in wonder.

"Well, sweetheart, if you came out of your shell a bit more often you'd be able to answer that yourself."

"I know," Abby agreed, and for the first time she felt that she'd made a huge mistake in sequestering herself so.

Her mother slid the plastic key into the lock and opened the door. The maid had been by and the room had been cleaned.

"I have to change my shoes," Linda said as she bent over and retrieved a pair from the closet floor.

For the first time Abby noticed her mother was wearing slippers. "I'm saving my feet for dancing at the reception. I did tell you I talked your father into taking ballroom dancing classes, didn't I?"

"Daddy?" Her father was the last person Abby would have expected to agree to dance classes.

"I never thought it'd happen but we got hooked on that television show, rooting for our favorite couple each week."

Abby watched the program herself, but the idea that it would influence her parents to take dancing classes was hard to take in.

"Your father is no slouch on the dance floor. He loves it."

Wow, things had changed.

Her mother straightened and then arched her back. "We're not that old, you know."

"Speaking of being old, I'm parked on the far side of the parking lot," Abby remembered. "Why don't I go get the car and bring it around front and you can meet me there."

"Are you sure, sweetie? I don't mind walking out that way."

"No problem, Mom."

Abby had started toward the door when her mother stopped her. "Sweetie. I hope I didn't embarrass you by bringing up grandchildren. Your father said I need to be more sensitive."

Abby reassured her with a smile. "You didn't embarrass me."

"Oh, good. I wouldn't want anything to ruin this day. Your father and I are so happy for Roger. We've waited for our children to marry for a very long time."

Abby hugged her mother and left the room. She was rummaging inside her purse for her car keys when she nearly bumped into a man who was hurrying down the hallway. He rammed into her shoulder.

Abby would have been spun off balance but the man grabbed her by the upper arms.

"I'm so sorry!" He paused and looked straight at her. "Abby?"

"Yes." She barely managed to get the word out. Abby didn't need to ask who he was. She recognized him immediately.

"It's me, Steve. Steve Hooks."

"I . . . know." Her mouth felt as dry as an abandoned well. She'd wanted to ask her brother about Steve, but she never had. She supposed she hadn't wanted to hear that he was happily married and had completely forgotten her. She'd certainly given him reason enough.

"So you remember me?"

Oh yes, she remembered him. "It's . . . good to see you again," she finally managed, although it felt as if the words had flowed from her lips like molasses.

He dropped his hands from her shoulders, although he seemed reluctant to do so. "You look great."

"You're here for the wedding?" That was probably the stupidest question she could have asked.

"Yes, Roger asked me to be one of the ushers."

"You weren't at the rehearsal last night," Abby blurted out before she realized it would be obvious that she'd been looking for him.

"No, my flight got delayed and I didn't land until after the dinner."

"I'm glad you made it." She wanted to talk more, but with her mother waiting she didn't feel she should linger. Hopefully she'd be able to catch up with him at some point later on in the day.

He took one step back, in retreat, seeming as hesitant as she was to end their conversation. "I'll see you later this afternoon, then."

"At the wedding," Abby said unnecessarily. Her cheeks flushed with color. The night she and Angela had gone shopping her friend had told her how excited she was to meet Steve. And Abby had droned on and on about how wonderful he was.

Roger had invited Steve to join their family for Thanksgiving because Steve's family lived on the East Coast and he couldn't afford a second ticket home within a few weeks of Christmas. Abby and Steve had been emailing back and forth nonstop since their initial introduction. Angela had spent Thanksgiving with her grandparents in Spokane.

Abby had fallen hard for Steve. Following the accident, he'd sent flowers and notes and letters, but she hadn't answered him because it felt wrong for her to have a great guy in her life when her friend was dead. The kicker came when a young man Angela had been dating stopped by the hospital. Abby had still been under sedation and in a lot of pain. He'd sat by her bedside, and pressed his forehead against the side railing and wept. He hadn't shouted the way Angela's mother had, but his grief had pained her in ways that angry words never could. He left soon afterward and she never saw him again.

Caught up in her thoughts, Abby nearly walked into the glass door leading to the parking lot.

"Get a grip," she muttered to herself as she headed toward the rear of the lot where she'd left her car. Following her release from the hospital and a period of recuperation, it'd taken real courage for her to get behind the wheel of a car again. In fact, it'd taken almost a year.

After unlocking the door, she slid into the driver's seat and placed her hands on the steering wheel. So Angela wanted her to visit her parents while she was in town.

That was an impossible request. She couldn't face them. She'd tried, but they'd been too caught up in their grief to find it in their hearts to forgive her. According to Angela, the years had done little to change their attitude.

Abby gave herself a mental shake. "You don't know that," she said aloud. What woman in her right mind listened to voices coming from beyond the grave? Enough of this silliness.

Enough.

The entire scene at the cemetery had been a figment of Abby's imagination. She'd waited far too long to visit her friend's grave site and as a result she'd mentally built it up to this huge event. The result was that she'd become delusional.

And hadn't her own mother just said she didn't want anything to ruin this perfectly wonderful day? Her brother was about to wed his bride. This was not the time or the place for Abby to step back in time in an effort to right past wrongs. The best way for her to handle this situation was to go to her brother's wedding and enjoy this special time with family. And then she would leave Cedar Cove; pack up her suitcase and simply put all this anxiety and pain behind her.

She waited, half expecting Angela to express her opinion on the matter. How silly she must look, sitting behind the wheel of her car, waiting for someone who was dead and buried to argue with her internal monologue.

Abby started the engine and drove around to the front of the hotel. Her mother stepped outside as soon as she appeared. Linda's face broke into a wide smile as she opened the passenger door and climbed inside.

"You will never guess who I just saw!"

"I bet I can," Abby returned.

"Steve Hooks!" Her mother cast Abby a meaningful glance.

"I saw him, too. We almost ran into each other in the hallway outside your room. Well, actually, we did run into each other."

"His plane got delayed," her mother went on to explain.

"I . . . I'm glad he made it in time."

"Me, too. By the way, Roger mentioned that Steve isn't married." Again her mother looked pointedly in Abby's direction.

"Oh?" Her heart instantly started to beat at double time, although it was ridiculous to think they could pick up where they'd left off all those years ago.

"Roger said Steve had asked about you, too."

Abby decided to ignore that comment. "Mom, you need to put on your seat belt."

"Oh, right." She reached behind her and stretched the strap across her body and clicked it into place.

How Abby wished she'd insisted Angela put on her seat belt. Even now, all these years later, her mind shouted out the warning.

After she'd finished, Linda returned her gaze to Abby. "Well, sweetie, what did Steve have to say?"

"Unfortunately we didn't get much of a chance to talk."

"But you will later, right?"

"Yes, I imagine we will."

Her mother didn't say anything for a long moment, and then with a soft sigh she added, "That's a start."

A start. Yes, indeed it was.

Chapter 26

Josh took his time rinsing out the two mugs and placing them in the dishwasher while Michelle went to check on Richard.

The door to Richard's bedroom opened and closed and Michelle joined him. Josh glanced up expectantly. He wasn't sure what he was looking for from her but she met his gaze and quietly went to sit in the living room.

"How is he?" Josh asked, tucking the tips of his fingers in his jeans pockets.

"The same; sometimes a little better, sometimes a bit worse. At this point it's difficult to tell."

Josh nodded, unsure of what he should say. The tension between Michelle and him was stretched thin. While he was reluctant to wade into the emotional quagmire of their shared kisses, it seemed unavoidable.

"Perhaps we should talk about . . . what happened," he suggested.

Michelle gave him a quizzical look.

"You know," he insisted, wishing he was more experienced in these kinds of conversations. "I want to make sure you aren't reading anything into what happened . . . between us."

"I shouldn't?" she asked.

"No," he said quickly, thinking that he'd probably made a big mistake.

"Have you always avoided emotional entanglements, Josh?"

He blinked, definitely sorry that he'd said anything. "That's not what's going on here."

Her responding smile challenged him, but he wasn't looking for an argument or a confrontation. "Forget I said anything. I'm sorry I brought up the subject."

"If that's what you want, Josh, then I'm okay with it, but one day you're going to need to confront this issue."

She was probably right, but that time wasn't now. "Can we drop the subject?"

"That's fine with me. I didn't bring it up in the first place."

He felt an immediate sense of relief. "Good." Soon he'd be out of here and for all intents and purposes he never planned to return. And yet when he looked at her all he wanted to do was hold her close. This was crazy. One minute all he could think about was getting away, and the next he was overwhelmed with the urge to wrap this beautiful woman in his arms and hold on for dear life.

Michelle returned to the kitchen.

Not sure what he was thinking, Josh followed her.

She brought down a fresh coffee mug and when she turned around, Josh was standing directly behind her. For an awkward moment all they did was stare at each other. Josh didn't know what to say. He knew she was right. He had avoided emotional intimacy and he wasn't sure why. His job had always been a convenient excuse.

Without a word Michelle retrieved her coat and started out the front door.

Josh wanted to stop her, but every time he opened his mouth he seemed inclined to say something stupid. It was probably best just to let her go.

The front door made a soft clicking sound as it closed. So he was alone with Richard. The knowledge unnerved him. When Richard died, Josh would be truly alone.

Depressed now, he sank into a chair and closed his eyes.

Leaning forward, he braced his elbows against his

knees. He wasn't any good at this relationship business. Never had been. Michelle had hit the proverbial nail on the head. Josh was afraid of making a commitment, afraid of what the future might hold. He felt like he'd lost everyone he'd ever loved, and he wasn't sure that he could risk his heart again. His father had abandoned him and then his mother. That had been the first strike. The second had been his mother's death, followed by Dylan's. He didn't like to think about his stepbrother's death. It'd hit him hard, and Josh had never taken time to deal with the loss.

Perhaps it was fear of the unknown, fear of more loss that kept him trapped in this no-man's-land. He'd always assumed he'd marry one day, but he was quickly coming to realize that one day might mean never. It was far too easy to shove everything into the future.

Unexpectedly the front door opened again and Michelle came back inside the house. Josh leaped to his feet, his heart instantly glad to see her. She'd left without a word and he'd assumed that she wouldn't return. He'd wanted to follow her, talk to her, but he'd worried it would only make matters worse.

"You're back," he said, which was actually a pretty stupid comment. Thankfully she didn't say so.

Michelle held a box clenched in her hands. She set it on the kitchen countertop and then removed her coat.

"What's that?" Josh asked.

"Your mother's Bible."

"You have my mother's Bible?" Josh couldn't believe it. "How'd you find it?"

"Richard told me."

"He told you? You mean just now? Today?"

"Yes, just a few minutes ago, actually. He said it was in the garage and told me exactly where."

A realization dawned on Josh. "He said he wanted you to have it, didn't he?" Richard would naturally try to take away anything that he might possibly want.

"Me?" she repeated.

He nodded.

"No," she countered. "He wanted you to have it."

Josh's head shot up. "He said that?"

"Yes, don't look so shocked."

For one wild instant it actually felt as though his legs were about to go out from under him. Josh sank back down into the chair. "What happened?"

"You mean what changed Richard's mind?"

"Yes . . . just yesterday he seemed dead set against me getting that Bible, simply because he knew I wanted it."

"You'll have to ask him. Later though. He's sleeping now."

Josh reached for the Bible and opened it to the front page. Inside his mother had written her name in fountain pen. For as long as he could remember she had used a fountain pen. She said it was more distinctive. She'd certainly had beautiful handwriting that had lent itself to it. Her letters were filled with delicate loops and a gentle flourish. It was as if she'd studied cursive from the men who'd signed the Constitution.

Staring down at her name, Josh felt sadness descend upon him. He missed his mother as much as he ever had since she'd died. He raised his hand and ran his finger over her name.

Turning the page, he saw that she'd listed the dates of her two marriages and Josh's birth date as well. Richard—it could only be him—had entered the date of her birth and death. His abrupt, sharp-angled handwriting was in stark contrast to Teresa's.

Turning through the pages of the Old Testament, he saw that many of the verses were underlined, with notes written in the margins.

"I wish I'd known her better," Michelle whispered.

Josh had almost forgotten that Michelle was in the room. He wished he had known his mother better, too, but when she died he was a typical teenager, self-absorbed and selfish. He hadn't fully comprehended what losing his mother meant. He did now, and the loss was tremendous.

He wondered if that was the way he'd feel at some point in the future when it came to Richard, and doubted it. For all the bad blood between them, it would take more than the return of his mother's Bible for him to let go of the past.

Michelle sat down across from him and he offered

her a weak smile. He paged through his mother's Bible for a few more minutes and then decided to look in on Richard.

The bedroom door creaked softly as he opened it. Richard's eyes fluttered open and when he saw it was Josh, he rolled his head to the side as though to avoid eye contact.

Josh entered the bedroom and stopped at the foot of the bed. "I suppose I should thank you."

"Your mother would have wanted you to have it."

Josh bit his tongue to keep from saying that Richard could have given it to him a long time ago.

"Why give it to me now?"

Richard looked at him. "I loved her. You can hate me if you want—I know you do. I suppose I've given you reason enough."

"You have," Josh said. They were long past the point of sugarcoating the truth. "I needed a father and you were so cold, so unfeeling toward me—it was worse than not having one at all."

Richard briefly closed his eyes and said, "I may have failed you . . . I guess I did, but your mother was everything to me."

For Richard to admit his shortcomings stunned Josh, but he said nothing.

"I had a bad first marriage. Dylan's mother . . ." the rest faded as if he no longer had the strength to speak. "Teresa . . . was my soul mate."

Josh longed to ask the old man why he hated him

so much, but he already had the answer. In retrospect it was perfectly clear, perfectly understandable. Josh had been competition for Teresa's attention. She loved them both and each one had wanted, needed her to love them first and foremost. His mother had been in a no-win situation, loving her husband and her son and left to deal with this battle of wills between the two of them.

"Thank you for the Bible," Josh whispered.

"I kept it because I wanted to hold on to a piece of her."

Josh understood that.

"I'd left instructions for it to be placed in the casket with me . . . but I just dictated a note to change that. You can take it."

Josh planned to do exactly that, instructions or not. This Bible belonged with him, not in the cold ground with Richard.

Richard closed his eyes again. Whether it was because talking had exhausted him or he was asleep, Josh didn't know. He had what he wanted, or at least part of what he'd hoped to collect, and for now that was enough. Turning, he left the room, quietly closing the door behind him.

Michelle looked up when he emerged from Richard's bedroom.

"He didn't plan to give it to me," Josh told her. "He said he'd originally planned to have it buried with him."

"I know," she returned. "He had me write out a statement for him to sign that said he'd had a change of heart and wanted you to have the Bible."

"Big of him," Josh murmured.

"Yes, it was," she countered swiftly, heatedly. "What is it with you?" she demanded. "Don't you appreciate anything?"

"Apparently the fact that the Bible should rightly go to me in the first place doesn't mean anything," he shot back.

Their gazes clashed for several heartbeats. "I need some fresh air," she announced, and reached for her coat on her way out the door.

Josh thought to stop her. She was halfway outside when he raised his hand, but he didn't know what to say. Perhaps this was for the best.

His shoulders sank as the door clicked closed. Door after door had closed on him after his mother's death. Why this one should bother him as much as it did was beyond him.

Chapter 27

I was looking forward to my visit to the library. I've always been a big reader and thought I might eventually volunteer as a Friend of the Library.

Meeting Grace and Judge Olivia earlier over lunch had been a welcome surprise. I hadn't thought I'd make connections in my new home so quickly. I'd worried I'd be a bit isolated in this town where I knew no one. I recognized right away that these two successful women would be excellent role models for me. I could learn a good deal about business and life from them, and hoped to cultivate their friendship.

The walk to the library took only a few moments.

The building was made of cement blocks with a large mural on the side that faced the marina. The wind blew off the water and boats gently bobbed in the swells.

The library mural depicted a woman from the 1800s holding a lantern and looking out to sea, presumably waiting for the return of her husband, a fisherman or sailor. Two small children were at her side. It seemed to be freshly painted.

The double glass doors opened automatically as I approached. Once inside I felt a welcome rush of warm air. I noticed a long counter for checking out books was set off to one side. An information booth was more centrally located. Both counters were manned.

"Jo Marie."

I heard my name and turned around to discover Grace walking toward me.

"Oh, hi! I came in to sign up for a library card," I told her.

"Wonderful," Grace said, brightening. "If you'll follow me, I'll show you where you can fill out the form."

"Perfect." She led me to a computer stand and brought up the appropriate page. She'd just finished explaining what I needed to do when an employee approached her with a request.

"If you'll excuse me for a moment," Grace said.

"Of course." I hadn't expected her to drop everything just for me. It only took me a few minutes to complete the form and submit the information. I was told that my name would be entered into the system and I would be issued a card within five to seven working days.

Grace returned. "Would you like a tour of the library?"

"That would be great if you have the time."

We started toward the back of the large open area that was clearly for children. "We recently started a 'Reading with Rover' program for children with reading difficulties," she explained. "Beth Morehouse brings in dogs for the children."

"Dogs?" I asked.

"Yes, the children read to them—it puts them at ease and helps them relax. A dog isn't judgmental if they stumble over a word, and volunteers are available to help. I know it sounds funny, but you'd be amazed at how much this program has helped these slow readers."

"Do you need any more volunteers?" I asked.

"How kind of you to offer, but thankfully we have more than enough volunteers. You never know when that could change, though. I'll put your name down for the future. However, if you're looking . . ." she paused and studied me. "How are you with animals?"

I wasn't quite sure how to respond. "Fine, I guess."

"Do you like dogs?"

"I love them. But while I was working full-time it

didn't seem fair to have one that I left home alone all day."

Grace beamed me a huge smile. "How would you feel about adopting a dog?"

"Adopting a dog?"

"I volunteer at the local animal shelter," she explained, "and we've currently got a large dog population. I was thinking you might want to adopt a pet."

Instantly a long list of reasons to reject the idea came to mind. First off, having a dog would limit my business at the inn—anyone allergic or simply not fond of animals would certainly pass me over. I'm fond of dogs but I haven't had one since I was a kid. Did I really have the time to care for a dog? They could be labor intensive. I'd already made several big changes in my life and I wasn't sure I was up to another.

Grace must have read the reluctance in my expression because she added, "A dog, especially a larger one, would offer you protection and is such pleasant company." She smiled. "Years ago now, when I was single, I got a sweet-natured golden retriever named Buttercup. She was my constant companion. It was the first time in my life that I lived alone and I can't tell you what a comfort Buttercup was to me."

I'd been on my own nearly my entire adult life, so it wasn't the same for me. Still, Grace brought up a good point. A dog, especially of a larger breed, could offer me a certain amount of security. The world is full of men like Spenser who would be eager to take advantage of me. And when it came to taking in guests, well, I couldn't be sure what type of people they would be—having a large dog at my side wasn't such a bad idea.

"I think getting a dog is an excellent suggestion," I said, mulling it over. I was tempted but concerned, too. "My only worry is that it might be an issue for my guests."

"Think about it," Grace said. "I bet it's something you could work around. For dog lovers, it would probably be a selling point for the inn."

"I do like the idea . . ."

Grace appeared delighted by my interest. "Now is an especially good time. Like I said, the shelter has a big selection with several breeds available for adoption." She led me over to the counter and wrote down the address and tore the sheet of paper from the tablet.

A dog. Well, this should be interesting. I might take a look later and see what animals were available.

My errands completed, I walked back to the inn, thinking long and hard about adopting a dog. I'd always heard German shepherds were excellent dogs. A German shepherd would make a superb guard dog. It wouldn't hurt to check out the shelter and get the necessary information before I made a final decision. I'd also need to get the name of a dog trainer and find out about obedience classes.

With a sense of purpose, I got into my car and entered the address in my navigational system. The shelter was only ten minutes away, and as I drove, I could almost feel Paul's approval. Getting a dog would have pleased him. I remember him talking about his childhood pet named Rover, an Alaskan husky.

As soon as I entered, I could hear dogs barking in the background. I approached the counter and was greeted by a volunteer.

"Hello," I said. "I've come to see the animals . . . I'm thinking of adopting a dog—preferably a larger breed."

"We have several. You'll need to fill out the paperwork first. Once you've been approved you'll be able to make your selection."

Approved? All I wanted to do was take a look, but it might make sense to get all the paperwork out of the way just in case I found an animal I felt I could adopt. Owning any pet was a responsibility, so I could understand why the shelter wanted to be sure the animals in their care went into healthy living environments.

I was handed a clipboard with the application. I found a quiet corner where I could sit and fill it out.

It took me a few minutes and when I was finished I had to wait to hand the clipboard back to the volunteer.

"Thanks—a member of our staff will review the application and let you know in a few minutes. You can wait here if you'd like."

"Oh, sure." I had to wonder if things were moving more quickly than I wanted them to. After all, I'd just come to look. I hadn't made a decision, and yet I could feel myself leaning toward the idea. I wasn't an impulsive person by nature, and yet I'd made a number of major decisions in the last few months based on emotion. That wasn't like me. I suppose this sudden departure from my usual behavior could be part of the grieving process, but I couldn't say that for sure. I shifted, suddenly uncomfortable, and glanced toward the door, briefly wondering if anyone would notice if I simply left. My heart started to pound and my knees felt as if they wouldn't support me. What did I really know about dogs? Very little. I'd had enough change in my life and I certainly didn't need to add more.

Feeling unusually warm, I unbuttoned my coat. I continued to waver, but just when I was about to leave, a volunteer approached me. He smiled and said, "Come this way."

"I . . . I've had a change of heart," I said, stumbling over the sentence. "I mean I like animals but . . ."

"Hmm . . . I understand, but why don't you take a look at the dogs available for adoption, before you make up your mind."

"Ah . . ." Still, I hesitated.

This young man wasn't taking no for an answer. "This way," he said, and ushered me into the back of the shelter. He held open the door for me, and I noticed the clipboard with my application was in his hand. "My name's Neal, by the way."

"Hello Neal . . . I'm Jo Marie. Do you know Grace Harding?" I asked, to cover my nervousness. "She's the one who recommended I adopt a pet."

Neal broke into a big grin. "Grace and I both volunteer on Saturdays. She got called into work this morning unfortunately. I see she's still doing her best even when she's not here to find good homes for the shelter animals." He led the way down a long hallway with cages on both sides. The dogs inside lay sprawled out, most of them napping. Water and food dishes were set off to one side of the enclosure.

"It's like they're in jail," I commented, instantly sympathizing with the canines.

"They're only in the cages for part of the day," Neal assured me. "Volunteers walk them regularly and see to it that they have food and water. You don't need to worry—every animal in this shelter is well loved and cared for until we can find them a permanent home. Unfortunately, we have an overabundance lately. With a slower economy, some families can no longer afford to keep their pets."

"Like I said, I'm not sure about this."

"Don't make a decision just yet, okay?"

"Okay," I murmured.

Slowly we progressed down the wide hallway. "What about a German shepherd?" I asked.

"We have a few."

"Could I see them?" I asked, thinking I was wasting both his time and mine.

"Of course. Shep and Tinny are on the left-hand side about three-quarters of the way down." He stepped up his pace.

Apparently the dogs were accustomed to people walking past because only a handful seemed to even notice me. A couple lifted their heads but then they put their chins back down on their paws and closed their eyes.

With one exception.

As soon as he saw me, a small dog of mixed breeding instantly leaped to his feet and raced to the front of the cage.

"Well, hello there," I said, crouching down so that I could get a better look at the black and white dog. "And who might you be?" He was a cute thing, but much smaller than what I was looking to adopt. If I **did** adopt.

"Oh my," Neal said.

Perplexed by the volunteer's reaction, I glanced up. "Is something wrong?"

"That's Rover."

"Rover?" Paul's dog had been named Rover, too.

"Not very original, is it? We sort of run through a lot of names here and it looked like he'd been roving for a good long while, so that's what we picked."

"Oh." My gaze went back to the scraggly looking pooch who stared back at me with dark brown eyes. His gaze was unwavering, as if he expected something from me in return. I had nothing to give him.

"Rover was abandoned and was half-starved when he was found. It's the first time I've seen him react to anyone. I think he must like you."

"Well, Rover, I'm sorry but I need a much bigger dog." Slowly I straightened. I started to walk away when Rover let loose with a pitched howl that startled both Neal and me.

I turned around. "Is he all right?"

"I don't know," Neal admitted. "I've never seen him do anything like that before. In fact, I've never seen him show interest in anyone the whole time he's been here."

"Has that been long?" As cute as he was, in a scruffy sort of way, I had to assume if Rover hadn't been adopted before now, then there must be a good reason.

"Well, longer than most dogs his size. Because of the shape he was in when we found him, it took us several weeks to get him to the point, health-wise, where he could be adopted, and . . ." Neal hesitated.

"And?" I said, wanting him to supply the information.

"He seems to be a bit prickly."

"How do you mean?"

Neal shrugged. "He takes a disliking to some people and a liking to others, but you're the first he's responded to like this."

I guess I should have been flattered.

"Actually, every time any potential owner showed interest, Rover did something that caused them to choose another dog," Neal elaborated, "that is, until he saw you."

I shrugged it off. "He probably smells my lunch or something."

Neal didn't look as if he believed me, but he seemed willing to accept my explanation. We continued down the wide aisle and the further we got from Rover, the louder he howled.

I ignored him until we reached the pen that held the first of the two German shepherds. "What's his name?" I asked.

"This is Shep."

"Hello, Shep," I said and squatted down.

Shep lifted his head and gave me a disinterested look, and then nestled his chin on his paw once more.

In the meantime, Rover was up on his hind legs,

his paws against the lower bar, howling and making all kinds of a ruckus.

Neal stood with his clipboard pressed against his chest. "I've never seen Rover behave like this."

"I don't want a small dog," I emphasized. I was looking to adopt a watchdog that would give the likes of Spenser reason to pause. An eleven-pound mixed breed dog wasn't going to frighten anyone beyond the postman.

"This one is Tinny," Neal said, moving down one pen. "Like in Rin Tin Tin."

"Tinny," I repeated. Tinny was sprawled out, too, and couldn't have cared less that company had arrived to inspect him as a possible adoptee.

Rover continued to howl.

"Perhaps you should take Rover out for a walk," Neal suggested.

"I don't want Rover," I insisted.

Neal grinned and shook his head. "Apparently Rover wants you."

"Oh for the love of heaven, all right, I'll take Rover out for a walk." As far as I was concerned all this fuss was probably because Rover was housebroken and knew enough to let someone know he wanted outside.

Neal retrieved a leash and opened the pen door. I half expected Rover to race out of the cage and exercise his freedom. Instead he walked out with all the dignity of visiting royalty, and stopped directly in front of me. He sat on his haunches and looked up.

"Well, all right," I said, and took the leash from Neal's hands and connected one end to Rover's collar. Neal led the way to the door and that was where we started. I felt a bit ridiculous, walking this silly dog around the grassy area outside the shelter.

We had just crossed through the door when Rover turned his head and looked at me. Our eyes connected and it felt as if an electric shock jolted through me. Neal had joked about Rover choosing me, but I could see that this was no exaggeration. This dog had already claimed me as his owner. He was determined to go home with me.

I pulled my gaze away and returned to the shelter where Neal waited. "That was quick," he said.

"Tell me more about Rover," I asked.

"Well, like I said, he was half-starved and in poor shape physically when he was found." He flipped the pages and paused with a frown. "We believe he was an abused animal."

"Abused in what way?"

"It's difficult to tell, but the notes here suggest that he was physically and psychologically harmed."

"Which explains his reaction with other potential owners," I murmured softly, thinking out loud.

A dog that needed healing. I wondered if it was possible that Rover had recognized the pain in my own heart. Rover continued to hold my gaze, his look intent. I knew I should give this decision more thought—factor in the issues it might cause for the inn, especially if it turned out that he had a prickly personality. Yet something inside me said it would be okay . . . more than okay. Rover belonged with me at Rose Harbor Inn.

I squinted down at the dog and blinked back tears. "Did Paul send you?" I whispered.

Rover's gaze remained unwavering. It was because of Paul that I was living in Cedar Cove. He'd sent two wounded souls to be the first guests at the B&B and now he had thrust a dog in my path. Not just any dog, either, but one wounded in spirit and heart. The decision was made. I would bring Rover home with me.

Chapter 28

Abby and her mother pulled into the parking lot at the Pancake Palace where Patty had suggested they meet for lunch. Already Abby's heart palpitated as she mentally prepared herself for seeing some of her old schoolmates. Friends she'd once considered sisters but had blatantly ignored since Angela's funeral. She wondered if they'd be as welcoming as Patty, or if they would be so bold as to bring up the accident. Did people still think she might have been drunk or reckless behind the wheel that night?

Her mother seemed unnaturally silent, too. She appeared to feel Abby's hesitation and doubts. Linda

Kincaid placed her hand on top of Abby's. "You ready?" she asked softly.

Abby nodded, although dread built up like bile in the back of her throat. It shouldn't be this hard, and it wouldn't be if she hadn't shut everyone off so completely. Despite Patty's reassurances, Abby's fears ran rampant. What would she say if someone brought up Angela or the accident? She decided she would just be honest and tell them the accident had changed the course of her life. Perhaps she'd need to defend herself against their accusations; if that happened, she wasn't sure what she'd do.

"It will be good to see your friends," her mother said, her voice unnaturally high, as if she was trying to reassure herself as well as Abby. "You had so many good friends in high school."

"Yes," Abby concurred, forcing herself to smile. "Everything went well yesterday when I ran into Patty at the pharmacy. It will now, too." She hoped.

Abby opened the car door and climbed outside. The blast of the damp and cold was instantaneous.

Her mother joined her, wrapping her arm around her elbow. Together the two walked into the Pancake Palace. Right away the crusty old waitress that Abby remembered from her youth crossed their path in her pink uniform and white apron, moving from table to table wielding a glass coffeepot.

"Is that Goldie?" her mother asked. "My goodness, I would have thought she'd have retired by now."

Apparently Goldie's hearing was just fine because she turned to glance in their direction. She squinted as though she didn't immediately recognize Abby or Linda. The older woman shifted her weight and pressed her hand against her hip before walking toward them. "I remember you . . . now don't tell me your name," she instructed, wagging her index finger at Abby.

Since her picture and the scene of the accident had been plastered across the local newspaper for what had seemed like weeks on end, Abby had no doubt Goldie would remember her, despite the years.

"Kincaid, right?"

"Right," Abby said, grinning despite her nervousness.

"You with Patty's group?" She didn't give them an opportunity to answer. "She reserved the party room in the back. There's a whole gang of girls back there, making more racket than they did as teenagers." She winked at Abby. "Good to see you, Lambcakes."

"Lambcakes?" Abby repeated softly as a warm sensation filled her. She led the way to the rear of the restaurant where the party room was situated. Lambcakes was the pet name Goldie had dubbed her as a teenager. The waitress had remembered.

The party room was behind two glass doors with square wood panels. It was relatively small, with just enough space for one long table that seated twelve to fifteen. Abby could hear the happy chatter even before she reached the area.

The conversation died the instant Abby and her mother walked into the room. For an instant Abby was sure she was about to relive her worst nightmare. But the lull lasted no longer than a couple of heartbeats before she was instantly surrounded by friends she'd known nearly her entire childhood. And from the corner of her eye, she could see Patty's mother embracing Linda warmly.

"Abby, Abby." Marie, one of her closest childhood friends quickly hugged her. "I've missed you so much."

"You look fabulous."

"You haven't changed a bit since high school."

"How long are you in town for?"

"We've missed you at the reunions."

"Oh, it's just so good to see you."

Questions and comments seemed to come at Abby from every direction as her friends surrounded her. Abby tried to answer but before she was able to respond, another question or comment was thrust at her.

"Girls, girls." Patty broke into the fray, raising her hands above her head in order to attract their attention. "For the love of heaven give Abby room to breathe."

Her friends started to spread out, granting Abby and her mother the opportunity to find their seats.

"Let's all sit down," Patty instructed next.

"Patty always was a take-charge sort of person,"

Suzie reminded Abby, as she gave her a squeeze around her waist.

"Bossy, you mean," Marie added and then laughed. "But we wouldn't have it any other way."

"We love her for it," Amy added. "If it wasn't for Patty, we wouldn't have known Abby was in town. Remember the time you, Patty, and I snuck into the boys locker room in junior high?"

Abby would never forget how embarrassed they were when the assistant coach walked out of the shower and into the locker area. The girls had assumed they were alone. They had screamed and raced out of the room. The memory immediately produced giggles from everyone.

Abby was directed to a chair in the middle of the table and her mother sat down next to her, beside Patty's mom.

"What brings you to town?" Laurie asked.

"I'm here for my brother's wedding," Abby explained.

"Roger's getting married?" Allison said, pressing her hand over her heart. "I had the biggest crush on him in high school."

Abby grinned. All her friends had thought Roger was a hunk—she wondered if girls used the same terminology these days.

"Is he still as handsome as he was when we were teenagers?" Suzie asked, folding her hands and pressing them below her chin as she released a slow sigh of adoration.

"More so," Abby's mother insisted. "He's marrying Victoria Templeton."

"I know her family," Amy said. "They're good people."

"Lucky Victoria," Marie muttered.

"Can we stop talking about Roger? We're all married and Roger is about to be, so it's a lost cause. I want to find out about Abby." This comment came from Allison, who sat across from Abby.

Marie pressed her elbows against the table. "Shame on you. You haven't attended a single reunion," she charged, "and might I remind you, Abby Kincaid, you were the senior class president."

"Well, yes . . ." Abby started to say and was interrupted.

"Just tell us about you," Suzie said, leaning against the table. "Update us on your life. Are you married? Children? I have identical twins, can you believe it? And I just found out I'm pregnant again."

Her news was followed by a round of congratulations.

"Enough about you, Suzie," Patty said, "we want to hear from Abby."

Once again the questions came at Abby from all directions, but thankfully Patty stepped in again. "One at a time, okay? Marie, you're sitting the closest to Abby, so you go first."

For a full hour they didn't even glance at their menus. Goldie, all on her own, brought them salty, hot French fries with ice-cold sodas, which had been a favorite of Abby and Angela's, and just about everyone else, too.

"I just started a diet," Suzie cried. "It's my third one this week."

"Diet tomorrow," Marie insisted, reaching in the middle of the table for a French fry. "Besides, this is diet soda, right, Goldie?"

"Wouldn't serve you girls anything else," their waitress said as she moved around the outside of the table, refilling the tall glasses.

"All right, all right, I'll have a French fry," Suzie agreed, "but only one."

Abby laughed. Suzie had been on a diet for as long as she could remember. They used to jog together and had even joined the cross-country team as sophomores, but that had only lasted the one year.

"Yogurt again?" Abby teased, remembering the diet Suzie had been on before graduation. She ate yogurt three times a day for a week and gained a pound.

"You know, I've joined Weight Watchers so many times, when I last signed up, I used a pseudonym."

They all laughed.

Suzie reached for a French fry and popped it in her mouth. "I'll have a salad for lunch."

"Remember you're eating for two or three," Abby teased and they all laughed.

"Chef salad with dressing on the side," Goldie said, shaking her head as though amused.

The conversation continued throughout lunch. When Abby glanced at her watch she was shocked to see that two hours had lapsed. She'd ordered a side salad along with Suzie but she'd barely had a chance to eat a bite. It felt so incredibly good to be with her old friends again. They laughed, joked, reminisced, and updated one another on their lives since high school and college. Abby was the only one unmarried and without children.

Sitting with her friends, it struck Abby that each one of them had moved forward in their lives. She was the only one stuck in the past, fearing the future, in a holding pattern, waiting . . . and for what she didn't know. The endless before and after of Angela's death. With this realization came another. Chatter continued around her and she realized that her friends were genuinely happy to see her. What she'd been waiting for, Abby understood, was for someone to punish her. It was what she'd expected; what she'd been holding her breath anticipating. Only it hadn't happened. She had spent the last fifteen years punishing herself.

"I'd like to apologize to all of you," she said, and paused to clear her throat.

The room went shockingly quiet as her high school friends all locked their eyes on her.

"I realize I was rude and unfriendly following the . . . accident," Abby continued. "Each one of you contacted me and I . . . I was feeling so wretched and guilty that I wasn't able to deal with anything beyond my own grief. I can't tell you how much it means to see you all now." Tears flooded her eyes and she quickly wiped them away. "Thank you for being my friends when I wasn't even a friend to myself."

"Oh Abby . . ."

"We love you," Patty said and reached for Abby's hand and gave it a gentle squeeze. "Everyone knew you were having an impossibly hard time after the accident. The heart heals at its own pace. We're just happy to have you back."

"I'll forgive you," Marie added, "but only if you promise to attend the next class reunion."

"I promise," Abby answered.

"And if you never mention that yogurt diet again," Suzie added.

They all laughed and the laughter was a healing balm. Everyone spoke at once, offering excuses, understanding, eager to resume their friendships.

Abby's mother reached for Abby's hand and locked their fingers together, offering her silent support.

Abby looked back at her friends. "I dreaded returning to Cedar Cove for the wedding, but I'm so pleased I did. It's been wonderful to see everyone again."

"Let's throw Suzie a baby shower," Allison suggested. "You always planned the best parties. You'd fly back to Cedar Cove for that, wouldn't you?"

Abby laughed. "It would be easier if everyone came to me," she teased.

"Very funny," Suzie joked and then growing serious asked, "Is anyone interested in the rest of those French fries?"

Again they all laughed.

Laurie, the quietest of the bunch, reached for her purse in order to pay her share of the bill.

"Listen," Abby said, gathering her resolve. "Before everyone gets ready to leave I'd like to ask a question."

"Sure." Again Patty answered for the group. "Fire away."

"Do . . . do you ever see Angela's family?"

Her question brought up a pregnant pause.

"Her parents still live in town," Laurie said.

"Her brother is in the Spokane area, I think," Amy added.

"How are Angela's parents?" Abby asked next. They'd been so bitter and angry the last time Abby had attempted to talk to them, especially Angela's mother.

"Okay, I guess," Patty said, looking around the table for someone to add more details. "Charlene stops by the pharmacy now and again, but we don't really have a lot to say to each other."

"The Whites stay mostly to themselves these days."

"Mike White used to play golf," Patty's mother remembered.

"Yes," Abby's mother said. "Mike and Tom were often a twosome on the golf course. Unfortunately that changed after . . ." She didn't need to finish for Abby to know what she'd intended to say. After the accident . . . their relationship was strained to the breaking point and they no longer spoke to each other.

"Do you ever talk to them?" Amy asked Abby.

Abby shook her head. "I tried several times in the year after the accident, but they didn't want anything to do with me."

"You should try again," Patty's mother suggested. "I know how hard it will be for you."

"Maybe you'll feel better if you make one more effort," Linda said, "and really that's all you can do. At least you'll have the satisfaction of knowing you reached out to them."

"Use your own judgment," Amy urged with that same gentleness of spirit Abby remembered from their school days.

After paying their tabs, her friends stood to leave. Abby hugged each one as they left the party room until only the two mothers and Patty remained.

Patty and Abby hugged. "Thank you," Abby whispered, giving her friend an extra long hug. "I can't tell you how much this meant to me." It had helped her find a way back to all that had once been good in her life. It had filled Abby with hope for the future.

"It was my pleasure." Slowly they broke apart.

Linda hugged Patty, too.

"I'm sorry so few of our mothers could make it.

This is a busy weekend and I really didn't have much time to plan it."

"It worked out beautifully," Abby's mother assured her.

The four women left the Pancake Palace together. Abby's spirits were high. Her welcome to Cedar Cove had been so much more than she'd ever expected, or even hoped.

Patty's vehicle was parked on the other side of the building so they parted ways. Abby climbed into her rental car and immediately started the engine and turned up the heat. The blast of air was immediate.

Her mother slid into the passenger side and slipped her seat belt into place. Rubbing her palms together to generate heat, Linda Kincaid turned to look at Abby.

"Are you going to do it?" she asked.

Her mother didn't need to elaborate for Abby to understand the question. She wanted to know if Abby would stop by to see Angela's parents.

Abby hesitated. "I didn't mention where I was earlier. I went out to the cemetery to visit Angela's grave."

"Oh, sweetheart, that must have been so hard."

"I expected it would be, but it wasn't nearly as difficult as I assumed."

"About her parents . . . ?" Linda left the rest of the question hanging in the air between them.

"I know this sounds impossible, but while I was at

the cemetery I felt like Angela asked me to try to talk to her parents."

"Oh, Abby."

"It's been weighing on my mind ever since. I didn't think I could do it."

"And now?"

"Being with my friends just now convinced me that I have to try. If the Whites don't want to see me, then fine, but I think Angela would want me to at least try." If her mother thought it was odd that Abby was talking to a friend fifteen years in the grave she didn't say anything.

"The two of you were always so very close," she murmured. "I'm sure she would want you to see her parents."

"You think I should?" Abby asked, seeking confirmation.

Her mother hesitated and then nodded.

"Then I will."

When Abby glanced at her mother, she saw tears in Linda's eyes. "You make me very proud, Abby."

"Oh, Mom."

"I mean it. You've carried a heavy burden . . . one that you should never have had to carry."

"It's time," Abby said, and for the first time since Angela's death she was ready to lay aside the mantle of guilt.

"Do you want me to go with you?" her mother asked.

It was a generous offer. Nevertheless, Abby shook her head.

"Thanks, but this is something I need to do alone."

Abby held her mother's look for a long time before she was able to offer her a reassuring smile.

Chapter 29

Josh sat with his mother's Bible resting in his lap. Reverently he turned the pages and read her notes in the margins, finding solace in the fact that she had made her peace with God and seemed to have no fear of death.

After hating Richard all these years, accepting that his stepfather was capable of any act of benevolence overwhelmed him.

A gruff noise came from behind the closed bedroom door.

"Richard's awake," Michelle said and started down the hallway toward the master bedroom.

Josh joined her.

When she opened the door, Josh saw that Richard was leaning on his side against one elbow, struggling to sit upright. Michelle and Josh both rushed to him.

"What are you doing?" Michelle cried.

"I thought you'd left," Richard murmured, directing the comment at Josh. His voice was barely above a rasp as he struggled to breathe. Apparently the attempt to sit up had completely drained him of energy.

"All in good time," Josh said, his voice low as he struggled to find the words to thank his stepfather. "I've been reading through Mom's Bible. I'm grateful to have it. Thank you."

Josh helped ease his stepfather back onto his pillow and then sat on the edge of the mattress, pulling up the covers until they were tucked under Richard's chin.

His stepfather focused on Josh. "Teresa read that Bible every day. She made me a better man . . . without her . . . I failed you and I failed Dylan." Tears rolled down the older man's cheeks. "I loved her . . . nothing was right after she died." Richard's eyes were rheumy and moist and he seemed to have trouble keeping them open.

"There's . . . more." He choked out the words as if speaking caused him pain and sapped what little strength he possessed. He brought his arm out from beneath the blankets and grabbed hold of Josh's forearm, his grip so weak that Josh barely felt it.

"More?" Josh asked.

"Garage."

"Tell me later," Josh advised, seeing how difficult it was for his stepfather to speak. "After you've had a chance to rest."

"No time."

"Okay," Josh said and bent his ear closer to the old man's face.

"Garage."

"It's in the garage?" Josh asked.

Richard nodded ever so slightly. "Boxes."

"In boxes," Josh clarified.

Again the old man responded with a faint nod and pointed his finger at the ceiling.

"He wants you to give him a moment," Michelle said. "He can barely speak."

Richard's gaze sought out Josh's and he shook his head. Again he raised his finger.

Josh looked over at Michelle, who was sitting on the other side of the bed. She was holding Richard's hand, gently rubbing it with her own, as though to encourage him.

"Back . . . far back."

"Okay," Josh said.

"Teresa's name."

"Is on the boxes?" Josh asked.

Richard closed his eyes as though completely drained of strength and slumped against his pillow.

"We should let him rest now," Michelle whispered.

Josh agreed. Slowly he stood and stepped back from the bed.

Michelle studied him. "Do you want to check this out?" she asked.

He nodded, but his focus remained on Richard. The old man seemed to be resting peacefully. After a moment, Josh turned and followed Michelle out of the bedroom, softly closing the door behind him. His hand remained on the knob when he spoke.

"Thank you for everything," he told her. He wouldn't have lasted a single day if not for her and it was important for her to understand how much she'd helped him. It made Josh feel that much worse about having misled her romantically.

She shrugged off his appreciation.

Michelle was responsible for him getting his mother's Bible. And it went without saying that Richard wouldn't have mentioned the boxes either if not for Michelle's influence and calming presence.

Michelle was already halfway out the front door before Josh joined her. Moving down the icy walkway, she led him to the side door to the garage and turned on the light.

The car parked inside was the same one Richard had owned when Josh joined the military all those years ago. The only tools on the thick wooden workbench were a screwdriver and hammer.

As kids, Josh and Dylan had often used the garage as a meeting area where they could talk without the fear of their parents listening in. They'd shared secrets and plans in this old building. The basketball hoop remained positioned at the front of the garage but the net had long since been removed. Or it might have rotted away, for all Josh knew.

"Over here," Michelle said. She rushed toward the back and then abruptly turned to look at Josh. "There aren't any boxes here." The garage was barren, unlike what Josh remembered. Richard must have gotten rid of everything other than the necessities. A rake and a shovel hung next to a stepladder on the wall.

Josh glanced around and saw that Michelle was right. The garage was basically empty.

"Above," he said. "There's a storage area up above." He craned his neck to look up. "That's what he meant when he raised his finger. He was trying to tell us to look up." Josh retrieved the ladder and set it below the opening.

Michelle held on to the two back legs as Josh started the climb. "Be careful," she warned.

He kept his attention focused upward until he reached the last rung of the ladder. He lifted the square lid that led to the storage area and slid it aside.

"Here," Michelle called.

When he glanced down he saw that she'd found a flashlight. She handed it up to him and Josh switched it on. Standing on the top rung, he was able to look inside the storage area. Using the flashlight he surveyed the space and found a series of boxes crammed into the tight space. Reaching for a box, he read "Christmas Decorations" written in large letters with a thick black felt pen. Shoving that aside, he reached for a second box. That, too, was marked for Christmas. In fact every box appeared to be related to Christmas.

"Find anything?" Michelle asked.

"Not yet." It looked like he was going to have to crawl up there to investigate further.

"Look inside one of the Christmas boxes," Michelle suggested.

"Okay." He opened the closest one, and sure enough discovered tree ornaments. "That's not it," he called down, knowing Michelle was curious.

"Try another one."

Josh did and hit pay dirt. Inside the box was another smaller box. Penned by the same hand was his mother's name. Excited now, Josh scooted it toward the opening.

"Give it to me," Michelle said, raising her arms to receive the box.

Josh carefully lowered it into her waiting arms.

"Got it," she called out.

Josh continued his search until he located three other boxes, each one with his mother's name spelled across the top and tucked inside a box marked for Christmas. If he hadn't looked inside as Michelle had suggested, he would have missed them entirely.

"Let's go back inside," Michelle said.

Cold now, Josh was eager to comply. He came back down, closed up the crawl space, and then folded the ladder, putting it back where he'd found it. Then he reached for two of the boxes, stacking them one on top of the other. Michelle took the other one. Bringing them into the house, Josh set them on the kitchen table.

The first box contained items he barely remembered and had never hoped to see again. The first thing he pulled out was the blue padded baby book his mother had started for him after he was born. Reverently he opened it to find the newspaper clipping announcing his birth along with a copy of the birth announcement his parents had mailed to family and friends. The gentle slope and loopy letters of his mother's handwriting caught him by surprise as a rush of emotion hit him.

Turning the page, he discovered a picture of himself as a newborn with a scrunched-up red face and a tiny blue bow in his hair. He certainly hadn't won any baby beauty contests.

"You were handsome even back then," Michelle teased.

"Yeah, right."

He closed the book. He'd examine it later. Next he removed a small box that held a tiny blue baby outfit.

"I bet that's the outfit your mother brought you home from the hospital in. My mother saved mine, too."

As he dug deeper into the box Josh found a journal in his mother's favorite color—lime green.

"What's that?" Michelle asked.

"Mom's diary. She kept one for as long as I can remember."

The second box held an equal bounty. He discovered a cookbook that had belonged to his father's mother and a series of letters his parents had exchanged while dating.

"Oh, Josh, this is amazing," Michelle said.

It was indeed amazing. The full significance had yet to hit him. Josh realized that these three boxes contained the missing pieces of his past that he had never expected to find.

Earlier he'd been concerned about his high school letterman's jacket, mostly because he'd paid for it himself and it had seemed so hard-earned. But he wasn't any sports hero—the fact that Richard had destroyed it had annoyed him, but the truth was it didn't hold much significance for him. Not like this.

The contents of these boxes were directly related to him . . . to his heritage. Treasures from his past. It went without saying that Richard had purposely hidden them from him. After his stepfather's death, the house would have been sold and the contents donated to a charitable organization. No one would have thought twice about boxes marked "Christmas." It was unlikely anyone would have thought to look inside before giving them away.

The only person who would value these items was Josh. Anyone else would likely have tossed them in the garbage bin but to him they were everything.

"Richard disguised these boxes so you wouldn't find them," Michelle said and looked saddened by the thought. She was slowly beginning to understand the depth of Richard's maliciousness toward Josh.

Josh didn't bother to comment.

Michelle pressed her hand over his forearm. "You thanked me earlier, but I'm the one who should be thanking you."

"I can't imagine why," he said as he tucked his mother's journal back inside the box. Josh felt as if he were on an emotional roller coaster—with Richard and with Michelle, too. For years he'd comfortably ignored his emotions, stuffing them down rather than confronting them head-on. Now they seemed to be staring him in the face and so he did what was most comfortable. He pretended to feel nothing.

Chapter 30

Neal, the volunteer from the Cedar Cove Animal Shelter, filled out the necessary paperwork and handed it to me. I gave him my debit card and after I signed on the appropriate line, it was time for me to take Rover home. It dawned on me as I quickly scanned the shelter's adoption papers that I had absolutely nothing at the house for a dog. Not a leash, nor dog food, a carrier, or anything else. To be perfectly honest, I wasn't even sure what all I'd need. But I was fairly confident that the local pet store would be more than happy to fill in the blanks.

"Can I leave Rover here for an hour or two?" I

asked as I checked my watch. I assumed I had plenty of time to run to the store and back to the shelter.

Neal's eyes widened momentarily with surprise. "I thought you were eager to take Rover with you."

"I am, but I need to run to the store. I don't have a leash or anything else."

"Well, sure. I'll put him back in the pen until you return. Just a reminder—we close at four on Saturdays."

"Oh, I'll be back long before then," I promised. I intended to head to the pet store, get what I needed, and then return right away for Rover.

As soon as I turned to leave, Rover, who was inside a carrier, released a long, low howl that startled me. "It's all right, fellow, I'll be back," I said with as much reassurance as I could muster.

"I've never heard him make that sound before," Neal said, looking somewhat taken aback.

I started to leave a second time and again Rover howled as though in terrible pain. He didn't stop with one low howl this time, but continued with the pitiful, mournful cry that sounded as if he were in the throes of pain and terrible grief.

Several people who were sitting in the waiting area glanced up. The manager, who'd been working with another couple, turned to Neal.

"What's wrong?" she asked, clearly concerned.

Neal did his best to explain. "The dog doesn't want her to leave without him."

"Rover's been adopted?" She looked surprised but pleased.

"Yes . . ."

"Then she should take him."

"Yes," Neal agreed.

I wasn't sure what to do.

"Rover doesn't understand that you're coming back," Neal explained, speaking above the sound of Rover's moans.

"Oh dear."

"I'll tell you what," Neal said, lowering his voice. "I'll loan you this pet carrier as long as you promise to return it this afternoon. That way you can take Rover now."

"Sure, no problem." At least I hoped it wouldn't be a problem. My one concern was leaving him in the car while I went into the shop. But I doubted the pet store would object to me bringing a dog inside, especially if he was already in a carrier.

I crouched down on the floor so that Rover could see me. He raised his paw against the bars and barked once as though to get my attention. Slowly he lowered his paw and regarded me with deep, dark, soulful eyes that seemed to plead with me not to leave him behind.

"Don't worry," I whispered and thought myself ridiculous for believing a dog would understand.

"I'll walk out with you," Neal said, lifting the carrier.

I straightened, looped my purse strap over my shoulder, retrieved my car keys, and led the way into the parking lot. "Is this behavior common?" I asked Neal. As a volunteer, he must have seen literally hundreds of dogs find homes.

"No," he was quick to tell me. "I've never seen anything like it. Marnie, the manager, and I, feared we wouldn't be able to place Rover. Until you, his behavior has made placement nearly impossible. I don't know how to explain it. It isn't possible, of course, but it's almost as if he was waiting for you and he rejected everyone else until you walked through the door."

It was odd. I'd hoped that Rover would lose his ferocity now that he had a home with me. If not, it could be a serious problem with guests at the inn. That said, I didn't second guess my decision for an instant.

"Would it be all right if I stopped by the inn in a week or so to see how Rover is adjusting?" Neal asked as he loaded the carrier into the rear seat of my car.

"Of course."

"I can't help being curious."

As a matter of fact, I was interested in how Rover and I would adjust, too. I remembered Paul had loved dogs and when he originally enlisted in the military he'd hoped to work with the canine unit. But following basic training he'd gone into the Ranger program instead.

As soon as he realized he wasn't being left behind, Rover laid down in the carrier, head forward, and promptly closed his eyes. After saying good-bye and my thanking him, Neal returned to the shelter and I turned on the car engine. Before pulling out of the parking lot, I twisted around to glance at Rover.

"Did Paul send you?" I asked again in a whisper.

Rover lifted his head and cocked it quizzically.

"Never mind; I have a very strong feeling that he did." As I drove away from the shelter I felt sure that Paul had intervened in my life once again, this time bringing me this small companion. We would help each other, I believed.

The stop at the pet store took longer than I anticipated. By the time I'd accumulated all the paraphernalia required for a dog an hour had passed. I'd never intended to be away from the inn this long, so I hurried back to the shelter to return the carrier. Rover had made the transfer to the new one I'd purchased without a qualm, almost as if he knew exactly what was required of him.

Neal wasn't around when I carted the carrier back into the shelter. I didn't stay longer than necessary and hurried back to where I'd left the car. When I opened the driver's-side door Rover looked up, saw it was me, and immediately put his head back down, resting his chin on his front paws.

I drove directly back to the inn. At breakfast both my guests had said not to expect them for tea that afternoon. If life had taught me anything it was that plans change, though, and I wanted to be prepared in case either of them found themselves at loose ends and returned to the inn.

After parking my car I was relieved to see that both my guests' vehicles were nowhere in sight. I brought Rover out of the car and unzipped the carrier, attached his leash, and lifted him out.

"You might want to acquaint yourself with the grass," I told him. The woman who'd waited on me at the pet store said that Rover would want to mark his territory.

He shivered in the cold and looked up at me doubtfully.

"Do your thing," I said, waving him forward, eager to get inside where it was warm.

He twisted his head around and looked at me a second time with the same questioning look.

"You know . . . relieve yourself," I elaborated, gesturing with my hand once more.

After a moment he apparently got the idea and lifted his hind leg against a bush. Then, as if he knew exactly where to go, he trotted toward the inn, leading me up the steps.

"All right, all right," I said, smiling to myself. I unlocked the front door and swung it open. "It's a big house, you're welcome to look around," I told him.

I unfastened the leash and expected Rover to immediately go exploring. To my surprise he sat down on his back haunches and studied me.

"What?" I asked. This was the most peculiar dog.

Rover just continued to stare up at me as though he was waiting—for what I could only speculate.

"Well fine," I muttered. "You can stay right here if you want, I've got things to do." I traipsed back to the car and lugged in the two heavy bags of supplies I'd purchased at the pet store. First things first, I made room in the pantry for the bag of dry dog food and the cans.

I was still rearranging the storage area when I was interrupted by the chime of the doorbell. Immediately Rover barked ferociously and raced so fast into the entryway that his hind legs nearly went out from under him on the polished wood floor.

I took a deep breath, hoping he wouldn't be aggressive or overly protective with visitors. When I opened the door I was surprised to find Grace Harding from the library on the other side.

"Grace," I said, welcoming her. "This is a surprise. Come in." I pulled the door farther open and then realized Rover was in the way, greeting her with a low growl. "Rover," I said, chastising him, "this is a friend." To my relief, he immediately backed off and sat down.

"I apologize for stopping in unannounced," Grace said. "Neal phoned and told me you'd adopted Rover and I was concerned."

"Concerned?" I straightened and led the way into

the kitchen. Without asking, I automatically put water on the stove for a pot of tea. I hoped Grace would stay long enough to join me.

Rover found the braided rug in front of the refrigerator, curled up, and watched me as I moved about the kitchen.

"Rover is . . . a troubled dog."

"Really?" I hid a smile. What Grace and Neal didn't know was that this dog and I had already bonded. I was pretty sure we understood each other.

"Well, he certainly looks content now," she added, and seemed surprised. "Neal said that Rover had the most unusual reaction to you." She paused as though she expected me to fill in the blanks; only I didn't know what to tell her. We had barely met and I wasn't comfortable explaining that I had just come through a major loss, which was why my heart felt wide open to this small dog. It was impossible to know exactly what had transpired in Rover's short life, but apparently he hadn't had such an easy time of it either.

Years ago I remember reading the story of a construction worker who'd been hurt on the job, losing the use of his arm. A friend had suggested he adopt a dog and he'd gone to the shelter. That dog chose him. I knew without a doubt that Rover had chosen me.

"It looks like you're adapting to each other just fine."

"We are," I assured her.

Grace continued to frown. "He hasn't . . . well, you've only had him a short while."

"Hasn't what?" I asked.

"Never mind."

"No, tell me," I said. The kettle on the stove whistled. I removed it, poured the hot water into the teapot, and automatically brought down two cups.

"Perhaps another time. I really can't stay long. Cliff is at home waiting for me and I told him I would only be a few minutes."

"Do you have time for tea?" I asked.

She hesitated. "It does look inviting."

"You have time," I assured her. I was sure her husband wouldn't begrudge her a cup of tea.

Grace unfastened her coat and slipped it over the back of a chair and then sat on one of the stools by the kitchen counter.

I poured the tea and placed the sugar bowl and milk in the center of the counter. Then I scooted a stool to the other side, so we could sit directly across from each other.

"A few weeks ago we had a couple of men come through the shelter," Grace said. "They asked to see what dogs were available for adoption. I had my suspicions right away—something didn't feel right about those two. They lingered for a bit and wandered out to where we walk the dogs. Another volunteer happened to have Rover on a leash and the dog went ballistic when he saw the two men, barking crazily and tugging at his leash."

"Perhaps he knew them?"

Grace reached for her teacup and held it with both hands. "Perhaps. We'll never know for sure. One thing was certain, he had the same feeling I did."

"Have you learned anything about them since that time?"

Grace shook her head. "It was just a feeling. If they'd applied to adopt one of the animals, I would have found an excuse to refuse them. They gave me the creeps."

I sipped my tea, wondering how Rover had known. Grace, too, for that matter. Perhaps the men ran a puppy mill. Well, it wouldn't do any good to speculate. They didn't get any of the dogs.

"Given the opportunity, I feel Rover would have gladly taken a chunk off their legs."

"In other words, you're afraid Rover might be a biter?"

Grace looked down and then nodded. "Keep an eye on him, okay?"

"Will do."

"Let me know if there are any problems, all right?"

"I will," I promised, but in my heart of hearts, damaged as it was, I knew that wouldn't be the case. After all, it wasn't every day that someone got adopted by a dog.

Chapter 31

Very little had changed about Angela's family home, Abby noticed, as she eased to a stop in front of the Whites' residence. The rambler with its shuttered windows and large three-car garage was as familiar to her as her own childhood home.

At one time Abby had spent as much time at Angela's house as she had at her own. More Fridays than she could count, Abby had spent the night with her best friend. Often they'd stayed awake until dawn, chattering and laughing, so young and silly. The most pressing decision was which boy's invitation they would accept for prom. Those days seemed a lifetime ago now.

The Whites were never the same after burying their daughter, or so Abby had repeatedly heard. Did parents ever recover from the death of a child? She prayed she would never have to answer that question herself.

With her hands braced against the steering wheel, she sucked in a deep breath and then reluctantly turned off the car engine. Her resolve weakened as she approached the house, clenching her purse in her hands. The hedge along the walkway was missing, she noticed. Funny how that small detail would catch her attention. In its place, Charlene White had cut out two foot-wide flower beds.

A memory flashed through her mind and she smiled. It had happened shortly after Angela started wearing Brandon Edmond's class ring. She'd hidden her arm behind her back to surprise Abby. She'd wanted to dramatically whip her arm around to show her friend the ring.

The surprise had been all Angela's though. The ring had flown off her finger, landing deep inside the hedge. The two of them had spent hours on their hands and knees searching for Brandon's ring. Thankfully they'd eventually found it, but not before a lot of angst.

Pausing halfway up the walkway, Abby felt herself drowning in the memories of her friend. After all these years she still missed Angela's easy laugh, her quick wit, and her zest for life.

"I don't know that this is such a good idea," she muttered under her breath just as if Angela was standing next to her.

"**Just do it.**" Angela seemed to be telling her.

Oh great, Abby thought to herself, not only am I hearing voices, they are speaking in clichés. This is ridiculous.

Still, she couldn't make herself turn away. It was now or never. Her brother's wedding was due to start in three hours and the rest of the day would be consumed with the ceremony and the wedding reception. Then in the morning, she'd leave for Florida at the crack of dawn. A late night, an early morning, and a flight home—if she was going to confront Angela's parents, it had to be now.

With renewed resolve, Abby approached the front door. Her one hope was that Angela's family wouldn't be home. Then she would feel that she'd done her duty, and could leave in good conscience.

Angela couldn't fault her if that happened. She was going to be in town for such a limited time, that this would have to be it.

Holding in her breath, she rang the doorbell. Her finger bounced against that round white button, her touch light and hesitant.

Almost right away Abby's hopes were dashed as she heard movement on the other side of the door.

"Coming," Michael White, Angela's father, called out.

Abby held her breath as the front door was unlatched and opened. Mr. White stopped and stared at her. Abby watched as the blood drained from his face.

"Hello, Mr. White."

He appeared to be in shock and didn't acknowledge her.

"Who is it?" Angela's mother called from the kitchen, and then joined her husband.

Charlene White stood next to Mike and stared at Abby with widening eyes. "You have a lot of nerve," she whispered, almost as if the words were being wrenched from her throat.

"I'm in town for my brother's wedding," Abby blurted out, saying the first thing that came to mind, as if she needed an excuse, an explanation.

"Oh yes, your parents must be happy to be able to attend their child's wedding. Unfortunately Mike and I—"

"Charlene," Mr. White said, cutting her off. He reached forward and unlocked the screen door. "Come inside, Abby," he said.

"Mike, no . . ."

Not sure what to do, Abby hesitated.

Mr. White turned toward his wife. "It's time, Char. Angela would have wanted us to welcome her friend."

"How can you say that?" Mrs. White quietly turned and left the room.

Stunned, Abby remained frozen, standing outside as the cold wind whipped about her. Her hair flew in her face, slapping against her cheek as if to punish her for her audacity.

Calmly, ignoring his wife's outburst, Mr. White held open the screen door. "Come inside, Abby, it's chilly out there."

With her feet weighed down with reluctance, Abby stepped into the house. "Thank you," she whispered, as the warmth welcomed her. The first thing she noticed was that they had rearranged their living room and bought new chairs and a sofa. Pictures of what she could only assume were their grandchildren lined the shelves of the bookcases on each side of the fireplace.

"Sit down, please," Mr. White invited, indicating the sofa. "It's time we talked—past time, really."

"Yes, it is," Abby agreed, although the words nearly stuck in her throat. She kept her coat on and sat on the very edge of the cushion.

"You'll need to forgive Charlene; losing Angela remains difficult for her. She's had a hard time of it."

Abby folded her hands, placing them on her knees. "I visited Angela's grave for the first time. I know it sounds unbelievable, but it was as if I could hear her speaking to me. She asked me to contact you and Mrs. White."

He smiled briefly. "As a matter of fact I've had a few conversations with my daughter myself. Unfortunately they are all one-sided and I'm doing all the talking."

Abby didn't elaborate on her experience. If she did, she feared the Whites might think she was nuts.

"Tell me about yourself," Angela's father asked, making polite conversation. "Are you married? Children?"

"I haven't married . . ."

"Yet," he finished for her, "you're much too pretty to remain single much longer."

Embarrassed, Abby glanced down at her clenched hands.

"Greg's married now. He has two children, and lives in the Spokane area."

Angela's brother was older by two years and he'd lived on campus in Pullman for their last couple of years of high school.

"Sarah's nine and Andy's seven," he added.

Abby glanced again at the framed photo of two youngsters on the fireside bookcase. Their gleaming faces smiled into the camera, sweet and innocent. Angela would have been a wonderful aunt to these two precious children.

Until then, Abby had avoided looking at Angela's high school graduation photo, which was prominently displayed on the wall above the fireplace. It nearly filled the entire space. Angela had never been fond of that particular pose and was probably outraged that her mother had chosen to display that shot. Actually, Abby agreed with Mrs. White. Angela looked . . . perfect. The mantel was covered with a dozen or more candles in varying sizes as if it were a shrine to her memory.

Mrs. White returned to the living room, her hands knotted into fists at her sides. "You have a lot of nerve to show up here out of the blue."

"Charlene, please," Mr. White pleaded. "You must know how difficult this is for Abby."

"As it should be." The older woman glared at Abby, her eyes filled with accusation.

"Sit down, honey," Mr. White said as though pleading with his wife.

Mrs. White looked like she wanted to defy her husband, but she must have read something warm and encouraging in his eyes, because she took the chair next to him.

"Do you have something you want to say?" Charlene asked Abby.

"Yes, of course." The lump in Abby's throat felt watermelon-size. "First off I want to tell you how very sorry I am—"

"Sorry. You came to say you're sorry? It's far too late for that."

"Charlene," Mr. White said softly, "let her finish."

"If Angela had been driving that night, you would have been the one killed," Mrs. White continued, ignoring her husband.

"I wish Angela had been driving. I would much

rather have been the one who died." It wasn't like this was a new thought. Abby had gone through all the might-have-beens a thousand times or more.

If only they'd stayed later at the mall.

If they hadn't stopped for dinner after shopping; if they hadn't lingered over their meal, then Angela might be alive today.

If only she'd been paying more attention to the road instead of singing Christmas songs.

The what-ifs had hounded Abby for years, and they didn't seem to get any better with time.

Charlene sat with her back stiff, and avoided looking at Abby as if the mere sight of her alive and well was a painful reminder that her own daughter was buried in a graveyard only a few minutes away.

"That night ended Angela's life and it forever altered mine." Abby's voice cracked and she swallowed hard in an effort to hold back the threatening emotion. "I drove the car that killed my best friend. That isn't something one ever forgets . . ."

"Or forgives," Mrs. White inserted.

"I don't imagine it is," Abby whispered. Her hands were clenched so tightly that her fingers had gone white. "And I should know because I've never been able to forgive myself."

Her statement was met with silence. Mrs. White angled her neck toward the ceiling and appeared to be fighting back tears.

"I miss Angela every single day," the older woman

whispered. "Not a night passes that I don't yearn for my daughter."

"I miss her, too," Abby whispered back.

"Every day?" Mrs. White challenged.

"Most days . . . over the years the ache has gotten lighter, but that doesn't mean I don't think about her often and—"

Again Angela's mother interrupted her. "But the bottom line is that you're alive and she's not. You can marry and give your parents grandchildren."

"I haven't married," Abby said, cutting her off, her hands stretching toward them pleadingly. "In fact, it's as if someone pressed the 'pause' button on my life since the night of the accident. I don't date; I avoid relationships. I live in a town where I don't have family. I just do my job and stick to my own business. I've carried this load of guilt and grief until it's become too heavy for me to haul around any longer."

Both of Angela's parents stared at her.

"I assumed that everyone else blamed me for the accident, too, but they don't. I met Patty Morris at the downtown pharmacy and waited for her to reject me . . . only she didn't. She was happy to see me. So happy in fact that she invited several of my closest high school friends to meet me for lunch this afternoon. And while no one overtly mentioned Angela, she was there; she was with us. I could almost hear her laugh. I could feel her smile. And because she smiled so could I."

Tears flowed down Mrs. White's cheeks. Mr. White's, too. He reached in his rear pocket for his handkerchief and dabbed at his eyes and then loudly blew his nose.

"Angela is gone and as much as I would like to bring her back, I can't. I'm so sorry I can't. This trip home has shown me something that I've overlooked all these years." Abby sniffled and reached for her purse to search for a tissue.

Before she could locate one, Mrs. White handed her one from the box that rested on the lamp stand next to her.

"Thank you," Abby whispered.

"You were about to say something," Mr. White said, gesturing for her to continue. "Something important."

After blowing her nose, Abby scrunched up the tissue in her hand. "What I've overlooked all these years is that this grieving, this guilt, isn't what Angela would have wanted for any of us. She was the most generous, happy person I ever knew. I couldn't be around her and not want to laugh. The minute she walked into a room, the light got brighter. She'd be shocked at what's happened to me . . . "

"And me," Mrs. White added. "I've grown into an old woman."

"A cranky old woman," Mr. White added, reaching for her hand to show his affection in spite of his comment.

"Michael James White, you will apologize for saying that," Charlene insisted.

"Well it's true, and I've done the same thing. We let our bitterness nearly destroy us . . . and our marriage. Abby's right; Angela was a happy person and she would have wanted us to be happy. She would hate what we've become."

"How am I supposed to live without my daughter?" Charlene cried out as the tears streaked her cheeks. "How am I supposed to forget she died and is forever lost to me?"

"We don't want to forget Angela," Mr. White answered. "We had her for nineteen wonderful years. She was our treasure, our joy. We have our memories and until we see her again that will have to carry us. Do you seriously think Angela would want us to destroy our lives because she died?"

"No, she wouldn't," Abby answered. "She'd be the first one to tell me to live and to enjoy life. She'd be the first person to reassure me that while it was tragic that she died, it was an accident. She'd be first in line to tell me I can't accept the blame for a freak accident. I hit ice on the road. Other than the ice, the only one to blame is God Himself, and frankly, I'm unwilling to take on the man upstairs."

Mr. White stood and walked over to where Abby sat. Automatically she stood, too, and he reached for her hands, holding them in his own. "If you came to us today to seek absolution then I'm giving it to you,

Abby. You've punished yourself enough. Be happy, child. Give your parents grandchildren and perhaps . . . perhaps you'll consider sharing them with us. I think Angela would be pleased if you did."

"I think she would be, too," Abby concurred.

"You mentioned earlier that Angela wanted you to seek us out," he continued with the question.

Abby nodded.

"She wants us to give you what you need."

Abby blinked back tears. Mr. White dropped her hands and reached for her to give her a hug.

Abby started to sob and so did he. "God called our daughter home. It isn't your fault, but if you feel you need our forgiveness then you have it."

"Thank you," Abby whispered, mumbling the words as it was impossible to speak clearly.

When Mr. White released her, Angela's mother wrapped her arms around Abby and buried her head in her shoulder as the two of them wept together.

By the time she left the Whites, Abby had received far more from Angela's parents than she dared think was possible. They had given her their permission to enjoy life again.

Chapter 32

Sitting in the living room with Michelle while Richard slept peacefully, Josh relaxed against the back of the chair. He'd finished sorting through the boxes filled with his mother's belongings from before her marriage to Richard. What he'd found was a treasure trove of memorabilia from his early childhood.

It went without saying that anger and pure stubbornness had nearly cost him all of this. Michelle had helped him to look beyond his petty grievances against his stepfather, and he suspected that if he hadn't thanked Richard for relinquishing his mother's Bible he might never have found out about these hidden boxes.

Looking up, Josh found Michelle sitting on the ottoman, leafing through his baby book. A smile lit up her eyes as she turned the pages, examining each photograph.

"I was adorable, wasn't I?" he teased. His mother had taken countless pictures of him. It used to embarrass him when he was little.

"You were the cutest boy in the universe," she confirmed. "I wrote that once on my school binder."

Josh knew that was probably a slight exaggeration.

Michelle glanced up and seemed to read the doubt in his eyes. "You don't believe me, do you?"

"You loved Dylan."

"For a time," she agreed. "Then I got a clue about who the **really** great guy was."

He chuckled. "You always did know how to flatter me."

"Not that it ever did me any good," she muttered, and then as if she'd suddenly remembered something she glanced at her watch. "It's time for Richard's medication."

"I'll give it to him," Josh offered, but Michelle was already on her feet.

"Let me. You can talk to him once the painkillers have set in. He gets pretty grumpy when he's in pain."

"Don't we all." Josh was in a mood to feel generous toward the older man. The sentiment generally didn't last long. No doubt, within five minutes Richard would start berating him and all that goodwill would swish down the drain.

Michelle disappeared down the hallway to the bathroom where Richard's medications were kept. He was taking some pretty heavy painkillers, and while the high dosages had concerned Josh, he could understand that the physician's main priority was keeping Richard comfortable and as pain free as possible in his remaining time. Knowing how stubborn the old man could be, that probably wouldn't be soon. For the first time since his arrival, Josh was glad of that. He found himself hoping for the opportunity to talk more about his mother and, if possible, Dylan.

Michelle was in and out of the bedroom so fast that Josh leaped to his feet, certain something had happened. Her eyes quickly met his and she drew in a deep breath.

"What's wrong?"

"Richard isn't responding and his breathing is only intermittent." Tears filled her eyes and spilled down her cheeks. "It's time, Josh, he's dying," she choked out.

The words came at him like a baseball bat in the dark and clobbered him directly in his chest. "Now?" he asked, frozen with shock.

Michelle nodded. "I have the phone number for

hospice. They know how to handle this . . . we should probably call them." She hurried into the kitchen and reached for the pad on the counter. "Would you mind making the call . . . please." Talking was beyond her at the moment.

Josh reached for the card the hospice worker had left and grabbed the telephone receiver from the wall. To his amazement his own hand trembled as he pressed out the numbers and waited for three excruciating long rings before the hospice line responded. After relaying the necessary information, Josh headed for the bedroom.

While he wasn't exactly the best stepson in the world, he wasn't going to allow Richard to die alone. He'd been with his mother when she'd taken her last breath, and though it wasn't an experience he wanted to repeat, he needed to thank Richard. He needed to let the old man know he appreciated Richard returning Josh's belongings to him.

When Josh opened the bedroom door, Richard's eyes stayed closed. For one frantic moment, Josh feared he was too late and that Richard was already gone. He sat on the edge of the mattress and pressed two fingers against his stepfather's neck. He felt a pulse, but it was weak and intermittent. Michelle hadn't exaggerated the situation. Richard was close to death.

By heaven, the old man intended to thwart him once again. Well, if these were the last words Richard ever heard, then that was fine by Josh. "I found the boxes," he said. He spoke loudly enough for Michelle to hear him all the way in the living room. He wasn't sure how much hearing Richard possessed at this point, and he wanted to be sure to get through to him.

No response.

"Thank you," he said, even louder this time.

Michelle appeared in the doorway. "Josh," she whispered, "what are you doing?"

"Waking the dead," he said.

"He can probably hear you. I've read that hearing is one of the last functions to leave the body."

"I found the boxes in the garage," Josh repeated. "You didn't have to tell me where they were," he added, wanting Richard to understand that he was well aware the old man had intended to hide those boxes, "but I'll be forever grateful that you did."

"Being able to have his mother's things means a lot to Josh," Michelle added, and sat down on the opposite side of the bed. She took Richard's limp hand and held on to it with both of her own.

Richard's eyes opened and he looked up, and seemed to be staring at the ceiling. He didn't appear able to speak, however.

"Thank you," Josh whispered.

Richard's eyes moved and focused squarely on Josh. To Josh's surprise a tenderness rose up inside of him, a sense of impending loss. Part of him wanted to leap off the bed and demand that Richard not die so they could have a relationship. One that wasn't based on competitive jealousy or one-upmanship.

And now it was too late.

Josh felt like weeping. He pressed his forehead against Richard's hand as he struggled with regret.

"Josh." Michelle's voice stirred him and Josh glanced up.

"Look," she whispered. "Look at Richard."

Josh turned his attention to his stepfather's face and was astonished to see that a solitary tear was rolling down the older man's weathered cheek. It was as if he was telling Josh he had his own share of regrets and he, too, was sorry.

Michelle checked Richard's pulse and then bit into her lower lip before she whispered. "He's gone."

"No." Josh refused to believe it. "No, it can't be." Two days ago Richard had been angry enough to demand that Josh vacate his property. He'd nearly screamed in outrage and now he was . . . gone.

Dead.

The release must have been instantaneous for the old man. One minute he was suffering and fighting the pain and the next he'd walked across the chasm between this world and the next. On the other side Josh's mother and Dylan waited with outstretched arms, eager and happy to have Richard join them, welcoming him to the afterlife.

Reaching across Richard's body, Michelle gently squeezed Josh's shoulder. "I'm so sorry."

"No." Again Josh shook his head, refusing to acknowledge his stepfather's death. To his surprise, tears welled in his eyes. Abruptly he turned away, not wanting Michelle to see.

For years there'd been no love lost between Richard and him. The old man had been a real bastard. Still, he was the only remaining link between Josh and his mother. Richard was the man who'd brought happiness back into Teresa's life, and now he was gone.

Dead.

A sob rose in his chest that he managed to choke off.

He felt the mattress shift as Michelle stood. She came around the foot of the bed and stood before him. Bending down she wrapped her arms around his shoulders. Josh hadn't expected comfort. Hadn't ever imagined he would need it.

Looping his own arms around Michelle's waist, he buried his face in her stomach and silently wept. His shoulders shook and then after a few moments he dropped his arms.

He was embarrassed that Michelle had witnessed his breakdown. He wanted to offer excuses and found he had none to give. Before he could say anything the doorbell chimed.

Michelle left the bedroom to answer the door.

Josh was grateful she was gone. He needed a couple

of minutes to compose himself before he was obliged to deal with more mundane matters.

"It happened just a few minutes ago," Michelle was saying as she led the hospice worker into the bedroom.

Josh stood. This was someone he hadn't met. "Josh Weaver," he said and extended his hand to the middle-aged woman in the long black coat. "I'm Richard's son." He stopped and immediately corrected himself. "His stepson."

Michelle came and stood beside him. "I'm a family friend. We were with Richard when he passed."

"Lois Freeland," the woman said softly. "I'm sorry for your loss. I'm here to help you in any way I can."

"Thank you," Josh said.

Lois asked a number of questions, all of which seemed to go over Josh's head. Thankfully Michelle had her wits about her and she answered on Josh's behalf. He felt emotionally incapable of dealing with anything more than this tightening ache in his chest.

After a few minutes he excused himself and returned to the living room, sitting in the recliner that had belonged to Richard. He felt close to his stepfather there, knowing how many hours of the day he had spent in this very chair. Josh leaned forward as he tried to make sense of the churning emotions that seemed to be attacking him from every direction.

Watching someone die wasn't a new experience,

and both his mother's death and Richard's had been peaceful, expected. This time Josh felt a rush of tremendous loss, of having been cheated, robbed. He swallowed his anger like a piece of tough meat, struggling to get it down his throat.

Michelle and Lois joined him. They seemed to be talking but none of what they said made sense. Tuning them out was easy to do as the memories rolled like marbles in his mind.

Josh recalled the first time he'd met Richard and Dylan. His mother had been so pleased to introduce him to her "friend." Teresa had dated before, but none of those relationships had lasted for more than a few weeks. Josh had sensed that Richard was different almost from the first. After spending time with Richard, his mother had seemed almost giddy with happiness.

Some of the men she'd dated made her so angry she'd come home and clean house as a means of venting her displeasure. He smiled at the memory of her on her hands and knees scrubbing out the bottom of the oven, furious over some guy for things she wouldn't discuss with her son.

After her dates with Richard, she'd come home, put on music, and dance by herself, whirling around the room as if she was on some imaginary ballroom floor.

Still, they had dated for several months before she was ready to introduce him to Josh. Josh and Dylan had instantly clicked and the two boys had compared notes. Josh learned that Richard had returned from his dates with Teresa in an equally good mood. The two boys wondered where they went or what they did to make them each so goofy.

In the years since, Josh had come to understand—at least on paper—that this was what it was like when people fell in love.

Teresa and Richard were meant to be together and now they would share eternity.

"Josh."

Breaking off his thoughts, he looked up to discover that Michelle was alone. Apparently the woman from hospice had left or was outside.

"Lois contacted the coroner," Michelle told him. "He'll be here in a few minutes, and once the body has been released, the funeral home will be by."

"What funeral home did you call?"

"Richard had already made the arrangements. He did that as soon as he learned that he was dying, and he gave my family the paperwork to make sure his wishes were carried out as stipulated."

"Okay." At this point Josh was grateful not to have to make decisions.

"He asked to be buried next to your mother."

Josh nodded. That was the way it should be. "He loved her very much," he said.

"And in his own way he loved you. I don't think he realized it until the end."

"That's funny," Josh whispered, swallowing hard.

"How do you mean?"

Josh's gaze met hers and he felt the moisture gathering in his eyes. "I was just thinking the same thing. I hated him for so long . . . but I didn't realize how close love and hate could be. I suspect he didn't either."

Chapter 33

After my assurances regarding Rover, Grace left, seemingly relieved at how well my adopted protector had settled into his new environment. Eager to step back into my role as innkeeper, I set up a plate of cheese and crackers in case my two guests decided to return. If neither showed then I'd enjoy a cheese and cracker dinner along with a glass of wine—preferably Merlot or maybe a Malbec.

Rover had finished exploring the downstairs and then, with a sense of proprietorship, he curled up again on the braided rug in front of the fireplace and promptly went to sleep.

"You look mighty comfortable," I muttered to Rover as I carried the cheese plate into the dining room.

Rover lifted his head from his paw and regarded me for just a moment before peacefully returning to his nap. I brought out a bottle of red wine and wineglasses, and a large pot of tea. I'd add the hot water later, if anyone was interested.

In the distance, I could hear a car door closing. Rover heard it, too, and was instantly on his feet. I watched him carefully. If he was going to remain with me, then he would need to adjust to a series of strangers taking up residence for short periods of time.

Barking, he went to the front door and waited.

No more than a minute later the door swung open and Abby Kincaid breezed in out of the cold.

The instant Rover saw her, he stopped barking and wagged his tail furiously, welcoming her.

"Who do we have here?" Abby asked, bending over and petting my newly adopted guardian.

I released a silent breath of relief as Rover seemed to immediately recognize that Abby was a friend.

"This is Rover," I answered. "I got him from the animal shelter this afternoon."

"Really? Well, he sure is a friendly fellow."

I grinned, relieved and reassured at the same time. "I just brought out a few snacks," I told her. "Please, help yourself."

Abby glanced at her watch. "I need to change for the wedding first but I should have a couple of minutes to spare before I head to the church."

I returned to the kitchen and put on the hot water for tea so she would have the option. I added a few cookies to a second plate and delivered those to the table, setting the cookies next to the cheese and cracker selection. I'd already set out small appetizer plates and napkins. The table looked charming, if I did say so myself.

Rover returned to his place in front of the fireplace and resumed his nap. He seemed utterly content in his new life. And while the deep ache of missing Paul remained, I felt content, too.

I'd just finished putting the finishing touches on the table when Abby reappeared. She was wearing a lovely pastel dress with cap sleeves and a lacy knit shawl was slung over one of her arms.

"Oh my," I said, watching her. "You look absolutely stunning."

"I do?"

This was no exaggeration. She was a pretty girl, but something had changed in the last two days. When Abby had first arrived it was as if the weight of the world was resting squarely on her shoulders.

"Tea?" I asked, when it became obvious that I was staring. "Or wine?"

"Tea, please." She reached for a small plate and took a couple of pieces of cheese and a few crackers.

"Your lunch with your friends went well?" I asked.

She smiled and her eyes brightened with joy. "It was amazing. I've known most of them my whole childhood. We didn't stay in touch after high school graduation and, well, actually, the fault was mine. I wasn't sure anyone would want to hear from me."

"Oh Abby, I'm sure they did."

"Well, you're right." She pulled out a chair and sat down next to me. "We had a marvelous time. My mother came, too, and she loved seeing my friends again nearly as much as I did."

"That's wonderful."

Abby ate the cheese and crackers and sipped her tea.

"Lunch took a long time, didn't it," I mentioned casually. Abby had been gone for several hours. I assumed she'd spent the rest of the afternoon chatting about old times with her schoolmates.

"We were only together a couple of hours. I stopped to visit with the parents of a friend after lunch," she explained.

I realized my comment might have come off as nosy, but that wasn't my intent. Her hand shook slightly and she lowered the cup to the saucer and placed her hands in her lap.

After a brief pause, she continued. "I'm so very glad I did," she added. "It was . . . at the home of Angela's parents."

I didn't know who Angela was, but I didn't want to interrupt.

"Angela was my best friend. She died in a car accident and her parents took her death hard . . . and because I was driving, they blamed me."

"Oh dear." I hardly knew what to say. While I fumbled for words of comfort, Abby spoke again.

"It was the first time since it happened fifteen years ago that we've been able to console each other and make peace," she explained.

"Peace," I repeated softly. I looked away and momentarily closed my eyes, savoring the word and all it meant in my own life.

"Are you okay?" Abby asked, her eyes wide with concern.

"Yes, of course, what makes you ask?"

She blinked and frowned ever so slightly. "When I spoke, your hand flew to your heart as though you were in pain or something."

"No, no, I'm fine."

"I think you must be," she concurred, "because as soon as your hand was on your heart a look of serenity came over you."

"I'm healing too," I whispered.

"You?"

"I lost someone I loved very much."

Abby blinked and reached for her teacup again. "I'm so sorry; I really am. I've known the pain loss brings." We sat quietly for a few minutes, and then she glanced at her watch and then seeming surprised at the time she reached for her shawl and leaped to her feet. "I'm off to the wedding festivities."

I stood, too. "I'll keep the light on for you," I said and walked her to the front door as she gathered her coat and purse. I waved Abby off.

As she backed out of the parking space a second dark vehicle pulled in.

Josh was back, too, but just from the way he climbed out of his vehicle I could see that his mood was as dour as Abby's mood was joyful. Apparently matters weren't going nearly as well for him.

Again Rover came to his feet the instant he heard Josh's car door close. My ever-ready guardian waited by my side as I held the front door open for Josh.

Rover barked furiously several times until I bent down and patted his head. "Josh is a friend," I assured him. Amazingly Rover seemed to understand and he returned to his post in front of the warm fireplace even before Josh walked inside.

"You're just in time for a late-afternoon snack," I announced as my guest entered the inn.

He paused just inside the front door as if he'd heard my invitation but hadn't assimilated it.

"There's a cheese platter and some wine available, if you're interested," I told him.

He removed his coat and hat and then ran his fingers through his tousled hair. "Wine would be nice."

I gestured toward the dining room. "I have both Merlot and Malbec in the reds and . . ."

"Merlot."

As I poured the wine into a stemless wineglass I asked, "So how did your afternoon go?"

He hesitated before he spoke. "My stepfather died a short while ago."

I set the wine bottle down with the finality of his words. "Oh, Josh, I'm so sorry."

He shook his head, accepting my condolences. "This morning I would have told you I wouldn't feel a blasted thing when the old man died. To my way of thinking he was finally going to get what he deserved in death. I had nothing good to say about him."

I did my best to disguise my surprise. "And now?" I pressed.

"And now . . . I wish he'd lived longer. After all these years of bitterness, the two of us finally found common ground."

"So you made peace?"

Josh reached for the wine, sat down, and brushed the hair from his forehead. "Yes, I suppose you could say we made peace. Peace," he repeated as if hearing the word pronounced for the first time. "For most of my adulthood I hated him. And he deserved it. After my mother died he threw me out of the house."

"How old were you?" I asked, already disliking this man for being so heartless.

"A teenager, just weeks from high school graduation."

"You did graduate though, right?"

"Yes, with help from friends who let me live with them."

How anyone could do that to a motherless boy I didn't know, but then I was only hearing one side of the situation.

"In many ways Richard shaped me into the man I am. I got tough because I had to be tough. The military was the best thing that could have happened to me at the time. I was forced to be a man and accept responsibility for my own life instead of relying on anyone else."

"Did you have any contact with your stepfather after you left the military?"

He looked away and shrugged. "As little as possible."

I sipped my tea. This was a difficult conversation and so very different from the one I'd just had with Abby.

"I was back in Cedar Cove for Dylan's funeral," he told me, "but that was years ago." Then he seemed to realize I had no idea who Dylan was, and he added, "He was my stepbrother. We got along fine. Early on I accepted that Dylan would always be the favored son and I was fine with that."

"What happened to your stepfather after he lost Dylan?"

Josh shook his head. "Frankly, I don't know. I

didn't stick around Cedar Cove long after Dylan's funeral. I didn't hear from Richard for several years and probably never would have, if one of his neighbors, an old friend, hadn't contacted me."

So that was the reason he'd returned.

"I came, but not out of any concern for Richard. There were some things of my mother's I hoped to collect. The timing worked out at the job and this friend seemed to think it was important that I come. Personally, I thought it would be a waste of time, but I agreed to visit."

"And now?"

"And now I can honestly say I'm glad I came. Richard gave me a few of the things that my mother brought into the marriage and . . . more."

Josh's gaze mellowed and I wasn't sure if it was the wine or the events of the afternoon. "Richard sincerely loved my mother."

"And so did you." Instinctively I recognized that the bond between these two men had been Josh's mother. Love for her was the thing that had finally brought them together. I found that thought comforting. Love had reached beyond the grave to touch Josh and his stepfather. Paul's love for me had done the same.

"I loved my mother very much," Josh murmured. "I wish now I'd taken the time to try harder with Richard." His words echoed with regret.

"But you made your peace with him?"

Josh nodded, and he appeared to be deep in thought.

"What now?" I asked.

"Once the coroner has released the body I'll see to the burial arrangements," he stated matter-of-factly.

"So you'll be staying on for the funeral?" I only had him scheduled for these three nights, but it would be easy enough to extend his visit, as I didn't have anyone else on the books until the following weekend.

"No, I'll be checking out on schedule."

My surprise must have shown because he added, "Richard requested there be no services. There's nothing here for me any longer. There never really was, but at least I'll have the things that once belonged to my mother."

"I'm pleased for you, Josh."

"Yes, I'm pleased, too." He took another sip of his wine and then set the glass on the table. "I better head over to the funeral home before they close. I don't imagine much is required of me, but I feel I should check in." He stood and hesitated as if he'd just thought of something.

Before I could ask if there was anything more I could do, he turned and went upstairs to his room, taking the stairs quickly as if in a rush.

Chapter 34

The wedding ceremony was lovely. Abby sat with her extended family and watched as her father reached for her mother's hand. While Roger and Victoria exchanged vows, Abby saw her mother dab at her eyes, a tissue clenched in her hands.

Abby felt tears blur her own vision a couple of times herself, but they were tears of joy, of shared happiness for her brother.

The dresses the maid of honor and bridesmaids were wearing were all various shades of lavender, each in a style most flattering to the woman who wore it. Abby thought fondly of Angela as she took in the dress styles, remembering her friend's wedding plans and sketches. The church was decorated with lavender pew bows and the altar was surrounded by white and green calla lilies. The colors, the music, the words . . . it was all just so lovely, so perfect.

At one point during the service, Steve Hooks, Roger's former roommate, turned and caught Abby's gaze. Then, completely out of the blue, he winked at her. Silly as it was, Abby felt herself blushing uncontrollably. She was over thirty, well **just** over, a mature woman. Far too mature to let a wink from a handsome man fluster her to this extent. Nevertheless she was flattered and excited.

The wedding reception was held at the country club, and Abby drove there separately so she could leave earlier than her parents if they wanted to stay late.

As soon as they arrived at the reception, they were given their dinner table assignments. To Abby's surprise she found she wasn't sitting with her parents or any of her cousins.

"You're not at our table?" her mother protested, and seemed about to call for the maître'd, when Steve Hooks approached.

"Mrs. Kincaid, I hope you don't mind, but I asked to have Abby at my table."

Her mother opened her mouth to protest and then quickly snapped it shut.

"That is," Steve continued, looking at Abby, "if Abby doesn't mind."

"She doesn't mind," Linda Kincaid said, far too quickly.

"Mother, I can speak for myself."

"Do you mind?" Steve asked, his eyes holding hers.

Abby would like to meet the woman who could refuse him. She nearly melted in a puddle right at his feet. "Ah, no problem. I don't mind." Her tongue appeared to twist into huge knots whenever she tried to speak to him. Oh how she wished she'd come up with something witty and clever.

"I know I've probably upset the entire seating chart, but I figured this might be the only chance Abby and I had to talk. I refuse to be thwarted."

This time Abby didn't bother to speak—she simply nodded. In gentlemanly fashion, he pulled out a chair for her and then claimed the seat next to hers.

"It was a beautiful wedding, wasn't it?" she said, reaching for the lavender-colored linen napkin and unfolding it over her lap. If she could keep her hands busy then perhaps there was a chance she would get through this dinner without acting like a naive teenager on her first date . . . although that was exactly how she felt.

"The wedding," Steve repeated. "Yes, it was very nice."

The three other couples who were assigned to

their table joined them. Steve made introductions, and Abby realized that he'd arranged for them to be seated with Victoria's family and friends, which was fine. She wondered just how many nameplates he'd altered in order to get the two of them to sit together. His efforts flattered her.

Soon the other couples were deep in conversation, giving the two of them a bit of privacy to chat and get reacquainted.

"Did I hear right," he asked, "that you live in Florida?"

Abby nodded. "Port St. Lucie. And you?"

"Vero Beach."

"Oh my gosh, we're practically neighbors."

"If only I'd known earlier," he mumbled under his breath.

"Really?"

"I would have called; we could have gotten together. I had assumed you'd be married by now. We were just starting to get to know each other when you were in that car accident, and afterward you just closed up. Roger said you needed space. The last time I saw you I asked you to give me a call when you were up to company."

Abby had never contacted him, and while she didn't recall that specific conversation, she hadn't been ready. What she did remember was the number of times he'd tried to connect with her. She'd thwarted every one. Abby had to give him credit, though: he hadn't given up easily.

"I don't understand why you never married," he said.

"How do you know that?" she asked, teasing him. It did feel like she was back in high school again, flirting with him like this.

"You mean you did marry? You're divorced?" He frowned, clearly confused.

"Answer my question first," she said.

"How did I know?" he repeated and then answered in the same breath. "How else? I asked."

"So you made inquiries about me?"

"I cornered Roger so fast it would have made your head spin."

Abby laughed, loving the way he made no effort to disguise his attraction. Truth be known, she felt it, too. It was as if all those years had melted away and they were both in college again.

"How is it you never married?" she asked, turning the question around on him.

"How do you know I didn't?" he asked, playing her game. "Did you ask?"

Abby hedged, but only a little. "I didn't."

He looked disappointed, his lower lip jutting out just slightly in a rather handsome pout.

"Roger volunteered the information before I had the opportunity."

"In other words you would have asked, if your brother hadn't been so quick to tell you."

"Exactly."

They smiled at each other and continued bantering back and forth all through dinner. When the dancing started Roger led his bride onto the dance floor and whirled her around the room.

"Did Roger take dancing classes?" Steve asked. He stood behind Abby at the edge of the dance floor, his hands cupping her shoulders.

"My lips are sealed," Abby joked.

"He must have," Steve countered. "I certainly don't remember him being this light on his feet."

"So you've danced with my brother?" Abby teased.

Steve laughed outright. "Not lately, but I know I would enjoy dancing with his sister."

Abby instantly tensed. "Oh, Steve, I don't know if I'm up to the challenge; it's been a very long time since I've been on a dance floor." She didn't dare admit how long. To the best of her memory it'd been her first year of college.

"You should be more worried about me stomping all over your feet," he chided.

Then, without asking, as soon as the dance floor opened up, Steve led her onto the polished surface. Abby thought about protesting, but this was such a magical time and she wasn't about to do or say anything that would burst her bubble of happiness. The guilt, burden, and shame had been lifted from her shoulders and she was finally free.

With Steve's arms around her, she closed her eyes and let her body move naturally to the beat of the music, instinctively following his cues as he led, their arms wrapped tightly around each other.

"You're good," he whispered close to her ear.

"Thank you."

"Abby, Abby."

She opened her eyes to find her mother and father close by. "You two look really good together," her mother trilled.

"Thanks, Mom," Abby said, smiling over at her parents.

As soon as they were out of hearing range, Abby looked up at Steve. "You'll have to forgive my mother. She couldn't be more obvious, could she?"

"Obvious?"

"Oh come on, Steve, she's all but spelling it out. She wants to pair me off and the sooner the better."

"Oh? Apparently she's been talking to my mother."

"Is she here?"

"No, thank heavens. The last thing we need is for the two of them to start scheming." He smiled down on her and then added, "I don't need any help, how about you?"

"No thanks."

"Good."

They continued dancing and were interrupted by Roger and Victoria, the bride and groom. "Hey, bro, can we trade partners for a couple of minutes?" Roger asked.

"I'm not even his wife twenty-four hours and he's already handing me off to someone else," Victoria joked. She kissed Roger's cheek and then swiftly made the transition into Steve's arms as the music continued.

Her brother held her loosely and Abby told him what was in her heart. "Oh Roger, the wedding was just perfect."

"You have Victoria and her mother to thank for that. They've been working on all the details for months. I was simply the yes-man. I gave the two of them free rein and they handled whatever needed to be done."

"Well, they did an amazing job."

"I married an incredible woman."

"So you did," Abby agreed.

"How's it going with you and Steve?" her brother asked, not bothering to hide his interest.

"Really well."

"You know you broke his heart," Roger told her.

"Oh stop."

"Steve was smitten, big time."

That was nice to hear. "Why isn't he married?" she asked, curiosity getting the better of her. They only had a few minutes and she intended to make the most of them.

"He would like to be. First off he got involved in

a big computer contract with the army that sent him to Afghanistan, and then he was working long hours when he came back to the States. If you ask me, he's looking, but Steve is picky."

"Picky?" This didn't sound promising.

"He isn't willing to settle for second best, which is one reason he's waited. That's something the two of us have in common. We have high standards."

Abby's gaze followed her brother's as he sought out his wife. His eyes warmed with love and in that moment Abby understood what he meant. Her brother had been willing to wait, but when he met Victoria, he didn't hesitate.

"Be happy, Roger," she whispered.

"I have every intention of doing exactly that."

"And hurry up and give Mom and Dad grandchildren, won't you?" she muttered.

"I'll do my best," he teased.

They switched partners a couple of minutes later.

Steve stayed by Abby's side for the remainder of the evening, dancing, helping her dish out the cake. While her intention had been to leave early, it didn't happen. It was after eleven before she decided she had better make her excuses. By that time Roger and Victoria had left and the dancing had dwindled down to only a few couples. Abby's parents lingered with the last of the guests.

Abby hugged her mother and father. "I won't see you again this visit," she said.

"Are you sure you're all right to drive?" her mother worried.

"I'm fine, Mom," Abby assured her. It was a normal question but one that, until recently, would have brought back painful memories. Her mother was oblivious to the possible subtext though, which meant she'd put the past behind her.

"I'll follow her," Steve offered, "just to make sure."

"Oh thank you, Steve. You always were a gentleman." Abby's mother leaned forward and kissed his cheek.

At first Abby wanted to object that she didn't need an escort to the inn, but she quickly realized it would give her and Steve an opportunity to be alone before they parted.

Sure enough, Steve followed her to Rose Harbor Inn. She parked, turned off the engine, and climbed out of the car. Steve did, too, and he walked her up to the porch.

"I better say good night," he said.

"Thank you for a wonderful evening," Abby told him sincerely. She didn't want to gush, but that was the way she felt on the inside. "I meant to leave hours ago . . . I have an early-morning flight out."

Steve took a step back from her. "I do, too. Is it possible we're on the same flight?"

"I'm flying into West Palm Beach."

His eyes brightened. "Me, too."

"My flight leaves from Seattle at eight-thirty a.m."

"Mine too," he confirmed.

"We're on the same flight!"

His smile broadened. "So it seems."

"Fate," she said.

Steve shook his head. "I prefer to think of it as divine intervention." And with that he lowered his mouth to hers.

Abby slipped her arms around his neck and opened herself to his kiss. Perhaps it was the effect of Roger's wedding. Or even the night itself—cold, clear, and crisp. Whatever it was, Abby felt as if the whole world had opened up to her with a wealth of emotion and happiness.

When they broke apart, Steve's gaze held hers for the longest moment. "I'll see you tomorrow then?"

"Tomorrow," she echoed.

Steve checked his watch. "In seven hours. I'll meet you at the airport by the gate."

"I'll be there." Seven hours until she'd see him again, Abby mused. It couldn't come soon enough to suit her.

Chapter 35

Josh waited for Michelle at the funeral home. He sat in a chair in the foyer and did his best to keep his mind focused on the future and not his stepfather. He was pleased the two of them had made peace; it was more than he'd hoped would come of this visit.

He wanted to find a way to thank Michelle. She'd been a godsend and he was grateful. He planned to ask her to dinner, though he wasn't in the mood to eat and he suspected she wasn't either. Dinner would seem like a celebration.

The door opened and Michelle appeared. She paused just inside the doorway before catching sight of him.

Josh stood. "Thank you for coming."

"No problem. Have you met with the funeral director yet?"

"No. I was waiting for you."

She offered him a half smile of appreciation. "I phoned my parents to let them know about Richard's death. They asked me to give you their condolences."

He nodded.

George Thompson, the funeral director, joined them and after offering his sympathies, he directed them into his office.

Michelle and Josh followed the older man down the hallway and into a private room.

Mr. Thompson gestured to two chairs on the opposite side of his large mahogany desk and then settled down into his own seat. He maintained a demure façade as he reached for a file, which he opened.

"As you know," he said, looking up, "Mr. Lambert has already made his own funeral arrangements."

Josh nodded.

"He asked to be buried next to his wife, Teresa. He purchased the grave site adjacent to hers at the time of her death."

Josh hadn't been aware of that. When his mother died he'd been too caught up in his loss to pay attention to much of anything.

Michelle and Mr. Thompson were looking at him as though they were awaiting his response. "Okay," Josh said, unsure what was required of him.

"He was quite adamant that there were to be no services."

"So he said," Josh replied. Richard had been "quite adamant" when it came to most everything.

"Would you like to attend the burial?" Mr. Thompson asked next. "It will be very simple with no formal ceremony."

"No," Josh replied.

"I would," Michelle responded.

"Fine. I'll let you know the time." He made a notation in the file. Straightening, he sat back in his chair. "A couple of minor details. First off, we'll need the clothes you would like Mr. Lambert to be buried in."

Josh looked to Michelle for assistance.

"I can get those to you," she offered.

"It would be best to bring them tomorrow," Mr. Thompson told her. "We're about to close the office."

"Okay," she agreed.

"Anything else?" Josh asked, eager to make his departure.

"Yes." He flipped the pages of the file and handed Josh a sealed envelope. "Mr. Lambert asked me to give this to you at the time of his interment, if you were present."

Surprise must have shown in Josh's face because the funeral director continued.

"I explained at the time that if this was a legal document, it would be best to have it delivered by an attorney."

Josh accepted the envelope and immediately recognized his stepfather's cursive scrawl, which spelled out his name.

The funeral director did his best to swallow a smile with limited success. "As I recall, when I suggested an attorney, Mr. Lambert was unwavering in his opinion of lawyers and claimed he wasn't paying one to hand over a piece of paper."

"Sounds like Richard," Josh said, smiling himself.

"I believe that's it then," George Thompson said, closing the file.

"I'll get Richard's burial clothes to you first thing tomorrow morning," Michelle said as they stood in unison.

Mr. Thompson walked them back to the foyer. "I'll see you then," he said in parting to Michelle.

When they were outside the funeral home, she asked Josh, "Where will you be Monday?" She made the question almost an accusation, as if it was his legal obligation to stay in town for the burial.

"Away from here," he said. "I came back because it seemed the right thing to do, but there's no reason for me to stick around any longer. Richard didn't want any formal services and it wouldn't have mattered one iota to him if I'm here for the burial or not."

"Maybe not to him, but . . ." she let the rest fade.

"But what?"

"Where will you go?"

Josh hadn't really stopped to think about it. The new job would be starting up soon. At most he'd have a day or two before he needed to be there. "There's not much point in driving back to California before I head to Montana. I thought I'd take a couple of days for a trip to the ocean."

Her response was a half smile.

"Would you like me to help you choose the clothes?" he asked.

She shook her head. "No thanks. Richard had a favorite sweater he wore quite a bit. I think your mother might have knit it for him. It's pretty well worn but it seems appropriate, don't you think?"

"Sure, whatever you think is best."

She glanced down at the envelope in his hand. "When are you going to read that?"

He shrugged. He wasn't in the mood to do it anytime soon. "I don't know. In a while I guess. Do you want to read it?"

"Good grief, no," she returned and took a step in retreat. "That letter is meant for you, not me. But aren't you the least bit curious?"

He wasn't and he realized why. "I already know what it says."

"You do?"

"Richard made it clear when I first arrived. I will inherit nothing, which doesn't surprise me. The fact is, I could care less about the house and I never really wanted anything from Richard."

"You were his son," Michelle argued.

"Stepson," he corrected. Although the two men had made peace in the end, Josh had never been a son to Richard nor had Richard been a father to him. He was unwilling to turn Richard's memory into something it wasn't.

Michelle frowned. "When are you leaving?" she asked.

"Sometime tomorrow, probably early."

"That soon?" She refused to make eye contact.

"That disappoints you?" he asked, reading her displeasure.

"Yes . . . no, I don't know what I think."

Michelle seemed as disoriented as he was himself. Nothing felt real and yet reality was hitting him in the face. They were standing outside the funeral home. Nothing could be more real than that.

"Everything is confusing," he murmured.

Michelle dug inside her purse for her car keys.

"We need a drink," Josh announced. "Preferably something strong."

"What about the Pink Poodle?" Michelle suggested.

"Sure." Josh wasn't sure they served anything stronger than beer though. They'd find out soon enough.

He left the funeral home and met Michelle in the parking lot of the Pink Poodle. Several bulbs on the neon sign had burned out, so it read INK P O LE, which might have indicated a tattoo parlor as much as a beer hall. Things hadn't really changed that much in town since he'd left, Josh mused.

A couple of men sitting at the bar looked up when Michelle and Josh entered the tavern. Sawdust covered the floor. He led Michelle to an empty booth and they slipped into it, sitting across from each other.

The waitress approached their table and Josh ordered a beer. He was surprised when Michelle asked for a diet soda, but he didn't comment.

"You okay?" he asked after a few minutes.

Refusing to meet his gaze, she shrugged.

"I know you and Richard were close . . ."

"We weren't that close." She kept her chin up and again avoided eye contact.

Josh continued to study her, and after a moment he noticed that her bottom lip was quivering slightly.

"This is hard," he said, reaching across the table to take hold of her hand.

Michelle pulled her hand from his grasp and rested it in her lap.

Surprised, Josh leaned against the stiff wooden back of the booth. They'd both been dealt a shock. While they'd known Richard's death was imminent, it still unsettled them. Dealing with death, no matter whose it was, wasn't easy.

"I know you cared a great deal for Richard," he said in what he hoped was a soothing voice. "I'm grateful to you and your family for looking after him. After my mother and Dylan died you were probably the only people left in his world who cared about him." Consumed by grief, Richard had made an art form out of rejecting family and friends. He'd isolated himself. His world had fallen off its axis the day he buried his son. At one time Richard had been different. Josh remembered the sound of Richard's laughter when Teresa had been alive and the pride that shone in his eyes as he watched Dylan play football. At one time he'd had it all.

The waitress delivered their drinks and Josh paid her, including a generous tip. He took a sip of his beer, but Michelle did nothing more than hold on to her glass with both hands while staring off into space.

Because she seemed so curious about the letter, Josh pulled it out of his coat pocket, scanned the contents for any surprises, and found none. When he'd finished, he handed her the single typed sheet.

Michelle looked surprised as she accepted the letter. She, too, quickly read the few lines and then set it down on the table.

"He asked you to look after Teresa and Dylan's graves, but not his own."

Josh chuckled. "He expected me to plant weeds over his grave and frankly the thought is tempting."

"Josh."

"Pretty ones," he clarified, hoping to get her to smile.

"You don't have a problem with the monies from the sale of the house going to charity?"

"None whatsoever." In fact, he was pleased his stepfather had settled upon those particular charities. Cancer research in honor of Teresa and brain trauma research in memory of Dylan.

Once again, she looked away.

"You okay?" he felt obliged to ask again.

"I'm fine." She took one small sip of her soda and then pushed the glass aside. "So this is it then?"

"How do you mean?"

"You said you're leaving tomorrow morning."

"Yes."

"I already told you I have Richard's clothes picked out for his burial so there's no need for you to stop by the house again, is there?"

"No, I guess not." He hadn't thought it through. "I'll stop by to say good-bye in the morning."

"Just like that," she whispered, sadness rimming her eyes. "You really mean to just drive away and not look back?"

The question hung in the air between them.

From Josh's point of view the answer was obvious. "Is there a reason I should stay?" he asked, genuinely curious as to how she would respond.

"I think there is," she countered.

"And that is?"

"Us, Josh. I know this discussion probably makes you terribly uncomfortable, but I won't apologize."

She was right, but he wasn't about to admit it.

"Before you say anything, allow me to make a simple observation. When you left Cedar Cove . . ."

"You mean after Richard kicked me out of the house?"

She ignored his sarcastic tone. "You left and you've been wandering ever since—first in the military and now with your job."

"I don't want or need roots," he insisted. "I haven't since I was seventeen years old."

"Everyone needs someone, Josh." Her voice was soft, gentle, knowing. "Who is that person in your life?"

He shook his head, indicating that he didn't have an answer.

"You have a choice now," she said in the same even tones. "You can continue wandering through the desert, living with a chip on your shoulder—"

"Or?" he asked, interrupting her. He wasn't entirely sure what she meant, but he had a fairly good idea it wasn't good.

"You can—"

"Stay in Cedar Cove," he offered, breaking in a second time.

"No," she countered swiftly. "That's not what I was going to say." She held his gaze for a long time and then shrugged and slid out of the booth. "In fact, forget I said anything. You've already made up your mind. I wish you well, Josh, I really do. I appreciate that you came. Although he'd never admit it, I'm sure Richard did, too. I wish you peace."

Without a backward glance she walked out of the Pink Poodle.

Stunned, Josh sat in the booth for several seconds while he attempted to assimilate what had just happened. The two of them had been through a great deal in the last two days and he wasn't about to let it end like this.

He found her standing by her car, one hand on the hood and the other over her eyes.

When she heard him, she quickly reached inside her purse for her car keys.

"Michelle," he said, rushing into the parking lot. "Wait, okay . . ."

She straightened and turned to face him, her eyes wide. Josh didn't know what to tell her, what to say. He wasn't even sure he knew what she wanted from him. What he did know was that he couldn't just let her walk away. Not like this. He might never see her again and the thought saddened him. The sensation was akin to the way he'd felt when he realized Richard was close to death. Unfamiliar emotions tugged at him.

"Did you have something you wanted to say?" Michelle prompted.

He thrust his hands into his pant pockets "I don't want us to part like this."

Again she appeared to be waiting, looking for him

to say something more. "I want to be sure you know how much I appreciate your help," he said, stumbling to find the right words. If she wanted him to stay in Cedar Cove, surely she knew that was impossible.

"You're welcome," she whispered. "Have a good trip to the ocean and to the new job site."

"I will," he said, and still found it hard to leave. He backed up a few steps. Really there wasn't any reason to stick around. He unlocked his car. He paused and waited, thinking she might say or do something to stop him.

She didn't.

Josh tried to think of an excuse to not leave, but none immediately came to mind. He slid behind the steering wheel, started the engine—the whole time feeling this incredible need to call a halt to all this, take her in his arms, and hold her against him. The pull felt magnetic and strong, tugging at him, but still he resisted.

Michelle stood tall and proud. Without another word she climbed into her car and drove off.

With a sinking heart Josh watched her go.

Wandering in the desert? How was he supposed to know what that meant? But he did. On some level Josh had understood the instant the words were out of her mouth. He'd been running nearly his entire adult life, refusing to become involved in anything more than his work. He was good at what he did for the simple fact that his work dominated his life, leaving room for nothing else. Not a wife. Not a real home. Not a family.

With nothing else left to do, Josh drove off, too. The closer he got to Rose Harbor Inn, the heavier his heart felt. By the time he realized what he wanted, what he needed, Josh was less than a mile from the inn.

Suddenly, without the least bit of warning, he made a sharp U-turn and then paused in the middle of the road. It came to him in a mad rush that he didn't want this . . . didn't want to leave . . . didn't want to continue on this same path—a path that could leave him alone and bitter, just like Richard. He wanted Michelle, to love her and make her part of his life.

He didn't stop to count the number of traffic laws he was breaking on his way back to Richard's, hoping, praying that she'd returned to the house to collect Richard's clothes. His heart sank when he saw that her car wasn't at Richard's or her parents' home.

Josh remembered Michelle telling him she owned a condo in the Manchester area east of Cedar Cove. He didn't know where but by heaven he'd find out. It didn't take long to scout out the area. Sure enough a three-story condo building had been built along the waterfront with a bottom-floor restaurant and a small grocery.

He parked, taking up two spaces, and went inside the store.

"Two twelve," the man behind the counter told

him when Josh asked about her. "She's been gone for a few days, but I thought I saw her pull in a few minutes ago."

With his heart racing, Josh headed toward the staircase, taking the steps two at a time. He rang the doorbell but got no response. Knocking hard got him nowhere either. If she wasn't inside, where could she be? That was when he noticed the newspapers piled in front of her door. Apparently the grocer was mistaken. Michelle hadn't returned.

The only thing Josh could think to do was to return to his car and wait. He was too keyed up to sit, though. He wanted to talk to Michelle. This was what he got for being so oblivious, so obstinate. Everything she said about him was true, only he'd been too pigheaded to see it.

The wind off the water carried with it the scent of the sea. Josh walked down to the short pier, intent on walking off his pent-up anxiety. He'd only gone a few feet along the boardwalk when he saw her.

Michelle stood with her back to him, looking out over the water. He paused as a surge of happiness filled him.

"Michelle." His voice carried in the breeze and she turned and saw that it was him. He started toward her, half-walking, half-running.

Josh wasn't sure what he expected. In his mind, he'd envisioned that she'd come racing forward, that she'd meet him halfway.

She didn't.

Instead she remained motionless, her hands buried in her coat pockets, her shoulders stiff and proud.

He slowed his pace as he reached her. "I'm glad I found you."

She said nothing.

"Listen," he said, "I don't know what's been happening between us over the last couple of days, but I think it could be significant."

Still no response.

"Whatever this is with us, it's important; I don't want to lose it."

"You're the one who couldn't get away from here fast enough. In fact I'm surprised you're still here."

He ignored that and realized she wasn't going to make this easy for him. He didn't blame her. "Can we go somewhere and talk?" he asked.

"I've already said what was on my mind."

"Yes, and I'm grateful because it made me think. I don't want to wander in that desert any longer. I want to put down roots. You said everyone needs someone and asked me who that is in my life. I didn't have an answer earlier but I do now. I want that someone to be you, Michelle. You." He talked fast, as if he couldn't get the words out quickly enough.

She blinked a couple of times as if she wasn't sure she'd heard him correctly. Then with a soft sad smile, she shook her head. "Sorry, Josh. I'm no longer that overweight teenage girl who gets dissed at the prom.

It's going to take more than a few pretty words to convince me you're serious."

"I am serious. Give me a chance and I'll prove how serious I am."

A smile tweaked her lips. "A chance?"

"That's all I'm asking. I'm going to woo you as you've never been wooed in your life."

She started walking back toward the condo. Josh matched his steps to hers.

"I want more than flowers and sweet talk, Josh."

"Will my heart do?"

She smiled up at him, her eyes bright. "For starters."

He reached for her hand, gripping it with his own, and then raised it to his lips. "I've lived so much of my life alone that I have trouble admitting that I need anyone. But when you drove off, I knew then that I needed **you**."

"It took you long enough; you're an idiot, a very lovable idiot, but still an idiot."

He grinned and kissed the top of her head. "No longer, Michelle, no longer." He closed his eyes and then spread kisses up and down the side of her face until she turned and their mouths met.

He'd found home, Josh realized. Home was in Michelle's arms.

Chapter 36

Rover spent a good night, sleeping on the rug next to my bed. I wasn't sure what to expect, this being his first night in a new environment. Surprisingly he adjusted without a qualm. Despite the short amount of time he'd been with me I felt that this special dog would become a big part of my life. It felt as if he'd always been with me.

I heard Abby return to the inn close to midnight. Josh had turned in for the night sometime earlier. I didn't chat with either one for long. I did hear Josh whistling, which was a surprise, and then he asked if it would be possible for him to stay on for a couple of extra days. I assured him it wouldn't be a problem.

Abby seemed to have her head in the clouds as she went on about how wonderful her brother's wedding had been. Because she had such an early flight I wasn't sure I'd see her in the morning.

The contrast between when the two had arrived and now was dramatic to say the least, and the difference left me feeling like whistling and humming myself. The transformation was nothing short of amazing.

The master bedroom was large enough for me to have a small sofa and a television, and I tended to relax there rather than in the common areas of the inn. I needed my own space and had carved this area out just for me.

I had a fire going in the fireplace and I read for several minutes with Rover sitting at my feet. After a while I set the book aside, and, basking in the warmth of the fire, I momentarily closed my eyes, content and at peace. I wasn't sure how long I sat there. Maybe twenty minutes, maybe longer. What did strike me as I lingered by the warmth of the fire was that I didn't feel that stark aloneness I'd experienced since learning about Paul's death.

Yes, I had the dog, but this feeling, this sensation was more than the company of the dog asleep at my feet.

I felt Paul's presence. And this time I wasn't asleep. Even though I knew it was impossible, my dead husband filled the room. I refused to open my eyes for fear it would dispel the moment and I wanted to grab hold of it for as long as humanly possible. I knew it wasn't real. It couldn't be. Paul was gone, and yet it felt so profoundly authentic.

For months there'd been a huge gaping hole in my life. Now, my husband was back. Though I couldn't reach out and touch him, hold him, his spirit was with me. Nothing could convince me otherwise. I clenched my eyes tightly shut, and held my breath, longing to feel my husband's arms around me once again, hungering for the comfort of his embrace.

I didn't hear audible words, but he did speak to me, and what he said would always remain with me.

This house, this inn would be a place of healing. Not only for those who came to stay here but for me, too.

After a moment my pulse returned to normal and I whispered. "Thank you."

I rose early, as I tend to do, and was already downstairs with the coffee brewing when I heard Abby carting her suitcase down the stairs, doing her best to make as little noise as possible.

"Good morning," I called out to her from the

kitchen. "Do you want a cup of coffee before you leave?"

She seemed surprised to find me up and about. "That would be great, thanks."

I poured her a mug from the freshly brewed pot and carried it out to her. "I hope you had a good stay."

"It was wonderful," she said, gratefully accepting the coffee, cupping the mug with both hands. She followed me back into the kitchen and leaned against the kitchen counter.

"I'm pleased your brother's wedding went so well."

She smiled and nodded. "It was magical. I don't think I've attended a more beautiful wedding."

Paul had told me this inn would be a special place but in the light of day it seemed likely that the presence I'd felt the night before had been a dream. While I wanted to believe it was real, I'm too much of a realist to put stock in what could so easily have been nothing more than a figment of my imagination. Perhaps I'd made up the entire fantasy because I was so badly in need of solace myself.

But here was evidence to the contrary. I couldn't deny the changes in Abby from when she'd first arrived.

"Can I make you breakfast?" I asked. I was prepared to cook whatever she wanted although it was still early.

"No thanks," she said, quickly dismissing my offer. "I'll pick up something at the airport." Abby blushed, almost as if she was embarrassed or perhaps excited. "I . . . met an old friend at the wedding," she added, lowering her gaze as though she wanted to hide her reaction from me.

"How nice." She didn't mention if this friend was male or female, but from the way she acted, I thought I knew.

"Yes, Steve was my brother's college roommate. He was one of the ushers."

I stirred my coffee and grinned. So a man **was** involved. No wonder Abby was struggling to squelch her excitement. She hadn't given me a lot of details, but I had the impression that whatever weight she'd been carrying when she arrived had been dealt with, too.

"Steve and I dated at one time."

"So the two of you had the chance to get reacquainted," I said.

"Yes and . . . amazingly . . . he's single and also lives and works in Florida."

Goose bumps appeared on my arms. This was more than a little amazing, and it hardly seemed like a coincidence.

"He's actually within easy driving distance from where I live. I'm meeting him at the airport this morning."

"You're on the same flight?"

She nodded, sipped her coffee, and then set the mug on the kitchen counter. "Steve sent me a text this morning. He's getting to the airport early. He's hoping to change his seat so we can sit next to each other on the flight."

I could see that romance was already in play. Just the way her eyes gleamed reminded me how I'd felt when I first met Paul. Right when I'd more or less given up on finding Mr. Right. I'd kissed so many frogs I was in danger of getting warts.

Then I met Paul and he turned my entire world upside down and sideways, too. Even if I'd known from the start that we would only be together for a short time, I would have changed nothing. Not a single thing. I knew what it was to love completely. While losing him was the most painful experience of my life, I wouldn't ever trade what we'd had.

"Thank you for an incredible weekend," Abby said as she reached for her purse.

"I'm pleased you enjoyed your stay." I followed her back to the foyer where she'd left her suitcase at the bottom of the stairs.

"Oh, I did enjoy it. So much." Impulsively, it seemed, she hugged me and then she was out the door.

Standing in the open doorway, I watched her pull out of the parking area, with Rover by my side, a cup of warm coffee in my hand. I felt a swell of affection for this young woman I had barely gotten to know.

The first of my two guests had departed. I didn't expect to see Abby again, but I had the satisfaction of knowing that she had left a happier person than when she'd arrived.

By contrast, Josh didn't come downstairs until almost nine that morning. I had cooked bacon and was ready to fix eggs however he preferred. The orange juice was ready and the table set.

"Good morning," I greeted when he appeared.

He grinned and helped himself to the coffee. "I can't believe I slept this late."

"Apparently you needed it," I said. "How would you like your eggs?"

He sipped the coffee and hesitated as if the question were a weighty one. "Over easy. No, make that scrambled."

"You got it." I returned to the kitchen and was surprised when Josh followed me. Rover had returned to the rug in front of the fireplace for another nap so it was just Josh and me.

He leaned against the doorjamb and crossed his ankles. "I hope it's not a problem for me to stay on a couple of days."

"None whatsoever." I got out the eggs and cracked two into a bowl and reached for my fork.

"I was able to make the funeral arrangements for my stepfather."

I paused as I added the eggs to the melted butter

in the pan on the stove. "I am sorry for your loss," I told him.

"Thank you. It does feel like a loss. I'm just relieved we were able to come to terms before he died. Clearing the air helped tremendously."

"I'm glad."

"I am, too," he said and then went into the dining room and waited for his breakfast.

After breakfast, Josh left.

Rover followed me upstairs while I removed the sheets from the bed in Abby's room and then he followed me down to the laundry room. He was quickly turning into my shadow. I nearly tripped over him as I stuffed the sheets into the machine.

As I returned to the main part of the house I noticed a man wearing a dark coat walking around the front yard, carrying a shovel.

It looked like Mark. I grabbed my coat, quickly stuffing my arms into the sleeves, and walked onto the front porch. Rover followed me and stood at my side at the top of the steps. Surprisingly he didn't bark or make a fuss at the stranger in my yard.

"Mark?" I called out.

He turned and looked at me. "Morning," he said. His gaze went from me to Rover. "I didn't know you had a dog."

"I just got him. The pound named him Rover but I'm thinking of changing his name once we get better acquainted." I wrapped my arms around my middle as a chill settled over me.

"Rover's a fine name," he said, and leaned on his shovel. "Can't see changing it, but then you didn't ask my opinion."

That hadn't seemed to bother him earlier, I noticed. "What are you doing here?" I asked, more curious than anything. Our last meeting had been a bit strained. I wasn't sure what to think of this handyman. Yet despite our awkward beginning, I rather liked him.

Mark leaned on the shovel. "You wanted a price quote on setting up a garden area, didn't you?"

"Well, yes, but . . ." He'd led me to believe that it would be some time before he was ready to start a project of such magnitude. I hadn't expected him to get back to me this soon.

"But what?"

"Nothing; it's just that I didn't expect to see you so soon."

"Do you want me to come back another time?"

He grinned as he said it, knowing full well I didn't. "Of course not." I hesitated and then decided to forge ahead. "Can I ask you something?"

"Nothing has stopped you before." He gestured with his hand as if granting me permission.

"Why do you need a shovel?" It was an estimate, and as far as I could see, that required a tape measure and not a shovel.

He chuckled, the sound of his amusement causing his breath to come in foggy bursts. "I'm not burying a body if that concerns you."

I smiled. "The thought hadn't entered my mind."

He grinned and I was surprised by how warm his eyes got when he smiled.

"I needed it to see how deep some of the roots went, nothing more," he said.

I was getting colder by the minute and I noticed Rover had wandered back inside the house. "Come in for coffee when you're finished, if you want."

He paused as though tempted. "Can't today, but thanks for the offer."

"Can't or won't?" I asked.

He shrugged as though the question had caught him off guard. "Perhaps a little of both."

I heard the phone ring, and the sound seemed inordinately loud, coming from my small office.

"You better get that," Mark suggested.

I nodded, turned away, and rushed into the house.

"Rose Harbor Inn," I answered, a bit breathless by the time I grabbed the receiver.

"Hello," a female voice returned, almost as if she had dialed a wrong number.

"Can I help you?" I asked.

Again the hesitation. "Yes, I was wondering if you have a room available in May, around high school graduation time."

I checked my book. "I do." In fact I didn't have anyone down that far in advance.

"Wonderful." She sounded surprised and disappointed all in one.

"Would you like to make a reservation?"

She hesitated and then said with some reluctance, "Yes, perhaps that would be best." She didn't seem the least bit convinced that this was what she wanted.

"The name?"

Again she hesitated and after a moment rushed the words. "Smith. Mary Smith."

"All right, Mary, I have you down. Would you like to secure the date with a credit card?"

"No . . . would it be all right if I sent you a cashier's check?"

"No problem." A cashier's check? Interesting. I had to wonder if it was because she didn't want to use her real name.

No sooner had I hung up the phone then I got a second call regarding the same weekend. It was a man this time.

"I'd like to make a reservation for my wife and me for our anniversary. It's in May," he said, sounding matter-of-fact. "If possible."

"It's possible. The name?" I asked.

"Kent and Julie Shivers."

"Okay, Kent, I have you down. I'll see you in May." How odd that I'd received two separate reservations, four months down the road, for the same weekend.

I hung up again and immediately wondered about the mysterious Mary Smith. Was that really her name? I wouldn't have given it a second thought if she hadn't sounded so unsure herself.

And Kent Shivers. He'd seemed oddly flat and emotionless when he'd booked the room.

I returned to the laundry room and added the detergent to the washer. As I closed the lid, I hesitated. "You were right, Paul," I whispered, as I stood motionless in front of the washing machine. My mood instantly lightened. Rose Harbor Inn would welcome its guests whatever their needs. I wasn't alone. I had Paul with me, and Rover, too.

As to Mary Smith and Kent Shivers and his wife, I couldn't help wondering what it was that required healing in their lives.

But then, I'd find out soon enough.

Knitting Patterns

Jo Marie's Crochet Shawl
Designed by Ellen Gormley

FINISHED MEASUREMENTS
Length: 35"
Depth: 14"

MATERIALS
Debbie Macomber's Blossom Street Collection
Petals Socks (100g/462 yds; 50% fine merino, 30% nylon, 20% angora) Color 601 Cherry Blossom—1 ball

Jo Marie's Crochet Shawl

Hook: US Size F-5 (3.75 mm) hook or size to obtain gauge

Notions: 6 lock-ring stitch markers

GAUGE

16 sts x 11 rows = 4" in patt st, blocked

Save time, check your gauge.

PATTERN NOTES

Chain 2 at the beg of row counts as 1 dc.

Markers are placed at the increases. Move markers as work progresses.

Jo Marie's Crochet Shawl

SPECIAL STITCHES

Cluster (CL): * Yo, insert hook in first specified st and draw up a lp to height of dc; yo and draw through 2 lps; yo, insert hook in next st and draw up a lp to height of dc, yo and draw through 2 lps **; sk next st, rep from * to ** once in next 2 sts; yo and draw through all 5 lps on hook; CL made. (After the foundation ch, all CL will be worked in ch-3 sps straddling a dc.)

SHAWLETTE

Ch 186. **Row 1 (RS):** Sc in 2nd ch from hook; * ch 4, sk next ch, CL over next 5 chs, ch 4, sk next ch, sc in next ch; rep from * across; with RS facing, counting in from the beginning of the row, pm (place marker) in the 4th, 8th, 12th, 16th, and 20th CL, ch 4, turn—23 CL. **Row 2:** * Sc in top of next CL, ch 3, dc in next sc, ch 3; rep from * across, ending last rep with ch 1, dc in last sc; ch 3, turn—24 dc, 23 sc. **Row 3:** Sc in next sc, ** * ch 4, CL in next 2 ch-3 sps, working half of CL in each ch-3 sp, ch 4, sc in next sc; rep from * twice, to next marker: [ch 4, CL in next 2 ch-3 sps, working half of CL in each ch-3 sp, ch 4, sc in **same** ch-3 sp, ch 7, sk sc, sc in next ch-3 sp, ch 4, CL in **same** ch-3 sp and next ch-3 sp, ch 4, sc in next sc]; rep from * to * twice to next marker, rep from [to] one time, rep from ** in pattern across, ending last rep with ch sc in **last sc, leaving remaining sts unworked;** ch 1, turn. Move the markers to

437

the ch-7 spaces—22 CL, 5 ch-7 sps. **Row 4:** Sc in first CL; [* ch 3, dc in next sc, ch 3, sc in top of next CL; rep from * to marked ch-7 sp, ch 3, dc in sc before ch-7 loop, ch 3, sc in ch-7 sp, ch 3, dc in sc after ch-7 loop, ch 3, sc in CL]; rep from [to] across, ending last rep with sc in **last CL, leaving remaining sts unworked;** ch 4, turn. **Row 5:** * CL in next 2 ch-3 sps, ch 4, sc in next sc; rep from *, ending last rep with sc in last sc, ch 4, turn—26 CL. **Row 6:** * Sc in top of next CL, ch 3, dc in next sc, ch 3; rep from * across, ending last rep with sc in last CL; ch 4, turn. **Row 7:** Rep row 5—25 CL. **Row 8:** Rep row 6. **Row 9:** Sc in next sc, ** * ch 4, CL in next 2 ch-3 sps, ch 4, sc in next sc *; rep from * to * twice, [ch 4, CL in next 2 ch-3 sps, working half of CL in each ch-3 sp, ch 4, sc in **same** ch-3 sp, ch 7, sk sc, sc in next ch-3 sp, ch 4, CL in **same** ch-3 sp and next ch-3 sp, ch 4, sc in next sc]; rep from * to * twice, rep from [to] one time, rep from ** in pattern across, ending last rep with sc in **last sc,** leaving remaining sts unworked; ch 4, turn. Move the markers to the ch-7 spaces—24 CL, 5 ch-7 sps. **Row 10:** Rep row 4. **Row 11:** Rep row 5—28 CL. **Row 12:** Rep row 6. **Row 13:** Rep row 5—27 CL. **Row 14:** Rep row 6. **Row 15:** Sc in next sc, ch 4, CL in next 2 ch-3 sps, ch 4, sc in next sc, ** * ch 4, CL in next 2 ch-3 sps, ch 4, sc in next sc *; rep from * to * twice, [ch 4, CL in next 2 ch-3 sps, working half of CL in each ch-3 sp, ch 4, sc in same ch-3 sp, ch 7, sk sc, sc in next ch-3 sp, ch 4, CL in **same** ch-3 sp and next ch-3 sp, ch 4, sc in next sc]; rep from * to * twice, rep from [to] one time, rep from ** in pattern across, ending last rep with ch 4, CL in next 2 ch-3 sps, ch 4, sc in **last sc,** leaving remaining sts unworked; ch 4, turn. Move the markers to the ch-7 spaces—26 CL, 5 ch-7 sps. **Row 16:** Rep row 4. **Row 17:** Rep row 5—30 CL. **Row 18:** Rep row 6. **Row 19:** Rep row 5—29 CL. **Row 20:** Rep row 6. **Row 21:** Sc in next sc, * ch 4, CL in next 2 ch-3 sps, ch 4, sc in next sc *; rep from * to * 5 more times, ** [ch 4, CL in next 2 ch-3 sps, working half of CL in each ch-3 sp, ch 4, sc in **same** ch-3 sp, ch 7, sk sc, sc in next ch-3 sp, ch 4, CL in **same** ch-3 sp and next ch-3 sp, ch 4, sc in next sc], rep from * to * 5 times; rep from ** across; leaving remaining sts unworked; ch 4, turn. Move the markers to the ch-7 spaces—28 CL, 3 ch-7 sps. **Row 22:** Rep row 4. **Row 23:** Rep row 5—30 CL. **Row 24:** Rep row 6. **Row 25:** Rep row 5—29 CL. **Row 26:** Rep row 6. **Row 27:** Rep row 21—28 CL, 3 ch-7 sps. **Row 28:** Rep row 4. **Row 29:** Rep row 5 –30 CL. **Row 30:** Rep row 6. **Row 31:** Rep row 5—29 CL. **Row 32:** Rep row 6. **Row 33:** Rep row 9 (same as row 21)—28 CL, 3 ch-7 sps. **Row 34:** Rep row 4. **Row 35:** Rep row 5—30 CL. **Row 36:** Rep row 6. **Row 37:** Rep row 5—29 CL. Fasten off. Block to enhance lace effect.

Jo Marie's Crochet Shawl

ABBREVIATIONS
Beg—Beginning; Ch(s)—Chain(s); CL—Cluster; Dc—Double Crochet; Lp(s)—Loop(s); Patt—Pattern; Pm—Place marker; RS—Right side; Rep—Repeat; Sc—Single Crochet; Sk—Skip; Sp(s)—Space(s); St(s)—Stitch(es); Yo—Yarnover

Jo Marie's Knitted Shawl

Jo Marie's Knitted Shawl
Designed by Michael del Vecchio

FINISHED MEASUREMENTS
Length (Along Top Edge): 72"
Depth: 6½"

MATERIALS
Debbie Macomber's Blossom Street Collection (distributed by Universal Yarn) Petals Sock

(100g/462 yds; 50% fine merino, 30% nylon, 20% angora) Color # 602 Alpine Strawberry—1 ball
Needles: US 9 (5.5 mm) 29" circular ndl **or size to obtain gauge**
Notions: Stitch markers, tapestry needle

GAUGE
14 sts x 31 rows = 4" in Garter st, blocked
Save time, check your gauge.

SHAWLETTE
Cast on 179 sts. **Set-up row (WS):** K2, place marker (pm), [k21, pm, k1, pm] 7 times, k21, pm, k2. **Inc row (RS): K2,** slip marker (sl m), [yo, knit to marker (m), yo, sl m, k1, sl m] 7 times, yo, knit to m, yo, sl m, k2—16 sts inc'd. Knit 1 WS row. Rep these 2 rows, 7 more times—307 sts.

BORDER
Row 1 (RS): K2, sl m, yo, [k1, * yo, k1, sl1-k2tog-psso, k1, yo, k1; rep from * to m, yo, sl m, k1, sl m, yo] 7 times, k1, * yo, k1, sl1-k2tog-psso, k1, yo, k1; rep from * to m, yo, k2—323 sts. **Row 2 (and all rem WS rows):** Knit. **Row 3:** K2, sl m, yo, k1, [k1, * yo, k1, sl1-k2tog-psso, k1, yo, k1; rep from * to 1 st before m, k1, yo, sl m, k1, sl m, yo, k1] 7 times, k1, * yo, k1, sl1-k2tog-psso, k1, yo, k1; rep from * to 1 st before m, k1, yo, k2—339 sts. **Row 5:** K2, sl m, yo, k2, [k1, * yo, k1, sl1-k2tog-psso, k1, yo, k1; rep from

* to 2 sts before m, k2, yo, sl m, k1, sl m, yo, k2] 7 times, k1, * yo, k1, sl1-k2tog-psso, k1, yo, k1; rep from * to 2 sts before m, k2, yo, k2—355 sts. Knit 1 WS row. Bind off all sts very loosely. Weave in ends and block, stretching to enhance length and lace effect.

ABBREVIATIONS

Inc—increase; K—knit; M—marker; Ndl—needle; Pm—place marker; RS—right side; Rem—remain(ing); Rep—repeat; Sl1-k2tog-psso: Slip 1 stitch as if to knit, knit 2 stitches together, pass the slipped stitch over the knit 2 together; Sl m—slip marker; St(s)—stitch(es); WS—wrong side; Yo—yarnover

Acknowledgments

It has long been my contention that the only people who bother to read the acknowledgments page are those who are hoping to see their names listed. Keep reading . . . who knows.

Early on in my career I learned the importance of surrounding myself with highly competent people, and so as the years went by I built my own publishing team. One of the first people I hired was my personal assistant, Renate Roth, who has been with me over seventeen years. I tell people, and it's true, Renate is my right and my left hand. In later years I

Acknowledgments

added Heidi Pollard to my staff, along with Wanda Roberts and Carol Bass. The most recent hiree is my daughter Adele LaCombe who serves as my business and brand manager. These five incredible women work with me in Port Orchard. They keep my life relatively sane and—to use a cliché—are the wind beneath my wings.

Nancy Berland has been my personal publicist for sixteen years. I wouldn't make a move without her. She manages my website, sends out the monthly e-letters, and is responsible for a dozen or more aspects of my career. Theresa Park, my fiction agent, has guided me through the swift current in the rapidly changing world of publishing for the last six years. I am forever indebted to Theresa for her wisdom, intelligence, and business acumen.

The story you are holding in your hands is due in large part to three of the finest women in publishing: Libby McGuire, Jennifer Hershey, and Shauna Summers. They have each added texture and depth to this book. I am grateful for their insights and their faith in me.

Now if this was the Academy Awards there would probably be music playing in the background, telling me to wind this up and get on with the program. So in one final breath, I want to thank my husband, Wayne, and my children for their love and support. And Wayne, you aren't fooling me one bit when you

Acknowledgments

lie down on the sofa and tell me not to disturb you because you are plotting. I know a nap when I see one.

Debbie Macomber
August 2012

ABOUT THE AUTHOR

DEBBIE MACOMBER, the author of **A Turn in the Road, 1105 Yakima Street, Hannah's List,** and **Twenty Wishes**, is a leading voice in women's fiction. Seven of her novels have hit #1 on the **New York Times** bestseller list, with three debuting at #1 on the **New York Times, USA Today,** and **Publishers Weekly** lists. Debbie Macomber's **Mrs. Miracle** (2009) and **Call Me Mrs. Miracle** (2010) were Hallmark Channel's top-watched movies for the year. Debbie has more than 160 million copies of her books in print worldwide.

www.debbiemacomber.com